Chittagong
Summer of 1930

Manoshi Bhattacharya is a former Indian Navy physician. Having discovered her passion for history and storytelling, she has to her credit *Charting the Deep: A History of the Indian Naval Hydrographic Department* and *The Royal Rajputs: Strange Tales Stranger Truths.* She currently works as a general physician in Gurgaon.

CHITTAGONG
Summer of 1930

MANOSHI BHATTACHARYA

First published in India in 2012 by
HarperCollins *Publishers* India

HarperCollins Publishers India, Cyber City, Building 10-A, Gurugram,
Haryana-122002, India
www.harpercollins.co.in

ISBN: 978-93-5029-212-9

2 4 6 8 10 9 7 5 3 1

Typeset in Adobe Thai 13/14
Jojy Philip, New Delhi 110 015

Printed and bound at
MicroPrints India, New Delhi

HarperCollins Publishers, Macken House, 39/40 Mayor Street
Upper, Dublin 1, D01 C9W8, Ireland

AUTHOR'S NOTE

This is a true story crafted from personal memoirs, diaries, personal letters, secret police files, official speeches, newspapers, etc. The narrative style has been employed for the sake of easy reading and to preserve the style in which the revolutionaries first told their stories. A minimal amount of fiction has been used to create settings that enable the telling of side stories which cannot be accommodated in the normal flow. These fictitious settings have been meticulously researched and counterchecked with the families. This story belongs to the revolutionaries and the British officers and their wives. I have merely facilitated them and helped provide flow and continuity. Research material and songs that could not be accommodated in the text have been shared in https://www.facebook.com/pages/The-Summer-of-1930/181204375236724.

ONE

Ananda Prasad Gupta, 1923

The radio crackled to life. Jogendramohan Babu's body stiffened. He had been leaning forward in his easy chair twiddling the knobs, when the few discernible words of the headlines stilled the lines of his body. Unable to withdraw his fingers, he sat as if glued into position.

A small dark head appeared from under the flowered kantha in the next room. Dark eyes peered across, ready to snap shut should his older brother turn around. Dada stood concealing himself behind the door-jamb, peeping into the living room where his father had turned on the radio. Deboprasad was all of twelve and worldly-wise. He had an opinion on most things and knew, it seemed, nearly everything. He could predict with confidence the outcome of most news items, and they fell from his lips like pearls of wisdom whenever Baba was not around. Rarely would he express them in the presence of his family, for they generated a predictable chain of responses: a cold grunt or nothing at all from his Baba, admiration shining through Ma's unsmiling face and a look of repressed amusement from Thakur-Ma. But Ananda's little face would stare in wonder, his mind hurriedly going over the precious words, trying to push them deeper into his head. They would come in handy before his classmates. It was useless to ask Dada what they meant or how he came to such conclusions, for he would either pretend not to hear or curl the corner of his upper lip in a sneer. Three years, Dada was three years older and that gave him such an advantage, such a wealth of knowledge and understanding.

Dada had raised himself on his toes, leaning at almost a dangerous angle, craning his neck to get at the words that had so excited the newsreader. Chatga was in the news again.

Chatga. The word ended with a nasal sound.

Ananda played around with it silently. That was not the way the genteel would pronounce it.

Chattogram. Now that was the way Baba would say it and so would the teachers at school. But old Thakur-Ma, who had cut her hair short and worn only white since the day Thakur-Dada died, would often lapse into the nasal Chatga. It was all right when she said it but if it slipped out of his mouth, it did not fail to attract Dada's unforgiving notice. A short snort and Ananda would quickly be reduced to embarrassment.

'Chittagong.' The British liked to call it Chittagong. It had a nice ring to it.

A movement caught the corner of his eye and biting his lip to keep himself from breaking into a wicked grin, he drew his eyes shut as if they never had been open.

Ma drew Dada away, her hands fondly caressing his right ear. It had not really been pulled and in any case it was time for school.

It was time to get up. Kneeling, he plunged his hands between the mosquito net and the side of the mattress that sat heavily upon the loose edge. Taking a good grip on the fabric, he tugged hard but lost balance and fell backwards. As he geared up once again to liberate himself he saw that a corner had come undone leaving a gap large enough to wriggle through. The four-poster bed towered over him. It would be many years before he would be tall and strong enough to pull out the fine drapes of netting and toss them onto the hammock-like top that stretched over the ornate wooden posts. He went to stand by the window sill. Dada would still be bathing and it would be best not to come across Thakur-Ma while still in yesterday's set of clothes.

Dada was at the table. 'Eat slowly, Khoka,' Ma was admonishing him. The breakfast was being wolfed down. Dada was visibly excited.

'Aye.' Ma looked up at Ananda. 'Come. Sit.'

Slipping into his chair, Ananda pulled at his thala until it was below his chin. It was past eleven and Baba's chair was empty. Ma placed a gleaming golden kansha bowl filled with warm milk before him. Refusing the freshly fried luchis, he reached out for the sandesh. Deboprasad did not wait for his brother to finish. Rinsing his mouth with the water that had been kept overnight in an earthenware pot, he took a long draught.

'Aashi.' He called out. 'I'll be back.'

Broad steps cut into the hillside leading the way out of the gate, past the European padre's garden hedged off with its border of young greens that needed careful minding by hurrying feet. Ananda raced down the hill, scarcely feeling the cold wind that stung his cheeks making them glow. Chattogram was in the news. The full story would be relished only once he and his classmates had put together the little nuggets they had imbibed. These were adult matters. Not to be discussed in the presence of adults.

Little lanes wound past the houses leading to the broad tarmac road that led to school. The ground had long been trampled into submission but here and there, after the night's rain, it had turned into muddy patches and little puddles. But the sun was high in the sky, having cleared the last of the mists and drenching the rain-washed gardens with its pale rays. Himangshu waited at the bottom of the tila. That was their daily meeting point. Deftly skipping past the glistening pools, for, Gobindo-da's eyes never ceased to burn the back of his neck, he turned down the slope and into the school lane. Makhon – Jibon Ghoshal – was puffing his way up. The Ghoshals' house was amongst the largest in the valley standing across the street from the Sadarghat Kali Bari. Jibon was a year ahead in school but the two were thick as thieves.

'Did you hear?' Jibon called out. 'Master-da Surjya Sen has confounded the British again.'

Ananda doubled up, holding onto his stomach as Himangshu took a flying leap kicking at the air. He landed with all the finesse of a martial arts warrior. The winter woollies did little to hamper his style.

'They can't catch him.'

'They never will.' Ananda laughed. He danced a couple of steps out of sheer joy before sprinting down the street with Gobindo-da chasing after them. He had relieved them all of their satchels and though his legs no longer found it easy to keep up with the flying warriors, he succeeded in getting them to the school gates on time.

Gobindo-da was well past his prime now, having begun his

innings at the Gupta household as a twelve-year-old accompanying the new bride – Thakur-Ma – from her maternal home. He had been her personal errand boy, always at her beck and call. Since then, his role in the household had grown from picking quarrels with her to keep her amused, to a position of authority. Jogendramohan Babu acknowledged Gobindo-da's place amongst the elders of the family and often meekly accepted a lashing from that rapier-like tongue. But the children knew they had him wound around their little fingers.

Master-da had surpassed all heroes, past and present. He could move like lightning, fly from rooftop to rooftop and disappear from sight at will. The British with their cumbersome police could do nothing. Their lathis and bullets could never find their mark. Dull-witted and slow, they continued to gape at the crowds that milled around them, failing to nab that veiled woman that brushed past them. No, they were no match at all.

School buzzed with news. Would a holiday be declared? After all, the Assam Bengal Rail Company had been looted. Seventeen thousand rupees had been stolen. It was being called the AB Railway Dacoity. A holiday had to be declared. The boys were ushered into the classrooms as usual at the stroke of twelve but even then it was obvious that the teachers were far too preoccupied. There would be no serious study today. Where were Sahayram and Subodh? Would they have heard the news? The little boys gulped down the information greedily.

'But who could it be?' 'Who could be such a daredevil?' Their eyes shone with anticipation.

'It is Master-da.' Ananda was confident.

All day, boys hurried up and down the corridor smuggling juicy little titbits of news. The robbery had taken place in broad daylight. The horse-drawn coach carrying the AB Railway's money had been robbed at gunpoint. The details were still not clear. But it was quite like the sensational swadeshi robbery that had taken place a couple of months ago. It had made such news. The British administration had been busy herding the peaceful and docile Congress workers into the jails for having started a non-cooperation movement, when forty men armed with revolvers occupied the village of Paraikora. They had held it captive for two whole days and decamped with thousands of rupees. Every one had suspected the hand of Master-da but there was just no proof. Nothing could link him to the robbery. But Ananda had overheard Baba say that the account had been wildly exaggerated. That it had been conducted by a handful of people and barely a couple of hundred rupees had been taken. And for this handful of money Chattogram's good name was being sullied. Not that Baba admired Gandhi-ji's way but this certainly was not the gentleman's way either.

This time, however, it did not take long for the police to swing into action. Within days, Suluk Bahar Kuthi, an abandoned house six miles away from Chattogram had been raided and a stash of weapons discovered. The presence of the Hindu youths in a predominantly Muslim area had not failed to attract attention. The police officer – Abdul Majid, had come in a phaeton; peeped through the window startling the Hindus and fled, having instructed the villagers to keep watch until he returned with reinforcements. Master-da had raced out of the house but by that time the phaeton had set off. The villagers had begun crowding around and, as Master-da and his colleagues ran towards the security of the hills, they followed at a distance pelting stones. The bullets fired into the air had not scared Master-da and his colleagues. They had run up the Nagarkhana Hill but by then DSP Braj Bihari Burman had arrived with his men. A running gun battle had ensued and carried on for a couple of hours. A police havaldar had lost his life and a few others had been injured. Master-da Surjya Sen and two of his colleagues had been found unconscious and taken alive. It had been the first civilian versus police encounter to be witnessed on Chattogram's soil.

'A disgrace. An absolute disgrace.' Baba could not hide his contempt for the man.

His voice had been raised for Dada's benefit. Ma muttered something inaudible.

'For this does one bring up a son?' Baba raged. 'A common murderer; about to be hanged.'

A strange prickling broke out over Ananda's back.

'Like he is going to sit around in jail and wait,' snorted Dada. 'Even the cyanide could not kill him.'

Ananda felt instantly better. Cyanide, even cyanide could not kill him.

'Ah! That poor wife!' Ma clicked her tongue.

Then she dropped her voice. The boys strained to listen with Ananda pretending he had no real interest in the matter.

So the superhero had a wife. The piece of information had the potential to set a young imagination on fire. The superhero's wife – a superwoman herself. She must be a secret partner. Ananda shut his eyes. A mysterious young woman, dressed in black, scaled the walls of the Chattogram Jail. For a moment she turned and the bright red of her sheedur flashed at him. He smiled at the vision as she stepped lightly over the wall disappearing from view.

RAM KRISHNA BISWAS

Running feet thundered up the wooden staircase. Horen, Khoka and Sachin, the Sen family boys, burst into the room chattering brightly as parrots and flung themselves on to the floor. The house with its thickly plastered mud walls and woven bamboo roof was a cool one – a good place to while away a summer morning.

This was followed by a familiar measured tread, making its way up the stairs. Baba! Ram Krishna could imagine Durgakripa Babu on his wooden chowki, eyes shut tight against the world, concentrating on a patient's pulse; starting at the noisy entrance of his friends; counting out the kaalboris before excusing himself. Something had played on his father's mind since the day he had stopped to watch the four friends perched on the edge of the Bhuvan-Biswas Pul, their naked feet dangling over the flowing waters of the khal, staring past the expanse of rice fields into the darkening evening sky. Baba had watched silently and then gone his way, but Ram Krishna could feel that he was working himself up for one of those talks.

'This age is for karma and dharma,' Baba began without preamble. 'If this country has to be uplifted it will not be until we all come down to mother earth.'

The boys were taken aback. But they maintained a respectful silence.

'Lofty dreams will never materialize if we do not wake up first. If a new Bharat has to be sculpted, you have to be the sculptors. Do not flutter about like a kite struggling at the end of its string or like mercury that slips through the fingers. Steady your minds.' Durgakripa Babu left as abruptly as he had come.

The big room on the ground floor was full that day with patients squatting on the white sheet stretched over the shataranji-covered floor, the queue spilling onto the verandah. Malaria was a heavy burden on this starving population and they came for Durgakripa Babu's kaalboris, little medicinal pellets concocted from his own recipe of mixed herbs, as the government-issued quinine was hard to come by. Anything that helped bring the fever down in these hard times was welcome. In the afternoon, Durgakripa Babu would make his rounds of the little huts carrying his black umbrella and bag, calling out the names of the skeletal figures that lived there. They were either to be found under tattered kanthas dragged to a spot where the scorching sunrays could reach, shivering as if on the heights of the snowy Himalayas; or in a dark corner boiling a little rice in a clay pot as sweat streamed from their bodies indicating that the chills and rigours had passed; or out in the fields making the best of a symptom-free day. They called it the alternating fever.

When the kaalbori refused to work its magic and the spleen grew hard and tender, Durgakripa Babu handed out money, from his own meagre savings, to buy quinine.

The boys looked sheepishly at each other. During idle moments of leisure they had toyed around with the ways and means to help. But money and manpower had always been the issue. A beginning would have to be made. Ram Krishna lay on the bed staring vacantly at the ceiling. His father had chosen to name him after the devotee of Ma Kali – Sri Ramkrishna Paramahansa – the one who embodied the soul of modern India. You, he had told Ram Krishna once, the youngest of my four sons and three daughters, came on a night so dark and stormy that we had been unable to call for help. There was nobody by your mother's side that night, no one to sound the conch but we welcomed you with a dab of honey in your tiny mouth. Like the paramahansa or the swan you too must learn to drink the pure and clean water of the ponds skimming over the dirt and murk in the depths.

Ram Krishna wished he had the vision of the man he had been named after.

But the Devi will not grant such a little boy like you her powers. At least not before you have grown into a man. A man with strong arms that people will depend on, and a good heart that will earn you a name as a trustworthy friend.

The voice was soft but clear as if the speaker were right by his side. It had assumed a character over the years, low and melodious, and had become associated with the scent of flowers and incense that hung about the temple of Kalchand in Haola village. He remembered the moist grip of his mother's hand as she led him there to seek blessings on his fifth birthday. But once in the temple, she had become busy with the flowers and fruit that were a part of the offering and had forgotten about him. And he had found the saffron-clad sadhu right outside. It was a tale that he had got to hear several times during his childhood. Nayantara Devi had been recounting the names of each of the members of her young family, bringing their individual needs to the notice of the Lord. As her Ledu's name came to mind she had become suddenly aware that his fist no longer clutched the end of her sari. He was nowhere to be seen. She had rushed out, frantic with worry, but had found him right outside, squatting on his haunches. A sadhu, a patient old man, had resigned himself to becoming the object of the little boy's attentions.

Shakti? Ram Krishna was saying to the sadhu. You are trying to gain power? Sitting here? You don't know much, do you? Come, I will take you to where the men and boys exercise. You can learn to be strong.

The sadhu had considered the suggestion quite gravely and had clarified, No, that is not quite what I meant. You are talking of physical strength whereas I am talking of mental strength.

The child had quickly arranged his limbs into the lotus position saying, I want to learn too! The old man had shut his eyes and given the matter some thought. Then he had spoken in the lilting voice that is used with little ones. He had said, Can that be possible? No, the Devi will not grant such a little boy like you her powers …

The moment had been fixed in Ram Krishna's mind. The way he had looked him deep in the eye, the warmth of his blunt, calloused fingers as he reached out to cup his chin and the solemn way he had said, You have a long way to go. Sanyas is not for the young. Your country and your people need you. Learn to be respectful of your parents and elders, fair to those of your own age and kind to those who are younger.

The words had tumbled about in his head for days, and for many years thereafter it had remained a story he asked for repeatedly and one his mother never tired of telling.

'Ma!' Ram Krishna stole into the kitchen to discuss the feasibility of his plans.

ANANDA PRASAD GUPTA, 1928

Ma sat beside her charcoal stove, her wok brimming with dark-yellow mustard oil. The slices of brinjal slipped into the hot oil with a loud sizzle and rose to the surface. The gram flour batter bubbled crisp and golden leaving long trails like beads on a necklace. Her bangles jingled as Ma wiped the excess batter from her fingers. She pushed them firmly towards her elbow until they remained in position. But the ones closer to the wrist would not retain their hold on that rounded arm and slid down within seconds, much to her annoyance.

A hand tapped the top of his head lightly. Thakur-Ma broke the spell, urging him to get on with his meal. Ananda broke the neat cup-shaped mound of rice with his fingers and waited until she poured a lava of simmering ghee onto the fragrant grains. Drawing the salt and the lemon wedge from the edge of the kansha thala, he leaned forward resting his chest against the edge of the table and began to eat. There would be many courses today. Three thalas had been laid out, each one ringed by a set of gleaming bowls. Thakur-Ma paced around the table, her sharp eyes keeping a lookout for items that seemed to be the quickest to disappear on the thalas.

Two, still sizzling, fritters landed on Dada's plate. His head jerked up in surprise. Baba wore a broad smile. Ma had served Dada first. It was a special day. Dada had passed his matriculation exam. Baba had personally supervised the buying of the hilsa that was to be cooked that day. His son was a star student. The teachers had expressed great hopes and the admission into Chattogram College had been a cakewalk. Deboprasad was now a first year intermediate student.

Ananda had fared well too. He had been promoted to class eight at the Chattogram Collegiate School, as had Himangshu. His thoughts went to Moti, as Ma served slices of steaming hilsa and ladled the rich mustard gravy over them. Moti had graduated minor school at the same time as him and the two had met for the first time at Collegiate School the previous year. It was unlikely that he could be sitting down to a meal half as splendid as this one, thought Ananda as he worked a green chilly into his rice, mixing it with the gravy. His family could not afford it. But then again there was little that they could afford. He had visited their house several times. Moti's mother had always been pleased to see him, and his brood of little brothers and sisters never failed to accord an exuberant welcome. But the signs of abject poverty that were evident in the Kanungo home never ceased to strike him as exceptionally cruel. That Moti was able to continue his education was because the British educationists had recognised his ability and granted him a scholarship that was seeing him through.

Tegra? Tegra had also made it. The teachers at school and the Bal household had let out a collective sigh of relief. That wayward boy with his flamboyant looks and personality was like a young colt raring to go. Trying to hold onto him, much less getting him to sit at his books, could wear down the patience of the most dedicated of teachers. Baba had voiced his disapproval. Associating with Tegra could only spell trouble. Trouble ran in his blood. Tegra's dada – Lokenath-da – was an upcoming swadeshi. It was barely discussed openly at school and never at home. But it gave Tegra a certain air about him. The children had sensed it on the very day he had joined Collegiate School. It hadn't escaped the school's notice either. His heart appeared to be in the right place but the boy could not seem to keep away from a good fight. It was the sight of his well-scrubbed face, round, plump and cheerful, the curls of his brown hair tamed to submission by a mother's hand and the sheer innocence that lit his eyes that kept Tegra inside the classroom and not constantly, on one leg, outside its door.

Ram Krishna Biswas

'Oh, mashima! The container is empty,' a young lad called out. Then winking, he added, 'It will not bring good fortune to your store of rice.'

The lady smiled indulgently. 'Help yourself, baba. Take some from the large sack,' she called back.

It was Sunday, a school holiday. Horen and Sachin had joined Ram Krishna and Tarakeshwar early in the morning and had set off with three jute sacks slung across their shoulders. Containers had been handed out, earlier that week, to all homemakers with the request that one handful of rice be put aside for every meal they cooked. The four boys had distributed the collection duties amongst themselves. They would bring it all to the clubhouse by afternoon.

Tarakeshwar Dastidar, Phutu-da to all his juniors at school, had heard of him and his plans and had sent word requesting a meeting. He had left Saroatali village and had joined the BSc course at Chattogram College but whenever he came home for the holidays he liked to pay the old school a visit and meet the youngsters. Ram Krishna had been ready that day at the school gate, pencil and notebook in hand; his newly acquired spectacles perched on his nose and his thick curls smoothed down with a little water. Phutu-da was tall and thin, and sported a very manly moustache, but at first glance Ram Krishna had classified him as the gentle poetic sort. The moustache had failed to disguise the sensitive mouth. Together they had made their way along the raised mud track that led through the flooded rice fields. Green shoots had raised their heads above the standing water. A pale-green snake had coiled itself along a stalk pretending to be the tender curling tip of a marrow vine and a brown freshwater snake had swum along, hunting amongst shoals of small fish that flashed about catching the evening light. A sudden clap of wings and the herons had taken off in a great white cloud, settling down a little distance away from the young men. They had walked with practised ease, ignoring the slippery, dark, clinging clay and the overcast sky – two madmen so lost in their thoughts that they had been oblivious to the richness of the surroundings. The pair had settled under a tree on the banks of the Jora Dighi and watched as the evening darkened.

There is need for pain in life, Phutu-da had said. The blacksmith uses blows to tame the iron and fire to make it stronger. Water hardens to ice only after being subjected to intense cold. Life, Ram Krishna, will not bloom until one faces reversals and troubles.

Ram Krishna had listened without uttering a word but with a quickening within his chest.

You want to work for the poor … help relieve the poverty? Tell me, Ram Krishna, who is responsible for creating these conditions? Who has heaped these miseries upon our heads? Who drains the wealth of India? It is time for us to break these bonds, if we are to survive.

Where shall I begin? Shall I begin with Purulia where the people survive on boiled corn alone? Survive? Is that the right word to be used for those who drag their half-naked skeletons about? Or shall I tell you about the people of Singhbhum and Manbhum[1] who live on boiled mahua flowers? Can you imagine that? Adults and children living off flowers? And the people in Bihar and Orissa who would rather stay drunk on toddy than wake up to the pangs of hunger? Remember Ram Krishna, remember the famine of 1876. Six zilas, a total population of fourteen crores starved not because there was a dearth of food but because there was no money to buy it! Fifty lakhs perished in the belt between the river Krishna and Kanyakumari. Did their cries reach the ears of the British government officials? No, they were too busy raising taxes that would fund the festivities planned for the durbar at Delhi. You can pull out the *Amrita Bazaar Patrika* of 23 November 1876 … it has all the details of Lord Lytton's[2] extravaganza. A famine caused by taxation. What next?

What came next was, of course, the series of Afghan Wars. No one was exempt from taxation; not even the forest tribes that till no fields, nor conduct any kind of business. Where will people who live off the fruits, shoots and roots of the forest find money? It is said that the Roompas of the Godavari zila were charged for the firewood they gathered from the forest. No one knows about the exact numbers of lives that were lost but it is said that numbers of skeletons that littered the forest floor were enough to make your skin crawl. Their blood had been drained to the last drop not by the lion of the forest but by the British lion.

Phutu-da's voice had trailed off and still there had been no response. Sensing the battle raging within, he had said kindly, Die we all will, Ram Krishna. Death is the one certainty that lies ahead of each one of us. But can we give a new meaning to that death? Mitthey joto hridaye jurey eibala shob jak na poorey, Moron majhey tor jiboney hok rey porichoy ... Burn away the falsehoods we have believed in with heart and soul. In death let your life find a new meaning. Ram Krishna, remember no one is going to give you credit for the things that your father has achieved. You will be remembered only for the work that you have done.

Tarakeshwar's words had set off something within Ram Krishna that day. A strangeness filled him, an emotion he could not explain. For days there had been no appetite, no desire to open his books, nor a wink of sleep. But if Tarakeshwar had touched Ram Krishna's soul, he had not escaped being deeply affected either. It brought him back every Sunday to help with the collections.

'Ha rey? Begging? What does your father have to say about this?' An old lady was pouring the rice she had kept aside.

'Nothing, Thakur-Ma. Today is the day we spend in the worship of mankind. You stick to your bel pata, phool and chandan for your Lokkhi Thakur.'

In the clubhouse Ram Krishna handed out lists. They bore the names of those that were sick, in need of money and without any relatives; widows with no clothes; people who were in need but would never come forward with demands. Some money had been collected. The unclaimed dead would be buried or cremated according to the faith they had followed while they lived.

The afternoon was hot, and sweat trickled down freely. The boys had spent the better part of the morning in ferrying the sacks to the clubhouse. The next part of the job would begin only when the sun went down. They stretched their legs out on the floor and rested their aching muscles.

Ananda Prasad Gupta, 1928

It was Tegra that had brought the news. His dada had said that the swadeshis had come home from jail. The boys crowded around in curiosity. What was jail like? Had they killed someone? They were really strong, weren't they? What did they feed swadeshis in jail?

Tegra's chest swelled with pride.

'Hari Gopal Bal!' The master barked at Tegra.

The boys nipped back into their seats.

'Master-da is back.' Jibon announced as they met up after class. He pushed his spectacles up the bridge of his nose. He was still not used to them. They fitted uncomfortably. His face, it was assumed, would grow into them in time. A light fuzz had begun to appear where a moustache hoped to sprout.

Ananda nodded his head in affirmation. For four years there had been little news since the brilliant defence conducted by Deshpriya Jatindra Mohan Sengupta. Everybody had been taken by surprise. No one, especially not the authorities, had anticipated it, least of all the accused. The swadeshis had been acquitted. But Baba had instantly predicted a backlash, and within a month, an order to arrest all extremists in Bengal had been promulgated. They called it the ordinance which granted the police temporary powers of detention as specified under Bharat Raksha Rule or the Defence of India Act. Arrests had begun almost instantly. The Bengal Legislature had refused to pass it but Lord Lytton,[3] the governor of Bengal at that time, had used his special powers to turn the BCLA Act[4] into law. Of Master-da there had been no news. It had come eventually in October 1926 when after two years of effort the police had succeeded in hunting him down. Since then, barring a small insert in the papers, there had been little talk of the superhero.

Chattogram seemed to have changed overnight. There was a charge in its atmosphere that was impossible to deny. With Master-da had come the heavily bearded Ambika Charan Chakraborty; dark-skinned Nirmal Sen with his unusual height, who peered benignly down at everyone; muscleman Ananta Lal Singh; the moustached Ganesh Ghosh; and Charu Bikash Dutt who walked with a limp. They were referred to as the ex-detenues. Young and old kept their eyes peeled should one of these demigods deign to step onto the road. Spotting one meant a rush of gossip. An instant allegiance had made itself apparent amongst the children of Chattogram. 'Lame Park!' the little ones would scream at those that eulogized Charu Bikash Dutt and they would lower their eyes when cries of 'Beard Square' would break out, indicating they had sold their hearts to Ambika Chakraborty.[5]

The classrooms were abuzz with memories.

'And Ananta Lal Singh,' said Ananda.

The boys traded smiles. He was the one that had paid those surprise visits to the schools during the non-cooperation movement of 1921. Ananda had a vague recollection of those days. The junior classes had not faced the intrusions and the seniors that had been targeted had long since left for college. But the little bits he had picked up from Dada's conversations remained glued in his head. When Gandhi-ji's call had come, Master-da's party had responded and taken part in the non-cooperation movement as members of the Congress.

'Strike' had been the operative word for the non-cooperation movement.[6] It had been straight up Ananta-da's street. The people flocked to his side, hanging onto every word he uttered: Schools, colleges, offices and businesses must respond to this call. We are together. Let us show them.

But it was the sight of him swaggering onto school and college lawns that drew the maximum attention. Ananta-da. It was impossible to keep the boys away from the windows. Lectures would come to an abrupt end and despite appeals to maintain discipline, there would be a mad dash for the door. Ananta-da would storm into a classroom, spring onto a table and deliver a grand speech: Two hundred years of foreign rule … this all consuming fear that binds our countrymen in its coils … pride in oneself … sense of right and wrong … the thirst to live an independent life …

Some would gaze in open admiration, some followed every word, its import dawning upon them, but a number of students and teachers resented the disruptions: You aren't even a student. Get out.

Ananta-da would respond with a: An impotent lot. That's what you are. What will their education do for you? You were paralysed since the day you drew your first breath!

A brawl would be the invariable outcome and Ananta-da would leave, his face glowing with evangelical zeal. He had been given the charge of motivating students. He was a natural leader – one that could captivate the hearts of youngsters. He was everything that young boys idolized. At eighteen, he had been an incredibly handsome youth at the peak of physical fitness; tall and strapping with a thick mop of dark hair. The girls had swooned and mothers had wished their sons were more like him. And his body, the outcome of regular workouts, was one that every young Chittagonian hoped to achieve. His was a spirit on fire. When impassioned he could be driven to such eloquence that he was impossible to resist.

The little ones had listened with rapt attention as the older brothers described their day at school: Ananta-da had visited yet again.

'And during the Khilafat Movement?' Jibon smiled. 'The day Deshpriya Jatindra Mohan Sengupta delivered his address at the Double Mooring Jetty?'

That morning the Bullock Brothers Steamer Company had been shocked to discover that their loyal khalasis had turned into nationalists overnight. The deck had been rent with cries of Bande Mataram and Allah ho Akbar and when the engines were started, the horrified captain had watched helplessly as his defiant workers leapt overboard. It had been rumoured that a sampan had been doing the rounds all night despite the heavy security and had contacted all Indian workers.

That had been Ananta-da again.

Ram Krishna Biswas

The crowd that thronged the edge of the field parted to make way for the teams. The boys streamed out on to the field in their shorts and blazers. The coach blew his whistle and the game began. The spectators on the touchline shouted encouragement.

'Saroatali!' they yelled, in rolling waves of sound, holding on to the last note of the cry until their breath ran out.

The play swept from one goalmouth to the other. The forwards had the ball now and were attacking strongly. A long, low, swerving shot came in from the left and Horen, in goal for Saroatali, dived to make a brilliant save.

'Good save!' called a chorus of voices.

The ball was cleared and away went the Saroatali forwards, Ram Krishna, at the outside-left, streaking down the field with the ball at his toes.

Tarakeshwar had been away for many months now. He was in the big city, pursuing his dreams … a degree in chemistry at Chattogram College. He returned only during the holidays. For Ram Krishna it had meant intellectual isolation. He could empathize with the legendary prince Lakshman who never wished to leave his older brother Lord Ram's side.

It was the opposing goalkeeper's turn to dive and gather the ball safely to his chest before kicking it clear.

A dutiful cheer went up for the opposing team. All through the first half the battle raged evenly with neither side scoring. But Ram Krishna's concentration was suddenly no longer on the ball. Somebody was waving to him from the edge of the field.

It was Tarakeshwar. Ram Krishna turned and ran. His friend was back!

The two hugged each other.

'Phutu-da, I've been offered the position of team captain,' said Ram Krishna breathlessly.

'Koroldanga … tomorrow.' Tarakeshwar whispered back. He was tucking something into Ram Krishna's waistband. 'Careful, this could mean six months of jail,' he smiled, motioning to him to return to the field.

Ram Krishna tugged at his jersey, pulling it down while scrambling back to take up position. A new excitement was bubbling up within him. The precious secret, whatever it was, lay cool and smooth next to his skin never letting him forget its presence.

The game ended and the boys trooped home. The secret could not be uncovered until he was safe in the privacy of his study.

That night, after dinner, Ram Krishna sat in the glow of the hurricane lantern and undid the little parcel. It was a small book with a bright-red cover. In bold letters it said, *KANAILAL DUTTA*. The author was Motilal Rai.

That captaincy would have to wait.

Ananda Prasad Gupta

Ananda sat up on the bench on which he had been stretched out until now. The sweat poured down his back and he pinched at his vest, flapping it a little to cool himself. He had flocked with the rest to Ananta-da's akhara – the physical culture club. Ananta-da was in the ring showing Swadesh a couple of moves.

Swadesh Roy was plump, soft and yet so eager. Ananda repressed the laugh that had been bubbling in his throat ever since the young contractor had jumped into the ring.

'Dekhli?' Swadesh swung himself down. 'Did you see?' His face had turned into a dark shade of pink, the flush unable to contain itself behind that light-coloured skin. Everything about Swadesh gave away his background: an overpowering mother who personally oversaw his every meal, obsessing that the slightest negligence could ruin his health; servants that kneaded his flesh with warmed mustard oil and the teachers that were employed to train his voice. Swadesh came from an affluent family, one that did not believe in tiring him out unnecessarily. So what was he doing here?

'Dekhli?' Swadesh's eyeballs swivelled in the direction. 'Ganesh Ghosh!'

An elegant young man with a moustache was sitting on a chair, his legs stretched before him, one well-shod foot resting on the other. He was watching the practice sessions. Well, not quite. He was watching nobody in particular. He shifted lazily in his chair and Ananda half suspected that his eyes had drawn shut behind the spectacles.

'Ananta-da's friend?'

'From Municipal School.' Swadesh filled him in. 'But not a dropout.'

'Why was he arrested?'

'Bombs!' Swadesh rolled his eyes. 'He was caught experimenting with explosives in the laboratory.' He waited until Ananda looked him in the eye. 'At BT College in Jadavpur.'[7]

'Engineering student?' Ananda looked suitably impressed.

'No real proof of course, but they arrested him anyway.'

Swadesh straightened his features and sat up. Ananta-da was walking up to them, a towel draped around his shoulders. He polished his spectacles, held them up to the light and then put them on.

'You need to be quicker on your feet; a little more chot-potey. He slapped Swadesh on the back, setting off a ripple that spread to his belly and chest. 'Chol,' He cocked an eyebrow at Ananda, 'let's walk down to the river.'

Ananda got up to leave. Ganesh-da, he noticed, was sitting up in his chair looking interested for the first time. Bidhu-da and Naresh-da were climbing into the ring – it would be Kumilla versus Mymensingh. These two budding doctors were well matched.

The Sadarghat Club was one of the many akharas that had mushroomed in the city. The revolutionaries, it seemed, had decided to spend their time establishing an ethos of physical fitness amongst the sleepy Bengali youths. Coaching was available in boxing, ring and knife throwing, bamboo wielding – the lathi khela and parallel bars. Lessons were also available in driving, boat racing, shooting and horse riding. It drew the youths by droves. The elders had nothing to complain about. It was a healthy trend.

Cheers and shouts could be heard from the river. Tegra, hot and sweaty, was spotted in one of the boats. A voice called encouragement from the top of the bridge. Ananda turned to look up. Phutu-da – Tarakeshwar Dastidar, who was a couple of years senior to Dada at college – was egging on the rowers. Standing by Phutu-da's side was Dada, staring down at him with narrowed eyes. Ananda looked away grimacing as if he had caught the sun in his eye.

Ananta-da had missed none of it. 'Would you like to learn to drive?' His voice held a note of amusement.

Ram Krishna Biswas

Koroldanga Hill stood wreathed in a fine mist of clouds. Ram Krishna made his way up the slope picking his way through the thorny bushes wondering what it was that drew Phutu-da here. Perhaps he would find him sitting cross-legged, meditating with his eyes shut as if he were on Mount Kailash.

He peeped behind every rock and scanned the shade beneath every tree. Where was Phutu-da?

'Why, Ram Krishna? Look at your hair … it has been blown about by the wind … and your lips are dry and parched. Are you not well?'

Ram Krishna burst into a grin. There he was. 'I walked down right after school. I didn't stop for a wash or a drink. What a place this is. Where would one even begin to look for something to eat?' He had walked the three miles that lay between the school and this place without so much as a drink of water.

'Come,' said Tarakeshwar as he led him to an orchard. 'Remember, Ram Krishna, health is wealth,' he said as they sat down to eat. 'Let me tell you about the nutritional properties of various foods and their effect on our bodies ...'

It was to be the first of many such Saturday afternoons.

'You are a bookworm and have not begun to think about these matters, so I have to point them out to you. Stay away from women and girls until you are certain that you cannot fall prey to their charms. Womankind for us can only be viewed as the divine mother. Tea, tobacco ... stay away from them as well. Do you know what these self-sacrifices are? They are your strengths, your band of students, upon whom you must invest your time and your knowledge. It is the responsibility that is taken on by students in every age; for it is they who sculpt the destiny of their countries. You have taken a great vow but your work has only just begun. You have to grant the crores of men and women that are content with their daily lives the amrit mantra of bhrahmacharya, which will enable them to make sacrifices. The Bharatvarshis have lost their self-respect. It has to be won back. None of these, by the way, are my words. These are the orders that Master-da has issued for you.'

'Master-da? Who is this Master-da?'

'He is our leader,' said Tarakeshwar. 'Come let us talk no more. Let us forget our sadness and enjoy the evening sunshine.'

There was a new book for that day: *Desher Kotha* – About our country – by Sakharam Daushekar.

Ananda Prasad Gupta, 17 November 1928

A host of proscribed literature had made its way into Chattogram. It was being passed around with great care. The elders were not to get even a whiff of it. Some were banned; liable to throw parents into jail. But Ananda was at that age when a young man's fancy took flight. He sighed deeply and often appeared listless whenever he was at home and answered in monosyllables. Ma fussed over him and advised Baba to be patient.

The madhobilata curled its tendrils entwining the bars of the window, thrusting the flowers into the room. The heady fragrance filled the night air. Absent-mindedly, Ananda stood uncoiling a tendril. But the tiny green shoot held a death-like grip over the iron. Lala Lajpat Rai had died that day. Word had it that the police were responsible; that Superintendent of Police J.A. Scott had ordered a lathi charge and had personally taken his baton to Lala-ji. The elderly leader had collapsed. All he had been guilty of was having led the peaceful protest march of 30 October 1928 at Lahore. The Simon Commission had arrived that day to deliberate on India's fate and did not want to take Indian opinion into consideration.

Shaat koti shontanerey hey mugdho janani
Rekhechho bangali korey, manush koroni

Seven crore children! Oh, besotted mother,
You have kept them as Bengalis but not allowed them to grow up.

The poet's raised finger struck a chord in Ananda's soul. The poet had not forgiven the bhiru Bangali, the cowardly Bengali. Theirs was such a useless existence. Anguish welled up deep within, and Ananda relished every drop, mouthing the remaining lines. A hand fell on his shoulder. Too stunned and almost embarrassed to turn around, he realized it was Baba's. They remained still for a few moments and then Baba left. Not a word had been exchanged but despite his palpitating heart, Ananda had felt the sadness that had washed over his father.

ANANDA PRASAD GUPTA

The sight of the raised hand brought Ananda to a stop.

'Eki? Bidhu-da, you are here?' Ananda dropped onto the bench beside him. Bidhu-da called for another cha. The little waiter with his shaved head rushed between the tables.

'Going home for lunch?'

Ananda nodded. 'What did you do today? In class?'

Bidhu-da laughed. 'The real thing will take place now in the afternoon session.' He was enjoying the anticipation in the youngster's face. 'The skin has all been removed from the thigh. Today we will scrape the fat out. It's a bright yellow now, having been steeped in all that formalin.'

Looking away he added casually, 'Looks like the custard they serve in the mess.'

He had achieved his desired effect.

'That Naresh. Poor fellow. Wonder what he is eating down at the mess hall.'

Ananda made a face and got up to leave. Bidhu Bhattacharya was known for his wicked sense of humour. But, he suspected, Bidhu-da probably did not have the money to pay for lunch.

He knew how the two medical students had come to be friends with Ananta-da. A man had died of smallpox and the people had been too scared to lend their shoulders to that final journey. Ananta-da had rushed about trying to gather some support when the two medical students had come forward voluntarily. Since that day a firm bond had formed.

Thakur-Ma's raised voice came from the Upasana griha. She was complaining once again to Thakur-Dada's photograph. 'Hey griher swami! Tumi to bahar diya choila geley. Aar aamarer rakhia geley Gobindor bhoroshayey … O master of the house! You have cheated me and gone away leaving me dependent on that Gobindo …'

Ma was busy feeding Chotkun at the table and smiled her tight-lipped smile, her forehead knitted into a frown. It was a warning against being cheeky. Gobindo-da retained his clueless look, the one he adopted on such occasions. Taking the books from Ananda's hands, he gave him a push towards the washroom.

'Here, give him to me.' Thakur-Ma had emerged from the prayer room. She clasped the squirming child and seating him on her lap, pulled his thala close to her. 'When he goes home next,' she raised her voice, 'I will pray that the Karnaphuli will flood. Let us see if there is a single person left to light a lamp in his name! … Listen,' she said to the struggling child. 'I will tell you the story of a tiger … a real bagh.'

Chotkun's face puckered as his little fingers curled into claws. Gobindo-da ignored Thakur-Ma. He had heard her threats before and knew that she would make sure he would get to hear them many a time again. Wordlessly, he filled the bowls and brought them to the table. Ananda surrendered himself to Ma's ministrations and resisted the urge to tease his grandmother. Thakur-Ma kneaded the rice on

Chotkun's plate moulding them into little balls while he chewed on the first one that had been popped into his mouth.

'Joteen Mookerjee was a little older than you,' Thakur-Ma's story was tailoring itself to the requirements of the moment. 'He lived with his mother and sister … wait, I will tell you his sister's name … Binodbala. One day Joteen and Binodbala were walking back from school. The path led through the jungle to the river, beyond which lay their home. It was a very dense jungle with tall trees, so tall that their branches formed an umbrella overhead. No light could get through.' Thakur-Ma prodded Chotkun's cheek, reminding him to chew. 'Binodbala hated this part of the walk and like every other day she began to run dragging Joteen by the arm. Where was the need, Joteen wondered, for did he not have his trusty Gurkha kukri tucked into his belt?' The pace would have to be quickened for the little one's face was a picture of disappointment. 'Suddenly Binodbala stopped. She was shaking as she pointed to the side where the long grass grew. Joteen looked carefully. There was the print of a paw.'

The child's eye held a glint.

'It was wet. A little moisture glistened within it. As they stared at it horrified, the wetness sank away before their very eyes.'

'Wait.' Chotkun had clamped his hands over Thakur-Ma's mouth. 'Binodbala will die.'

'No, no,' comforted Ananda.

'Then Joteen will die.'

'If you chew that mouthful I will tell you the rest,' scolded Thakur-Ma. 'Joteen killed the tiger that day and Binodbala helped her nearly dead brother home. A doctor came to bandage him and when he heard the story he named Joteen – Bagha Joteen or Tiger Joteen.'[8]

The story was over and the child had shot out of Thakur-Ma's grasp. Gobindo-da picked up the thala with the half-eaten meal and chased after him.

The rest of the story was abandoned but Ananda knew it all. Tiger Joteen had become a stenographer in the service of the Government of Bengal. As a young man he had come into contact with the likes of Professor Aurobindo Ghose and Swami Vivekananda. A desire to serve his people had awakened in him. What began as volunteering with flood relief missions grew into a realization of the need for an organization that would keep the British from squandering the Indian budget upon their interests in China. Joteen had been tried in several conspiracy cases but acquitted each time for want of evidence. He had finally been dismissed from service and had taken to living as an underground party worker, eventually ending up as the commander-in-chief of the revolutionaries. A flamboyant leader, he had become the hero of every heart in Bengal – Joteen astride Sundari, had been immortalized in the sketch that came with the banned book *Revolutionaries of Bengal: their methods and ideals* by Hemanta Kumar Sarkar. The final encounter with the police had taken place at Balasore on 9 September 1915, when Joteen Mookerjee had been martyred.

Ananda Prasad Gupta, January 1929

An air of tension had hung about the house ever since Dada had returned home. Baba had retreated into the office room and refused to join the family at the table. He had become so quiet that he barely said two words to Ananda and glowered when approached. Dada too had a new attitude: sullen and angry.

Later one night, Ananda was passing by when he overheard Baba speaking to Ma. He pressed his ear to the closed door.

'… grateful that he is back,' Ma was saying.

Ananda heard the sneer in Baba's voice. 'I should not have let him back into the house. Gone to Kolkata!'

'He is a good boy. You should talk to him.'

'Both you and Ma. You are spoiling him.'

Dada had left, ostensibly to visit cousins, but had confessed to having spent all his time with the Congress volunteers.

'It's not riff-raff that he keeps company with … they are all sons of respectable families, all good boys.'

'It has nothing to do with that.'

'No?'

'No.'

'Then?'

Ananda heard the rocking chair creak as Baba shifted on it. He pressed his ear even harder against the door.

'Rashik Nandi came to me in tears yesterday. Amarendra has left home – renounced the world to become a sanyasi! But he too is in with them. Admission into Chattogram College and he gives it all up for the sake of sanyas. I told him to keep an eye on the nephew, Phoni. They, the English, have a saying … it is the same thing … the case of the bad apple. These are troubled times. Boys at this age get so easily out of hand. Without a good education what will become of him? Politicians prey upon the sons of the middle class.'

Ananda tiptoed back to his room. The news that Dada had attended the forty-fourth session of the Indian National Congress on 29 December was driving Baba round the bend. The Bengali papers had not stopped talking of the spectacle that had taken place: Motilal Nehru had been elected president; Subhas Bose, the chairman of the reception committee, had led a volunteer corps to man the session. It was this second piece of news that had grabbed all the attention. Instead of the Gandhian white, the participants had worn khaki shirts and shorts and behaved like a well-drilled military unit. Bose had played the role of a general in command of the corps, leading it on horseback. He had made women march alongside the men. That Oxford-educated woman, Ananda had heard Baba say with contempt … the Oxford-educated woman had been Lalita Ghose, who had put on a colonel's uniform and led a 300-strong women's contingent – some recruited from Bethune College, Victoria Institute and some from amongst the teachers of the Calcutta Corporation. Baba feared that the Congress was drawing the best and the brightest away from their studies. They would then be dropped once they had served their purpose. But by then perhaps it would be too late for many.

Jatin Das, a student of the Bengal Technical Institute, had become the talk of Chittagong. He had taken a leading part in training Subhas Bose's volunteers and had attracted a great deal of attention dressed in the uniform of a major. It was apparent to all parents: here was a bright future well on its way to being blighted.

TWO

Lady Kathleen Tegart, 2 February 1929

The governor's motorcade had arrived. Kathleen waited with the ladies for the men to escort Sir Stanley and Lady Jackson in. They were all coming in from the Dum Dum Aerodrome,[1] having inaugurated the first two machines gifted to the Bengal Flying Club. Sir Stanley had declared the club open and the Gypsy-Moth, gifted by the generous Sir Victor Sassoon, had been christened by the first lady of Bengal after her own name. Characteristically, as it always is on such occasions, the bottle of champagne had displayed a will all of its own. The manufacturers always succeed in slipping one made of reinforced glass into the case and destiny decrees that it will unerringly be chosen. Despite the raucous encouragements from the onlookers, it had held together defiantly, yielding against the spinner only when Julia's arm swung in the widest possible arc gathering momentum with all the violence she could muster.

Kathleen had been the first passenger that morning to accompany Captain Leete on the test flight. It had been a perfect morning with clear skies and the land, with its unending green laced by the fingers of racing water which led the Ganges to the sea, made for a charming sight. The second aircraft, a gift from the Government of India, had been honoured by the presence of Princess Ila Devi, the eldest daughter of the maharani of Cooch Bihar. The two Gypsy-Moths had been followed by an Avro 'Avian' belonging to the Bengal Air Transport Company and then Baron Köenig had taken off in his monoplane – the 'Kamerad', which he had flown in the previous year from Germany. The three light aeroplanes had flown in formation and performed combined stunts.

The speeches had begun. The Outram Institute[2] had become the Flying Club's new headquarters and Sir Rajendranath Mookerjee was hosting lunch to celebrate the occasion. It was a historical building which had served as the old Bengal Artillery Mess, the first mess incidentally, which Earl Roberts had joined at the beginning of his service in India.

'No great city,' Sir Stanley was saying, 'can afford to be without facilities for aviation. Our membership is open to all communities and I anticipate that within a short time, aviation in Bengal will become a popular sport and prove to be of great commercial and public utility.'

Justice Costello, the president, had taken the floor. 'The Light Aeroplane Club at Delhi has recently held its inaugural ceremony. To tell the truth,' he declared, knitting his bushy eyebrows together, 'they pinched our programme and forestalled us!'

'And it's the last time we will be so indiscreet as to send them our plans in advance,' said Sir Charles Augustus Tegart, his Irish drawl distinct amidst the shout of general laughter.

'Light aeroplane clubs have been founded in India,' continued Justice Costello, 'with the support of the government, to foster civil aviation. The Bengal Club has been brought into existence by the energies of Mr Arthur Moore. He is unable to be with us here today but has sent a message wishing us success, especially in competing for the Wakefield Presentation Plate! I hope that this meeting will yield more members and the rich and public-minded individuals will follow the example of Sir Victor Sassoon and present us with more aeroplanes. We owe a great deal to our patrons: Sir Rajendranath Mookerjee and His Excellency Sir Stanley Jackson. It is our desire that Lady Jackson become an honorary member. I request Her Excellency to accept this enamel and gold broach, which will serve as an open sesame to all future gatherings.'[3]

A tour of the premises had begun. It was amply spacious and included two lounges, a dance room, a ladies room and a reading room. Two tennis courts lay outside and there was some unused land adjoining them which could always be used as an extension at a later date.

'Strange name – Dum Dum?' observed Lady Jackson.

'Dom Dom actually!' said the princess speculatively. 'Perhaps it is the equivalent of the English bang bang, considering the British artillery unit was stationed there.

'Excellent point!' said Sir Rajendranath Mookerjee. 'Why, of course! There are several old firing ranges in the vicinity and all that the locals would have heard in those days, was dom dom!'

'And the first of the soft-nosed bullets that were developed here, by Captain N.S. Bertie Clay, took the name 'Dum Dum' from this very place,' said Sir Charles.

'Soft-nosed?' the ladies were intrigued.

'Well,' said Sir Charles, 'the soldiers realized that a hard-nosed bullet passed cleanly through the victim causing minimal injury. But on cutting the jacket away from the nose, the soft interior would expand as it came in touch with the victim's body, slowing down its progress and inflicting, as a result, colossal damage as it travelled through the flesh.'

'Mike's[4] memory … legendary!' laughed Sir Stanley. 'And now you have the ladies cringing.'

'Oh, we can't use it any more. The horror of it all led to far too many complaints by the Germans!' Sir Charles' eyes twinkled. 'The Hague Convention outlawed it and Britain gave it up the very year I came out to India. I've never seen it in use.'

'Did you know Sir Stanley before he came out to India, Mike?' Kathleen buttered a piece of toast as she looked across at Sir Charles.

'Saw him play cricket you mean?' Colson, chief of police, had joined the Tegarts for breakfast. He had spent the early hours of the morning exercising and practising revolver shooting on the roof where Mike had rigged up a canvas with a life-size sketch of a Bengali assassin levelling a pistol. It was either him or F.J. Lowman of the Special Branch who took part in these sessions, during which no member of the household dared venture upstairs. It was customary for one or the other to give a sudden, unpremeditated yell; upon which the other had to switch around and shoot the canvas gunman in some vital part of his anatomy. 'Who didn't know old Jackers?' he laughed.

'Well, to answer your question,' said Sir Charles, 'I spent considerable time those days following cricket news. Sir Stanley played for his alma mater Trinity, Cambridge, for several years. And of course I went home in 1905, to watch him captain England: won all five tosses; topped the batting and bowling averages for both sides. Two wins and three draws – we retained the Ashes.' He nodded to the bearer who set the coffee pot on the table. Adjusting his copy of the local Bengali daily with care against it, he added, 'Had a fair bit of hair in those days. The Boers took most of it away and the parliament the rest.'[5]

'But nothing was better than when he jumped in and drove the ball over the bowler's head,' added Colson. 'And that nice easy bowling, plenty of spin and a good length!' He jumped to his feet. The commissioner was ready to leave. They would have to be in office by eleven.

'Dinner at the Hugh-Bullers, darling ...' Kathleen's voice trailed off as Sir Charles dropped a brisk kiss on her upturned face and rushed out with Colson close behind. It was business as usual for him. He would be back for a quick lunch before rushing back to Lalbazar and then it would be time for the evening round of golf or polo. She hurried to the verandah in time to see Subah Khan in his red pugree open the door and Tim, the Sealyham, leap lightly on the footboard up onto the back seat and look back to make certain that the master was following before jumping onto the folded hood of the car. There was an air of expectancy. The gardeners had jumped to attention, hosepipes and rakes held discreetly away from view. There was hardly a trace of the limp as Mike went down the steps. He had his good days and his bad.

Subah Khan slammed the doors shut and the Fiat[6] began to roll down the deep-red sweep of the gravel drive which twisted its way between the lawns, until it was obscured by the tall casuarinas. It was a lovely, spacious expanse that went with the old houses and Number 2 Kyd Street dated from the time of Warren Hastings.[7] The call came to her ears: the long-drawn cautionary word of command, followed by the sharp guttural orders, the stamping of boot heels and the slapping of rifle butts. They would be passing through the large iron gates now, Tim standing up in excitement, his tail wagging deceitfully. He was the master's dog alone, though he also permitted the mistress and Subah Khan to pet him. But others, mistaking his laughing demeanour for friendliness, were quickly rewarded by a sharp bite. Her husband, sighed Kathleen to herself, was devoted to Tim and took him everywhere even though he was a dead giveaway. The morning breeze ruffled the pleats of her yellow patterned dress and she was suddenly conscious of the eyes that stared at her. They would not break out of position until she went back in.

She made her way to the morning room, the dinner invitation still playing on her mind. Mike had sealed his own reputation. Since the day she had been married, she had come to hear the oft repeated consolation other wives offered their husbands in case of an unavoidable delay: It's all right, the Tegarts are going. We can't possibly be later than they are.

It was only fair to say that her husband tried very hard to be on time but was usually genuinely delayed by work at the last moment; often by secret assignments which became impossible to explain. He was gregarious by nature and so loved to dance that he usually pushed their bedtime to anything between midnight and 4 a.m. But her Irish half still struggled with the need for punctuality. In vain would she extract promises to make that special-effort-for-next-time; for lateness was a sign of bad manners. But when next-time came, there was always that last-minute scramble and the breathless, unpunctual arrival.

Kathleen sat at her writing table. The pigeonholes were docketed into sections: letters unanswered, letters to keep, household, estate, menus, miscellaneous, addresses. Hers was a precise and orderly nature. Today she sifted through the cards in her visitor's box, as she sorted the day's issues with the khansama. In the old days, every married woman was expected to affix a not-at-home box to the gatepost when she was out. But the population had so increased since the early 1900s that the practice had been altered. It now remained available at all times. Being the wife of the commissioner of police was a responsibility, and the social side of life, though pleasurable, a duty. The bulk of the European population were expected to call on them, for after all, Mike was a member of the administration. And when they were not entertaining, they were out attending dinners or some other form of gaiety. Both made prodigious efforts to keep their appointments on time, but some curious chance always seemed to intervene. In the early days, before they were married, Mike was known as much for his reliability at work as for his streak of irresponsibility with regard to social affairs. Many a host, Kathleen had learnt, had, after patience had run out, rung him up to find him seated at his own dinner table. But the apology would be made with such commingling of contrition and drollery that he would always be forgiven.

But it was a prominent Calcutta lady who had taught him a salutary lesson. She was in London at a time when Mike was on leave and had invited him to dinner. Lady X, as Mike referred to her mysteriously, was a dear and personal friend and he had accepted joyfully. But as he carried no diary, the engagement entirely slipped his mind until, at a subsequent chance meeting, he received a sound scolding. He could only grovel and express hope that forgiveness would be shown in the shape of a fresh invitation. The invitation, Mike said, duly arrived and this time he made no mistake. He was there on time; one amongst a considerable number of guests. Once the cocktails were disposed off, he marched in with the rest into the dining room but none of the cards round the table bore his name! Everyone sat down. He alone was left standing, beginning to feel rather hot and bothered.

Turning to the hostess, he began diffidently, Lady X, you did ask me to dinner tonight, didn't you?

Yes, I did, Mike, she replied, but of course I never expected you would come.

Kathleen drew out a leather-bound guest book from one of the drawers. It held a complete record of the year that told her at a glance, almost to the hour, which guests had been entertained; who had spent which night under her roof; where they had slept and what she had given them to eat. She loved this room with its light and air, looking out onto the lawns. It was one she had decorated herself, choosing every piece with care so that each chair, each vase, every fragile little item was in harmony with her. Reaching for a pencil, she ran through the items on the menu marking the ones that did not please her with little crosses. Theirs was a hectic lifestyle but, despite the lateness of the hour, Mike, a middle-aged thirty-eight-year-old, still managed to be up fresh and alert by 6.30 in the morning, ready for a walk or ride or a practice session on the roof. Kathleen breathed a word of prayer, pressing her hand lightly to her throat. She thanked the Lord for making him the way he was and giving him the ability and the temperament to endure the kind of strain his work called upon him. Alterations of cloud and sunshine in the summer sky: that was her Mike. David[8] had once painted for her a picture of Mike at work: A Bengali officer had been reading from an article containing the crudest incitement to murder. Mike's face was set as grimly as the day of judgement ... and then without warning it had widened into a grin of irresistible drollery. The cornflower-blue eyes that had sparkled with indignation moments ago disappeared into his head as he threw it back and dissolved into laughter. A saucy piece of writing, he had summed it up before dismissing the bewildered officer.

The sunlight came in through the window glancing off the thick ivory-coloured letter paper with its golden crest. Her neat slanting hand filled the sheet rapidly. The months between November and March were the busiest. Some six or seven hundred cards had been presented that season and though they had succeeded in having most of the callers over, a sizable number still remained. She added her signature to the end: K.F.T. Blotting the sheet carefully she tore it off and moved onto the next.

Ananda Prasad Gupta

Dada was settling down. He was now a final year intermediate student showing a definite inclination towards the sciences. Phutu-da – Tarakeshwar Dastidar – who had finished his intermediate and had been enrolled as a chemistry student in the same college, had taken him under his wing. He was soft-spoken and courteous and had an air of gentleness about him. Ma and Thakur-Ma had taken to him immediately and he had a calming influence over Baba. Although Baba and Dada still existed in different spheres within the same house, there was peace at last.

Sometimes Phutu-da would hold chemistry demonstrations. Dada had brought home a couple of test tubes and a Bunsen burner. And Ananda had been allowed to invite Moti and Himangshu. The boys' study room had been converted into a laboratory. The experiments were simple enough and the chemicals changed colour or form almost at Phutu-da's command. That year, Jibon joined college as did Rajat-da – Rajat Sen, the son of a family friend who joined the intermediate course at Chattogram College. Since the college stood at the base of their hill, they soon became a part of those that trooped in and out of the house. A boy new to Chattogram also visited sometimes. He was Phutu-da's friend Ram Krishna Biswas.

Sadarghat Club continued to flourish and it was no longer possible to keep track of the newcomers. But the Bal brothers never ceased to be the centre of attention, the latest entrant being Probhash, Tegra and Lokenath-da's kaka's son. It had been Kalipada Chakraborty – the Sanskrit scholar who was better known as Pundit-da – who had introduced him. And it had been Pundit-da who had also caught him smoking. The chastisement of Probhash Bal had been a great source of amusement. He was reminded of his great lineage: their surname was actually Bose but an ancestor had acquired the title Bal – the powerful one – for lore had it that he had once crushed a handful of mustard seeds and rubbed the oil on his skin before a bath.

'Physical strength and mental strength must go hand in hand,' rebuked Pundit-da.

'I have to think,' Probhash said, fiddling with the curls that dropped onto his forehead.

'Think?' cried Pundit-da and Ananta-da in unison. 'A son of such a family needs to *think*?'

'What if I give my word and then discover myself incapable of quitting?'

Probhash earned his two days of reprieve. Ananta-da flicked Ananda on the ear and the pair made their way down to the river. A light drizzle had set in. They were walking as usual towards the Sadarghat Bridge discussing the news headlines for the day. Dual systems, reserved portfolios, economic development – these were part of the new post-war jargon that danced on every lip in Chittagong. Ananda read copiously and was proud of the knowledge he had acquired.

Sitting by the river's edge was Ganesh-da. Ananta-da nodded briefly at him. Ganesh-da smiled and motioned to him to sit. 'Desher kaajey jog dibi?'

The question was an abrupt one.

'Will you help out with the nation's work?' Ananta-da repeated looking directly into Ananda's eyes.

He *really* meant it.

Ananda gulped at the droplets that beaded over his face. His mouth had gone terribly dry.

'Will a wooden spinning wheel win us independence?' Ganesh-da clapped a hand on his back, his voice soft and gentle.

Ananda had no answer.

'How much money do we save by not buying British cloth?'

'Eighty lakhs.' The amount seemed ridiculously high in his head.

Ananta-da and Ganesh-da made no comment.

'The Howrah zila Congress president – Shri Sharat Chandra Chattopadhyay had made a speech at the Bongiyo Jubo Shommelon[9],' said Ananda with the modest air of one who, without undue ostentation, has no wish to hide his knowledge under a bushel. He had saved the little paper cutting and had memorized all of it. 'He had pointed out that we were fighting a political battle for independence and not quibbling over business. The British machine-made fabric costs them some twenty lakhs and Britain actually makes some eighty lakhs out of us.'

'The point is,' said Ganesh-da, 'that by just sitting at our spinning wheels all day long, we are not going to get swaraj. Even Gandhi-ji has figured out that not all his so-called followers are completely convinced about the ahimsa policy. Did he not have to put an end to his 1921 aandolan even though people readily abandoned schools and offices to support his theory? Tell me, do you know what prompted him to do so?'

'The Chauri Chaura case. The emotions let loose in the aandolan workers in the Chauri Chaura village of Gorakhpur zila in the United Provinces, had overcome all thoughts of ahimsa and they had unleashed their fury upon the perceived centre of torture – the local jail – setting it on fire, killing some twenty-one policemen and chowkidars.'

'And why did that take place … wait I will tell you. It was because the British had run a veritable steamroller over the quiet and meek ahimsa aandolan workers all over the country. Every action must beget its just reaction. Can you now believe that non-cooperation and non-violence are the answers we are seeking? Will they help us fight the British government?'

Ganesh-da's voice dropped to a whisper. 'Let me tell you once and for all that the Tory government is the cruellest government in the world. No one can beat them at the art of fashioning shackles. That is the only reason why we are being ruled by a country of traders.'

He could feel the heat in his ears and the sudden panic within. Talking against the British government was inviting very serious trouble ... and anti-Gandhian sentiments? No Indian ought to tolerate it. He glanced at Ananta-da, who smiled at him and said kindly, 'Wagging our tails in an attempt to please may earn us scraps from the master's table but not one amongst those scraps will be *independence*.'

'The first thing to remember is the need for absolute secrecy. Don't discuss any of this with anyone.' Ganesh-da continued.

The drizzle turned to rain. Ananta-da and Ganesh-da showed no signs of getting up or leaving the grey and turbulent Karnaphuli behind. A hundred questions whirled in Ananda's mind. It would be a while before he would even begin to articulate his thoughts. But, wonder of wonders, he was in the revolution – he had a chance to change the destiny of this great country.

'The British have a system of prevention of cruelty to animals,' Ganesh-da continued, 'but not even a cowrie is put aside for an Indian life. The stray dogs caught by the corporation are treated better than the natives who are killed as if they were locusts. Boot-shod feet claim lives. In the name of justice great injustice rules. Their justice is nothing but a farce, for their judges let off such offenders with nothing but a nominal fine. Will they ever permit these murderers to be tried by Indian judges?' He looked meaningfully at Ananda. 'The best example of this mindset is the way in which Poona's plague commissioner – Rand sahib – behaved as the epidemic swept through the city. Rand ordered the most atrocious culling possible. People began to fear Rand and his men, more than the disease and the inevitable death. How many women have been molested in the process and how many mothers have needlessly lost their children? Think of the wives that were turned out of their homes even as they mourned their husbands. Those for whom the Plague Control Committee was put together, became its victims. Not a thought was spared for them. Rand sahib, the messenger of death, seated himself on Poona's breast and tortured its people. It was not that the workers were culling the sick voluntarily, they were following government orders. It led to people being turned out of homes, properties being looted. All the while money was being siphoned off because the Ganeshkind Sarkari Bhavan was in the midst of celebrations – Queen Victoria's diamond jubilee.'

'Ever wonder what they did with the sick?' Ananta-da asked. 'I mean removing corpses and burning them is one thing, sealing homes and throwing out grieving families to brave the elements another ... but just think ... what did they do when they discovered a sick person or a sick child?' Ananta-da leant back putting his weight on his arms. His face was upturned catching the light rain. His big burly presence inspired a sense of security. 'The barbaric behaviour set the peoples' blood on fire. Damodar Chapekar could take it no more. With his brothers Balkrishna and Vasudev, they set out at night and tarred the marble statue of Queen Victoria. But the three, otherwise tame Brahmins, who could boast of little education save the practice of Brahminical rituals, had not finished their work. Rand would be made to pay.'

Ananda sensed that the long-winded story was about to get somewhere.

'On 22 June 1897,' continued Ganesh-da, 'fireworks lit up the night sky above the Sarkari Bhavan. Crowds gathered to witness the display. As the festivities ended, a carriage rolled out. Lt Ayerst and Rand sahib were returning home after a night of revelry and merrymaking. As it made its way down the leafy lane, Vasudev ran behind it crying 'gondiya ala rey'. Balkrishna jumped on top of the man holding the reins and shot him. Realizing that it was the wrong man, Damodar entered the carriage and shot Rand. Damodar Chapekar was hanged for his crime and became the first martyr in British India.[10] Balkrishna soon followed him to the gallows. These incidents called out to Savarkar and a dream was born.'

'That dream is in our hands now,' said Ananta-da quietly. 'Whether it will fructify depends on us.'

Ananda clenched and unclenched his hands. He clasped his chest tucking his bony fingers within the warmth of his armpits.

Lady Kathleen Tegart, April 1929

The guard of honour snapped to attention and the company commander saluted, as the governor's car drove up Birch Hill, rolling to a stop before the Government House. It was a clear day, but a fine mist had wrapped itself around the Kanchenjunga. The pale sunrays picked out the Lebong Racecourse in the distance. The Tegarts and the Jacksons had taken out a few days to holiday at Darjeeling.

Julia drew Kathleen by the arm towards the flat green that lay between the main house and the ADC quarters. Like Kathleen, she was tall and broad-shouldered, very handsome, with a determined set to her jawline.

An exclamation of delight broke out from Kathleen's lips. 'And you worried they wouldn't grow in the cold!'

Water lilies bloomed in the sunken water garden; Julia had designed it the previous year. Lady Jackson walked around its periphery, triumphantly counting the number of blooms and the buds that needed nurturing. 'But come my dear,' she said, 'I simply must have a wash and a cup of tea.'

Garden chairs had been laid out in the terrace garden which had been Lady Lytton's contribution to the Government House. As they settled down, the chief steward's nod brought forth a stream of liveried bearers. Lt Julian Gascoigne, the governor's ADC hovered shyly behind. Julia beckoned to him. She was a motherly sort, with a soft spot for youngsters, having married her only son off the previous year. He dropped into a chair, glad for the company and a cup of tea.

'Now, Julian's been curious about the old days,' said Lady Jackson sipping her favourite China tea.

The Government House staff had laid on a virtual feast with the gleaming silver, the snowy tablecloth, piping hot crumpets dripping with butter, floury scones and those mysteriously flavoured sandwiches, the recipe of which Kathleen had never quite deciphered.

'Calcutta has changed drastically since you arrived, hasn't it?'

'Well,' said Kathleen, her fingers wavering between the Angel cake that melted in the mouth and the very special Government House gingerbread, settling eventually for the former, 'Mike should really be the one to tell that story. Calcutta, being the second largest city in the empire, always prided itself on its modernity and cosmopolitan atmosphere. The bit of modernity that I first experienced was the tramways which had come with the start of the Edwardian era. It was used by the poorer sections of society and they of course also had bicycles. Cars had not come into general use and the upper classes still drove about in dog carts and carriages.' Kathleen looked up to smile at Julian. 'For young people like you, calling was an important rite and in Calcutta there were special peculiarities attached to it. With the exception of all but the most highly placed officials, on whom everyone of inferior rank called as a matter of duty, it was the newcomer's business to call on the older and more established residents.'

'Very sensible too,' observed Julia. 'It would certainly have made things easier for the newcomer and dispensed with the lengthy wait for recognition, as is known to happen all too often in the English country districts.'

'When Mike moved from Patna to Calcutta as acting deputy commissioner in 1906, personal calls were still de rigueur. They were supposed to last for exactly ten minutes and the well-conducted caller was always accompanied by a top hat!'

Julian leaned forward, the cup of tea in his hands forgotten. 'I hear they were wild,' he said.

'Well,' Kathleen laughed. 'They were a group of bachelors that shared a chummery ... John Nixon being one of them.' At this point they all began laughing, for John Nixon of the ICS was Sir John Nixon now and a well-respected figure.

'They were wild!' she continued, 'theatre every Saturday night with the local theatre ready and waiting. Rarely would the night end without an exchange of missiles which ranged, I am told, from bowler hats to the box carpet. The actors on the stage faithfully flung the items back at the box and so the exchange would continue through the night. But Saturday was uneventful compared to other evenings spent at the chummery.'

'I dare say,' laughed Julia. 'Practising revolver shooting by aiming at flying bats?'

'Much to the alarm of the bearers and orderlies, mock fights were routine and minor injuries common. One young man had his ribs broken by a hog spear and Mike broke his ankle when bicycling downstairs, the night before he was to be best man to Frank Halliday!'

'Frank Halliday, the commissioner?' Julian's eyes sparkled.

'Deputy commissioner in those days; came from a hunting family with a passion for horses and became, as a result, Mike's greatest friend. In fact they had both got their MVOs[11] together after the TMs' visit in 1911. Actually, Mike got his King's Police Medal that year, and the next year, both of them got the MVO.'

'The TMs visited twice, didn't they?' said Julia. 'First as prince and princess of Wales and later as King George and Queen Mary. I've heard they were a runaway success.'

'And it had been Frank and Mike at their service both the times. Before the first visit in 1905, there had been a suggestion of a general boycott in Calcutta but once they actually arrived, they received a tumultuous welcome. Lord Minto had had a successful talk with Gokhale.'

'And the general masses back then were not infested with anti-British feeling,' said Julia.

'Calcutta was en fête for days: massed bands on the maidan, the best conjurers and musicians. They had been brought in from all over India. The most brilliant of them was said to be a forger who was serving a severe sentence at the time but had been temporarily released to entertain Their Royal Highnesses. Frank had been a part of the escort as the royal party had driven in state. When the TMs returned in 1911, to hold the Delhi Durbar, they stayed for a part of the time in Calcutta. The police commissioner had been occupied in riding escort and the responsibility for practical arrangements had fallen once again on Frank and Mike. David Petrie, then assistant to the deputy inspector general of the Punjab Criminal Investigation Department, had described the atmosphere of Bengal as supercharged and had warned that it was on the cards that anything might happen. Mike was in the CID at the time, and it was on him that the ultimate responsibility rested. Their Majesties were always considerate, very punctual and gave far less trouble than the others that had accompanied them. But despite the fact that terrorism had been on the rise, there had been no anti-British demonstrations. On the contrary, the crowds had nearly mobbed the royal carriage and had swarmed into the roadway to throw dust from the carriage wheels over their heads.'

'The dust from the feet of royals absolves Indians of sins accumulated through the past lives and assures them of release from the cycle of life and death,' explained Lady Jackson to Julian. 'But, Kathleen, you digress. Tell us about the top-hatted callers.'

'Yes,' laughed Kathleen. 'When duty dictated an afternoon calling, two or three young men would set out gaily in a tum-tum, which was a dog cart, wearing topees and frock coats, carrying a top hat between them and arrive at a house where the hostess was home. One young man would remove his topee, seize the top hat and vanish into the house where, for exactly ten minutes, he would make polite conversation. On his reappearance he would hand the top hat to the second caller who would go through exactly the same performance which would be repeated until all the callers had had their turns.'

'Chummery tales!' The men had come to join them.

'Have you told them about the time Mike and his opponent decided to have it out?' Sir Stanley laughed. 'For someone whose beginnings lay in standing on a hassock – his head barely showing above the lectern – reading the lessons in a treble brogue, Mike could land a terrific punch. His opponent's broken jaw had them both surprised. What was it that Headmaster Dickie Biggs said to you before you passed out of Portora Royal? First turn to the right and straight on … good advice, guaranteed to stick in a young boy's memory.' Sir Stanley sat down and reached for a cup. 'Old days … the best part of one's life.'

'Good days, yes.' Sir Charles agreed. 'The caning, the master supervising the cold water showers making sure no one escaped … I remember a particularly memorable end-of-Christmas-term pillow fight which was interrupted by the fearsome bearded Dickie who strode into the dormitory, candle in one hand and cane in the other. After receiving the necessary application to the rear end, we spent the night shivering, locked up in the kitchen passage … And remember the endless service one had to dish out for one's fag-master?'

'Warming toilet seats during the winters!' added Julian.

'Lloyd George said to me, as Winston introduced us in the House of Commons dining room, "I have been looking all my life for the man who gave Winston Churchill a hiding at school." Winston had been my fag at Harrow,' chuckled Sir Stanley. 'Ladies, we are off for a walk. I am sure Julian will take good care of you.'

The receding figures remained distinguishable as they made their way down the slope: the lean six-foot figure of the governor and the powerfully built police commissioner. The sun was low in the sky and rocks and grass shimmered in a golden glow. Blue harebells glistened, catching the last rays.

'How is it that Mike came to choose the police service?' asked Lady Julia softly.

'It just happened to him,' smiled Kathleen, realizing the import of the question. The police services had neither the glamour of the army nor the prestige that came with the ICS. 'A notice that said two riding tests were compulsory caught his eye and that made him take the test. It was during his first year at Trinity, Dublin; Mike still had no vision of what he wanted from life. He had been orphaned early and, with his younger brother Edward, had spent his schooldays at Portora. That had taken care of the teenage years.'

Lady Julia raised her eyebrows. 'Portora! Oscar Wilde?' she looked questioningly at Julian.

'And Henry Lyte, of '*Abide with me*' fame,' he said.

Kathleen nodded and continued, 'As you know, he comes from a humble southern Irish background. His father was rector at Dunboyne, County Meath, but he died by the time Mike was twelve and his mother followed soon after. Mike was really his father's companion and accompanied him everywhere – even to the meetings of the Royal Dublin Society. The rector would ride an old fashioned tricycle and Mike his own child's tricycle. The journey, each way, was a whole twelve Irish miles and they would return the same day itself. They took to using trains only after Edward was old enough to join them.'

'I can just imagine,' said Julia, 'plump little legs pedalling furiously along the country roads. It's remarkable, such stamina at such a tender age.'

'It was his father really, who tamed the lively young animal that resided in my husband and in my brother-in-law, both of whom had a natural dislike for sitting still. He was an erudite man; a fine classical scholar who introduced them to the excitement and variety in life. Sadly, he suffered from a fatal illness and awoke one Sunday morning to discover that his failing sight had completely gone.'

'And that was when Mike took over his duties at the church!'

Kathleen smiled wistfully. 'His father continued taking the usual services for he knew them by heart, but the lessons he delegated to Mike. But to come back to the story, he qualified in the entrance exam. It wasn't a particularly stiff one, about the same level as the entrance to Sandhurst, but the competition was excessive. Only seventeen had been selected. Then came the difficult part, for he had no contacts in India, no hereditary link with the country and only the vaguest of ideas of what was expected of a policeman in India. But the fact that horsemanship was a requisite seemed to suggest an open and active life. He tells me that it had been the visions conjured by the *Boy's Own Paper* that had made him join up even though he had been heartbroken at having to leave Trinity. The age restriction was strict – between nineteen and twenty-one only – he could not afford to take a chance and apply again. But it has been a good life, providing him with the necessary excitement. He often says to me: "I was made for the wild life. The frills of urbanization bore me."'

'The fine he has levied on Mr Gandhi for burning foreign cloth was a rich one,' laughed Julian. 'Treating the Mahatma like an errant schoolboy! They are sure to fight it all the way to the high court.'

Mr Gandhi had been on a whirlwind tour of the country and had been in Calcutta from 3 to 5 March during which time he had encouraged the masses to throw out all their fine foreign clothes and burn them on the streets. The rich and poor had come out alike pulling out the clothing articles they had treasured all their lives. Sir Charles had swooped down on Mr Gandhi, prosecuting him for creating a disturbance and imposed a token fine of one rupee. Mr Gandhi had continued with his tour schedule but was due to return again to Calcutta by the end of the month.

'Mike's sense of the absurd!' laughed Julia. 'He can extract humour out of the strangest of situations.'

'It quite vexes me most of the time,' said Kathleen. 'Have I told you about the time we were driving past the maidan when we spotted three atrociously drunk British soldiers troubling a few Bengalis out on a walk with their womenfolk? My husband charged out off the car like a wounded bull to chastise the offenders with his baton. Seeing them being herded towards our car, I stepped out in a hurry and got into the front seat beside Subah Khan. Sure enough, Mike bundled the lot into the back seat and kept guard over the, by now, corpse-like Tommies until we reached the hospital. I scolded him the rest of the way. After all, he should have simply driven to the nearest station and sent a sergeant to take care of the situation!'

A cold breeze had begun to play about their shoulders. Lady Julia patted Kathleen's knee sympathetically and rose to move indoors. 'I can well imagine. Being the wife of a police officer cannot be anything but trying.'

The bearers had a log fire going and it blazed away merrily bathing the room in a pleasant glow. Two more months to go before their sailing date, thought Kathleen. She couldn't wait to get back home and to the driving holiday they took each year. They would be away from the tribulations of India until December.

Sir Charles Tegart

The two men strolled down the hill, walking sticks in hand. They had fallen into a serious conversation.

'S.R. Das, the advocate general, had come to see me at home,' said Sir Charles. 'He wanted to discuss a draft resolution regarding the release of political prisoners in our custody in those days. Gandhi had proposed to bring it up at a public meeting in Calcutta. Das pointed out and commented on the fact that the resolution "prayed" and not "demanded" the release of the prisoners. I was against it. It would only result in the resumption of secret revolutionary propaganda if not immediate recrudescence of revolutionary activity. Das, I could see, was prepared to admit the force of this contention. He then said that he had been asked by Gandhi to see me and that Gandhi would like to see me himself. I replied that if Gandhi wished to see me, I was naturally quite prepared to see him but it would have to be distinctly understood that I would be seeing him in my personal capacity; that any views I expressed would be taken as an expression of my own opinion. It would not reflect either the government's or that of the Intelligence Branch. The interview, I stipulated, would have to be strictly private. The next morning I received a letter from Das saying that Gandhi would meet me at 6.30 in the evening at the Das residence.'

'And this was ...?'

'On 25 June 1925. Gandhi was waiting for me when I arrived. Das repeated the conditions under which the meeting was going to be conducted and remained present throughout. We made no notes but I recorded the conversation later for the secret files.[12] I waited for him to broach the topic but he wouldn't start. So I began with the fact that Das had shown me the draft. He then started off at considerable length expressing great grief at the death of the Deshbandhu.'

'Chittaranjan Das?'[13]

Sir Charles nodded. 'The Indian word for patriot – friend of the nation. I think Gandhi believed it was a feeling shared by all sections of the community including the government and the European community. He thought it was an opportunity to seize on to try and bring together the various parties in the province under the shadow of a personal sense of grief. He then proceeded to enunciate his absolute adherence to the policy of non-violence and his detestation for assassination as a political weapon.

'He next proceeded to assure me with great emphasis that in the last three months of C.R. Das's life, he had been in close contact with him and the Deshbandhu had become an adherent to the policy of non-violence. He said very frankly that he made no reference to any views that C.R. Das might have held on the subject previously and nor did he propose to discuss the exigencies that caused him to switch off the policy of non-violence.

'I replied that on this issue we were on common ground but surely Mr Gandhi realized the fact that the Bengal revolutionary was a tough proposition to tackle. They were as thoroughly convinced in the efficacy and righteousness of their cause and deeds as Gandhi was in his own cause. And that they had shown time and again that they were, as a whole, prepared to go through a great deal of hardship and suffering for their cause without any hope for reward. I said that C.R. Das had himself admitted that they were a difficult body to control even by him and, therefore, Gandhi would have to admit that it would be very difficult for him to exercise control – given that, in addition to the difficulties confronted by C.R. Das, he was not a native nor a resident of the province and was not likely to stay indefinitely. I then said to him that I understood his resolution to be an omnibus one, which made no exception. To that he replied in the affirmative.

'I then said that I had read a certain correspondence which had been published early in the year in his own paper *Young India* between a Bengali revolutionary, whose name was not given, and Gandhi. At this point, Gandhi remarked that contrary to the usual custom amongst journalists, he accepted and published anonymous communications and had done so, he considered, with useful results. I said he would have to admit that the writer of the letter was a hard nut to crack and that Gandhi had failed to convert him. This he admitted. I reminded him that the revolutionary had asked Gandhi to retire from the political field because he had led the thousands of young men who had followed him during the last four years to nothing but absolute failure; that his philosophy was a philosophy of despair, and any progress that had been made on the road to swaraj had been made entirely by the acts of revolutionists. I also reminded him that his attempt at argument had only earned him a rebuff and with this too Gandhi was in full agreement. I then said, "For the sake of argument, if the writer of this letter were now in custody without trial, would you propose to release him?" To this Gandhi replied, "No." I then said that in considering this question, the individual cases of the men held in custody must be considered on their merits. Gandhi said, "Yes," but added that though he had failed to convert one revolutionary through the columns in his paper, he would not despair of converting him if personal touch could be established.'

Sir Stanley hid a smile. 'I am prepared to concede the fact that if he could get an ardent revolutionist in close personal contact with himself for a considerable length of time and isolate him from his revolutionary confrères, he might probably succeed. Unfortunately, they are so numerous and scattered over such a wide area. But no; out of the question.'

'My thoughts exactly. Gandhi went on to say that he would visit all the prisoners in the jails and have a talk with them. If they gave him their assurance, he was certain they would not revert to violence. But, I pointed out that some of them had previously given undertakings and broken them. Gandhi replied that they would look at it in a different light if they gave an assurance to him.'

Both men shook their heads in frustration.

'The responsibility for detaining or releasing lies solely with the government,' said Sir Stanley. 'And it cannot transfer any portion of that responsibility to anyone, no matter how exalted his position. And Gandhi himself would find great difficulty in assessing each man unless he first knew his history. What the man had done in the past would determine what he is capable of in the future.'

'Of course his reply turned to the sentimental side of the case and he insisted that he could override all the difficulties I had suggested. And besides, even when considering each case individually, the government was bound to consider the general state of the province from which the terrorist hailed. I asked him if he would admit that the failure of his non-cooperation programme gave a definite impetus to terrorist activity. He admitted it but insisted that his non-cooperation policy had failed because he had promised swaraj within a definite period, but the swaraj policy as such had not failed; for the swarajists laid down no such definite period.

'Then he spoke at considerable length on the three things that particularly weighed on C.R. Das's mind during the closing weeks of his life and he had no doubt that these had hastened his death: first the internment of prominent swarajists; the second, the case of the fakir – a grave error had been committed in allowing his burial in the New Market, and C.R. Das felt absolutely at a loss about the steps to take to rectify the error without alienating the sympathy of and possibly even using violence towards the Muslims; the third sorrow was the silence maintained by the Secretary of State for India about his gesture at Faridpore. C.R. Das kept waiting for the response until the last day of his life, so that could not have been as great a sorrow as the first two.

'Gandhi was of the opinion that the internment had been done with a political end in view and that the police subordinates concocted false reports implicating prominent politicians in the terrorist movement. He also said that he had been unimpressed with the Rowlatt Committe report and had opposed its findings and deductions. I responded that had he read the evidence or been present during the sittings of the Rowlatt Comittee, he too would have signed the report. At this he laughed.

'I asked whether he had gone through the literature on the subject by the revolutionists themselves. He said he had read some of it. I pointed out that nowhere in the writing had they urged that they and others arrested along with them were innocent, wrongly dealt with, or victims of police conspiracy. His answer was, "I can accept their statements as regards themselves but I cannot accept them regarding the others."

'Gandhi then proceeded to give me a long account of the trouble which had occurred in the Yervada Jail when he was incarcerated. I do not know the details, but understood from what he said that there was considerable trouble among the convicts; that he had suggested a manner of dealing with this which was unorthodox from the official point of view; that he pressed the point until the officials gave in and the trouble was allayed. I told him that I could not see the parallel between the trouble at Yervada and the trouble caused by terrorists in Bengal. He then proceeded to tell me of the revolutionists he had successfully converted in the past and the only name he could come up with was V. V. S. Ayyer, the one whose death has been recently reported in the papers.'

Sir Charles heaved a sigh and continued. 'Then we got to the actual issue. I asked him if it would meet his views if the government considered afresh the cases of all the people held in custody without trial with a view to seeing how many could be released without taking undue risks and endangering the peace of the province. He said, "Yes, provided the government said they were doing it at this particular juncture as a gesture in memory of C. R. Das." I said the government would be bound by facts and not by sentiment but he repeated that he would attach great importance to this proviso.

'Then he asked when the absolute recalcitrants were likely to be released. I said nobody would be kept in custody a day longer than was considered absolutely necessary; that those in jail would be removed at the earliest and placed under less rigorous control such as home or foreign domicile. The absolute recalcitrants, I imagined, would be released when the soil was arid and the seeds of terrorism, which they would try and sow, would have no chance of germinating. "But", said Gandhi, "Would they not themselves take to bombs and revolvers?" I said there were different grades in the terrorist ranks: recruiters who train and equip the rank and file; the actual assassins were usually young men for assassination was a young man's job. Gandhi said, "I see. So you will keep them in jail until they are too old to commit assassinations." I told him that was not what I meant. The ones in jail now may not come under the assassin category. Gandhi said, "Then they are cowards and none would follow a coward." I said this did not follow and then instanced the case of Biren Dutt Gupta who had shot Shamsul Alam in the Calcutta High Court and had been hanged for the crime.

'I told him that Biren had narrated to me and subsequently to the chief presidency magistrate the whole history: he did not know the victim personally, he had no personal knowledge as to whether Shamsul Alam was a good man or a bad man and that in killing him he had merely carried out the orders of his leader Joteen Mookerjee whom he described as a divine man. I asked Biren, "Why did Joteen Mookerjee not commit the crime himself?" To this the answer was: "He is the leader of the revolutionaries; it is not his job to commit assassinations himself and so risk his life which is far more valuable to the country than mine." I said to Gandhi, "Yet no one in Bengal will call Joteen Mookerjee a coward."

'I then asked him a question: Did he believe that if the Deshbandhu were alive today, he would have advocated and welcomed a proposal such as this one? Gandhi said "yes". I asked whether it was not a fact that C.R. Das could not control the revolutionary element in Faridpore; that he did not himself wish to press for an omnibus release, though this was urged on him with great force by the revolutionists; that during the interview C.R. Das had asked them if they were pressing for release of all these people on the ground that they were innocent? The reply had been: "Yes until they have been proved guilty", on which C.R. Das had countered: "do you suggest that Sachin Sanyal is innocent?"'

'I had read it in a journal and believed it to be true since it had not been challenged and Gandhi agreed that he had knowledge of the incidence. It was clear the Deshbandhu had himself apprehended trouble if all the terrorists were released at once.

'Finally Gandhi said to me, "If I were to ask you as a friend whether you would like me to move this resolution, what would you say?" I said, "Most certainly not." Gandhi replied, "Then I will not move it." Later, S.R. Das told me that his own opinion was that Gandhi believed Subhas Bose had been interned for political reasons and he personally did not think that any releases which did not include Subhas Bose would satisfy him.'

Darkness had descended and the yellow light of the street lamps had come on. The two men made their way back to the Government House, immersed in thought.

THREE

Ananda Prasad Gupta

That was pretty much it. Nothing spectacular took place for the next couple of months. It was really quite uncomfortable and Ananda found himself almost sneaking around. He actively avoided his classmates for fear that he would let slip the secret. Himangshu, he could not steer clear of, for the Sen house lay at the bottom of the hill on the way to school. The walks back and forth were carried out in near silence, the growing levels of discomfort becoming apparent.

The boys had become good at keeping track of ongoing politics. The Congress party in Bengal was struggling, with the differences between J.M. Sengupta and Subhas Chandra Bose coming to the fore. And though J.M. Sengupta was a Chattogram man and the one who had defended Master-da, Ambika-da and Ananta-da so ably in 1924, Master-da veered towards Subhas Bose. And Anushilan backed Sengupta. In February 1929, a Congress committee had formed in Chattogram with Mohim Chandra Das, a Sengupta man, as president and Master-da as secretary. In addition, a Youth Congress had been formed with Ganesh-da as secretary and a Students' Union with Tegra's dada – Lokenath-da – as secretary. The associations encouraged the building and promotion of gymnasiums and a grant of Rs 300/- was sanctioned, by the Chittagong Municipality, which was used to appoint Ananta-da as instructor to various clubs on a monthly salary of fifty rupees.

About two months after that initial conversation, Ananta-da called out to him after gym. Ananda could not but help notice the look on Himangshu's face. Avoiding his eye he hurried to Ananta-da's side.

'You have to meet the top boss. Come to my place after school tomorrow. You know his name don't you? Surjya Sen. We call him Master-da.'

The words sent a delicious thrill down Ananda's spine. He felt the gooseflesh prickle over his arms and shoulders. Master-da. He was going to meet Master-da. The name was associated with not just revolution but with armed revolution. In times such as these, the word 'revolution' was ominous in itself and strong men paled at its mention – but 'armed revolution'? Toying with the words was unthinkable. And bringing them to one's lips? No, that was just not possible.

The British guarded their hold over India with an iron hand. Nothing would ever keep them from letting the goose and her golden eggs slip from their grasp. Should she make an attempt to flap her wings, the retaliation would be swift and brutal. So brutal that it would never be allowed to die from public memory. The common man would rather turn in his own blood than allow such a chastisement to be inflicted upon society. The exploits of Khudiram Bose, Kanailal Dutta and Bagha Joteen made for good reading, but the masses had paid for their actions.

Ananda spent the rest of the day quietly at home. Thoughts rushed in and out of his head. A hundred questions posed themselves to his young sense of responsibility, but a particularly disquieting one kept sneaking in. What would Master-da think of him? Of Ananda Prasad Gupta? He did not look like a runt. Ruefully, he flexed his arm. The mirror caught his eye. A short, slight figure stared back. Slowly it turned, bringing its hands ever so insidiously to the hips. Then suddenly, without warning both pistols flashed.

Ananda peeped past the door. His face was scrubbed and his hair parted neatly down one side. Ananta-da sat in the corner, chatting quietly with a middle-aged man. Ananda's eyes swept the rest of the room. There was nobody else there. Perhaps he was early.

Ananta-da looked up. 'Here he is.' He motioned towards the chair he vacated as he rose and left the room saying, 'This is Ananda.'

Leaving his shoes outside the door, Ananda went in feeling more than bewildered. This could not be Master-da. Where was Master-da?

This man was nearly the same age as his father, a little shorter perhaps and with a receding hairline. Where was that muscular body that he had been trying to emulate? He transferred his attentions to the floor. The sheen of the rich red mosaic reflected a confused boy, whose eyes stared rigidly back at him. His toes, seemed to have grown extremely long. They were awkward and wriggly against the reflection of his face; his nails disgustingly neglected for weeks.

'Ananda?'

The eyes could see right through him.

Ganesh-da couldn't stop laughing. 'Imagine my plight. Here I had talked endlessly about him to my friends in the Anushilan party. The opportunity to introduce them came when the ordinance under the Bharat Raksha Rule brought us all together at the Medinipur[1] Central Jail. Master-da was the last to be brought in and the day he was arrested, there had been great excitement. I took Satish Pakrashi and Niranjan Sengupta to meet him. Master-da had been keen that the Jugantar party – the one we are cooperating with – and the Anushilan party put their energies together for the cause. After the experience of the non-cooperation movement both parties had lost faith in Gandhi-ji's ahimsa policy and were arriving at the conclusion that more needed to be done.

'It seems Niranjan had ideas similar to yours.' Ganesh-da looked at Ananda kindly. 'And he is more my age than yours. I too felt I had let Niranjan down. I was almost apologetic. This was our Master-da? The wallflower? The one that shied away from addressing the public and refused to be chief guest at any gathering. What could I say? But I need not have troubled myself so for within days Niranjan had fallen under his spell and was calling him Master-da. Master-da is the brain behind the revolution. He leaves the fiery oration and the antics to the other. You won't catch him making grand speeches or adorning the chairman's seat on a dais with a chest loaded with garlands.' Ganesh-da winked.

Ananta-da put on a look of mock hurt. He personally loved attention and what was so wrong with it anyway? 'Not easy at all to resist Master-da. All I wanted to do was to win his approval.' He burst out laughing. 'We were preparing for the Congress's non-cooperation movement. My boys and I had volunteered our services at the Congress Swaraj Sangh office. That was routine stuff – going from home to home collecting rice and money, supervising the food that was to be cooked for the masses that were gathering, maintaining discipline and looking after the arrangements for the processions. But that had not been enough for me. A hartal, I knew, was being planned.[2] And that kept going round and round in my head. The masses had to feel involved to make the strike a success. Nothing came to mind and to give myself a break I went to watch a jatra.

'The show had been organized on the grounds of the Assam Bengal Railway Company. An absolute sea of humanity had assembled. Men, women and children jostled for space on the durries elbowing and manipulating themselves into better viewing positions. The stage, you would have seen many such, was a simple one with planks of wood arranged over a wooden frame. A painted cloth screen, stretched between two bamboo poles, was to serve as the backdrop and allowed the actors to smoke or change costumes hidden from public gaze.

'It was getting uncomfortable. A little smiling old lady kneed me in the back and I extricated myself and moved to the edge. But one thought and one thought alone kept playing in my mind. The hartal. It had to succeed. Succeed not just for the liberation of India. Somewhere deep inside me I knew that I wanted it to succeed for Master-da. The show began and a hush descended upon the audience.

'The actors took the stage by storm. What a sight it was – the colours, the costumes, the make-up, the dramatic inflections of the actor's voices ... the dialogues rang loud and clear through the grounds. The audience sat spellbound, unable to move a muscle. There were tense, action-packed sequences interspersed with pretty song-and-dance interludes that added a bit of light relief. Then an idea flashed through my head.'

'Bujhli? You understand?' Ganesh-da raised an eyebrow at Ananda. 'Ananta had a brainwave.'

Repressing the retort that rose to his lips, Ananta-da continued. 'I couldn't remain still after that. I was shaking with excitement. The people around me probably put it down to emotion, for a hair-raising scene was about to begin. The hero, a prince, was on the verge of being sacrificed as the goddess Kali looked on, her eyes bloodshot, her tongue the most unnatural shade of red against the blue paint that coated her body. A scimitar flashed overhead and the audience drew in a sharp breath. The executioner paused for effect and prepared to bring down the scimitar to the words, Jai Ma Kali. He had barely gotten past the word "Jai" when all hell broke loose. The executioner lost his balance and fell over the prince. Kali gathered her skirts and ran. And I, Ananta Lal Singh had taken the centre stage.'

Ananda gasped in delight.

'You should have seen me,' chuckled Ananta-da. 'I was in top form, in command of all the eloquence at my disposal. In Gandhi-ji's name I reminded them of their duty to our nation. "Go home," I said to them. "Stop the show and go home. The hartal tomorrow has to be a success."

'It was unbelievable. After the initial shock they all began shouting. The grounds were reverberating with cries of Bande Mataram, Allah ho Akbar and Gandhi-ji ki jai. I couldn't believe my ears and before my very eyes that massive crowd simply melted away.' Ananta looked triumphantly at Ananda.

'An honest appeal made from the heart is worth its weight in gold,' observed Ganesh-da.

'And what did Master-da have to say?'

Ananta-da stole a sideways look at Ganesh-da. 'He giggled like a schoolboy.'

'He is a good sport.' Ganesh-da added. 'He was embarrassed that he could not ride a bicycle. Ananta and I decided to teach him.'

The thought of Ananta-da holding the front end of the cycle and Ganesh-da the rear end and the pair letting a wobbling Master-da loose on the ground was funny. 'And where has he been all these years?' Ananda demanded. He was still unable to ask directly about the vision that had been a part of his life – that of a young superwoman; resplendent in black with the long streak of red that flashed from the centre of her head down to her forehead. The fact that her icily splendid features were softening gradually to resemble Ma's was discomfiting. But it was not his place to ask about the personal lives of grown-ups.

'Well, for about two years they moved him from jail to jail until they figured that it was too dangerous to keep him here in Bengal.

Finally, he was shipped off to a jail as far away from Chattogram as possible. After all, catching him had turned out to be a major challenge. For most of us it had been a long stretch in jail. We had barely been released for a month or so when we were rounded up again on 1 October 1924 under the secret ordinance and held until 1928. Master-da alone had eluded this second arrest.'

'We had simply waited in the comfort of our homes to be chauffeured back to jail,' laughed Ganesh-da. Though he said nothing about his previous internment, Ananda had heard of the 1923 Maniktala bomb conspiracy case[3] ... the one that Swadesh had hinted at the other day at the club. But they had found no proof and had let him go.

'No, Nirmal-da too had given them the slip.' Ananta-da corrected. 'He got caught[4] in July the next year. A few months after his arrest the police received a tip-off from a small-time arms dealer in Kolkata. He had made a sale of a small quantity of explosive material. The lead was followed up and there was a surprise raid on a house in Shobha Bazaar.[5] But of Master-da there was no sign. He had slipped down the drainpipe from the second floor of the building.'

'Our superhero did not manage to actually take flight and landed instead with a rather heavy thump,' said Ganesh-da. 'He was extremely fortunate to have escaped with just a wrenched knee and not a broken leg. He managed to limp away and hide himself near the Ganga's ghat. After a couple of hours, once the coast was clear, he made his way to Shyam Bazaar to a relative's house. But the poor cousin was petrified and pleaded to be spared.'

'Despite the agony he was in, I don't think the cousin even let him cross his threshold. And it wasn't unreasonable if you come to think of it, for men with families have their own responsibilities. Anyway a friend living in Maniktala received word and came to the rescue. After he recovered, Master-da spent his time moving about in disguise contacting workers of different revolutionary groups trying to get them to unite. That was until he was caught and taken to Medinipur Jail.'

'Anyway, to cut a long story short, Master-da was too hot to handle here in Bengal,' said Ganesh-da. 'He was transported to Ratnagiri Jail near Bombay and then to Belgaon. That was probably the furthest and the most secure jail the British could think of. Niranjan was being moved around with him. I got to hear a first-hand account as a result. They had had a great time amongst the Marathis and when they were being readied to move to Belgaon, the other prisoners bid them a very emotional farewell – the raja-babus were going away, they said. Master-da took care to meet every last man in jail before leaving. A car had been arranged, for the authorities were greatly apprehensive that Master-da's journey would attract great crowds. They left before dawn and travelled through the Western Ghats. Niranjan claims he will never forget the view – the high peaks, the waterfalls and the ravines set against the morning mist, not to mention the deer and the peacocks that abound in the area. Our Chattogram has low hills but the Western Ghats, I am told, are spectacular.

'By afternoon they had reached the village of Shakharpa. It was a chance to stretch their legs. A police van and a truck had followed them. The British police inspector, accompanying them, was a pleasant sort of person – a thorough gentleman – having moved only recently from the army to the reserve police force. He chatted comfortably with them and did not fuss when the villagers gathered around. Master-da was in his element. It made no difference to him that the villagers spoke no Bengali. A few tentative words of Hindi and a smattering of Marathi, picked up during the stay in Ratnagiri, and they got along like a house on fire. Word soon spread that Master-da was the swadeshi the local papers had been talking about and a schoolteacher at that. Little Konkani children broke through the crowds greeting him with folded hands. Niranjan, they took to be Deshpriya Jatindra Mohan Sengupta and had to be corrected, but then they insisted that he must be a close relative. The police stood around beaming. They quite clearly considered it an honour to be escorting them. The village postmaster took them to his office and the village headman invited them to his house for lunch. The sleepy little Konkan village had been jolted awake.

'The meal itself was an experience. Two places had been set and the women stood ready to wait on them. Women in those parts enjoy a near equal relationship with their men and do not hide behind veils or purdahs. And the food! The spread was so lavish that it was embarrassing. The headman sheepishly explained to Niranjan and Master-da that most homes had sent a little something for the swadeshis.'

Ganesh-da's face held a strange faraway kind of look. 'I think Master-da draws his sustenance from the fellow feeling displayed by the masses.' He laughed. 'Niranjan too commented on the glow that had appeared on his face. I guess he is a bit of a romantic at heart; wrote regularly to Amiya-Boudi, Niranjan's wife, while in jail, never letting her spirits flag; constantly spouted Rabindranath's verses – something he does even today. I think Master-da loves Rabindranath to a fault. But that got on Niranjan's nerves at times. The two were used to taking their daily walks while in Ratnagiri Jail trekking up a hillock, within the precincts, from where the great expanse of the Arabian Sea was visible. On one such afternoon, as the poet's words threatened to overcome Master-da's emotions, the look on Niranjan's face struck him dumb. It made them both choke with laughter. "Love of poetry will not kill the revolution, Niranjan," Master-da then assured him. "The poet is inextricably entwined with our lives."'

Ananda's unspoken question went unanswered.

Ram Krishna Biswas

It was Saturday. Ram Krishna could not wait for school to get over. Phutu-da would be waiting at Koroldanga. Today the path posed no problems. He remembered it well. Following him were the Sens – Sachin, Horen and Khoka. Ram Krishna led the way, leaping over the boulders and the puddles with ease, ignoring the nettle as it brushed against his bare legs. The day was bathed in the weak golden rays of the sun and the cold December wind swirled deliciously.

Neither was Phutu-da alone. A quick round of introductions was made. Apurva Sen – or Bhola, as he was referred to, the one with the beautiful voice – had come from Dhalghat. He had brought with him Ajit Biswas whom everyone knew as a quiet, calm and dependable lad. And there was a new boy from Saroatali – Ardhendu Dutt.

A hole had been dug in the ground in which a crackling fire had got going. A clay pot hung over it steaming.

'Today,' announced Phutu-da, 'we shall celebrate. We shall have a bon-bhojon – a feast in the woods. The day is just perfect for a picnic.'

The boys sat in a circle and Sachin and Khoka began a round

of recitation, choosing the verses of Rabindranath that Master-da loved. Soon everyone was engrossed and all thoughts of hunger had been driven from their minds until Phutu-da got up to give the pot a stir.

A stack of enormous and sturdy lotus leaves, washed and cleaned, stood on one side. Phutu-da had thought of everything. The boys got up and grabbed a pair each. They were a rich dark green and felt like velvet. One was to serve as the seat and the other the platter. The food was served. The rice was a little sticky and smelt a bit smoky – the bottom layer having been rescued just in time. Over it was ladled generous helpings of a steaming carp and vegetable stew. A squeeze of lemon juice was added to every plate and shiny green chillies placed by the side. Could it have compared with a mother's practised hand? The verdict was unanimous. It could not have been better.

The band of young revolutionaries turned their attentions to Horen. Horen Sen, the only son of a mother that knew nothing but ahimsa, worshipped the doctrine of love which demanded complete surrender to the dark-skinned flute bearer – Lord Krishna.

'The story of the poet Nobeen Sen …' he began. Then quoting from Kobi Nobeen Chandra Sen's writings, he said: '"An ominous darkness looms before India. Dependency and atrocities are now our constant companions."' Horen cleared his throat, and continued, 'The people of Bharatvarsh are helpless, steeped in poverty and humiliation. The poet Nobeen Chandra Sen who belonged to our Master-da's village of Noapara had done extremely well for himself in life. As a young man, he had been appointed magistrate but did that keep him from feeling for his people? He poured his soul into his autobiography *Aamar Jibon* – My Life. Of Nobeen Babu's literary talents there was never a doubt but while reviewing *Aamar Jibon*, Bankim Chandra Chattopadhyay wrote in the Kartik edition of the *Bongodarshan*: "When Nobeen Babu's soul cries for the country, then he calls a spade a spade. If the wail of agony can drown out all other sounds, if the fear of torture cannot overcome the desire to speak freely, if anger can be expressed like Sage Durvasa's, then this describes Nobeen Babu." The man who had composed "*Bande Mataram*" had described Kobi Nobeen Chandra Sen to the T.

'But in this dependent country could the foreign rulers boast of an open mind? Could they accept criticism? Could they refrain from dragging a good man's name in mud? What did *Aamar Jibon* speak of? The poet describes the pain of being dependent. He writes with great sorrow that the laws prevailing in England are not applied by the British in India. Why, even a common murderer in England is informed of the charges against him and is permitted to speak in his defence! But are the Indian deputies of the British government of India permitted such privileges? Are they informed of the nature of complaint made against them by secret demi-officials in whom the magistrates and the commissioners of the empire repose such blind trust? Are they given the luxury to defend themselves at court? Why is it that mere suspicion of harbouring softer feelings for one's country and countrymen invites harsh punishments?

'Had Nobeen Babu been born in an independent country he would have received much acclaim. But unfortunately, it was humiliation that lay in store for him. Was Nobeen Babu the only victim of such injustice? Has such an incidence never taken place before? Then tell me, why was Lokmanya Bal Gangadhar Tilak jailed in 1897? It was because he had arrived at the same conclusion and had voiced his opinion in his newspaper *Kesari* earlier that year: "Our first duty is to put to proper use this new knowledge of English. The people must be made aware of the law and of their rights. They must know the ways and means of lodging a protest and yet remain within the limits imposed by the law." The words had driven the white man mad. Nobeen Chandra Sen and Tilak are not the only examples. Many of the Indian intelligentsia have suffered. The country has come to such a point that there is no option but to remember Vivekananda's words: "To rock the foundation of the British Empire, the young minds will have to awaken and be filled with love for their country." He believes that the worth of men is far more than all the wealth of the country. Vivekananda says that the country needs strong people to come forward, not just people with strong sinews but ones cast in steel.

'Do not forget we have been born to die. Repeat after me: Bharat's well-being is my well-being and repeat day and night – Oh Gaurinath! Make a man out of me, O mother take away my fears and my weaknesses.'

Before the applause could begin Ram Krishna raised his hand to speak.

'Philosophy is fine, provided it yields results. Our capabilities will be proven only when we put them to the test. As for the character of the nation … why, it reflects our individual characters! It is but natural that the powerful will subdue the weak. There is no point in blaming the British. But what is it that we must do now? We have to make ourselves stronger than the enemy we face. We have to beat them at their own game.'

Rifle in hand, the band of budding revolutionaries moved about the small hills during the weekends. Their targets ranged from the wild deer, duck, to jungle fowl. The strong sun beat down upon them darkening their arms and faces and the sweat trickled freely, but they did not mind. Not a thought did they spare for the exhaustion that assailed them. They ran their prey down and did not flinch from the distasteful task of skinning the meat. They quenched their thirst at the clear streams that abounded, and at the end of the day looked forward to a feast of mutton curry and rice. While it cooked, they made sport of setting green coconuts afloat amidst the wild waters of the streams and used them as targets.

The orchard on Koroldanga hill had been turned into a centre for revolutionary activities. A secret shooting range and an akhara for physical exercise were set up. Here the twists and turns of ju-jitsu were taught and the mysteries behind the finesse of professional swimmers and boxers revealed. Pistols, revolvers and rifles yielded their secrets and the revolutionaries learnt to dismantle, clean and reassemble their weapons.

Under Phutu-da's guidance the youngsters' lives took on a new meaning. A newsletter *Purbachol Patrika* was conceptualized and published. Ram Krishna became its chief editor.

Ananda Prasad Gupta

The edge of the mattress sank a little as a comfortable presence lowered itself by Ananda's side. He turned without waking, adjusting himself slightly. His head found its place without guidance on to Monorama

Devi's lap. Ma liked to sit quietly and listen to their soft snoring. Her fingers curled themselves into his hair.

She leant across to stroke Dada's cheek. It fitted smoothly into the curve of her hand. She remained in that position, not taking her eyes or her hand off his face. Then suddenly touching the rim of her eye, as if to wipe away a tear, she reached out again to mark the corner of Dada's forehead with her kohl and added a quick dab to Ananda's as well. She had got Baba to take them to a photographer's studio, earlier that week. In the years to come, Ananda would think back to this moment and see what she had seen: Ananda growing so fast that his legs would soon be pressed against the wooden end of the bed; Dada – everything a Bengali mother's heart could wish for: the mop of dark curls, lotus-bud eyes fringed with thick eyelashes, the fine straight bridge of the nose, a beautifully shaped mouth and the gentle curve of that cheek untouched as yet by the prickly tokens of manhood.

Adjusting his head back on to his pillow, Ma got up to tuck the ends of the mosquito net tightly in again. Ananda's eyes followed her. She had found a book hidden under Dada's mattress. She turned it this way and that trying to catch the dim shaft of moonlight that cast silvery patterns on the wall. She held it for an eternity. A cool breeze blew the madhobilata's fragrance into the room. She shivered; pulled the windowpanes shut and returned the book to its secret place.

Ananda stole out of bed and took the book from where his mother had left it. Squinting he tried to make out the words on the cover.

My Fight for Irish Freedom. The author was Dan Breen.

A pair of eyes bore into the back of Ananda's neck. Dada had raised himself onto his elbow.

'Master-da, Ambika-da and I were labelled as cowards.' Ananta-da was leading Ananda and Jibon towards the Lotus theatre. Every time a war movie was screened, Ananta-da made it a point to see it. The mind too has to be prepared for what could lie in store, he would say. It had been a great relief when Jibon and Himangshu had disclosed they had been chosen as well. But Swadesh remained a problem. It was getting increasingly difficult to ignore the hurt so evident on his face. They had all been expressly warned to keep him away. His was a soft background – too many temptations; too luxurious a future; too many binds.

'We had believed ahimsa to be a tactical move on Gandhi-ji's part, one that would change to relentless struggle if the need arose. But the Congress stuck to it like a leech refusing to listen to reason. After two centuries of subjugation, was there even a memory of himsa that we were expected to learn the value of ahimsa? Their workers were being herded into jails and we were expected to lower our heads and comply. It was too much. True, their malicious whispers hurt for a while but then we had work to do.'

Every day after the exercise sessions, they would head towards Sadarghat Bridge to attend classes on boat racing, horse riding and even shooting. Sometimes secret meetings were held on the bridge while others continued with their lessons below. It was out in the open and yet the others would not catch on. But there were times when they assembled at the Congress office where Master-da and Ambika-da shacked out, or at Ganesh-da's or Ananta-da's residence or late in the night within the hostel rooms attached to the National Medical School where Naresh-da and Bidhu-da were training to be doctors.

'Have you heard of the Easter Rising?' Ananta-da whispered above the music as he settled into his seat. Ananda and Jibon nodded.

'Yes, yes, the teacher Pearse led the Irish Volunteers and seized the Dublin Post Office in 1916.' Jibon could not tear his eyes away from the screen.

Ananta-da's face registered the message and he retreated into his seat as Ananda dug Jibon in the ribs. He was a poor second to MGM's screen idol.

The three days from 11 to 13 May 1929 were earmarked for the Congress Assembly, Youth Assembly and Student Women's Assembly. It was to bring the likes of Subhas Chandra Bose, Deshpriya Jatindra Mohan Sengupta, Jyotish Ghose and Nripen Banerjee to Chattogram.

Months had gone into the preparations. Since March, Ananta-da, Ganesh-da, Lokenath-da, Ambika-da and Nirmal-da had been screening the hopefuls that had lined up to be recruited into the Volunteer Vahini. A hundred had been selected and since then, it had been march, march, march, with the new boots giving everybody hell.

'Come on, come on, move it.' Lokenath-da called from the rear as Naresh-da and Bidhu-da sprinted effortlessly alongside.

'On your heels. Dig in your heels.' The first couple of days were filled with mirth as they tried to match the rhythm being called.

'Once again. Start out with your left foot ... left foot, not the right. And swing those arms ... up to the shoulder ... No, the left arm swings out with the right leg ... that was impossible ... how on earth did you do that?' The two doctors collapsed helpless with laughter.

Lokenath-da decided to intervene. 'Sen. Over here.'

Tripura Sen came forward to demonstrate. He was a tall fifteen-year-old and had come from Dhaka to live with his maternal uncle and study at the Municipal School. Tripura was a natural. It didn't come as a surprise when he was chosen to lead his company. Lieutenant Tripura. The name stuck.

'Le-eft turn! At the double, qui-ick march! Left-right, left-right.'

The companies turned to jog along the periphery of the grounds.

It had come as a shock to most. They had been fit when they joined. What had happened over the last couple of days? As ribs heaved in agony, and muscles, hitherto unknown, made themselves felt, reflections began to creep in.

'Faster, faster ... one-two, one-two.'

The finish line was in sight. A part of Ananda believed that he would not make it alive. Blood was pounding in his ears. It was impossible to hear clearly.

'Round again boys ... once more round the track.' Naresh-da smiled affectionately.

Had Ananda not known him so well he could have sworn it was the most evil of smiles.

There were boys, young hopefuls that hung around at the edge of the grounds watching. Among them was Himangshu. He had not been selected either. There was some mystery about the way the selections had taken place. It had not exactly been based on physical attributes.

Ramani Majumdar

The day dawned and the Volunteer Vahini dressed in starched khaki-green uniforms made of the homespun khaddar turned out to be a crowd-puller. Multitudes gathered. They pushed and jostled for a chance to get to the ropes that marked the boundary of the parade ground bordering J.M. Sen Hall.

A police contingent was in attendance and Sub-Inspector Ramani Majumdar scribbled little notes that he would enter into the police diary that evening: Chattogram lads put up an incredible show … stunning displays of physical prowess; Lokenath Bal stopped a motor car in motion with his bare hands; Ananta Lal Singh twisted iron rods into a 'D' and a 'V'. Ganesh Ghosh was in command dressed in the uniform of a general. He chewed on the end of his pencil thoughtfully before adding: one similar to that worn by Bose in Calcutta five months ago! Flanked by Major Naresh Ray, Captain Ananta Lal Singh and Lieutenant Tripura Sen.

Ramani Majumdar walked along the halls, through the stalls examining the posters on display. Come young men, they cried out and quoted from Tagore: Shall the altar of the goddess of bondage remain forever standing?

The youth of Chittagong were being reminded of the youth movement taking place the world over. From their dormant states they were waking up like a rush of lava to sweep away the evils and usher in the golden age. The power of the youth had changed the fate of China and awakened new aspirations in the hearts of the Turks. Life had been infused into the decaying carcass of Russia. The posters continued: Today your unhappy motherland eagerly awaits the employment of the energy slumbering within you. Join at once the Chittagong Youth Association which is a meeting place of the servants of the country.

Chittagong Youth Association? Ramani Majumdar's heart skipped a beat. Could this be the New Violence Party the police in Calcutta were issuing warnings about? His intuition told him it was something to be reported and kept track of. Paradhinatar Bedona … the pain of being dependent! The appeal of words was difficult to ignore. Aagey Desh porey nyay aar dharmo . . . First the country. Justice and principles come later. The placard had been put up on the central pandal.

He was on duty again the next day. It was only the second day and already the placard had been torn. The concluding part of the slogan was missing. Some twenty or twenty-five volunteers armed with lengths of strong bamboo had gathered. They were being led by Ananta Lal Singh, Lokenath Bal, Naresh Ray and Tripura Sen. On the last and final day, one Radhika Dutt, who lived across the road, filed an official complaint. He had been brutally assaulted. A case was registered under Section 147 of the IPC and scheduled to be heard on 23 October 1929.

Ananta Lal Singh

The Congress Assembly in Chattogram had brought a pleasant surprise for Ananta and Ganesh. Subhas Chandra Bose, who had chaired the meetings, had sent word. There was to be a secret meeting. 'Bring Tripura Sen,' he had said.

The great man met with them in a secret vault at the Mahalaxmi Bank. The Chittagong show had impressed him, especially young Tripura.

'But we have no intention of being an ornamental part of the Congress,' Ananta and Ganesh confided. 'The motto of non-violence is only a cover. We will continue to prepare for the youth revolution!'

Subhas Chandra Bose nodded his assent.

FOUR

Ananda Prasad Gupta

Ananda settled onto the wooden bench beside Makhon – Jibon Ghoshal – and Ananta-da. The Bengali and British had this one habit in common, but whereas tea was welcome anytime for the Bengali, it was a late afternoon ceremony among the English. The little dhaba boy set down the cups with a clatter, spilling the hot fluid. Under Ananta-da's watchful eye he whipped out an old gamchha and rubbed the table vigorously.

'Ireland's tragedy has served to drive home the need for unification of all extremist groups,' said Ananta-da. 'Not me,' he shook his head piously as he touched the lobes of his ears. 'These are words from the speech delivered by Eamon de Valera at New York in 1920: "We of Ireland and you of India must each of us endeavour both as separate people and in combination to rid ourselves of the vampire that is fattening on our blood, and we must never allow ourselves to forget what weapon it was by which Washington rid his country of the same vampire."'

Ananda blew on the brown fluid and swished it around in his cup. Tegra had just breezed in. He squeezed himself in and signalled to the serving boy with a cocky wave of his hand. The child responded at once, grinning like an idiot. Tegra was his hero.

'The concept of armed revolution first gained momentum here in Bengal,' continued Ananta-da, 'but over the decades no single cohesive establishment evolved. As a result, numerous little groups are struggling to come up with a working plan. The younger generation is impatient and eager. It cannot abide by the restraints advised by the seniors. Clashes are inevitable. Differences of opinion are forcing the leaders into reaching out to one another. It has brought your Ganesh-da's Anushilan friends Niranjan Sengupta, Pratul Bhattacharya and Binoy Rai to Chattogram. A much-needed strategy is being worked upon and it has been agreed that individual action has to give way to meticulous planning. The groups must fit in neatly like a cog and wheel. Anushilan and Jugantar – these are the only two parties of note in Bengal … there is a group called the Bengal Volunteers but they are far too loosely organized. But, though we outwardly identify with the Jugantar Party as opposed to Anushilan, and cooperate with the Congress, we are really on our own. Master-da is our leader and we plan our own operations.'

The dregs had gone cold. Ananda stopped swirling the tea in his cup and called for another. The afternoon had been earmarked for a session of firing practice. The range was at Rajat-da's home. It stood at the southernmost edge of the city – a picturesque spot in the Firingee Bazaar area on the banks of the Karnaphuli. Tall leafy trees, with girths that spoke of their advanced years, shaded the sprawling lawns and the beautiful two-storeyed mansion. It had served them well and provided a secure place, far from prying eyes, to carry out weapons training. The other, was Ananda's own home which had become the revolution's northern centre.

A sheet of newspaper had been strung up amidst the branches. A Colt had been arranged and Ananta-da moved between the boys letting them have a feel of the unloaded revolver. They had learnt the basics and could identify the parts. Each one was taught to strip it down and clean it. The weather was warm and an inquisitive kokil cooed from the upper branches. Rajat-da's eyes dwelt lovingly on the Colt's sleek body. Tenderly he picked it up. 'Isn't she a beauty,' he crooned and suddenly whipping it up, aimed it at the surprised bird peeping from behind the dark leaves. 'Boom! … boom!' he intoned jerking the hand upwards each time.

Ananta-da laughed. 'Julu-da held this session for us … Julu-da? He was amongst the group leaders when I first joined. Besides Master-da, there was Anurup Sen – also a teacher, Nagendranath Sen, that is Julu-da who had served as an NCO during the Great War,

Ambika-da and Charu Bikash Dutt. Charu Babu left our group to join Anushilan, and sadly, Pramod, who had introduced me to Master-da, went with him.'

'Julu-da went to war?'

'Aah! Now that is another story.' Ananta-da could see that he had them eating out of his hands. 'The leaders had been given to believe that Home Rule would be awarded if the Indians helped the British. But once the Treaty of Versailles was signed, we received the Montague–Chelmsford Reforms instead – a lollipop! But getting back to our story, we chose for our first lesson not lovely surroundings such as these but Mr Twiddle's bungalow!'

'Mr Twiddle?'

Ananta-da nodded sagely. 'Yes, a judge who lived out his days here in Chittagong. He had turned Hindu and, as per his last request, was cremated on the banks of the Lal Dighi. He had died ten years ago, but,' Ananta-da shuddered deliciously, 'his spirit had never left. No one dared venture near that lone bungalow on top of the hill.'

'And for you that had to be the place to choose.'

Ananta-da bowed his head. 'We were trying to figure out why Master-da and Julu-da had desired such secrecy. Chanting mantras, we marched into the bungalow. The shock was too much. It stank. It stank so badly that it would have driven out any spirit that dared try a hand at haunting. The place was overgrown. Cows, lame horses, dogs and foxes had moved in. Crows, kites and vultures nested inside and the ceiling was a mass of bats. The lesson began with handkerchiefs pressed to our noses but when Julu-da displayed the six revolvers and pistols all the smells vanished. All I could think about was how to procure more weapons.' His eyebrows twitched up and down. 'Visions of the visit to my mamar-bari floated before my eyes. My mother's brother works at the palace of the maharaja of Tripura. Truly! What a palace! But what I could not get out of my mind was the sentries guarding the ...?'

'Armoury.' The boys said in unison. They huddled in a tight circle about him.

'I landed up at Agartala. Mama and mamima were only too pleased and plied me with food and planned various visits: to the maharaja's pleasure garden, a hunting trip with the maharaja ... But all I wanted to do was break into the armoury. Finally, I took Umesh, my cousin, into confidence. We spoke to my mama and got him to organize a visit. It was winter and we were dressed from head to foot in woollens. The great doors opened and I went giddy at the sight. Shining glass cases and their precious contents! Suppose I took one? Would anyone get to know? Master-da's face hovered about me and he wagged his finger severely in my face. My uncle was walking ahead talking about each weapon. "Mama!" I said. "There are so many cartridges. Can I take one?" He laughed and said, "Go ahead. But, mind you, just a few." He waited at the door while Umesh and I stuffed our pockets, our socks and even our shoes. What bore, what make … there was no time to think. As we left, we were both nervous. Every guard seemed to look at us suspiciously. But then Umesh was not only mama's son he was also the Crown Prince's best friend and riding partner. We got home without trouble. When we turned out our pockets, we had about a 1,000 between us. Then I roped in a distant relative who was a soldier. The day he was on guard duty at the armoury, twenty-five rifles and their bullets were removed, packed into gunny bags and sent to Chattogram via steamer. Master-da and Julu-da were ecstatic. Encouraged, I motivated Rakhal De, a friend of Master-da's students – Sukumar Biswas and Dalil Rehman – to go and stay in my mama's house. We planned to bring more rifles but then the leaders said no. A large firearm like a rifle would prove difficult to handle in a job like ours.' Ananta-da tsk'ed mournfully. 'The leaders were getting ready for a dacoity. They were busy collecting information: where was the target house located; how far was it from the police station; what kind of people lived close by; did anyone in the vicinity have a firearm; how far would one have to go before the money could be safely sent on its way.'

Giving the gun a final rub with the oily rag, Ananta-da gave the sky a suspicious look and abruptly waved the boys on their way, completely deaf to the moans and entreaties that welled up around him.

Ananda Prasad Gupta, 12 June 1929

Bhagat Singh and Batukeshwar Dutt had been sentenced to transportation for life. They had thrown bombs into the Central

Legislative Assembly on 8 April 1929. Harmless ones, but bombs nevertheless. It had made a good story and Ananda had followed the trial carefully. Bhagat Singh had meant to do nothing but call attention to the Indian question. But with the sentencing came the shocking news that another trial was to start, for Bhagat Singh had been implicated in the murder of Deputy Superintendent of Police J.P. Saunders. It had taken place the previous December soon after the death of Lala Lajpat Rai. Within days of this news, a bomb-manufacturing unit was uncovered in Lahore and news of another arrest was being flashed. A twenty-five-year-old Bengali from Kolkata had been picked up. He had been instructing Bhagat Singh's group on the art of assembling bombs. It was Ganesh-da's friend from college, Jatindranath Das – Jatin Das of the Anushilan Party, the one who had donned the major's uniform at the forty-fourth session of the Indian National Congress.

Needless to say, an alert was sounded through the country. And Chattogram in its remote corner did not fail to feel the effects. Word was passed around: the police had added the names of those who participated in the Volunteer Vahini to the list of those under surveillance. Every member was cautioned. They were all being followed.

But it was Jatin's arrest that was causing the sensation in Chattogram. He had been incarcerated at the Lahore Central Jail along with Bhagat Singh and a highly publicized trial had begun on 10 July 1929 at the Borstal Jail. True there were several others that were being tried in the Lahore Conspiracy Case, but it was Jatin's name in the papers, on every lip, and it had, quite strangely, not bypassed the ladies of Parade Square.

Ananda paused outside the door in surprise.

'No more than a boy! The poor child.' Ananda had never heard Thakur-Ma speak with such vehemence. 'Such shoddy conditions. No way to treat the son of a gentleman.'

'Common criminals are fed better. These boys are not thieves or murderers. Why, even the thieves and murderers have privileges so long as their skin is white!' Ananda was shocked to hear Ma's voice. 'And Lahore Jail ... an establishment like that? Surely, the conditions ought to be better. No, they do it on purpose. I am sure the rations make their way home to the memsahib's kitchens.'

Jatin Das continued to hog the limelight for a while. There would be news of his welfare every now and then. And then, barely a month after the arrest came the news: Jatin and his comrades had refused all food; the prison fare was intolerable; they were going to fight for the rights of political prisoners. A fast unto death had begun.

Even Baba could not hide his admiration. This was Jatin's second hunger strike. 'Twenty days!' said Baba. 'He had gone without food for twenty days when in the Mymensingh Jail. The jail superintendent had had to apologise personally.'

The state of his health, whether he appeared cheerful or depressed at court, details of his growing emaciation … people had begun discussing it on the streets. Then, on the thirteenth day there was a hush. Jatin Das had collapsed. He had been rushed to the jail hospital and was fighting for his life. Something had gone very wrong. He had appeared reasonably fit during the hearing earlier that day.

'They were trying to force-feed him.' Bidhu-da explained. 'They forced him to the ground, ran a rubber tube down his nose and were pouring in the milk oblivious to the fact that the tube had entered the trachea instead of the food pipe. Drowned him quite literally. With all those heavyweights pinning him down there was no question of recognizing the damage until it was too late.'

A sudden vivid scene flashed through Ananda's mind. Jail. He shook himself, trying to get rid of the vision. A kind of quiet had enveloped everyone at home. Ma tiptoed about and spoke in a near whisper as if Jatin lay in the next room.

But Jatin did not die. He survived that episode and the jail authorities heaved a sigh of relief. But the pneumonia that was inevitable took charge of his already wasted frame. Jatin continued to refuse all medication and nourishment. The medical authorities were helpless. Soon there were others. The beds in the jail hospital were filling up rapidly. The jail authorities advised release. The police insisted it was possible only on bail. A well-wisher went ahead and paid up. But Jatin refused. His fight was against the conditions in jail; the denial of a political prisoner's legitimate rights and not an attempt to get out of jail or the case instituted against him. The court proceedings had to be adjourned. A sense of gloom pervaded the whole country. A race towards death had begun.

'Horror stories! Pouring in.' He was making his way with Ananta-da past the police quarters. A youngster called Kishore had swallowed red chilli powder. His throat was so swollen that it was impossible to push the feeding tube down. Ananda had thought about it all day.

'There are some that swallow flies to induce vomits as soon as the feeding is over,' Ananta-da was saying. 'The authorities are furious. They have denied the prisoners water.' But Ananda was not listening. Himangshu, who had been missing from school the last few days, was sitting by himself beneath a tree. Ananda raised his hand, about to give voice to an Oiii! Andu! when Ananta-da jerked him by the arm.

'If they have to drink, it will have to be milk,' he said maintaining a strong grip.

The look in his eye prevented Ananda from asking questions.

❧

Political prisoners everywhere had begun hunger strikes protesting against the conditions in Lahore Jail. It caused a stir worldwide. Attention was focused on the conditions of the Indian jails. At home, people sat glued to their radios for news of Jatin. But Jatin was past caring. He had not heeded to Bhagat Singh's pleas to give up the fast. He could no longer talk or hear.

Elections in Chattogram were due on 21 September 1929. The chosen representatives would go to Kolkata to vote in the BPCC elections due in November. Campaigning had taken on a fevered pitch. But the elections brought with them their own political muck. Paid goons and hired hoodlums tracking the elections, made their way in. In the middle of it all Master-da called for a public meeting. The agenda was to demand the release of Jatin Das. Students turned out en masse. A few speakers had finished their addresses when a telegram arrived: JATIN DAS DEAD. 13 September 1929. Dead after sixty-three days of fasting. He had won his battle against the empire. Chattogram was thunderstruck. All words vapourized and a hush descended. It was as if they were in the presence of the dead. Consciences revolted against the low whispering that was seeping in from the periphery of the crowd, and yet the words found their way into every ear: Subhas

Bose had sent Jatin's brother Rs 600/- to have the body brought down to Kolkata; eighty eminent Punjab Congressmen and volunteers were to accompany the body to the railway station; shops in Lahore had downed shutters in protest.

Jatin's body reached Kolkata on 15 September. Six lakh people waited at Howrah and the funeral procession wound its way down the streets. Flowers were showered by the kilogram and posters proclaimed grimly: Let my son be like Jatin Das.[1]

In Chattogram, the mood was dark. A procession was organized. Flagged off from J.M. Sen Hall, it wound through Andarkilla, Teri Bazaar, Khatunganj, Firingee Bazaar and Sadarghat, making its way back to the starting point. A photograph of Jatin Das and a few banners were on display. Slogans were shouted all the way. Masses thronged the streets and picked up the buzzwords.

'Veer Jatindranath Ki Jai! Glory to brave Jatindranath!'

'He trampled fear with both his feet and his shackles call out to all!'

'Bande Mataram! Allah ho Akbar!'

The Municipal School boys joined in late. The principal had refused to give them the day off. The gates had been shut. But Tripura – Lieutenant Tripura – had forced his way out of his classroom and had called out to his mates. 'Brothers come out or else we will be insulting a martyr. As long as there is breath in my body, I cannot permit this to happen.'

The boys had hurtled past the angry teachers and spilled out onto the street.

'Jatindranath's memory is going to pave the way for the destruction of the British government!' called Lokenath-da.

Ananta-da had as usual taken centre stage. 'Our blood is boiling over. The floodgates of tolerance have been broken!'

'May Jatindranath's blood flow through our veins and give birth to a thousand Jatindranaths.' Ganesh-da lent his voice. 'May the hearts of the tyrants cower with fear!'

The dam had broken; the outpouring of grief unprecedented. The anger, observed Ananda, had changed shade.

Ananta Lal Singh

Within hours the Chattogram police had received instructions from Kolkata. The party detectives issued a warning that a twenty-four-hour watch was being instituted: each of the ex-detenues had been assigned one plain-clothes constable by day and two by night. A police inspector was to personally supervise the operation. The police had also become aware that some workers were forcing their parents into making heavy donations; that revolutionaries had been spotted moving about in Chattogram sometimes in regular shirts and dhutis, at times in khaki or Western wear and at other times in disguise. With elections looming, there was little time to pay attention to the warnings.

Six days went by in a flash. The counting had begun. The doors of the Town Hall were closed tight. By late evening the results were out: Master-da, Charu Babu, Ambika-da, Nirmal-da and Ganesh had made it. Master-da called for a private meeting and the youngsters were asked to go home. But within half an hour the doors of the Town Hall had been broken down and goondas swarmed the building.

Unintelligible shrieks echoing in the closed space; the sounds of furniture breaking; the smell of sweat and alcohol. The others were by his side. Ananta couldn't hear them or for that matter himself. Perhaps they were all screaming. Knuckles flashing in the air; broken furniture flying across the room; the salt taste of blood in his mouth. A cry at the door; Nirmal-da's tall form running out into the night; the sight of Master-da's face streaked with blood; the room bristling with crowds one moment, now suddenly emptied. It all happened at once.

'Let's take Master-da back to the Congress Office.' Ganesh's voice broke through the blur.

'Lock the doors.' Master-da said. He looked unsteady. Ganesh held him firmly by the arm.

'What sent them packing like that?'

'Somebody … not sure who … has been stabbed. Nirmal-da has gone to investigate.'

They walked slowly with Master-da in between. There was not a tikka gharry in sight. The streets were deserted.

A crowd had assembled before the Congress office. They had seen them coming. A cry went up. Blood. They wanted blood. It was their very own Volunteer Vahini. Sharpened lengths of bamboo; legs broken off tables and chairs were being wielded by every hand. Voices. Words. They came at him rapidly. He groped amongst them to filter the story: Sukhendu had been stabbed. Sukhendu Bikash Dutt of the Collegiate School. A group of boys, on their way home, had entered a dark alley, when they had suddenly been attacked from behind. The goons had turned tail leaving Sukhendu on the ground. When they turned him over, they had seen the knife wedged into his spine. The boy was alive but his legs were paralysed.

More words were coming at Ananta. His own were going wasted. But then there was a sudden silence. They were listening. Listening to Master-da.

'Will all our energies be spent in fighting members of the Congress?' he was saying. 'And shall we let the British sit back and watch happily?'

Master-da's bleeding forehead had riveted their attention.

'Go home now!' His voice was calm but it could not be ignored.

Nobody moved. Then Naresh held up his hand. 'Everyone deposit your weapons.' Aside he said, 'Sukhendu is being moved to the Government General Hospital.'

Nirmal-da and Bidhu were managing that end. Within the next few hours the Chattogram doctors decided to move Sukhendu to Carmichael Hospital in Kolkata. Nirmal-da, Ambika-da and Ganesh, it was decided, would accompany him. They would stay on to vote at the BPCC elections. Ananta turned to Master-da, his eyes wide and pleading.

He needed money immediately. He would be in Kolkata in two days' time. In his statement, Sukhendu had named ten of his attackers. Ananta had been informed that he would receive summons to bear witness but now he did not have the time to stick around in Chattogram.

He needed to meet Saroj immediately. Saroj Kanti Guha was not from as wealthy a family as Jibon Ghoshal, Sripati Choudhury or Haripada Mahajan but at that point in time he was at an advantage. The family was to leave by boat early the next day for their village home where his sister's wedding ceremony was to take place. The jewellers would have delivered by now. Handing Saroj a cloth bag full of heavy metal locks and keys, Ananta said, 'Be sure to remove about Rs 200/- worth of jewellery.' Saroj did not need to be told more. He would replace the stolen jewellery weight for weight with junk metal.

Ananta was in Anukul-da's house, in Kolkata, the next day. 'I need to buy a revolver.'

'You have the money?'

In fact, Saroj in his earnestness had removed close to Rs 1,000/- worth of jewellery. Later that day, Ananta held in his hands the first revolver that he had bought in his life. Buckling the leather holder against his skin, he pulled his vest over it tucking it into the waist of his dhuti. The long shirt that was worn loose hid every shred of evidence. He made his way to Belgachhia Medical College where Sukhendu lay awaiting death.

Subhas Bose was at the bedside. Ananta would have to bide his time. The Congressman came to see Sukhendu twice a day. 'We need him out of the way.' Ananta whispered to Ganesh.

At last he was alone with Sukhendu. The boy had lain unmoving in bed for days. Ananta knelt by his side and laid his hand on the forehead. Ananda, Tegra, Himangshu, Sahayram, Moti … this boy was their classmate. Sukhendu turned his tired eyes to look at him. He was a quiet boy, a hard worker, one that rarely spoke. Ananta reached out for the hands and placed the revolver in them. He watched the eyes light up. The fingers traced the silken outlines of the sleek little weapon.

He had been right. It was the dream of every young revolutionary – to hold a weapon in his hands. 'I promise you, Sukhendu,' he whispered. 'We will be successful.'

Sukhendu died a few days later and Subhas Bose came tearing down to the hospital. He was amongst the pall-bearers and walked barefoot all the way to the crematorium.

Blood for blood. The slogan was being raised again and again.

'My grief over Sukhendu's death is no less than yours but party infighting is just what the British want,' Master-da reiterated over and over again. Sukhendu had died earlier than expected. The train was bringing them back to Chattogram.

Ganesh remained strangely silent through the journey. Ananta could read his mind. He wanted revenge: for Sukhendu; for Jatin; for every Indian that suffered.

He had not met Ganesh in days. Leaning the cycle outside the shop, he looked around. It was curiously empty. None of the youngsters were around; the chiks had not been rolled up for the day and the showroom was dark. Ananta went through to the inner room. Sunlight slanted in, past the curtains and cast a triangular wedge of light on the cotton mattress on the floor. Ganesh was there sitting with his back to the wall. Ananta went into the kitchen and set the pan to boil. He knew where the tea leaves and sugar were kept. There seemed to be no milk. They would make do without it.

He set the cups down and settled on the mattress, resting his back against the wall.

'No more dacoities,' Ganesh said quietly. 'The funds will have to come from our homes and we will no longer try to source weapons from abroad. A few will do. We will use them to capture the weapons in the government armouries. We will make our own bombs. Team building … we will concentrate on building our teams.' His eyes brightened as he turned to face Ananta. 'Murder,' he said. 'Massacre the Europeans but keep the murder of Indian officers to a minimum. Lead by example.'

Ananta sat quietly elated as Ganesh went on to elaborate. The plan. It was fantastic. Till the last moment 'the team' would be together. They would fight together and die together. There would be no betrayals, no secrets, and no fear of being taken prisoner.

Ananta rose. He would be back.

Master-da had been brought to Ganesh's shop. He heard them out. 'If we can establish a revolutionary government in even one zila we would have shown India the way.'

His voice was grave. 'I believe in the two of you,' he said.

Ananta reached out to take Master-da's and Ganesh's hands piling them over each other. 'On this day, 15 October 1929, we make this pledge. It is no longer do or die. We will DO AND DIE.'

FIVE

Ananda Prasad Gupta

Ananda searched the rooms. Master-da was nowhere to be found. The Congress office looked deserted. But the chairs had been arranged as if a meeting had just taken place. Ardhendu-da had probably gone for his classes. He had joined the Homeopathic College since a big row with his father had forced him to leave home. Poor Ardhendu-da. He had been very depressed since. Dastidar Babu had not come to terms with his son's choice. They were both swadeshis but Dastidar Babu was a strict follower of the ahimsa way. Or perhaps Ardhendu-da had gone to the Ramkrishna Mission for a bit of solace. He had been volunteering with their relief work for many years now. How long, wondered Ananda, would he be able to continue his studies without financial aid from his father?

'Ah Ananda!' Master-da was bringing in a large vessel of steaming khichuri.

Ananda sprang to his side and helped him lower the vessel. 'You were cooking!'

A naughty smile played about Master-da's face. 'Do you see me living in my baba's hotel?' He wiped the sweat off his face with the gamchha that was slung over his right shoulder. 'I am just an underpaid Congress worker; so overworked that I am forced to live in the office day and night.'

It made Ananda grin sheepishly. He was used to the luxuries of the Gupta Hotel with Ma and Thakur-Ma catering to his every whim. 'You held a meeting last night?' He changed the topic.

'Meeting? No, no a court really. Not here but at the National Medical School hostel. Bidhu had brought in a culprit to be tried.

Ananda's eyes widened. ****. The expletive went unvoiced. He had missed all the fun.

'What had he done?'

'Or rather, what was he about to do? Bidhu had recognized him from an earlier encounter ... he is notorious that one ... and now Bidhu had caught him loitering outside the girls' school. The goon wanted to know if Bidhu was a policeman.'

Ananda could picture Bidhu-da holding the fellow by the neck. Police? He would have said. I am bigger than the police. In a couple of moves Bidhu-da would have had him on the ground.

'It was a sight,' laughed Master-da. 'A swadeshi adalat was set up with a great deal of fanfare. The hoodlum had already been frightened out of his wits. He could only make some feeble protests. A chair was set aside for the judge and a medical student officiated. It was all very proper. The prosecutor asked him his name, his father's name and accused him of lurking outside the Chittagong Khastagir Balika Vidyalaya with MALAFIDE intentions. The poor fellow fell at the judge's feet blubbering and swearing that he would give up his wicked ways. As punishment he was made to rub his nose on the ground.'

Ananda had missed something all right. It was a known fact that of late the mere mention of Surjya Sen's party sent shivers down the spines of the city hoodlums.

Everyone seemed to have gone off to Kolkata. Nirmal-da, Ambika-da and Ganesh-da were busy with the BPCC elections and the rest were there ostensibly to be helpful. Ananta-da had returned briefly with Lokenath-da, Naresh-da and Tripura to attend the court hearing on 23 October and then they had all gone off again. Ananta-da had been sentenced to four months of rigorous imprisonment but he had six months time to report to jail. The rest had been let off with a fine.

Ardhendu-da would soon be back from college. Master-da busied himself, setting out the thalas on the floor.

Ananta Lal Singh

Mr Peters's villa lay deep within a coconut grove. It was approached by a drive lined by tall shady gulmohars. The rich elderly Anglo-Indian owned a rice mill. The entrance to the drive was guarded by two columns on which were perched a pair of white winged lions that stared scornfully down at Ananta and Anukul-da as they made their way in. The house was immense, surrounded by acres of green lawn. Ananta followed Anukul-da up the steps of the colonnaded portico. A length of silken rope hung by the door and when this was pulled, a bell jangled somewhere inside. The massive wooden doors flew open and there stood a bearer, resplendent in a white-and-gold uniform. He bowed slightly and indicated the way in. His gloves, noticed Ananta, were spotless. He led them down a long corridor into a great gloomy room and pointed to the sofas. Ananta sat uncomfortably staring at the walls that were lined from ceiling to floor with bookshelves. Anukul-da was more at ease. He frequented the house often.

'Will offering more money help?' Ananta whispered for the nth time. Unlicensed weapons were hard to come by, for the smugglers had all been raided – making them extremely wary.

'Peyey boshbey,' Anukul-da whispered back. 'It will send the black market spiralling and in the end you will be feeding their greed.' He had taken Ananta a few days ago to the fakir who lived in Nabik basti behind Dr Bidhan Roy's home. They had touched the old man's feet and handed over the money. The fakir had reached into a handi and brought out two revolvers. As they left, he had said, 'Let me know in time.' But Anukul-da had expressly warned Ananta never to go back there again.

Mr Peters came into the room. He was a tall, powerful man with a great jutting hawk nose, sweeping flamboyant white moustache and a mane of white hair.

'Babu,' he nodded. 'Welcome.' He sat down and without preamble handed over a beautiful case which held a Belgian revolver. There were two boxes of cartridges of different bores.

In Anukul-da's presence, Ananta was unwilling to open his mouth. They left, thanking the elderly man and returned home. The next day, he cycled down to the villa without telling Anukul-da. 'Mr Peters,' he said cautiously, 'I must have cartridges for the Belgian revolver.'

The old man remained solemn for a few minutes and then scratched his chin.

'I will pay you Rs 2/- per cartridge,' volunteered Ananta.

'Well, babu,' he said. 'Come back day after tomorrow please. I must give you those cartridges.'

Anukul-da wasn't offended. In fact he accompanied Ananta and carried a bottle of Johnny Walker for the old man.

It was an issue of trust. Revolutionaries feared that the dealers could turn into police informers. In their turn, the dealers worried about walking into traps set by police agents posing as revolutionaries. Yakub, the Muslim shippie, insisted on changing the meeting place every time. He would drive down in a large private vehicle and pretend to go about his business during which time the parcel lying at the foot of the passenger seat would have to be removed.

SURESH DE

'Come,' Master-da called. Eat a little before you go.'

Suresh had kept himself out of sight. But Master-da had known all along that he was there. He came often, ever since Pundit-da had introduced him. The atmosphere around Master-da was intoxicating. The boy nipped out from behind the cupboard and sat down. Master-da ladled out the steaming khichuri.

'Now, Suresh,' he said, 'remember all that glitters is not gold. A costume can turn you into a king on a stage but not make a man out of you. Vidyasagar Mohashoy made a name for himself not because of what he wore. On the outside he was like an Ude-thakur.'

Suresh lowered his eyes in shame. Master-da had caught him out: he had been unable to take his eyes off Ananda Gupta from that first day he had laid eyes on him. It was the other reason that the Congress office attracted him so. Rajat Sen, Ananda, even the boy that was murdered – Sukhendu – he loved the way they spoke, their sense of style … these were the fashionable youth of Chattogram. But he had never worked up the courage to speak to them.

'I want you to stop coming to the Congress office. Ram Krishna will take over your training.' Master-da said, as he swept his hand around his thala, scooping up the last morsels. 'He will be waiting for you.'

Suresh was new to Chattogram, having moved only a couple of months ago from Dhaka. He would make his way to Patharghata that very afternoon, he decided. Ram Krishna lived there in his sister's house. Her husband, Kali Prasanna Choudhury, a promising young government servant with a bright future, had opened his home to his young brother-in-law, hoping to see the rather intelligent youth graduate and follow in his footsteps.

Suresh presented himself at the door. Ram Krishna-da came down from the second floor, where he lived and seemed pleased with his new charge. Suresh, on the other hand, was smitten at first glance: a calm gentle face and a voice that was soft and pleasant. He could have been allotted no better mentor … a glow arose within him as if lit by the presence of a divine being.

'Come early tomorrow morning,' Ram Krishna-da said, slipping him a little roll of paper. 'Read this every day.'

Suresh unrolled the little piece as he walked back. It read:

> Daily routine:
> Leave your bed by 5 a.m.
> Sit outside and contemplate on the vastness of the universe.
> Give up daydreaming and fickleness.
> Concentrate 100 per cent on every task no matter how simple it may be.
> Finish every task in the amount of time allotted.
> Success will come to him who aims high and follows the right path.
> Spend the day in preparing your mind.
> Criticize yourself every morning.
> Good behaviour, good principles, good intentions – if these are lacking, you will become unhappy.
> Give up prejudice.
> Remain alert always.
> Use your commonsense.
> Give women the kind of respect you will give your mother.
> Never share your bed with anybody.
> Read the Gita daily.
> Get rid of fear, anger and worries.

This meeting had gone off far better than the first meeting with Master-da. Master-da had given him a fraction of a glance and mumbled, Janani Janmabhumishcha swargadapi gariyasi ... Mother and the motherland are greater than even heaven ... remember these words always. And with that, he had gone back to his work. Today once again Suresh had felt that powerful magnetism that he associated with Master-da. It had emanated from Ram Krishna-da's body, enveloping him in a cloak of tranquillity. What was it, he wondered. The kind of power perhaps that Thakur Sri Ramkrishna used, to draw a worthy man like Naren Dutt to himself? The same power Sri Ma had used on the unbelieving playwright Girish Ghose?

Suresh spent a restless night and was up early the next day. He was at Ram Krishna-da's doorstep before dawn. Ram Krishna-da was ready and waiting. 'It is good to be an early riser,' he said. 'Nature is calm at this time and helps you concentrate.' Together they set off. They walked along a small road towards the Karnaphuli. 'Suresh, now that you have received the life of a man, do not waste it in sleeping, eating and chatting. Do not forget the worth of being born a man,' Ram Krishna-da handed him another slip of paper. 'Read this every morning. It will inspire you.' It had a long mantra which made his head buzz. He would have to figure it out later.

They had reached a small straw hut. Ram Krishna-da went in, beckoning to him to follow. A swami-ji greeted them. He sat amidst piles of books. They were all for sale at three annas each. The boys browsed through them. It was peaceful inside, with the hum of the Karnaphuli, right outside the door.

'Sit,' said the swami-ji. The boys sat on either side of him. He closed his eyes and sang. Then he placed his hand on both their heads. 'If you farm this life well you will reap in gold.'

Ram Krishna chose three books and paid for them. Handing them to Suresh, he said, 'Read these with care. Come and meet me again in a week's time.'

A week later, even before the crows could caw, he was at Ram Krishna-da's doorstep.

Ananda Prasad Gupta

Jibon had not come by for several days. Ananda went down to the Ghoshal house. Mashima sat him down in the living room. Jibon was indisposed. He couldn't come out to meet him. Mashima's face was strained, her eyes puffy. She sat by Ananda's side as he ate the sweets he was offered. As he got up to leave, she stroked his head in an absent kind of way. He wondered what had changed. Was it childhood that was coming to an end? Did it have to mean the severance of old friendships?

Mumbling something about not feeling well, Ananda went to bed without dinner. Ma and Thakur-Ma hovered anxiously around, constantly laying their hands on his brow. Even in his sleep he could feel the coolness of Ma's hands. He drifted off. She was sitting beside him again. A hand nudged him, then shook him slightly. It was Dada. He was sitting by his side.

'Makhon got into big trouble at home. It will be a while before they let him out.'

'Oh.'

'He forged his father's signature and removed eighteen hundred rupees from his account. But the bank manager called his father to check if Jibon had got home safely with the money. Now they won't let him out of the house. And his examinations are due. They are too embarrassed. It's understandable. His parents have even visited Ananta-da and Ganesh-da, pleading with them to drop him from the team.'

Of late Dada's aloof attitude had also got to him. He wanted to snap back and tell him to mind his own business.

'They insist he is too young and weak from the time he had the typhoid. Ananta-da used to spend a lot of time by his bedside during that time. They reminded him of all that, hoping to appeal to his tender feelings.'

'Oh.'

Deboprasad paused. Ananda felt his older brother was once again on the verge of breaking some news. He had felt it several times before that year but Dada had always drawn back. He could see his face despite the fact that he was not looking at him. The eyes would be narrowed and if he decided to speak it would be with a deliberate slowness as if expecting him to read his lips.

'Baba and Ma. They need you here. I have to go. You understand that.'

This had been it. Tears prickled behind Ananda's closed eyelids. He turned on his side pretending not to have heard. Deboprasad Gupta would get to go, would get to follow his heart. It was not about Ma and Baba. They had Chotkun, didn't they? But it hardly seemed worth voicing it. It was never about him … it was never about what Ananda wanted or hoped for.

Dada continued to sit by his side.

Suresh De

'You know, Suresh, I read China's history last night. Listen: China is the largest country in the world. Not just largest; it was once the leading nation in terms of education, civilization, science and wisdom … like Bharat. It predates Christ by 300 years. The Qin dynasty, they built the great wall that continues to be one of the great wonders even today. The day this great country came into contact with the Europeans, it began to decline. It became poor; drugged with opium. Suffering had become a way of life and their women … they had been left with little respect. When Sun Yat Sen came forward, he travelled from one end of the country to the other, reminding people of what China had once been. He made them aware of how far they had fallen. And he advised them to take their future into their own hands. His magnetic personality drew the people, and together they won independence for their country in 1912. Life did an about turn and the people prospered. Corruption was driven out. This mental revolution did not remain limited to China. The Chinese settled in India changed as well. They cut their hair, threw away their opium boxes and released their women from the centuries-old iron shoes. But all this did not happen in one day and not without its fair share of difficulties.'

By the time he finished, the sun had risen. 'Show me what you have written.'

Suresh was embarrassed. 'I couldn't … there was no time.'

Ram Krishna-da looked displeased. 'I never encourage laziness. If you are not thorough, you will be caught in loopholes.'

Suresh could have just disappeared into the ground. He had fallen short in the eyes of his idol. He plodded through muddy fields, skipping across little streams; keeping up with Ram Krishna-da who walked briskly ahead talking all the while: it was a monologue on Vivekananda. By the time he finished they had reached Chaktai.

'Will you be able to do it, Suresh? Convert yourself into a Vivekananda?'

For once, Suresh knew no answer was expected out of him.

'Do you realize we look at Bharat through the eyes of the white man … and that is why we look down upon our dharma, karma and shikkha-dikkha, the traditional wisdom and knowledge handed down to us. We must begin to think independently once again. The revolutionary cannot ask others for help. He has to help himself. Swami Vivekananda, though he was educated in the manner of the Europeans, managed to pull himself out of the binds they had placed and learnt to think for himself. No one will gift us independence. We have to ready ourselves to pay the correct price. Vivekananda has said: "May the world learn of this great ideal, may it be rid of corruption. Do not think of yourself as weak or sad. O all powerful. Rise. Awake. You think of yourself as a sinner … it is not worthy of you. Tell the world this. Tell yourself this. Look how it will reward you. See how, as if in a flash of lightning, everything will be revealed."'

Ram Krishna-da was a Vivekananda fan. It had been Master-da who had first told him about Vivekananda in such detail. And he worshipped Master-da's word.

They had turned around and begun walking again, taking the winding road, the one that led to Fairy Hill. There was no one about but them.

'You know, Suresh, this is the best part of life. The young mind can be moulded like clay and the impressions that it will take on now will last a lifetime. Whatever you strive to become now, you will achieve. Struggle, struggle, struggle … that itself can achieve a lot.'

They had reached the top of the hill. Ram Krishna-da stood in silence, overcome by the beauty of the dawn. It was his first visit there. Suresh pointed out the sights: to the south at the bottom of the hill stood the Municipal School where he studied; to the north, on a higher hill, nestled amongst the green trees was the district magistrate sahib's bungalow; to the east lay Andarkilla and the waters of the Lal Dighi. Most of Fairy Hill was occupied by the magnificent courthouse buildings from where cases were tried and verdicts read out.

Ram Krishna-da walked around slowly. He had become very quiet.

'One day all this will belong to us,' he said softly.

Tock! Suresh jerked awake. The hands of the clock pointed to 5 a.m. He had gone to bed telling himself that he would rise at 5 and go to Patharghata. He had woken on time without the help of an alarm.

His dada, Shri Satish Chandra De, habitually left every morning, walking stick in hand, for the banks of the Lal Dighi. The household would be pleased that Suresh was developing good habits. It was a cold winter morning, still pitch dark. Wrapping a warm chador about himself he set out. He could have passed for someone responding to the call of the Nishi – the spirit of the night. It was not the Nishi but the country that had called out to him.

Ram Krishna-da was in the middle of doing push-ups when Suresh came upon him. He was pleased to see him so early. 'It promises to be a lovely morning. And now that you are here I can see that it will be a wonderful day.'

'I was up last night and I have written a piece.'

Ram Krishna-da took the paper from his hand. 'You have a flair for writing and you think clearly. But you mix the pure form of Bengali with the colloquial.' He pursed his lips. 'That spoils the effect.' He read it again carefully; took out a pen and scratched out bits with red ink. He made some notes by the side and returned it to Suresh. 'Have you brought your swimming trunks?'

The boys made their way towards Lal Dighi. Most children in Bengal are natural swimmers. Perhaps they lack in grace and style but they can all make their way swiftly across the water. But to be of use to a revolutionary, these skills would have to be honed. Prafulla Babu waited to give lessons. He demonstrated the many commonly made mistakes and new styles that ought to be kept in mind: How do the fish swim against the current? By following a diagonal path! How to keep afloat for long hours? How to keep your head above water and how would you escape from a man-eating marine creature? It was a cold morning but the boys churned the Lal Dighi's waters till afternoon. When they clambered out, Chandra Shekhar-da announced an eight mile race in the Karnaphuli.

They jumped into the river the next day and floated in the manner prescribed. The current was strong and Suresh felt himself being pulled along like a bit of straw. Then, at the signal, they struck out. For two hours they swam steadily in one direction until Prafulla Babu raised his arm. Suresh saw him mouth the word ghurni – whirlpool. Not an inch of this river was unknown to this man. The boys turned back. The shore had by now filled with spectators.

The swell had begun to make itself felt. 'Switch to breaststroke. Keep your heads above the water.' Ram Krishna-da was in a sampan calling out encouragement. He leant over periodically and pushed lozenges into the mouths of the swimmers. Finally, he hauled Suresh onto the boat and draped a blanket around him.

Prafulla Babu, Biren De and a few others, whom Suresh did not recognize, continued to swim. By the time they reached the shore, the electric street lights had come on. Sadarghat was aglow. The crowds on the shore were going wild, congratulating those that actually finished.

Suresh huddled in the boat shivering, trying to squeeze his shoulders between knees that stuck up straight and knobbly into the air. Ram Krishna-da smiled. 'Tomorrow we will go for a dip in the sea.'

Sir Charles and Lady Kathleen Tegart

Sir Charles looked up from the table where he had been jotting notes in his personal diary for the day. He smiled quizzically. Kathleen was still busy scribbling in hers. The vacation was coming to an end. The initial hectic round of socializing had just about come to an end and it would be but a few days before the rounds of farewell parties started off and then they would be India-bound once again. These were their few precious days together.

'Not yet finished.' Carefully covering the freshly written page with a sheet of blotting paper, she smiled mischievously.

'Well,' said Sir Charles, 'let's see what I have here. Seely! This is my personal favourite. "Britain acquired her Empire in a fit of absence of mind …" Gladstone writing to his wife: "Ireland, Ireland! That cloud in the west, that coming storm, the minister of God's retribution upon cruel, inveterate and but half-atoned injustice. Ireland forces upon us these great social and religious questions."' He smiled as Kathleen laughed aloud. '… Peele's admission: "The creation of a police force has given me more trouble than anything I ever undertook in my life!"' He snapped the diary shut and came across to lean over the top of her head. 'Nothing intimate, nothing personal I hope.'

'None whatsoever, Mike,' said Kathleen. 'Would I tell the world about the great personal happiness I enjoy?' Her eyes gleamed with playful delight as she resisted the deep blue of his eyes that willed her to say all. The blotting paper had slipped.

'The bagh!' he exclaimed.

'All I know is the scraps I have picked up from the newspapers,' said Kathleen defensively.

'I have no time for fiction,' groaned Sir Charles as he went to stand by the window. 'Like those detective stories I picked up at the store … the legal impossibilities; the chancy detection; the inexplicable behaviour of the police … disgusting!'

'Then tell me the story your way.'

'Old history,' he said meditatively as he lit a cigarette. 'But so vital to the tale of the Empire.' Sir Charles inhaled deeply and began. 'I had been refused permission to serve king and country. David Petrie, who had wound up his investigation on the bomb attack on Lord Hardinge earlier that year, had been injured in gun battle with Sikh revolutionists in September at Budge Budge and had gone home to recuperate. The War was going badly for Britain and she could certainly spare no extra troops to quell rebellions.'

'And everyone dominated by Britain seized the opportunity to strike a blow.' Kathleen picked up her pen.

Sir Charles's face was obscured in a cloud of blue smoke. 'For some time I had my eye on a certain cloth shop in Calcutta which specialized in Indian-made goods. I had a tip-off that the owners were planning to keep a large arms dump on the premises. Money was comparatively easy to obtain and it was merely a question of planning one or two important dacoities. One plotted in a Bengal district in January 1915 failed but another succeeded and brought in Rs 11,000/-. The next month the gang received wind of a sum of Rs 18,000/- which was being taken to Messrs Bird & Co by three employees in a hired cab. That was grabbed and within the month two taxi-loads of young men of the educated class committed a dacoity in the Calcutta suburbs and raked in another 22,000/- for the fund.

'The party was now anxious to hear what Germany had up her sleeve, for Jitendra Nath Lahiri had returned from Europe bringing offers of help in general terms from the Germans.

'An emissary needed to be despatched to Batavia to discuss concrete proposals and Narendranath Bhattacharya, adopting the nom-de-guerre of C. Martin, set off. Bhola Nath Chatterji left for Bangkok to get in touch with the German Consul and Abani Mukherji for Japan. Contact was established with the revolutionaries in America. There were three points on the agenda:

'The Andaman Islands were to be captured, for a number of political prisoners including Barin Ghose, the owner of the Maniktala Bomb Garden, were there serving their time. A German disguised as a merchant was to land, get in touch with the released prisoners and persuade them to destroy the wireless station on a particular night when the German ships were due to arrive. These would carry a fighting crew on board and arms and ammunition picked up from a dump on the Nicobars. The islands were to be taken by storm and convicts, willing to serve under German leadership, would be taken off to join an army training camp near the Burma border. Germans of military age, stationed in Thailand and the Dutch East Indies, would be conscripted; Burma would be occupied and an invading force would then enter Bengal. But, before all this, the Burma Military Police would first have to be corrupted and persuaded to join the army of insurrection. In the meantime the Bengal revolutionaries would have, with the help of German arms, taken possession of the province.

'There was a second scheme for the North-West Frontier, and a third for the disaffected Mutiny Party Sikhs returning from South America to Punjab to raise a revolt there.

'It was all planned with typical German thoroughness and attention to detail. On paper it looked as though it might only be a question of months before India became the property of the Fatherland. But in making their calculations, the Germans showed their national tendency to disregard the human element and to underrate the intelligence of the enemy, which in this case, was the police.

'C. Martin of Chingripota, 24-Parganas, was no prentice hand. His hometown had the distinction of having been the first scene of a political dacoity, and evidence pointed to him having been connected with it. One of his co-villagers was the manager of Harry & Sons, which far from being a respectable English firm was merely a cover name for the rebel group. Martin was introduced, in Batavia, to Theodore Helfferich. Helfferich appeared to have everything organized down to the last button: The 'Maverick', carrying 30,000 rifles, ammunition and money was already making its way from California via Java; more money could be remitted to Harry & Sons … the sender would be named C. Martin and the money would be transmitted through a genuine trading firm. Martin suggested the ship be diverted to a little known place called Rai Mangal in the maze of waterways – the Sundarbans. Satisfied, Martin returned.

'The Big Five: that is Martin, Joteen Mookerjee, Jadu Gopal Mukherji, Bhola Nath Chatterji and Atul Ghose decided that the arms, when they arrived, were to be divided into three parts and distributed to eastern Bengal, Balasore and Calcutta; the three main railway lines into Bengal were to be sabotaged; a force would be raised which would first occupy eastern Bengal and then march onto Calcutta; the German officers would remain behind in eastern Bengal and continue to raise and train the army. Calcutta would be attacked and held by a separate party until the main group could come down from eastern Bengal.

'Joteen was to be in charge of the sabotage party, which was to blow up the chief bridge on the Madras Railway; others were detailed to take care of the Bengal Nagpur and the East Indian Railways. Jadu Gopal Mukherji was to take charge of the cargo landing of the 'Maverick' and Martin reserved for himself the big plum – Calcutta.

'I had a particular interest in Joteen-the-bagh, or Bagha Joteen as they call him. He was an energetic devil-may-care member who exercised a stiffening effect on any group he came into contact with. He and his gang had been responsible for the big arms theft from Messrs Rodda & Co, and he had personally instigated young

B.N. Dutt to murder Deputy Superintendent Shamsul Alam in the high court some five years before. I had had a long talk with the boy before his execution.

'The other members of the group were not desperadoes like Joteen but pretty much of his calibre. Martin had planned to attack all the arsenals in town, collect all arms available and storm Fort William before the civil or military authorities realized the extent of the rebellion.'

'One cannot help but admire the bold concept of this venture,' murmured Kathleen as she put down her pen and shook her aching fingers.

Sir Charles nodded. He came to sit by her side and reached out to take her hand, massaging it gently. 'Open warfare! Almost refreshing,' he said. 'The DCI had become concerned about what was going on in neutral Siam. Petrie was due back in August 1915, after his convalescence. He was moved instead to Bangkok for six months and attached to the British legation. His reports convinced the Government of India that it needed its own overseas intelligence network. Petrie was ordered to set one up and he recruited agents during a tour of Singapore, the Dutch East Indies, the Philippines, Hong Kong, China, and Japan, and subsequently directed their operations from August 1916 to November 1919, while ostensibly the vice consul in Shanghai. Getting back to the story, we, in India, spent months piecing together disconnected facts, following up clues and carrying out detective work. Preparations in India had begun in right earnest. Harry & Sons sent a cable to Batavia asking for another remittance while Jadu Gopal Mukherji enlisted the help of a landowner near Rai Mangal who was persuaded to provide men and the necessary small craft to unload the 'Maverick's' special cargo. The ship should have arrived by the end of June. The German signal to be given on any ship carrying arms was three horizontal white lights. The conspirators waited to acknowledge it by two horizontal red lights from the shore. A week went by and then another. They waited until July. Could the German genius for organization have side-slipped somewhere? Then a messenger arrived from Thailand: the German Consul in Bangkok was sending five thousand rifles, ammunition and a lakh of rupees to Rai Mangal in an unnamed vessel. What seemed to be good news at first, on reflection gave them little satisfaction. It appeared that the Germans had decided not to send the 'Maverick' after all and had arranged with the consul in Bangkok to substitute another vessel and cargo.'

Sir Charles lit a second cigarette and waited for Kathleen to finish writing. 'It was a shabby trick that Germany seemed to be playing. From the point of view of the recipients it was not at all an adequate exchange: half the money, one-sixth the amount of arms promised. It would inevitably delay the big day they were all looking forward to. They decided to despatch an urgent message to Helfferich begging him to stand by the original agreement. Of course, they could not send a letter or a telegram. The issue was far too delicate to be worded comprehensively keeping it, at the same time, innocent on the surface. The only way out was to persuade the Bengali messenger to return to Bangkok, calling at Batavia on the way.' Sir Charles caught the sharp look in Kathleen's eye and smiled. 'The message was that while they would rather not accept any substitute for the 'Maverick's' cargo they were only too willing to accept any addition to it. The other vessels would have to land their cargo at Batia in eastern Bengal and Balasore on the shores of the Bay of Bengal.'

'And all this while you were indulging your passion for automobiles driving unescorted in an open car through the city!' Kathleen pressed both her hands to her heart.

'Well, Tim's predecessor was always with me, my brave little Straffordshire Bull Terrier. There were a couple of telegrams that I scrutinized … all very innocent, and made enquiries of one or two trusted agents … who may have got wind of the trend. We instructed the bank to freeze the last 10,000/- that may arrive for Harry & Sons and paid the company premises a visit on 7th August. We had also planned a warm welcome for the 'Maverick' should she arrive at Rai Mangal, one far warmer than the revolutionaries had in mind.

'The revolutionaries kept their heads, though there must have been some consternation at the turn of events. A warning telegram was sent to the Germans at Java: MARKET LOW POSTPONE TRANSACTION TILL INFORMATION. C. MARTIN. Martin left for Batavia taking with him Phonindra Nath Chakraborty alias W.A. Payne.

'Acting on a clue, enquiries were made at Balasore and it was discovered that a brother of the manager at Harry & Sons had started a shop which bore the modest title of Universal Emporium. Oh! It sold gramophones and gramophone records and took in a little bicycle repairing on the side. But what was of interest to us was that the manager was a friend of the energetic Mr C. Martin in whose company he had made a journey to a remote habitation in the jungles. Some seditious literature was also found which the manager was unable to connect either with commercial activity or a love of music.

'Accordingly, the district magistrate and the police officers in charge thought it desirable to pay the jungle retreat a visit. They made their way to the remote village of Kabtipada and then followed a mile-long track through the jungles to a lonely house. The birds had flown but not without leaving traces of their sojourn: a map of the Sundarbans, a newspaper cutting about the 'Maverick' and a few other documents they had been unable to destroy. The trees in the vicinity were scored by bullet marks – the result of firing practice.

'The raiding party now worked out a plan to watch all lines of escape and before long, news was brought that the rebels had taken cover in a patch of jungle surrounded by open fields. They hurried to the spot and encircling the area advanced over open ground in extended order. They were met by Mauser fire but continued to advance while returning fire. Eventually, two Bengalis emerged from the wood and surrendered. It was then discovered that during the fire, Joteen Mookerjee had been killed and two others had been wounded.'[1]

'But Gopi Nath Saha, who had tried to kill you, said during his trial that it was a bullet from your gun that had killed Joteen!'

Sir Charles pretended not to have heard and continued. 'The discovery that the police knew so much shook up the group. The Germans developed cold feet and backed off, and as a result Martin received a severe snub when he reached Batavia. As regards the 'Maverick', she waited in vain at an island off Mexico for a rendezvous with the schooner 'Annie Larsen' and her cargo of arms. The schooner failed to make an appearance and instead on the horizon appeared two British warships, the 'Kent' and the 'Rainbow'. Search parties boarded the 'Maverick' but found nothing on her, for the five passengers, Sikhs of the Mutiny Party, had hurriedly burnt the contents of their four suitcases and four sacks. Meanwhile the 'Maverick's' crew bored by their inactivity, had turned garrulous and a secret destination was revealed in one of the war telegram slips. Germany was furious and recalled the ship. Another ship the 'Henry S.' which had been loaded with arms, destined for Bangkok, was caught by the Customs before leaving Manila and forced to disgorge her cargo. Martin still managed to work his way around Helfferich and the German consul to consider some plan, any plan. First, they were adamant in their refusal, but later agreed that the German consul at Shanghai would arrange for two shipments. Payne was instructed to make his way to Shanghai and finalize the details. He reached after a hazardous journey but Petrie was waiting. And Payne was promptly arrested. The same fate befell the Chinese messenger carrying money to Bengal. The grand German plan had fallen through. Martin decided against returning to Calcutta and left to join the Mutiny Party in America. He reached San Francisco, after a long circuitous journey, in the summer of 1916, where he was arrested on a charge that proved to be false. On his release he escaped to Mexico and, subsequently, made his way to Russia after the Revolution and became leader of the Communist International under the name he had assumed in the USA – M.N. Roy.'

The story had all the makings of a great spy thriller. Kathleen closed her diary but remained lost in thought. The grand German plan had been unravelled chiefly by David and it had taken a toll on his health. It had brought him the OBE in1918; the CBE in 1919 and with it an offer to become the new director of Central Intelligence. But he had turned it down on grounds of exhaustion and had gone home and got married. When Cecil Kaye retired in 1924, David eventually consented to becoming director[2] and changed the name of the department to the Intelligence Bureau. David Petrie and M.N. Roy continued with their cat-and-mouse games, the latter never giving up his attempts at establishing communist cells in India and the former constantly monitoring and thwarting his every effort.

Many questions had been left unanswered but Kathleen refrained from pushing her husband. Had he really rushed to Joteen's side[3] as he lay dying, acknowledging a brave man that fought from the trenches; did he really once say that had the man been born in England his statue would surely have stood in Trafalgar Square by Nelson's side? He would only laugh away her queries. But the one thing she could be sure about was that he viewed the moves of his opponents with disinterested appreciation but appreciation nevertheless.[4]

Ananta Lal Singh

The fund collection drive was on. Rajat Sen had been summoned. He was from a middle-class family but the rules were strict. 'No less than Rs 100/- and no more than Rs 200/-. You have two days' time but getting caught is not an option.'

Rajat came back dejected after two days. There was no way he could break into the family strong box.

Ananta sat him down. 'If I say let's go loot the Imperial Bank, you will be ready, won't you?' The boy nodded. 'This is the same thing. Remember Napoleon's words: Necessity knows no law. When I had to first do it I had drawn my dada and didi into my plans. Didi had opened the family strong box, for which she was responsible. "Tell Baba," I had said to her, "I am helping myself to my share of inheritance and no more."'

Within six hours Rajat brought his first instalment. He soon returned with more. His mother had handed over all the jewellery she had inherited from his Thakur-ma. His little sisters had come forward with their necklaces, earrings and bangles.

Lokenath came in that day to hand over a gold chain. 'Baba!' he said. 'That little sister of mine can scream … Maaa Shona Bhai niye gelo!' He mimicked in a high-pitched nasal tone. Another chain that came in that day was brought by Ananda. He had picked it up from the bathroom where his sister had left it. Ananta called for Debu.

'Now that he has brought it,' said Debu, 'keep it.'

But the loss of that chain resulted in a ruckus in the Gupta household. It had set Ananda's father off on a roaring rampage. He swore to get to the bottom of it and if need be, drag the information out of the clairvoyant Taracharan sadhu. Debu panicked and ran to meet Master-da.

'Should I plead with Taracharan Baba not to give away our secret?'

But Phutu, who was there that day, put an immediate perspective to the whole thing. 'If you go to the sadhu baba, it will be a virtual confession. Do you really think that the man, despite all his pretensions, will be able to resist the temptation to show off his great powers?'

As it happened, Taracharan Baba gave Ananda and Debu's father such a long-winded explanation that the affair of the chain died a natural death. The agony that the boys had gone through reminded Ananta of the times he had helped himself to his father's almirah. But the most difficult episode had been the one he had used to encourage Rajat with.

It had been in the months following the Paraikora dacoity. Ananta had not returned to school. He insisted on being sent to Kolkata to the college in which Ganesh studied. Ganesh had applied on his behalf and within weeks had sent a congratulatory telegram. Ananta had secured a seat in the Bengal Technical Institution. Master-da and Nirmal-da had not been happy. You think I am going to study like a good boy? I will meet Julu-da and discuss how to begin more work, he had assured them. Be a good boy, study, don't let me down, Ma had said repeatedly. Baba had warned him to stay away from the political parties. A part of him had been quite convinced. But once in Kolkata, the studies had turned out to be fairly boring. Student life hadn't proved particularly enjoyable, but with Julu-da, Ganesh and Jashoda Ranjan Pal the days had been pleasant enough. He learned the ways of smugglers, was introduced to Anukul Mukherji – Anukul-da and some of the old-time revolutionary dadas – Bipin Bihari Ganguli, Jyotish Ghose and Bhupen Dutt. The biplobi dadas read copiously and propagated the material amongst the youngsters but except for Anukul-da, the rest maintained an air of mystery and secrecy.

Within a few months of his reaching Kolkata, Santosh-da's group had gone into action. They had become a bit desperate and had not taken the precautions observed at Paraikora. One after another, several places had been looted – Kona, Ultodanga Post Office, an oil company, Shankharitola Post Office and a couple of other places. The police had swung into action and arrested Santosh-da and his group. One Nityananda Gopal had turned witness for the prosecution, driving several people into hiding. Among them had been Julu-da's contacts Deben De (Khoka) and Gopi Nath Saha, named in conjunction with murder. They had turned out to be young boys, no older than him or

Ganesh. Helping them go into hiding had been exciting; spending time with them in the underground thrilling. Meanwhile, the case had begun at Alipur with Jatindra Mohan Sengupta defending the accused. But at the helm of police affairs had been Sir Charles Tegart, an old India hand who had returned recently from England. Soon the elderly revolutionary dadas had been pushed into hiding. The government, it had been decided, needed to be punished for harassing revolutionaries. Ananta had volunteered to go on a fund-collecting mission to Chattogram.

He had reached home the very next day. After the pampering and cosseting the turn of the inevitable question came: how did you get home before the term got over? Pat had come the answer: the syllabus had been finished. What was the point in staying on and incurring hostel charges? Though Ma had looked ready to burst with pride, Baba had not been quite convinced. Wait. Didi had shot him a smouldering look that vaporized any chance of an argument. She helped Baba with the business and was in charge of the money. He would have to wait. Baba was due to leave home soon, for he was negotiating for Dada's wedding. He eventually left one day to meet the prospective bride's parents. By that time Ganesh had come home, as college had closed.

That day Didi had opened all seven locks on the steel almirah and Ananta had picked up two cloth bags and packed them into Didi's leather suitcase. There had been no time to count the money but he had known that it was approximately Rs 3,000/-. His cycle had been right outside and it had taken him no time at all to disappear from sight. Ambika-da had been waiting at the designated spot to take charge of the money and leave for Kolkata. For the rest of the day Ananta kept himself well hidden and had made his way that evening to the European Paltan Maidan where Dada and Premananda were waiting to update him on what had happened at home after his disappearance. Pishemoshai was very angry and wanted to inform the police but had been stopped by Ma's tears. A telegram had been sent to Baba to return immediately but he had not been told what had happened. Didi had enjoyed the situation the most; abusing Ananta and inventing frightening little details.It had been good to have Dada and Didi on his side. Baba had been livid and the memory still had the power to reduce him to a contrite little boy. He had decided he would catch the next train and board it at Bhatiari and not Chattogram to avoid being caught by Baba. But the next morning he had found Premananda waiting for him at the station with news: Pishemoshai and Ganesh had just boarded that very train, at Chattogram. Ganesh had been pretending to help Pishemoshai look for him.

The warning had come in the nick of time. He had taken a later train and had soon been back at the Taltola hideout with Gopi and Khoka. Ganesh had returned after the holidays and filled him in. He had accompanied Pishemoshai till the Chandpur station where he had bumped into Baba. Baba had been shocked to see them. Having calmed his fears and after assuring him that no one in the family was ill or dying, he had broken the news as gently as possible. Baba had had just one thing to say before he turned his face to the window: I consider Ananta dead; I'll will all my property to Nand Lal.

A lump still formed in Ananta's throat at the thought of what had happened that day. It was not being cut out of the will that hurt so much but the fact that he was so misunderstood. But all that was now long past. All fathers forgave eventually.

Rajat had come in with more jewellery. 'What is this, Rajat?' Ananta asked.

He laughed. 'I said to Ma … look I am not coming back alive. You will never get a chance to give your son's bride all this jewellery.'

Ananta stared at the boy quietly. 'And what is Mashima wearing now?'

'Nothing.'

'No,' he said shaking his head. Pulling out a necklace from the jumbled pile he handed it back.

'We cannot strip our mothers bare.'

SIX

Ananda Prasad Gupta

Ananda snuggled deep into the covers. Ananta-da was back. He had been waiting for him, for he wanted to introduce a couple of boys he believed to be competent. But Ananta-da would have to test them first. The entrance examination had many hilarious stories that went with it. There was the one about Rajen Das … not the one who was injured in the Nagarkhana Hill battle with Master-da and Ambika-da. This one was as old as Master-da and used to constantly harangue the group saying they talked too much and did too little. Ananta-da's words drifted into Ananda's sleepy mind:

We decided to test him. Over a tightly wrapped dhuti I put on a lungi. I rolled up the sleeves of a white shirt and wore a black waistcoat secured by one button so that I could remove it in a second. Then, once I pasted a beard and moustache on, I could not recognize myself in the mirror … I looked like a goonda. My neighbourhood was too civilized to be frequented by hoodlums, so we made use of the empty plot beside our house. It was a large plot, nearly five bighas, with a footpath that ran through it and served as a short cut to our house. I went and crouched on my haunches waiting for Rajen Das. Ambika-da was to send him down that way at 9 p.m. While I waited, I debated on all the possible outcomes: would Rajen attack me; would he come at me screaming; would he run away; or would he faint? I was ready for all eventualities. But what if he attacked me? Would I hit him back? He was after all a colleague. I was busy deliberating on the issues when I spotted him walking jauntily towards me. I saw him look at me. He slowed down. I rose and took a step towards him. He stopped. I walked up to him and gave him a nudge. He fell down. He remained rooted to the spot unable to scream, run or attack me and there I was struggling to hold onto the laughter that threatened to break out. I walked away quickly. Ambika-da was waiting impatiently on the verandah of the National High School. We were both busy laughing when we saw my dada, Rajen Das and a manservant from our house walking towards us. They all had sticks and the servant also carried a lantern. The funny bit was that my dada knew about the test but he was playing along. I looked at them in surprise. "Dada? Where are you going with lathis and lanterns?" Rajen was very agitated. "Do you know what happened? I was attacked by how many? Three! Three goondas. I fell down hurt. They ran off towards the east."

Ananta-da and Ambika-da had been all-concern. This cannot be permitted, Ananta-da had growled, Why even women use that path! Ananda drew the covers over his head. The story always brought on a fit of giggles. There had been others like Nobeen who had burst into fits of screaming and had brought all the neighbours running. Fortunately, Ananta-da had been able to dash behind a bush, tear off the disguise and rush back, pretending to be a well-wisher. Some men who had been sent to pounce on people walking along lonely stretches and rob them of their possessions had come back with the realization that they were not cut out for such work. They would help the revolution but from the wings.

Ananda glanced across at his dada. He was already fast asleep. But Baba and Ma weren't. And Baba was distinctly agitated. Snatches of their conversation wafted across.

'He asked me why I let them neglect their studies. Tell me, have they been visiting Ganesh Ghosh?' Baba was saying.

Ananda pricked up his ears.

'Sharada Babu seemed quite certain.'

Sharada Babu? Was Baba talking of Police Inspector Sharada Kumar Bhattacharya?

'Who else had been summoned?'

'Well, Nandi Babu was there. One of his sons has walked out of his home and now the nephew. Up to no good. And Jaitra Mohan Das. He was there receiving a warning to keep an eye over that nephew of his – that Haripada Mahajan.'

Ma made some soothing noises.

'Khoka will be sitting for his IA finals. Should he not be studying? Why is he constantly wandering about?'

There was a long and heavy silence. Ananda strained to hear more. Nothing. They had stopped talking.

Ma entered the room, her figure silhouetted against the dark.

She moved gently to avoid waking them. She was bending over Dada's head. Her hands patted the pillow back in shape. A book? Ma had tucked a book beneath his pillow. When had she taken to borrowing Dada's books? Did he not know that it had gone missing? It was then that he realized. Ma was in the habit of reading the material they had been secreting in.

SURESH DE

It was a long walk to the seashore. Ram Krishna-da started on a story:

> My beard, in those days, was long. Really long ... not like Robi Thakur's[1] ... something like the one shown in the Kuntala hair oil advertisement. I went with a group of friends one day just as we are going today, to bathe in the sea. We reached the shore and jhoop-jhoop, one after the other we jumped in. My friends were all the cautious kind and toop-toop they clambered out of the water as soon as they surfaced. They busied themselves collecting shells on the shore. But I did nothing of the sort. I took a deep breath, dived in once again and swam under water past Kutubdiya and Cox's Bazar to the southernmost island in the Bay of Bengal. But there I was faced with a problem, for I found I could not surface. The reason was the millions of prawns that clung to my beard. Within their territory they become extremely powerful. They waggled their antennae at me dragging me down as I struggled to rise. My beautifully oiled and carefully nurtured beard was in danger and I could not declare war upon them. My ahimsa policy had turned them into little British administrators. They dragged me swiftly through the blue-green waters until we were in the Indian Ocean. I was dragged past Lord Ram's

bridge, the ones the monkeys helped him build to get to the island kingdom of Lanka and I was in the Arabian Sea. I was allowed a glimpse of the sky as I swept past the Karachi harbour but the smoke from the British ships had turned it dark and gloomy. Past Basra, grazing my back along the coast of Aden I found myself pulled into the Lohit Sagar.[2] Then across the Bhumadhya Sagar,[3] until I was in the English Channel. By now the prawns had grown exhausted. They had not eaten nor rested since the beginning of the journey. They slowed down and surfaced near the city of London. No sooner had they done so, some Englishmen spotted them. Sadly for the prawns, these people had returned only recently from a trip to India and had developed a taste for fine dining. Mouths watering, jaws slavering, they came by the droves: young men and old, pretty young things and crones. They leapt into the waters for the kill. So intent were they in gathering all the prawns they could find that they ripped out my lovely long beard. It has never grown back again.

Ram Krishna-da finished his tale and another lad started one of his own.

Suresh had expected to see great waves, hear the ocean's roar but the waters of the Bay of Bengal were a flat calm. They spent the day splashing and playing until they had worked up a magnificent appetite.

Ram Krishna-da opened a bundle tied with cloth. He extracted an earthenware pot of curds, a bunch of ripe bananas, some khoi. He mixed it all together and crumbled a handful of sandesh over the top. There were several banana leaves that had been brought along and on these they ladled out the phalar. It was cool and refreshing. The afternoon wore on and their companions left one by one. In the end Suresh was left behind alone with Ram Krishna-da.

Ram Krishna-da hired a fishing boat … well, not exactly hire, as he paid to book their seats with a group of six fishermen. They were to go deep-sea fishing. They had taken sampans many times on the Karnaphuli and took great pride in their skills. But this was open sea. The fishermen took the name of Durga as they set the sampan afloat. Between the two boys they took turns at the tiller and the oar. The oars dipped, cutting through the silken waters and the boat surged ahead with an energy that seemed to seep through Suresh's arms, flooding his body. Now land had been lost from sight. It was water all around. The fishermen dropped anchor. The nets were swung overhead and cast. When they were hauled back in they had changed from black to silver, and were pulsating with life. There was a steady staccato purring noise of the tails as tolai-lotia, rup-chanda, prawns and phaisha flopped about on the floor of the boat. They had helped reel them in and though they had no claim on the catch, they felt a proprietary sense of pride. The fishermen were now in a hurry to get back in time for the evening market. They lifted the anchor and unfurled a large sail. With the wind behind them, they skimmed along. One man alone remained standing beside the tiller. 'Guiding is a skill by itself,' he said to the boys and offered them a turn at the tiller explaining the tricks used to keep the boat from capsizing. The setting sun painted the sky in the colour of the hibiscus and the sea reflected it faithfully. As Suresh jumped into the shallows a thought played on his mind: there was a purpose behind this seemingly playful jaunt.

'Suresh, do you believe that there is a God? Some say it is all false.'

It caught him off guard. 'How can that be? Durga Puja, Kali Puja … people do all this because they believe.'

'Many of these rituals have been created by clever people to fool the simple-minded.'

'But a lie? How can a lie survive for ages?'

Ram Krishna-da smiled. 'Meet me tomorrow, before midnight, in the funeral grounds.'

Meet him at the Maha-shashan bhumi? But how? Suresh was certain he was not scared. The real question was how would he leave the house at such an hour? Should he steal the keys from his mother? He couldn't think of a solution. He went to bed that night hoping to have an answer by the time he awoke.

Mahendra Choudhury was shaking him awake. It was pitch dark outside.

'How did you get in?'

'You dolt! I came to share the roshogollas. I even threw a couple at your verandah but you were dead to the world. I had to climb up.'

You climbed up two storeys?'

'Up the electric lamp post and then swung across to your verandah. Come, time for celebrations. I have Rs 500/- for the revolution's kitty ... dacoity in my own home.'

ANANTA LAL SINGH

The French sahib had a big house in Kolkata surrounded by high walls and hedges. A new Studebaker stood parked outside. Ananta had been to see him several times with Anukul-da. Today the butler led them straight into the bedroom. The sahib was in bed with gout and did not stir from under the covers. The lady of the house sat ready to conduct the requisite business. She was not a bit like Ananta had expected. He had visualized her either as tall, gaunt and forbidding, or a sinuous mysterious beauty married to the elderly man. She turned out to be neither. As she rose to her feet, Ananta saw that she was tiny, very fat and very pink and as dimpled as a rosebud. Her honey-coloured hair was piled high on her head, and under her permanently arched eyebrows were eyes so green that they riveted his attention. She removed two very nice pistols out of an iron almirah. They had extra magazines and 200 cartridges each.

'But we have bought no money today,' said Anukul-da.

'It does not matter,' she said sweetly. 'Have it sent later.'

A wave of nervousness rose in Ananta's throat. Was this a trap? But they got home safely that day.

The BPCC elections were over and Subhas Bose had won by a narrow margin defeating J.M. Sengupta as Congress chief. Master-da, Ambika-da, Nirmal-da and Ganesh had gone back to Chattogram leaving politics in Kolkata in a murky state. The Opposition was crying foul and Motilal Nehru had ordered a detailed inquiry which concluded that September elections in Chittagong had not been free and fair. The BPCC elections thus remained technically incomplete. Frantic telegrams flew up and down urging haste in the re-election process in Chittagong. The BPCC elections had to be completed before the AICC meeting on 21 March 1930.[4] Ever since he had been sentenced to four months in jail for the May fracas, Ananta had tried to spend as much time as possible in hiding. For him it was safer living with Anukul-da in Kolkata. The short money collection drives that he made to Chattogram were highly secret and few and far between. He dared not go back home, for it was most certainly being watched. He borrowed instead from a Kabuli-wallah. The hefty Pathans from Kabul who made moneylending their business charged Rs 100/- on every Rs 1,000/- and came personally to collect the principal amount in exactly a month's time. An Irish sea captain, a tall big-built man, with coppery skin and deep-blue eyes had promised to bring weapons back from Europe by the end of the month.

A new 'friend' made an offer and took Ananta to meet one Abdul Razzak Khan. There was some confusion about his identity. Perhaps he was in the Communist Party; perhaps he had some war experience. Ananta did not receive clear answers to his questions and was confused over what exactly it was that the Communist Party stood for or who they were. But the offer of receiving firearms was too tempting. Khan sahib was said to have many contacts in the merchant navy. He had promised to send four pistols. The 'friend' sent word that two pistols had been received and that Ananta could collect them from his house. He set off without informing Anukul-da.

Two fine pistols lay on the bed. The man wrapped them up with newspaper and handed the parcel over. Faint alarm bells had begun ringing.

'No.' Ananta refused to touch them. Bunching up spare newspapers, he wrapped them into a parcel the same size as the one he was to pick up. Tucking it under his arm he left. Nothing happened. Ananta returned to collect the pistols.

The man was amused. 'There are two more that I left at the paan shop. We will collect them at 8 p.m. sharp.'

'Why not now?'

'I am tired.' He looked faintly irritated. 'Besides, I have told the paan-wallah that we will come at eight.'

Suspicion made Ananta's hackles rise.

'It may be dangerous to go now,' warned the man.

'Now!' said Ananta placing a menacing arm around his neck.

'I am telling you it is dangerous.'

'And I am telling you I want them now.'

The 'friend' walked with Ananta, protesting feebly. There was no danger around. The unsuspecting paan-wallah handed over the parcel and Ananta made his way home.

Lady Kathleen Tegart, December 1929

It had started with the aggressive shrilling of the bedside phone at 1 a.m. Kathleen had never got used to her husband's sudden departures in the middle of the night and his returning like a blast from the North Pole. Mike still insisted on taking part in raids and maintaining personal contacts with agents. The six-month holiday back home might never have been. The attack on the viceroy's special train, the week before, had indicated the start of a new campaign. Lord Irwin had escaped unhurt but Bengal had been placed on alert. The Hindustan Socialist Republican Army that had carried out the atrocity had deep and powerful links in Bengal.

She lay uneasily in bed watching the hands of the clock. Subah Khan was with him, she reminded herself. He had been their driver ever since Mike had become commissioner and was known to follow him at a distance, with his revolver ready, unless expressly told not to. Mike's life had always been in danger and more so since he had become commissioner. But what annoyed her most was his tendency to bottle information, a point that drew loud criticism from his colleagues as well. There was, however, no denying the fact that his preference to err on the side of caution was a highly important factor in his success in the handling of underground agents. Every time any police officer kept a secret assignation he was taking a risk, for the agent could be shadowed; he might have turned traitor – though this hadn't happened until now; or the officer could himself be recognized and trailed either before or after the interview.

The door burst open. Mike was back. With a sigh of thankfulness Kathleen moved closer towards him. He drew up the sheets and snuggled in. 'An agent,' he said briefly, 'had done some invaluable work for us ... found himself being shadowed by several people.'

Kathleen waited patiently wondering if he would continue. Shadowing was a dangerous game for both sides and only too often the shadower found himself to be the one being shadowed. Once, four Indian officers who had been trailing suspects had been followed back to the house in which they were living. It had been a warm night and the officers, having let down their guard, had sat down to dinner leaving the windows open. The revolutionaries' bullets had claimed all four lives. Once a man discovers he is being shadowed, Mike had always said, his life depends on his keeping his head. If he looks back – and the temptation to do this is often irresistible, hurries unduly or dodges aside too suddenly, he makes it clear he is aware of the situation and his pursuer is forced to close in on him to take action quickly before he escapes.

'But he succeeded in following the golden rule. It was only after the most nerve-racking experience that he managed to shake them off temporarily and take refuge in a private house. Fortunately, it had a telephone and he was able to s.o.s me.' Mike's eyes were closed.

Closely linked with and auxiliary to Mike's secret service was his creation of a highly competent staff of watchers. Memories drifted in and out of Kathleen's head, driving all thoughts of sleep away. When the Great World War had broken out, Edward had joined up from Dublin and moved to the trenches in France. To his great disappointment, Mike's application had been turned down by the government of Bengal. And it was only the fascination of unravelling the great German–Bengali plot, in which Joteen Mookerjee was traced to Balasore and killed, that had kept him going. But Ireland's Easter Revolution that came with the following year had brought an uncontrollable surge of emotions to the fore. It had made Lord Lytton joke that they had placed a Sinn Feiner in charge of the Bengali revolutionists. And it had amused and confused many of his friends. Being by instinct 'agin' the government, they said, he knew exactly what people who wanted to make trouble felt like and was able to forestall their action. In 1917, Mike had been permitted to go back to Britain and given a commission in the Horse Transport of the ASC with a promise of a transfer to RA. But, much to his annoyance, even before he could join his unit he had been recalled to give evidence before the Rowlatt Committee. They had held some forty-six sessions in camera. Mike's memory could certainly be classified as above average. He could recall isolated scraps of information and had the power of accurate visual recollection and would often stun the committee with remarks like: I think there is material bearing on this in file number so-and-so of so-and-so year on page so-and-so. It had prompted Mr Rowlatt[5] to observe to a member of the Bengal government as he examined official documents and reports on terrorism in India: You've got a remarkable man in Tegart.

Mike had set sail once again for England, received a commission in RFA[6] and made his way to France. It had given him the chance to experience active service and the horrors of war. When it ended, he had remained behind with the army of occupation for nearly a year before being seconded for special intelligence duties at home. The Intelligence Branch in England had undergone a giant makeover. In the years before the war, German spies had overrun Britain. A counter-espionage programme had been initiated in 1908 but it had been Captain Vernon Bell, aided by nine officers of the Secret Service Bureau, who had blasted the spy ring on the eve of the war. The department had been renamed MI5 in 1916.

In 1923, Mike had accepted the post of police commissioner of Bengal. He and Kathleen had had endless discussions about this: the money was good, a point that could not be dismissed casually, and the accommodation that went with it tempting. But the factor that clinched the deal was that Mike would be free to pretty much run his own show. He got down to reorganizing the department with his usual energy, making it a model of efficiency. In an eastern city, the jostling loafers, hawkers, street vendors and beggars afforded useful cover and were ready-made aids to success, but even then the slips and pitfalls were endless, and in vain was the fowler's net spread in the sight of the bird. It had to be freely admitted that the proper use of agents was one of the hardest and most difficult tasks an intelligence officer could undertake. Bad and unreliable agents were far worse than none at all, and, in the political field, they became instruments of the cruellest injustice. No one was more alive to this danger than Mike and his pains to cross-check all that was brought to him were unremitting. As to maintaining the agent's security, it was with scrupulous respect to the point of sanctity that he observed the obligation to keep secret all that was imparted to him in confidence. If, wittingly or unwittingly, an employer exposed the identity of an agent, he would soon find himself without anyone worthwhile. Never, no matter how strong the temptation to 'blow', would Mike permit the sacrifice of an agent to gain some temporary advantage. Many a holiday had turned into a busman's vacation for her husband, obsessed as he was with the way the secret service was shaping up in Britain, would join up as a special constable and work with the MI5 for the six months that he was on leave.

But in the years that he had been away, much had changed in India. India's contribution to the success enjoyed by the Allies had been acknowledged and in December 1919, a royal proclamation had announced the release of the persons interned during the period from 1914 to 1917 under the Defence of India Act. Some 1,100 persons had already been freed. The hundred that remained had been sent home immediately and, in addition, the 130 ringleaders locked up under Regulation III had begun to be released in stages. Mr Gandhi, who had preached passive resistance when the Rowlatt Bills were being discussed, introduced his ideas for a non-cooperation movement. Support came from an unusual quarter with a group of Muslims joining in, rather illogically, for they disapproved of the Turkish peace terms. The movement rapidly gained adherents. In 1919, a disturbance broke out in Punjab when troops under General Dyer's orders fired at a peaceful crowd, at Jallianwala Bagh in Amritsar. Those killed had been attending a protest meeting against the Rowlatt Bills and against the deportation of Dr Satya Pal and Dr Kitchlew, the local organizers of the non-cooperation movement. In 1920, the Congress decided to support Mr Gandhi and bands of youth, calling themselves Congress National Volunteers, joined together in pseudo-military groups. As was expected, it wasn't long before things began to get out of hand. In August 1921, the Moplah rebellion took place in the Malabar. Fanatical Muslims rose and murdered the officials and then proceeded to murder the Hindus. Rioting became common all over India. Eventually, a mob got out of hand at Chauri Chaura in the United Provinces and burnt nearly twenty-one police constables to death. It was then that a horrified Mr Gandhi finally called for an end to the movement. With Mr Gandhi's arrest, the fragile Hindu–Muslim bonding fell apart. A section of the Congress began to think that they were mistaken in not having a destructive finger in the government pie and formed a separate party led by

C.R. Das and Motilal Nehru. The Swaraj Party had thus come into being. It was important to keep in mind that the troublemakers were not representative of the population, for the great masses of India neither knew nor cared about politics and had no reason to believe that a change of rule would benefit them in any way. Under these very disturbed conditions, the new Montague–Chelmsford Reforms made their uneasy debut. Centrally, the shift of power was with the Government of India in India and no longer with the Secretary of State in London. The provision which aroused the greatest passion was the dual system by which the governor-in-council took charge of the reserved portfolios while Indian ministers, chosen by the governor from the elected members of the provincial Legislative Council, took the transferred portfolios. On the reserved portfolios, Indian opinion was represented – usually as much as by 50 per cent – on the executive council. In the case of the transferred portfolios the governor could, if conscientiously unable to accept the advice of a minister, require action to be taken otherwise. These were special powers which were not to be used except in vital cases. But their very existence was resented.

She must have fallen asleep, for when she looked he was no longer there.

'Blasé,' she groaned. He treated the death threats he received like a part of everyday correspondence. Her head ached and she reached for the bottle of Aspros.

Careless. In the way he put himself out there; in the way he handled unexploded bombs recovered from the site of outrages. For years he had kept one on his desk as a paperweight assuming its contents had deteriorated. And then one day, while engaged in a friendly rag with Denham and another friend, he had picked it up and thrown it across the room at a map to point out a particularly unpleasant up-country station, saying: Lets have a shot at Bogra. When the dust cleared they had discovered a part of the wall had been blown out. It had taken sometime to explain to the department that there had been no attempt at assassination.

A woman was at the gates.

'She has walked all the way from her village; she has journeyed for many days memsahib, just to see you.' The chowkidar made a personal appeal.

'Bring her into the compound,' said Kathleen. The morning air, she hoped would do her head some good. They rarely turned down appeals, and Mike, when at home, met everybody that arrived at their doorstep. The first time when he as a very young officer, rode out with a senior officer to a village, Mike had said to her, he had been touched by the people's genuine expression of faith. The inhabitants had come into conflict with the interests of a landlord. Word reached that they had been spotted and the entire population had come running, salaaming and crying: Dohai sahib! Jan Kampani Bahadur insaf! (Have pity, Sir, we want John Company's justice.) It said so much in support of the old East India Company so often accused of malpractice.

The woman had fallen on her knees groping for Kathleen's feet. 'Please, memsahib,' she began, 'tell Tegart sahib to give my husband six bighas of land. We are very poor.'

'But,' said Kathleen, 'I am afraid he doesn't own any land in India.'

'Oh, lady sahib, we all know he owns the whole of Bengal. He has only to say the word. We don't want money. If he won't give six, perhaps he will give us four bighas? I have come all this way to ask it. It is very little out of the whole of Bengal.'

'But really, I assure you, he doesn't own any land. Even this garden isn't his. It belongs to the government.'

The woman laughed and shook her head. She was a jolly up-country woman. 'Oh, memsahib, I come from a little village far away from Kolkata and even I know Tegart sahib has power over all Bengal. Let him give two bighas … see I am down on my knees to ask it.'

No attempt at explanation would convince her that Mike was not, in fact, a combination of magician and autocrat within the sphere of the province. As the chowkidar led her away, an orderly explained, 'His honour has such a reputation that by the name of Mr Tegart, a pregnant lady suffering from delivery gives birth to child without having pain.'

Appeals begging for letters of recommendation were common, but the general public, which included his opponents, had begun to regard Mike with superstition. His many escapes and the fact that he seemed to know everything that went on both inside and outside the force had caused people to think he possessed supernatural powers.

Added to this was Mike's morbid dislike for press interviews and a natural shyness when it came to facing the camera. The press would not, however, be done out of a good story and made up for it by going ahead with their own accounts. When they first arrived in 1923, a spate of such stories had done the rounds. Kathleen had saved the cuttings in her scrapbook.

In August 1923, the *Sisir*, an Indian-owned newspaper of Calcutta, had published the following: It is said that a few days ago a gentleman, while passing along Central Avenue at night to procure a medicine for his sick wife, was accosted by a police constable who compelled him to hand over all the money he was carrying at the time. The gentleman proceeding in his distress further on met a European who was apparently a drunkard, being dressed to perfection for the part. The gentleman apprehending that he was to be robbed again, stated that he was penniless. The European drunkard, however, replied that he did not want money but only wished to know why the gentleman was in such distress. He asked the offending sentry to be pointed out to him, and it was only after a good deal of persuasion that the gentleman agreed to point him out. When this so-called drunken sahib met the sentry, he gave him a smart slap on the cheek. The sentry, recognizing in the so-called drunkard the commissioner of police, fell at his feet ... Whether true or false, these rumours redound to the credit of ...

The *Nayak* of Calcutta had reported in the same month: There is a wide spread rumour in Calcutta that Mr Tegart is visiting the house of ill fame in Calcutta, dressed as a dandy in up-to-date Bengali style. The story goes that recently, thus dressed as a babu, he visited the house of a woman of ill fame at Rambagan, where four men were drinking wine. They thought he was a likely victim and hence threateningly asked him to hand over his gold studs, rings, etc. Mr Tegart at first made a pretence of being very much frightened, but while he was making a show of hesitating about giving up the money with him, the drunkards brought out a dagger. Thereupon, Mr Tegart brought out his revolver and whistled, which brought to his aid a number of policemen, posted in disguise in the neighbourhood. These are of course rumours but the public take them as true. Considering the active efforts Mr Tegart is taking to suppress goonda-ism, such rumours are bound to prevail in this country and, after all, such rumours redound only to his credit. That is why we make it public for his information.

The *Dainik Basumati* and the *Bangabasi* carried another story: Mike had been dressed as a Bengal dandy when he was surrounded by goondas who were then caught. Mike had then instructed senior police officers to inspect the thanas daily. The editor of the *Bangabasi* felt that the ill repute he had earned by slapping a political prisoner would now be wiped off. Mike had put the Goonda Act of March 1923 to good use, known bad characters were deported outside the city boundaries and the section of the town where their crimes were most frequently committed were policed by augmented patrols. It produced excellent results and the figures for burglary and theft steadily declined.

The point of fact was that Mike never once disguised himself as a Bengali. His features were strongly marked, he was tall and muscular, his eyes a deep blue and his tan had a warm, reddish tinge. His nose was well defined and almost aquiline in its shape. No matter what aid he might have brought to his disguise, he would have stood out had he tried to pass himself off as a Bengali. But at night, wearing a beard and a pugree, he could become anyone from a Sikh taxi driver to a Kabuli-wallah or a Pathan. He and Mr Lowman used the Pathan disguise on more than one occasion when they wished to watch the movements of a certain suspect or check a report given by an agent.

It had been a phase of Mike's life that she had missed. He rarely used the disguises these days. It had been Lowman who had regaled her with the exploits of the early days. On one occasion, accompanied by two other policemen, they had set off. Raids were always carefully planned so as to ensure that the element of surprise was in their favour. The house in question was situated in a winding lane and surrounded by a wall too high to vault on to from the ground. Lowman had accordingly bent down to make a back, but for some reason Mike had sprung onto his shoulders before he was expecting it. The result was that they both had rolled in the dust, seized with a perverse and uncontrollable desire to laugh. The four of them had stood shaking with silent laughter, their hands clasped tightly over their mouths for more than several minutes before they had recovered their composure. That particular raid had continued to have a bizarre flavour about it. The absconder had been found in bed, rendered immobile with an attack of rheumatism; his guard, who was sleeping in the adjoining room, arrested in the act of pulling out a Mauser pistol from under his pillow; while the downstairs sentry had slept peacefully through it all, his pistol tucked beneath his pillow. But generally speaking, there was little relief in the grind of the counter-terrorist campaign.

Mike was coming up the driveway dressed in his usual khaki shirt and shorts, Tim at his heels.

Ananda Prasad Gupta, 1930

An emergency meeting had been called at Collegiate School. It was assumed that the teams would be announced and everyone assigned their specific tasks. The first-rankers buzzed with excitement. The teams would have to remain in a state of readiness as the call could come at any given time. But it would be the leaders who would have to exercise the maximum caution. They could not afford even a single arrest. The police should not be able to catch anyone in possession of material that could even remotely be labelled as dangerous. Perhaps they would now be asked to spend their nights away from home and keep away from places that were being watched. But Master-da had a different agenda that day.

'Deboprasad Gupta!' he personally addressed the issue. 'There have been complaints. Your IA final answer sheets were filled with rubbish.'

The invigilating officer had been startled, to say the least, to see the star pupil turn in doodles.

Dada managed a light laugh. 'By the time the results are out I will no longer be there.'

'This will not be tolerated.' Master-da said sharply turning to where Ananda, Himangshu, Tegra, Moti, and Sahayram sat in a row. 'Jibon and Tripura did well in the matriculation papers last year. Your lot still has three months to go. Like it or not, you will have to perform well.'

Suresh De

'*Tomar kormo tumi koro Ma, lokey boley kori aami* ...' Oh Mother, you keep working the strings and people think I am responsible.

Suresh left his room by 11.30 at night and made his way past the sahib's dighi. The night was darker than any that he remembered, a night when none of flesh and blood would venture out. Giant shapes had come alive, stooping, waving, calling out to him. He stood gulping the cold air, trying to gather courage. Ghosts spirits ... they do not exist. Do not think about them and they will disappear. These are nothing but the date and coconut palms. Suresh broke into a trot. He could pretend to be a horse with blinkers on. Surely, ghosts had no hold over the animal mind. As he turned into the burning grounds, he spied a familiar figure in the distance. Immediate relief washed over him and he slowed down to a dignified walk. Ram Krishna-da stood outside the temple of Shashan Kali – the form of the goddess that presides over the last rites – his figure just about visible in the dying glow of a little oil lamp. The purut would have left a while back. The dhoop had gone out but the fragrance lingered. The boys prostrated themselves before the image.

'Who says God has no roop, no form? Let the unbelievers come and see my Mother now.' Ram Krishna recited one of his own compositions: '*Ma-go tor moner majhey sneher shaagor, tai to Ma tui jagat janani, Shokoley tokey Ma boley dakey, tobey tui keno mundomalini?*' ... Oh, Mother, an ocean of love lies within your heart, you are the mother to all the world, then tell me why you garland yourself with human skulls?

A canal flowed past the shashan. It was full, the tide being high in the Karnaphuli. On its banks lay a half-eaten body being savaged by foxes and dogs. In the dark, the flap of vultures' wings came to Suresh's ears. Sometimes the birds let out an eerie cry and the dogs snarled, gnashing their teeth, while foxes threw back their heads and howled into the night. This was Kashi Mitra's shashan. The boys made room for themselves under a small plant.

'Suresh, do you not get frightened?'

'At first yes, but now I am all right.'

'Lajja, ghrina, bhoy ... shame, hate and fear ... if these remain, character cannot be built, one cannot become a man. Character building is a great achievement. Do you understand now? You know Suresh, when a man has a strong point or a talent, one must be loud in appreciating it. Virtue must be respected and that in itself is a virtue. The revolutionary needs strength of character. He needs to be a bhramachari. Then the atyachari's daggers cannot scare him.

'Look at Ma, Suresh. She holds in one hand a kharga for biplob. When the world is sunk in sin and law and order is neglected, when falsehood masquerades as truth, the great Mother kills the beasts and the demons, protecting the righteous. The other hand is held up in assurance – biplob's other roop: shanti – peace and prosperity. Look at the curling tongue with which she drinks the blood of the demon Raktabeej – whose seed lay in his blood, giving birth to thousands of progeny from every drop spilt on the ground. Look at her, Suresh. The great Mother, who is unable to stop once she is out fighting for justice, is at heart a loving wife. It is her husband, Lord Shiva – that ascetic with his ash-covered body and matted unkempt hair bleached brown by years of neglect – who alone can control her. See him lie across her path. See also the devoted wife bite her tongue in shame for having allowed her foot to accidentally strike the sacred person of her lord and master.

'Look at the pyre that burns away merrily, consuming the wealthy man's arrogance, the great man's pride and the learned man's learning. Here everybody becomes equal. There is no discrimination here – between the rich and the poor, the idiot and the pundit, the Brahmin and the chandal.'

The jail bell sounded thrice. Chattogram Jail had announced the end of the silent hours.

'You may come now, Suresh.' Ram Krishna-da had talked the night away.

Suresh got up to leave. He would have to be home before he was missed. As he walked out of the gates he heard Ram Krishna-da's voice:

Pakhi shob korey rob rati pohailo
Kanoney kusum koli shokoli phutilo
Poradhin Bharater mahanidra tutilo na.

Birds all twitter for the night is past
The flower buds in the garden have all bloomed
But dependent India does not stir from her deep sleep.

He turned for a last look. The first rays had lit up the plant beneath which Ram Krishna-da sat. It was a korobi. Its pink buds had opened out during the night, and as the gentle morning breeze stirred them, they dropped about him in a gentle shower.

SEVEN

ANANTA LAL SINGH

Ananta and Ganesh sat hidden in the bushes. They were keeping watch on the little changing room attached to the tennis grounds of the Paltan Maidan. The whites had finished their sets and were sitting around sipping their lemonades, whiskies and tea. The pair waited patiently. The Europeans would not leave until the sky darkened.

The sky clouded over and a light drizzle began. The place cleared up. Even the bearers left. There was no one in sight. But in the distance, two figures had materialized. They were moving towards them but quickly stepped into the changing room and shut the doors. A dim light lit up the two windows but the rain that sluiced down the panes obscured all vision. Ananta and Ganesh waited for the downpour to begin in right earnest before making a run for it. They had seen all they needed to.

Master-da was alone in the Congress office.

'Ganesh's source is right.'

Ganesh's friend, an assistant sub-inspector in the police, had sent word: a trusted first-ranker was meeting the deputy superintendent of police in secret.

Master-da absorbed the information calmly. 'He will still be of use to us.'

SURESH DE

Walking barefoot was the norm for a boy from his background and Suresh thought nothing of it until the cobbles stung his feet. It was a blazing hot day! Hot enough to pop rice grains into crispies.

Hurriedly, he leapt onto a patch of green by the road and stood cooling his scorched feet. Fury rose in waves as tears came unbidden to his eyes. Why had Ram Krishna-da chosen such a time … surely just to trouble him. And Patharghata was such a long way off. Today, he would have his answer. A mentor could not afford to be so careless. Then, without warning, Master-da's words rang in his ears: The path of revolution is not strewn with flowers. The revolutionary will have to step on thorns and move ahead with bloody feet.

Suresh hopped from one foot to the other and then planted one tentatively on the road. 'Rabindranath has said Poran diye bandhtey hobey setu … the bridge will have to be built with your life,' he said loudly. It didn't feel so bad, but then again the road would not reveal its true self until it reached a treacherous section with no relief in sight.

'Poran diye bandhtey hobey setu, Biplobi pashan boi to noy, Poran diye …' Suresh leapfrogged like a kola-bang keeping count of the number of grassy patches visible ahead. Biplobi pashan boi to noy … the revolutionary is nothing but hard rock. Sharat Chandra had said that in his *Pather Dabi*.

He was suddenly outside Ram Krishna-da's doorstep. Surely, he had achieved a record of sorts. He would have to prise that answer now. Three knocks. The door opened a crack and an arm pulled him in. It was pitch dark. Ram Krishna-da had the doors and windows all shut and the floor covered with a sheet.

He was still blinking stupidly when Ram Krishna-da moved the sheet and went back to work. Tiny pieces of machinery glittered back at him. As his eyes adjusted, he realized that Ram Krishna-da was hunched over a sheet of paper with instructions. Before his eyes a beautiful automatic pistol emerged. Ram Krishna-da held it out. It was sleek. It was shiny. It was perfect. It was an honour that Ram Krishna-da was sharing this moment with him. But Ram Krishna-da had become busy again. The chamber clicked open and shut again.

'Let's put you to a test! Can you pull the trigger with your little finger?'

Suresh took it lovingly into his hands. 'Please Ram Krishna-da, let me keep this for a few days.'

'All in good time,' he said, turning away.

Suresh sighed. The shefali, he knew, would not bloom until it was time for the pujas.

Ananta Lal Singh

On 22 February 1930, 200 boys armed with lathis and sharpened bamboo canes assembled outside the house of Karunamoy Dutt of Municipal School. The news sent Ganesh and Ananta running to the site.

'Ei! Ei! What is all this about?'

The doors of the Dutt household were firmly shut but the crowd milled around on the lawns and the verandahs looking for a way in.

'Hemendu and Gopal were beaten up.' Tegra yelled, trying to make himself heard above the din.

'Boys! Let us discuss this at the Kotwali,' called Sub-inspector Siddique Dewan trying to sound reasonable even as sweat patches appeared on his shirt despite the coolness of the afternoon.

Ananta hauled Tegra aside by the collar. 'Why are you here? Your school is not yet over.'

'Yesterday Karunamoy put up a notice on the school board.'

'On his school board or yours?'

'His.'

'So?'

'It was for a debate.'

'So?'

'The topic was: The pen is mightier than the sword.' The look on Tegra's face was one of sheer incredulity. He wrested himself from Ananta's grasp indignantly. 'That notice was torn down and the second would have been too if Gopal Dastidar had not been prevented by Karunamoy and his friends!' he said, adjusting his collar slowly and deliberately. 'Nripa Gopal, Krishna Choudhury and Hemendu Dastidar had caught Karunamoy today on the way home and were thrashing him when his father ran up and stopped them. A complaint has been made to the headmaster,' Tripura clarified. The two boys traded blank looks.

But they were misreading them. Nothing could have been clearer: anything an Anushilan boy did was good enough reason to declare war. The boys had been smarting for a good fight ever since Sukhendu had been attacked.

The crowd was paying little attention to the police. Siddique Dewan had sent word to the Kotwali for backup. The boys would have to be dispersed immediately.

But on 25 March 1930, Sub-inspector Abdul Azim began an investigation into the matter. A hunt for Tegra, Tripura and Bidhu was launched. They were nowhere to be found. The matter threw Ananta and Ganesh into absolute panic. Two months away from action … they could not afford any further trouble. Already, a cycle stolen from one of the team members and offered as evidence by the rival group had been forcibly reclaimed from the thana.

'My own four months in jail are pending,' said Ananta ruefully. It was true the boys had no clue about the proposed action, even though they had seen a decided move from mere bodybuilding and boxing at the gymnasiums to the secret lessons on bomb making, the art of firing revolvers and pistols, espionage and counter-espionage.

'It's time for a little natok … drama is the order of the day,' said Ganesh. He sent for the boys.

Ananta sat glumly, unwilling to talk; his eyes were downcast as if ashamed to let anyone see the emotion within. Ganesh was angry. He strode up and down the length of the shop. 'Do you know how many or what kind of weapons have been gathered? Though we have not revealed the details yet, you all know that we are getting ready to take action against the British government.' Ganesh paced up and down, wringing his hands as if unable to find words. 'But if you have no patience and are sure that our strength will not be getting dissipated, then here, take these.' He suddenly handed over his revolver.

Ananta removed his and slid it across the table. 'Go,' he said unwilling to look Bidhu and Tripura in the eye. 'Go take your revenge.'

As anticipated, in the sudden silence in which he found himself, the little speech splashed as loudly as a stone thrown into a placid pond on a summer night. After the ripples died away, a gamut of voices broke in. It was a while before the two of them could come out of their very emotional state.

'Then turn yourselves in,' said Ganesh fiercely. 'You know Azim has been hunting for you. I am going to make the telephone call.'

He was due to turn himself in for his four-month conviction period. Master-da had called for an emergency meeting.

'I could go into hiding right away,' suggested Ananta. 'If I serve my four months, we will have to postpone the action by another four or five months.'

Nirmal-da shook his head sorrowfully. 'Think of something bhai! You and Ganesh … you have such fertile brains.' But neither Ganesh nor Ananta could come up with anything.

'Go into hiding?' Master-da was doubtful. 'With the police keeping such a strict watch on us, your going into hiding would indicate we were up to something. Going into action within the next couple of days is out of the question. The only way out is for you to report for punishment and we could appeal in Kolkata. If the appeal is accepted, we can have you out on bail.'

'If that doesn't work, we will have to create a force, out of the first-rankers who have already been given their weapons and allotted their individual tasks, that will break into jail and rescue me.'

'It will not come to that.' Ambika-da spoke for the first time. 'I will personally make sure your appeal comes through.'

'How can you be so sure, Ambika Babu?'

'I feel it in my bones,' replied Ambika-da scowling with determination, the line of his jaw tensing beneath the thickness of his beard.

On 7 March 1930, Ananta presented himself at court and was sent to jail. Jail Superintendent Srigyan Chatterji, who was also civil surgeon in-charge of the government hospital and family physician to most families in Chattogram, was outraged. 'This is impossible,' he said many times. 'I know the family, seen the boy since he was so high … Jail? A jail sentence?' He tsk'ed his tongue several times. While he was in charge, he would never permit Ananta to dress in the kurta and underwear allotted to the common convict. The British system placed every Indian who was arrested under Division Three and made them dress the same, eat the same food, stand in a line, salute, etc.

No, Ananta Lal Singh would not be treated as if he were a criminal or a common goonda off the streets. 'Provisions will be made for you in your cell. You have the choice of cooking for yourself or having food delivered from your home.'

Ananta waited patiently. The first day went by, then the second and soon the third, fourth, fifth and sixth days came and went. There was no news. The seventh day, 14 March 1930, was Holi – a holiday. Surely, no news would come on that day. Ananta sat glumly. If Ambika-da had failed even then … he would have to wait till the offices opened before he got to know anything. At one o'clock, there was a call for him. The mukti aadesh-nama had come. In a flash, Ananta was at the jail gate. A grinning Lokenath was waiting with another ten or fifteen of their friends, fists bursting with abeer. And though Holi was a festival Ananta avoided, he had no choice. The boys were in a celebratory mood, and the coloured powder smeared his face and clothes, finding its way into his hair and down his shirt. He tried to make a run for it, laughing and twisting out of the way.

'The high court was at first on the verge of rejecting the appeal but Ambika-da succeeded in coming through.' Lokenath was jubilant. 'As soon as I got his telegram, I rushed to Srigyan Babu's house to have the aadesh-nama prepared.'

'Then we ran with it to jailor babu's house but his manservant told us he was enjoying his afternoon siesta and could not be disturbed before four,' laughed Naresh. 'We started hollering and banging on the door and jailor babu came out looking ready for human flesh. But the look on Lokenath's face made better sense prevail.'

They were running through a short cut across the fields. Ananta's house lay half a mile from the jail. The door was wide open. The news had reached before he had.

Ma was in the drawing room, her round face beaming. She turned to Boudi who quickly lit the little silver lamp set on the edge of a thala filled with flowers and more abeer. The flame gave off wisps of fragrance, as the wick sucked up the ghee. Ma held the thala to his forehead and moved it slowly in a circular motion to his chest and round again before dotting his forehead with abeer. Baba reached up to place a hand on his head. The boys had thrown themselves on the chairs unmindful of the coloured powder that fell off their bodies and worked its way indelibly into the fabric of the cushions. Nobody minded. The Holi Purnima had turned out an auspicious one. There was a boisterous gaiety in the house. There was no need to force sweets on this eager, ever hungry bunch and yet Didi and Dada were not about to lose their opportunity.

Ananta excused himself. He needed to wash the colour off and have a proper bath, one denied to him for nearly a week. Boudi was still pulling out a set of fresh clothes and a towel for him when Tegra stuck his head out of the living room and gave a full-throated cry. 'Ananta-da, there is someone here for you!'

Grumbling loudly for he had just been on the verge of stepping into the bathroom, Ananta went out again. A boy waited at the gate with his bicycle.

'Ki rey? … What is it that you want? Who are you?' He barked. He had never seen the boy before.

The youngster started stammering. 'Shankar … aaggey …,' he stuttered his eyes flickering nervously at the crowd that milled around him. Ananta shrugged and jerked his head.

'Explosion,' whispered the boy as others moved away. 'Ram Krishna-da has been burnt.'

Ananta's eyes narrowed in suspicion. It could not have been more bizarre. This was surely a set-up designed to put him back in jail.

'We were making percussion caps at Patharghata,' the boy panted.

Doubts began niggling at the back of the mind. Why had this Shankar not gone to Ganesh in the first place? How had he come to know that he had been released? He stared hard at the boy. His pistol had been lying in Didi's care these past seven days. Dashing into the house to retrieve it he whispered to Naresh. 'Follow us. Bring Bidhu along and bring your weapons. This may be a set-up.'

Pulling out the Baby Austin, Ananta turned to Shankar. 'Drop the cycle and get in.' Picking up Ganesh from his house, he explained the situation quickly. Ganesh's eyes were bright with suspicion. The circumstances of the Mechhua Bazaar arrests the previous December[1] had been similar. A plan was formulated on the way. Ananta would drive slowly enough to give Naresh and Bidhu time to reach. Neither he nor Ganesh would leave the car. Shankar would get off and go into the house. Once he was out of sight, the four of them would take up positions. In case it was a trap, they would disappear silently. Ganesh's Anushilan friend, Niranjan Sengupta, and Satish Pakrashi had been arrested at the Mechhua Bazaar hideout in Dhaka and the police had lain in wait inside the house. One by one as the team visited, they had all been picked up. The Chittagong group had had a narrow escape, for Ganesh had given Niranjan Subodh Choudhury's address in the Rail Class Quarters at Chattogram for any secret communication that needed to be sent. Subodh's house had been raided as a result, but fortunately, the police had found no incriminating material. It had been a wake-up call. The British were capable of crippling the revolution even before it could get the chance to take off.

It was three in the afternoon. Shankar was waving from the house. Ananta waved back. The boy helped Ram Krishna into the back of the car. Ananta and Naresh moved cautiously towards the car. Ram Krishna was a sight! Nearly half his body had been burnt. This was a calamity.

'We cannot even cover him with cloth … it will be too agonizing,' whispered Naresh. 'These are dangerous burns,' Bidhu poked his head in. 'Naresh, I think we need to call in a senior doctor.' The two young doctors had recently acquired their qualifications. Bidhu was a gold medallist but they had grasped the gravity of the situation in an instant.

'You boys go along with Ananta,' said Ganesh. 'I will inform Master-da.'

The Baby Austin was driven carefully. This was an unforeseen event. They should have had a shelter ready where disasters could be managed. The car stopped outside a house and Bidhu ran in. He was back within minutes. 'No,' he said. 'They sympathize all right but will not help with a burns case.'

Several homes turned them down, but in the end one person was willing to accommodate Ram Krishna for two days. Two days and no more!

Ananta returned to Ganesh's shop. Master-da was there. 'This is very unfortunate,' he said. 'The police will get to know. Ram Krishna's brother-in-law is an upcoming government officer and he will let nothing come in the way of his promotion. He will report. I do not want any of you first-rank leaders involved in his care. Send for Phutu. Let him take the responsibility.'

Tarakeshwar had been busy with his BSc finals and had kept a low profile. He had not involved himself with the clubs or the Volunteer Vahini. Out of police notice, he was the perfect choice. He swung into action. A house was taken on rent and Ram Krishna was moved out. Ganesh went to meet his family doctor, Dr Jagada Ranjan Biswas, who listened to the story and said, 'All I know is that the boy was frying luchis when the vessel toppled off the fire splashing him with hot oil.'

That night a worker in a tikka gharry took the doctor along the lane that ran north from the main road at the bottom of Collector's Hill. Ram Krishna had been brought into a little house on that lane. After the doctor left, Ram Krishna was moved back to his shelter.

❧

Ten days had passed since the accident when Jagada Babu's manservant knocked at Ganesh's door. It was a little before dawn. 'Babu, the police had come to doctor babu's house last evening.'

As the man spoke, Ananta, who had spent the night at the shop, dashed out to the Baby Austin. Ganesh and he would have to verify the story. Doctor babu confirmed the events. He had stuck to his story. 'But,' he added, 'the house where I examined the patient, I have had to tell them about it.'

It was already 6 a.m. and the sun was piercingly bright in the sky. The actual shelter lay on the slopes near the south-eastern corner of Askar Khan Dighi, barely 500 metres from the Congress office. Twelve hours had passed since the police had received the news. Could they now be lying in wait inside? Collecting Naresh and Bidhu on the way, they stopped a little distance from the shelter. Ganesh and Bidhu slipped out, their revolvers ready, and disappeared amongst the trees. Ananta and Naresh watched from the car. There appeared to be no signs of activity. Naresh left, revolver tucked behind his back. He went in and was soon leading Ram Krishna out. It was broad daylight. Ram Krishna's body had swollen up. He was practically unrecognizable. The burnt skin had begun to peel revealing raw flesh covered with pus … or was it a white ointment? The boy was leaning heavily on

Naresh, breathing with difficulty. If the police can manage to lay their hands on him now, he will not have the strength to resist, thought Ananta to himself.

'Keep driving for the next three hours. Avoid places where you may have to stop. I will have news for you at Nouko Ghat by that time,' said Ganesh.

Making Ram Krishna lie down in the back seat, Ananta drove off. That frightful sight was sure to attract attention on the roads, but in case they were caught, it would be just the two of them.

Ananta kept to the sparsely populated streets and speeded up every time he had to cross people. Sunlight streamed over the top of the half-doors onto Ram Krishna's body. Though he had taken care to draw the hood up, he could feel the burning rays as he rested his hand on the rubber bulb of the horn. The boy lay quietly and mumbled dreamily at times. Ananta's eye strayed to his watch. When would the three hours get over?

As he passed Nouko Ghat where the boatmen await customers, he recognized a familiar face. As the car slowed down, the youth came purposefully forward. Without a word, he opened the door. It was broad daylight but it did not appear to worry the youth. Slinging Ram Krishna across his shoulder he set off down the steps of the ghat. As Ananta drove off he could see a boat pulling out across the Karnaphuli, a figure shrouded in a sheet laid out as if the dead were being ferried. The youth had arranged for a bright garland that was draped over and visible for miles.

'First-rankers in the police eye must go into hiding.' Master-da had called for a secret late-night meeting at the Municipal School. 'The rest must remain at home but must not be in possession of any incriminating material.'

Ananda Prasad Gupta

On 26 March, a case was registered on Ram Krishna's name under the Explosive Substances Act. Sub-inspector Abdul Azim hunted for him at Saroatali, at the house of his brother-in-law and in the house near Collector's Hill. A few homes were raided at random. Nothing out of the ordinary was unearthed.

Ananda had never witnessed a raid before. But what startled him was the impact it had on the elders. They were suddenly reduced to abject cringing fear. It had let loose the floodgates of terror. Spectres, the khaki-clad apparitions, sprang out of their childhood nightmares and invaded their privacy, the security of their homes. They barged into bedrooms and kitchens with no thought for the women present, new mothers that suckled babes or the children that screamed in horror.

He was getting ready to spend the afternoon at the Sadarghat Club. There were driving classes to be attended in the evening. He would meet up with Himangshu and Moti later. Ma seemed to be spending more and more time by the window. Chotkun was growing up. He was less clingy these days. Ananda found him on the lane outside. The child was playing by himself.

'There's no telling as to when you will invite calamity upon our heads,' he had heard Ma say to Dada earlier that day.

'Achchha, tell me then do you not consider it an honour to be generous with one's life, to donate it to the cause of the nation?' Dada had countered.

There had been no reply. But Ananda knew that deep in her heart, like every parent, she believed in the cause and yet secretly hoped that the revolution, when it came with all its ills, would bypass her family.

Sir Charles Tegart

'November last year we had instructed Chittagong to keep a special watch on Surjya Sen, Ambika Chakraborty, Nirmal Sen, Charu Bikash Dutt, Ganesh Ghosh and Ananta Lal Singh. Accordingly, on 16 November they inducted twenty-four constables to act as watchers. A twenty-four hour watch was instituted: four constables to a suspect by day and two by night. In February, they had revised the system. Two constables were deputed per suspect and the remainder were posted at specified locations around town. Since 12 February, Johnson's men have been expressly instructed to cooperate with the DIB staff.

'The result of my visit is that Johnson has now taken over direct and complete charge of the DIB, which until now had been under the supervision of a deputy superintendent. Immediate steps have been taken to intensify the system and Lewis, the ASP, has been placed in charge of the revised watch arrangements. Daily written reports are to be submitted by the watchers and the DIB inspectors and sub-inspectors are to move around town keeping an eye on them.'

Colson had returned having spent the 24–26 March 1930 in the company of Johnson, the superintendent of police of Chittagong.[2] Colson, Lowman and Mills, of the Special Branch, sat around the commissioner's table. Sir Charles had returned from home leave. While he had been away, suspicious activities had been reported in that remote East Bengal area.

'A very close watch will have to be maintained,' said Sir Charles. 'We have been caught unawares before. The outbreaks of 1908 and 1915 ... we were without any supplementary powers to deal with the revolutionists or the press.'

'Johnson will institute a revised system, 2 April onwards. The message has been sent out to all districts.'

The officers turned their attention to the other disturbed district – Barisal.

Those in the room were all acutely aware that the Bengal Criminal Law Amendment Act of 1925 was due to expire on 1 April that year. For the last three years, no use had been made of the special powers and the government had taken a decision that the powers of detention should be allowed to lapse. As a result the officers had begun touring extensively, keeping close contact with various districts. District offices were being encouraged to maintain close links with Calcutta.

Lord Lytton came briefly to mind. Sir Charles recalled the letter of support he had received soon after his appointment as commissioner. It had seemed standard enough at the time. But true to his word, when trouble came, that ardent supporter of Home Rule took on the unenviable task of introducing the BCLA Act.

Since his appointment as police commissioner, he had succeeded in pushing the ordinary crime rate down drastically but the number of terrorist crimes had continued to rise and he had once again joined the ranks of the marked men. On 12 January 1924, a youth named Gopi Nath Saha who was gunning for him had killed Earnest Day, a Calcutta businessman. The following March, a youth had been brought to Calcutta, suffering from serious burn injuries. His colleagues had attempted to keep him hidden and had brought him to Calcutta only when his condition turned serious. His story that he had been making fireworks had not gone down well and he had been prosecuted under the Explosive Substances Act. Within the same month, a raid on a certain house had disgorged a Mauser pistol, a revolver and a large cache of ammunition. In April, a European, driving down a busy road, had been shot at. The matter had been reported. Bruce, Sir Charles recalled, was not unlike him in appearance. The car had been taken back to the scene of the crime and placed in the same position as it had been when the shooting had taken place. Mill's examination had proved that the bullet had entered the windscreen at an angle and he had inserted a bullet of similar calibre into the hole and with a long rod taken direction from it. The result had been significant. Whereas all the surrounding buildings were occupied by Marwaris, the rod pointed to a set of rooms whose inhabitant turned out to be a young Bengali on rent. The youth had been spotted earlier, loitering on Kyd Street.

There had been other attempts, but his army of agents had been on top of their game. At a Hindu bathing festival, his point of entry had been changed at the very last moment, bewildering the assassins lying in wait with bombs. The conspirators at the Santahar railway junction, through which he was due to pass, divining that the police had got wind of their intended action, had fled. But the secret societies never stopped looking for opportunities. A communal riot in June that year had arisen from a bizarre rumour that the Sikhs working at the construction site at the docks were kidnapping Muslim boys to sacrifice at the site. It was based on an ancient superstition that sacrifices like these helped the building stand for years. The suddenness and the scale on which the rioting began had taken them all by surprise. He had lost no time and had been out there every day, directing the operations. He had to be visible so that the common man could take heart. Eight Sikhs had been killed; many policemen and common people injured. He had not escaped the blows himself. But while he had been thus occupied, there had been armed youths moving about the city, taking position in places he was most likely to appear. But the would-be killers had failed to identify him and the riots had been brought under control without further incident.

To him it had become clear that, as foretold by the Rowlatt Committee, if the police were to control the revolutionary movement, the ramifications of which were extending every day, they would need special powers similar to those contained in the Defence of India Act. The Rowlatt Committee had, for the first time, based their recommendations on police inputs and had taken cognizance of the challenges they faced. But it had come under severe criticism by the Indians who viewed it as a conspiracy between the judiciary and the police. In the generous mood that followed the success of the Great World War, the Rowlatt Act – The Anarchical and Revolutionary Crimes Act – had been repealed[3] even before it had come into force.

Accordingly, Lord Lytton had gone to Simla in July 1924 to persuade the government to grant the powers. The governor's vivid presentation and his staunch refusal to accept anything less resulted in the government agreeing to grant the powers, provided they were submitted in bill form to the Bengal Legislative Council and passed in the ordinary way. It had been a setback, for it meant that the various societies would have enough time to despatch their ringleaders out of the province and destroy their incriminating documents. However, Sir Charles's point of view had been appreciated and the request for a six-month period of secrecy had been granted in the form of an ordinance. This had made it possible to take action before the bill came to be presented to the Legislative Council. He had launched into the preparation immediately, maintaining absolute secrecy even within the forces. A body of 600 officers and men had been mobilized in Calcutta alone and only a few select officers informed about the nature of the operation the evening before. The rest had been kept under the impression that excise raids would be taking place any day; the action was slated for 1 October and teams were kept in readiness to swoop down upon suspects at exactly 4.30 in the morning. Mills, assisted by L.N. Bird, the deputy commissioner, had carried out the preliminary organization while the actual arrests had been put into effect by two officers of the Special Branch. Fifteen persons in Calcutta had been arrested that day, under Regulation III and another fifteen under the new ordinance. Of these, two had been members of the Legislative Council and of them one was Subhas Chandra Bose. Bengal had broken out in demonstrations at the so-called stifling of legitimate political agitation. But it had been C.R. Das who had been hit the hardest, for his chief lieutenant Subhas Bose had been summarily removed from his side. The Swaraj Party had lost no time in eulogizing Gopi Nath Saha, Khudiram Bose and Joteen Mookerjee, whom they dug out from the pages of history. But the net effect had been a marked slump in terrorist activities.

By January 1925, time had come for Lord Lytton to present the Bill to the Bengal Legislative Council. In spite of the viceroy's and the governor's announcements of the reasons for its introduction, many Indian politicians seemed to believe that the police reports of terrorist activities were wildly exaggerated and that the ordinance had been instituted to strangle political agitation. Accusations and charges of planting evidence ran rife. The stock allegation of duplicity and dishonesty had always been a sore point with him and more so since the bombing of Deputy Superintendent Basanta Kumar Chatterji's home at Mussalmanpara. It had been in November 1914, shortly after the War had broken out, when they had all assembled in Chatterji's house. Chatterji was an efficient and popular officer with great influence over the younger generation. The meeting had been in progress when two bombs exploded in the premises. The officers had rushed to investigate: a head constable on guard outside had been killed; two constables and a relative of Chatterji, who had been inside the house, severely injured. An injured youth had been found lying on the street with a .380 Webley revolver beside him. It appeared that the second bomb, intended for the people inside the house, had hit a bar on the window and had exploded backwards. A phial of phosphorous and a used Mauser pistol cartridge were discovered. The youth had been taken to hospital where he underwent surgery. He turned out to be one Nagen Sengupta, a bright young student at Calcutta University and a ward of the court. The brothers of the Oxford Mission that had raised him would not believe a word the police had to say and vouched for him. According to them, he was of sterling character. The case against him came to be known as the Mussalmanpara Bomb Case and had been tried by a tribunal of three high court judges.

Nagen had pleaded that he had been a casual passer-by, who had been injured in the blast and knew nothing about the revolver lying beside him and it had been assumed that it had been planted there by the police. The youth had been unanimously acquitted and one of the judges had taken it upon himself to make caustic comments about the police. Among those that used the occasion to heap slander upon the police were a couple of glib Europeans who remained outside the arena. Sir Charles would never forget or cease to rage about it; short of having a magistrate or a judge on the spot who would himself discover an assailant in the act of throwing a bomb and carrying a basketful of ammunition, there seemed to be no way that the police could succeed in bringing home guilt. But a development had taken place by the time Lord Lytton was to make his speech. Nagen Sengupta had, in the intervening years, reformed and turned into a sincere and practising Christian. The governor had met with him; got him to admit his guilt publicly without having to give away his former colleagues; and the admission had been incorporated in the governor's speech of address to the Legislative Council. The police had at long last been vindicated. But the bombshell had turned out to be a damp squib, making not a mark on the emotions of the listeners. And why should it have, thought Sir Charles bitterly. The listeners had all along been aware of the true state of affairs. The bill had been rejected by a majority of nine votes and in the end Lord Lytton had been compelled to use his special powers to turn the BCLA Act into law.

And neither had it come as a surprise to him when the same body continually refused to accede to any of his desires, be it improving housing and living conditions for the rank and file in the police or installing mosquito netting for his men. It had all been turned down on the argument that they, like the rest of their brethren, were used to living in unhygienic conditions.

Sadly, the brave Basanta Kumar Chatterji, who had smilingly refused an early retirement despite the constant danger to his life, had been shot in 1916, as he cycled back from work accompanied by a guard. A group of young men armed with Mausers had taken them by surprise. Chatterji had not taken Sir Charles's advice to rest on his well-earned laurels. It had proved to be a heart-wrenching time. As the then deputy inspector general in charge of the Intelligence Branch, he had led the funeral under heavy security cover lest the terrorists saw it as a plum opportunity to dispatch the entire branch once and for all. On his appointment as police commissioner in 1923, he had addressed all his officers and offered honourable retirement to the ones that were marked. Not one had agreed to leave his side. Poor Bhupen,[4] who made that warm speech when the knighthood[5] was announced in 1926, had shared his gallant namesake's fate within a matter of months. He had been interviewing political prisoners at Alipore Jail, when he had been set on by a gang of men armed with an iron crowbar and brutally done to death. The loss of his trusted colleagues and friends had been a big blow to Sir Charles – a personal loss, the memory of which still caused great distress.

Too often he had been criticized for recruiting too few Bengalis to the ranks, but that was because few at that level passed the fairly stiff medical examination and physical requirements. The Bengali, he mused, tends to run to brains rather than brawn and does not take kindly to the discipline and order of a hard life; at the same time, he lacks neither courage nor ability, and shines in the higher ranks.

'A very, very close watch! Increase the number of watchers in the districts,' he said.

EIGHT

Ananta Lal Singh

A number of locations had been raided, including the shelter in which Ram Krishna had been kept. Quite strangely, none of the homes belonging to the first-rankers had been violated. Why? Did they have no evidence or was it yet another ploy? After a few days, Ananta and Ganesh decided they should move back home. Confidence. That is what they needed, in order to brazen their way out of every situation.

Precious days had been wasted. A major task remained. There were seventeen iron shells, cast under Dada's supervision at the AB Railway workshop, waiting to be filled with explosive powder. Now that Ram Krishna was out of action, the percussion caps were no longer a possibility. Ananta and Ganesh sent for Phutu. There was not enough time left, imported fuses would have to be used instead. Phutu was set to work filtering picric acid.

It was decided that one of the inner rooms in the Congress office would be converted into a lab and Ardhendu Dastidar, who lived there now with Master-da and Ambika-da, would help.

'You will keep in mind that you are working with extremely volatile acids.' Ganesh warned.

Phutu had done the task before. He had just got a bachelor's degree in chemistry. They went over the steps: nitric acid and sulphuric acid were to be mixed in equal proportions. A powder would settle at the bottom of the beaker. This would be boiled up with ammonium carbonate and lots of water. The ammonium picrate crystals formed would be filtered and dried carefully. They would then be pounded in a mortar with potash-chlorash, to form the powerful explosive that would go into the iron shells.

The police were getting surprisingly frisky. A number of watchers in white uniform loitered about, keeping their sights on all young men and scribbling on little paper pads.

'Ei shaala!' Ananta called out to one of them. The man came bounding up like a good little boy. 'Ki rey? Why are you loitering around? Don't you have anything better to do?' Ananta's size was daunting. 'Why are you following me like an idiot? You want a good hiding? You want me to report you and have you sacked?'

'Babu, forgive me, babu. You know it's a responsibility towards the mouths waiting at home to be fed. We are poor, babu.'

The increased manpower was noticeable. And they were constantly being ragged and threatened by the Chattogram youth.

❧

'Since 12 March, Gandhi-ji has begun his satyagraha. Subhas Bose has still not taken a decision on breaking the Salt Law in Bengal. But I think we, in Chattogram, should prepare ourselves to join in.' Master-da had called for a meeting in the first week of April. It included the youth that maintained contact with the DSP.

A cheer broke out. Most of the boys were thirsting for some action.

'It is a shame,' he continued, 'a matter of deep regret that Chattogram, the pioneer of the independence movement since 1921, should remain behind in the struggle.'

'In Kolkata,' Ganesh stood up, his voice rising amidst the cheering, 'disobedience of laws, other than the Salt Law, has already begun. The law on sedition is being openly flouted. We should also commence disobedience without delay.'

'Ganesh, the public must be prepared ... given time to prepare,' interrupted Master-da. 'We cannot rush into this. We want satyagrahi soldiers. We will also want people to come forward with donations.'

Ganesh held his hand up for silence. 'We will allot responsibilities. Picketing? Who are the volunteers?'

A number of voices clamoured for attention.

'A show of hands please,' said Ganesh, as Ambika-da made quick notes.

'Banners. Painting of banners? Whose house will be used?' He made a quick note of how much money would be required for the cloth, the paper and the paint.

'Putting up posters? … Master-da, we need pamphlets to be distributed. The public should also be given the chance to participate. I will have them printed, instructing the general public keen on volunteering to meet Ambika-da and me on 21 April 1930.'

Master-da nodded. 'You can begin with the words: Chattal-bashider Prati – To the residents of Chattogram.' He turned to the boys. 'Before you jump up and volunteer, know in your hearts that if the police are able to lay their hands on you it will mean jail!'

'We need volunteers for distribution.' Ganesh looked around.

The young man, who was the police agent, had not been given a task as yet, despite his enthusiasm. This time he was picked as one of those who would be distributing the leaflets on 17 April.

The summons came on 5 April. Ananta, Ganesh and Bidhu were to report to the police station. A hurried conference was held in Ganesh's shop.

'We will carry our revolvers strapped to our bodies under our shirts. We will have to make a quick getaway in case things get nasty.'

'Naresh and I will come along with you,' said Lokenath.

Ananta saw Makhon shoot him a look pleading not be sent home. 'And if they ask us about Ram Krishna? We cannot pretend we have no clue?'

'I can.' Ananta shrugged it off. 'Never heard of him.'

'Well,' said Ganesh reasonably. 'I will say that I know who he is and can point him out if they hold an identification parade. But more than that?' He upturned his hands.

The interview at the station went off smoothly and as they left, a thought struck Lokenath.

'Shall we pay Sharada Babu, the DIB Inspector, a visit? He is looking forward to a promotion, isn't he?' The boys grinned. Dead men do not look forward to promotions. They would explain it delicately to Sharada Bhattacharya: harassing and deliberately picking on this group of friends would not be advisable.

Ganesh's shop, the one opened by his father, served as the field headquarters. Bipin Bihari Ghose, who had been senior station master in charge of the prestigious Double Mooring station, had taken part in the 1921 Assam Bengal Railway strike. He had been a fiery orator, one who had decided to give up government service and set up a cloth shop in Sadarghat close to the Kali Bari, minutes away from the local police station. The big room that opened onto the street served as the showroom while the five rooms at the back were utilized by the family. Ganesh and his older brother, the doctor, managed the shop stocking only local weaves. When Ganesh's brother joined government service and was posted to Assam, he took their elderly parents with him, which left Ganesh managing the whole show. The shop had turned into the local headquarters where plans were discussed and new recruits taught the art of firing revolvers. Right under the nose of the police – that was where they were safest.

The meeting with Subodh Choudhury had gone well. The first-rankers had been given their responsibilities. There were targets that had to be studied. Every last detail needed to be gathered and an eye kept on the target until the zero hour. Ananta and Ganesh ensured that even the first-rankers were kept in the dark about each others' tasks, by meeting each one separately. They had all been forbidden from disclosing their duties to one another. Subodh lived in the Rail Class Quarters and passed the Auxiliary Forces of India Armoury every day. But his field of study had included not just that armoury but also the one at Double Mooring. Ananta's dada, Nand Lal Singh, worked at the AB Railway workshop. He was privy to what went on inside. But the responsibility of the main armoury at the police lines, Ananta and Ganesh had reserved for themselves. After three days of aimless hanging around, they had chanced upon the news that the sub-inspector in charge of the police lines was one Sanjiv Chandra Nag and his son studied in the eighth standard of the Kali Maji School. A worker was deputed to work on him with recruitment in mind and then bring the child for an interview. But recruitment was the last thing Ananta and Ganesh had in mind. The child was thrilled to have received a call and impressed by the burden of secrecy. He was completely under the influence of the idea of revolution. Proudly, Line Babu's son took his new friends and mentors on a guided trip of the lines. Not one but several.

They were keeping up with their timetable. Pleased with the day's proceedings, Ananta made his way back home for lunch. A cycle stood by the wall occupying the place meant for his own. Leaning his cycle by its side, he peered cautiously about. There was no one in the drawing room. As far as he could see, even the courtyard looked clear. He stepped in cautiously, scanning the courtyard, when his eyes were arrested by the sight of Didi standing at the entrance to the room she used for training her students. Tension was coiled into her body. She looked ready to spring. Looking past her, Ananta spotted a girl, her sari wrapped tightly around her youthful form, her raised arm descending through the air as if to strike the young man before her. In the wink of an eye she was bent over double, her arm twisted behind her back, her body curved helplessly into that of her intended victim.

Ananta strode away, keeping his eyes fixed to the ground, clearing his throat in displeasure. The girl was far too attractive. The couple made an extremely handsome pair.

Boudi was serving him lunch when Didi marched in defiantly.

'You have broken your word.' Ananta snapped, before she could get a word in. 'I had sent Saroj to train you alone. From tomorrow, he will not be available.'

Her constant complaint had been that he never helped out with the girls' training activities, but now she had axed her own foot. Baba nodded in approval. He was proud of the principles the Chittagong youth held dear.

It had been a good lunch. The rice and fish sat heavy on his stomach, sending delicious tendrils of sleep through his body. Ananta had stretched out on his bed for a glorious afternoon siesta when Boudi shook him awake. A boy waited at the door. The matter was urgent. Dragging his reluctant body, he made his way to the door, ready to bite off a head if given a chance.

'Explosion. Congress office.' The dilated pupils stood out in the large light-brown eyes. The terror in them exploded a reaction within

Ananta. Phutu and Ardhendu! They were the only two. But they were working with such tiny amounts: mixing fifty grams of picric acid with half that amount of potash. Neither of them were smokers.

'Not even the blows of a hammer can make it explode. Who lit the stove?' Ananta's voice bordered on a scream.

'All that I don't know.' The boy was holding on to his nerves. 'All I know is that you had better come quickly.'

The Baby Austin was racing towards Ganesh's shop.

'The mortar is in smithereens,' the youth filled him in. 'Both Phutu-da and Ardhendu were flung some five to six cubits away.'

Ganesh's face was unable to register emotions. Here they were in the first week of April and …

'Drive to Makhon's,' he said.

Ananta leant on the horn. The boy ran out at the first toot. 'Bring your new Essex to the Congress office,' called Ganesh as the Baby Austin moved off.

Thick smoke issued from the windows of the Congress office. Ananta ran through into the inner room. It was a shocking sight. The sickening smell of burnt flesh. Master-da, Bon Bihari Dutt and some of the others had dragged Phutu and Ardhendu to a room where the smoke was less. They had emptied out the first-aid kit and were squeezing tubes of Borafex.

Ardhendu took a few awkward steps, collapsed and made an attempt to pull himself up again. Burns covered his face and chest. Phutu who lay on the floor unmoving was suddenly caught in the throes of rigor. Chunks of flesh had been blown away. Bits of bone glimmered sickly and white.

'Ananta-da!'

It was Phutu. Ananta forced himself to go over to his side.

'Shoot me. Ananta-da, only you can do it.' The words came with effort. 'I can't stand it.'

Ananta stumbled out of the room. 'I think I had better shoot them right away.'

'Stop, stop. This is rubbish.' Ganesh screamed.

Master-da laid a hand on both their shoulders. 'Troubles will come. We have to deal with them and move on.'

The cold logic that was so apparent to both Phutu and himself had been lost on Ganesh and Master-da. Hadn't the Ram Krishna episode taught them enough?

Makhon's Essex had drawn up outside.

'Move,' said Master-da. 'The explosion must have been heard for miles.'

'Wait! Wait!' Bon Bihari hurried his five workers and ran to the adjacent field. He settled down with his flute and in next to no time a singing competition had begun in right earnest. His boys posted themselves on the road diverting the passers-by, leading them cheerfully by the arm to take a few minutes to encourage the participants. Master-da stood outside the Congress office, a smile on his face, sending the more reluctant of the lot back to the field. 'Two minutes of your precious time … it's for the children,' he said.

Very carefully, keeping him shielded from view, Ardhendu was brought out and laid on the back seat of the Essex. Beneath the seat, on a mattress on the floor, was Phutu.

'Keep driving. Do not stop,' whispered Ganesh as he left with the Baby Austin. 'I will meet you by 5 p.m. with a can of petrol.'

Ananta had been driving now for hours, keeping to the quieter part of the town. Five o'clock was approaching. There was still no sign of Ganesh. As he drove along the big road in front of the Rail Class Quarters, he spied Subodh Choudhury cycling down. The boy responded to the horn signal and as he peeped into the car his mouth fell open in horror.

Waving to Ananta to wait for him, he sprinted home and returned with two dhutis and two bed sheets. These were strung between the driver's and the passenger's seats and all around the windows, as was common in the cars that carried ladies from the aristocratic Muslim families who observed purdah. 'I will put just a little surma in your eyes, Ananta-da,' he said. 'Those who don't know you will assume you are Muslim and the rest will not know the difference. Drive up and down this road, I will be back with a can of petrol.'

He had been driving non-stop since he had begun. It was now six o'clock and there was still no sign of Ganesh. At last Ananta spied the Baby Austin waiting under a tree. Ganesh handed over a can of petrol. 'Still no shelter. Keep driving.'

Eight p.m. Still no news. No shelter had been arranged. Ananta was becoming increasingly nervous. The moans from the back seat were occasionally interspersed with a scream. The sounds worked like a balm on Ananta's heart. But it raced when the two passengers were quiet. He stepped on the accelerator skirting past a group of villagers walking along the road. It was getting dark now.

The Baby Austin appeared. 'Go to Lokenath's home in Patharghata. I will bring doctor babu.' It was 10 p.m.

Ananta parked the car flush with the door. Lokenath, Tegra, Naresh and Bidhu were waiting. Ardhendu was removed. Then it was Phutu's turn. The seat had been raised and holding the edges of the mattress, the boys pulled him out taking him inside. Phutu lay as limp as a rag doll, his body cold and clammy. Bidhu placed his ear to Phutu's chest as Tegra ran to bring some water.

Jagada Babu arrived. He gave some injections and left Naresh and Bidhu with a couple of ampoules of Coramine. As he turned to leave, he pondered for a second. He needed to get something off his chest. 'Look … it has been obstacle after obstacle. Give up the road you have chosen. Perhaps God does not will it.'

'It is God's way of testing us, doctor babu,' said Lokenath politely leading him to the door. 'Bless us so that we can accomplish what we have set out to do.'

Ganesh placed his hand on Jagada Babu's arm gently. He had to drop him back home and Ananta needed to get going. Phutu and Ardhendu would have to be moved to their individual shelters.

❧

The movie house – Lotus – stood on Fairy Hill, to the south of the courthouse, a little lower down on the slope. On the same hill, to the east stood the post office. Ten youths lazed in the seats. The movie was about to begin. Talkies were as yet a novelty and they could be seen only in Kolkata. Ananta and his boys were out as they usually were, enjoying life, eating at restaurants, competing loudly at every music concert. His up-to-no-good reputation had escalated lately to 'a bit strange … given to using Snow and face powder'. It tickled him immensely.

A nudge. A figure on the aisle gestured and a whisper passed around. The movie had begun to roll. The group left in twos and threes so as not to attract attention.

'Activity in DIB sub-inspector Rohini Bhowmik's house.' The party watchers keeping track had sent a runner.

'Post guards on the roads that lead to Ardhendu's shelter and Phutu's,' said Ananta as he set off at a run. Three newly sharpened swords had been stored in Ganesh's shop and all evidence of having tested guncotton would have to be got rid off at once. His boys set to work. Ganesh's shop had been cleaned out when word arrived that the police force was taking the route that led to Ardhendu's shelter. The Baby Austin was pressed into service and Ardhendu taken for a drive. Ananta kept to the streets until confirmed news arrived: the police were raiding a different house. Ardhendu could safely be dropped back and 8 April had passed off without any untoward incident.

Parking the car near Parade Square, Ananta made his way to Ananda and Debu's house. Ganesh had been there all evening, getting an early start to the night's work that lay ahead. The boys' study room had been converted into a laboratory.

The past couple of days had been a whirlwind of activity: irate parents, bewildered boys waiting to be counselled. Madhav Babu, a comparing clerk at the district judge's court, had filed an official police complaint against his son: Fakir Chandra Sen had stopped attending school since January and had stolen nearly eight to ten times from his mother, the amount adding up to nearly Rs 300/-; was associating with Ganesh Ghosh, Ananta Lal Singh and Rajat Sen and, or so Madhav Babu assumed, had made the money over to them.

Ananta checked the buckets of water in the room. They were full. Ganesh worked at one end of the table mixing carefully and lightly half an ounce of potash-chlorash and ammon picrate crystals on a two-inch by two-inch pasteboard. Once it was done, it was kept aside in a dry glass beaker before he got up to bring the next half-ounce from the stock room.

Phutu had pulled out his books as soon as the pain had become bearable. He had sent for Ganesh and made him read from them: When picric acid is made from sulphuric acid and nitric acid, traces of sulphuric acid are left behind along with the picric acid powder. When ammonium carbonate and picric acid are boiled with water to make ammon picrate crystals, the sulphuric acid is converted into tiny lumps of sulphur. It had been a revelation. Yellow sulphur is indistinguishable from ammon picrate crystals. And everybody knew that the explosive masala used to stuff fireworks was a mixture of sulphur and potash-chlorash.

Debu peeped in cautiously. The boys had been expressly told to stay away from the lab. He had returned from Kolkata, having escorted Pratul Babu to Chattogram earlier that day – a day devoted to Pratul Babu: driving him around; talking theoretically about the options available, for Ganesh had, a long time ago, promised never to go into action without including him in the plans. But today, when the man had actually been offered the chance, he had discovered responsibilities. He could not commit without first discussing the details with his party in Kolkata. Thank goodness, thought Ananta to himself, no details had been disclosed.

'The boy has settled in,' said Debu from the door. He had accepted Fakir's charge without question, without pressing for details. 'He will double up with Gobindo-da and remain out of sight.'

'Wish you'd sort this out for me.' Ganesh pushed across an envelope.

Debu stood uncertain for a moment; then came in and pulled out the letter. 'It has been brought to my notice,' he read rapidly, his words running into each other, 'by the guardians of a number of members of the institution that their wards do not attend schools and colleges, do not obey their guardians, do not even stay home at night and sometimes do such things which are against principles of morality. Some of the guardians directly accused me and the institution for the present state of affairs with regard to their wards. Personally, and as president of the institution, I am not prepared to accept the above accusations. Although I have every sympathy for physical culture, I have no sympathy for indiscipline, disobedience to parents and guardians and leaving present schools and colleges before such time as may be absolutely necessary for the interest of the country, or until educational institutions have been established on national needs. I do therefore ask you to call a general meeting at an early date to explain my position and, if need be, to tender my resignation which of course I shall do with a very heavy heart.'

'Suresh Babu's resignation?' said Ananta reaching for it. 'Here.' He folded the note and leaning forward, stuffed it into Ganesh's apron pocket. 'That's where it belongs.'

The wink and a toss of the head told Debu the conversation was over. Ganesh emptied his freshly mixed powder into the glass beaker with immense concentration and proceeded to clean the table. Underneath that moustache it was difficult to figure out what his lips were up to. The half-formed smile on Debu's face widened into a grin and he left.

Suresh Bandopadhyay, the respectable elderly businessman who had started a gymnasium in 1927 with great hopes of guiding and helping the youth and had appointed Ganesh secretary, was more than a little peeved. Unfortunately, they did not have the luxury of time now to comfort him.

There was enough powder in the beaker to fill a shell. Ananta placed one in the grasp of a vice fitted on to the table, counted out the requisite number of screws and settled down with a magnifying lens and a tiny brush. Meticulous cleaning was required. Not a trace of powder could be left on the screws. They worked in silence. It had been decided that no more youngsters would be permitted to try their hand at manufacturing explosives and there was no time to make TNT powder. They would fill ten shells with the ammon picrate and potash-chlorash mixture and the rest with smokeless gunpowder that the British used. It was time to put on their body shields. A sheet of tin had been hammered and moulded to cover the chest, arm and face. Two pinholes had been left. Carefully, they inserted the screws into the cork holders in the shell. A wrench was attached to the head of one screw and a long rope to its handle. Ganesh and Ananta took up positions outside the room, hiding behind the wall. They held the rope in their hands and twisted it carefully until it turned the handle of the wrench. Each screw would be tightened individually.

The Gupta house was just right for this kind of work, situated as it was on the top of the tila, with the study room about 30 feet away from the main house. The densely wooded hills behind had served them well, having been used for experimenting with time fuses – ones that would explode in five seconds and others that would take seven. There the boys had been taught the art of throwing bombs. The explosions could not be heard beyond a limited range. Those that did get to hear could not figure out where it came from.

Ananta had gotten off at Himangshu's house while Ganesh took the Baby Austin away. He would not be returning before two or three hours. He settled down to listen to Himangshu's report. The boy had been on duty, keeping watch on Inspector Sharada Bhattacharya's house. Together they went through his notes.

'His men have contacted Sarada Seel. Sub-inspector Rohini Bhowmik had brought him to the house.'

Ananta nodded. He had been aware of it. Phutu had warned him earlier and he had had a talk with the boy. They were all aware that Sarada's family struggled with poverty. They were trying to break him, he had warned. They would offer financial help, free tuitions, etc. The boy had steeled himself, and Ananta had interviewed him again after the visit to the inspector's house. The boy had succeeded in standing his ground. But boys reacted differently. Monoranjan Sen, whom he had personally recruited … in fact his first recruit after he had come out of jail, had flown into a rage. He had come to him demanding a revolver to shoot his father with. The man he had loved and worshipped all his life had approached him with the inspector's proposal: Money in return for all he knew. Mona had left home, threatening to return and pump a couple of bullets into his old and frail father. Ananta had hung on to him all day until he had calmed down.

'The inspector has contacted the purut moshai of Kali Bari.'

Of that too he was aware. The Kali Bari priest's sons Ashutosh and Bhabatosh Bhattacharya had joined them. Bhabatosh, who was in class eight, had reported to him that the inspector had suddenly discovered that they were related and had invited them to lunch on Sunday. Ananta had briefed the boy. Now he made a mental note to wait at Ganesh's shop on Sunday afternoon. He would place Jibon Ghoshal, whose house faced the temple, on duty and catch Bhabatosh the moment the family returned. A debriefing would then take place in Ganesh's shop.

'I need to take you off duty,' he said to Himangshu. 'Oh!' he said lightly, 'the police would also have noticed that you have been spotted around the inspector's home these last few days. So back to school with you,' he laughed.

The Baby Austin was tooting outside. Ganesh had returned earlier than expected.

'One of our guards is reporting movement on the route to Chor-Chaktai.'

Ananta got in, patting his waist to reassure himself that the revolver was with him.

'He has no clue as to the importance of Chor-Chaktai but has mercifully observed the movement and reported ... I hope on time.'

Ganesh was driving towards the home of a young worker, who had to be picked up. 'Police,' they mouthed and the lad jumped into the back seat without a question.

The car bumped its way through the fields leaving Patharghata behind. A quarter-mile of bumpy track still lay before them beyond which was a beel that marked the extreme edge of Chattogram – Chor-Chaktai. The lad jumped out and ran on ahead while Ganesh turned the car around. The engine was left running. Agonizing minutes ticked by before the worker was spotted helping Phutu across the uneven ground. He was struggling – there was simply no other word for it; his body a grotesque mesh of swollen tissue.

'But this is the life of a revolutionary.' Ananta heard Ganesh murmur. It was four in the afternoon and the April sun blazed down cruelly.

Phutu was in the car. He did not respond to their words. His breath came raspy and thin. Ganesh stepped on the accelerator. The worker was dropped off and the Baby Austin sped towards Ananda and Debu's home. 'Where is the choice?' he said though no question had been asked of him.

'But we can't make him walk up.'

'Just watch,' he said.

Though the motorable road ended at the base of the tila it was possible to push the car at least halfway up. But Ganesh stepped on the accelerator a good way ahead of the tila and the car shot all the way up through the garden of the British padre, leaving the lady of the house hysterical with rage, coming to a stop inside the Gupta compound. Phutu nipped out and disappeared into the study before Mashima and Jyotsna-di could come running out onto the verandah, shocked at the sight of a car within their gates. But they were their favourite young men and the ladies did not subject them to too much questioning.

Guards took up position immediately. Boys loitered in front of the Government College and along the path that led up the tila. They would be able to spot the police long before they approached the base. Phutu would be given enough time to disappear into the jungle behind the house.

In two days time, shelters had been arranged in the villages for both Ardhendu and Phutu. Ananta took Phutu to the Abdur Rehman Kheyaghat at midnight. The boy, Shankar, was waiting. He came nervously up to Ananta and placing his mouth right next to his ear said, 'Dui thaiya dui anna – two rupees two annas.'

'Why are you whispering?' Ananta barked as he backed away a little. 'Your behaviour reeks of illicit affairs! What are you so nervous about? Here, you are in charge of Phutu now. Go pay the boatman whatever you have agreed upon.'

He sat in the car watching. Relief washed over him as he saw the boatman pull strongly at the oars. Soon they had become a speck across the Karnaphuli. A smile played over his lips. Dui thaiya dui anna … this would go down as legend. Ei kheyechey! … again dui thaiya dui anna would become his response every time someone would begin to display signs of nervousness.

Raucous laughter spilled out on to the street. The area that served as the shop in Ganesh's house was filled with first-rankers. Boys came and went. Cycles zipped in and out. Cups of tea flowed as did poetry: lines laced with questions and the impromptu responses they generated. Cigarettes, beedis, alcohol were strictly forbidden. They were to be used only as disguise aides.

A tikka gharry clopped up to the door and Nirmal-da came in. He drew Ananta and Ganesh indoors. Surreptitiously, he shut all the doors and windows beaming all the while with a mysterious secret.

'Dara, dara … wait,' he said, 'it is a good omen … a godsend.' At last he was ready to part with his secret. 'Pravin Dada, our very own, has returned. Bai-rey-bai,' said Nirmal-da in his pronounced village accent and held on to Ananta's arm, 'my beloved brothers, let us all go and ask him to join us.'

A quiver of thrill seeped through Ananta. Pravin-da had come back at long last. It could be nothing but providence.

Nirmal-da was speaking with the earnestness of a simple revolutionary. 'Come let us introduce him to Rajat, Mona, Tripura, Naresh and Bidhu. Let us lay our weapons at his feet. Surely, seeing our resources, he will join us.'

Ananta tugged at Ganesh's arm. Leaving the boys to their hoi-hoolor and ruckus, they walked out. Himangshu ran out to see them to the door. A man in white stood in the distance watching as the Baby Austin's engine was started. Himangshu narrowed his eyes and levelled the stick in his hand at the watcher as if it were a gun. 'Gudum,' he said and then grinned like the devil. Ananta, watching in the rear-view mirror, burst into laughter. His heart was light and happy.

Ambika-da was completely taken in by the idea. Ananta waited for Master-da to give it his nod. It did not matter if Pravin-da took over the military command from him. At least he would be there.

But Master-da's words startled everybody. 'I agree with you. The responsibility must rest with the one that is most able. But I will not agree to disclose everything to him just to be able to attract him. Despite his prolonged absence, have we fallen short anywhere? True, we need to increase our strengths, so let us call him this evening and try to understand him. But our plans are not to be disclosed. Let us tell him an imaginary one and test him first.'

The evening meeting resulted in strange disclosures. Pravin-da had much to say. 'You need to work closely with Jugantar under Subhas's leadership and support the Congress. The time has long gone when little groups can take uncoordinated action on their own.'

It was blindingly clear. He had been sent by the police to get a feel of what this group was up to; his mission: pour oil over stormy seas. How could they have been so foolish? Had he not become a family man since the last time they met? And here they had been on the verge of disclosing their plans. Their plans that would surely have earned him large amounts of money.

It was Master-da who had saved the day. On 10 April 1930, they would have all been walking cheerfully up the garden path had it not been for Master-da. Ananta lay in bed that night. He had to see Master-da again.

Master-da was lying down for a bit, as he usually did in the afternoon, when Ananta burst upon him.

'Ki hey? Baipaar ki?' Master-da was startled. This was not the usual hour for Ananta to visit him. 'Any news?'

'I have to talk to you on a very serious issue.'

It did not have the desired effect on Master-da. He continued to lie as he was waving his hand indicating that Ananta should sit. Ananta pulled a chair up.

'I want to discuss my own feelings.'

Master-da nodded.

'Master-da, why is it that I cannot come to you and say that we are ready once and for all? Why is it that there are always ends left to be tied up? Am I not ready to fix my last day upon this earth?' He had become alive to the vacillations of his mind. The youngsters were raring to go. They had not yet formed strong attachments in life. But he? Was it he, a seasoned revolutionary used to fame and notoriety, who was unwilling to let life go? 'Would it not be nicer, Master-da, to spend a few more days rounding up lads; working up their feelings? Just enjoying the hold one has over the youth?'

Master-da was sitting up already. He had not uttered a word until now. 'It is good to hear your words. They've made me do a bit of soul-searching. The delays are due to a subconscious desire to live.'

'Let us fix the date and delay no more.'

'Tomorrow is Saturday. Call a meeting and decide.'

They sat in silence. The date would be fixed within twenty-four hours.

'How do you feel now, Master-da?'

He smiled. He did not look at him. 'Everything will get over so soon. Then … then … I cannot explain it. All our work will be done. We will never know what the outcome was … where the future would lead this country … life is so sweet. But to donate it for one's country … even sweeter.'

Master-da, Nirmal-da and Ambika-da were ready and waiting when Ananta and Ganesh walked into the Congress office. He had not told Ganesh about his conversation with Master-da. He had wanted to see what was there in his heart.

Ganesh sat down and opened a chart. It was a mobilization chart that he had corrected and redrawn several times over. It was the compilation of many thoughts, scribbles on bits of note paper, drawings and discussions. This final chart had been painstakingly printed at a secret press. The five men poured over it discussing every detail.

Then Ganesh folded the chart up announcing, 'This will be burnt the night before the action but now we have to fix the date and the time. The final arrangements cannot be made until then.' Ambika-da and Nirmal-da nodded in agreement.

Someone suggested Thursday, 17 April. But Ananta was uncomfortable. Since his childhood nothing had gone right on a Thursday for him. 'I suggest it be moved to Friday which is my lucky day.'

No one protested for everybody knew Ananta and his superstitions.

'It's a good day,' said Master-da immediately. '18 April 1930 – Good Friday. The day the Irish held their Easter Revolution.'

Five days to the day. Ananta's heart raced. Every beat was henceforth numbered.

NINE

Ananta Lal Singh, 18 April 1930, 5.30 a.m.

Ananta tossed in his bed: a rhythmic chant pounding itself again and again within his head:

Udayer pothey shooni kaar baani?
Bhoy nai orey bhoy nai
Nissheshey praan jey koribey daan
Khoy nai taar khoy nai

On the path that leads to the rising sun, whose words is it that I hear?
No fear, there is no fear
One who can donate his life, holding nothing back
For him there is nothing to lose.

The poet[1] would not let him sleep. The eastern sky had not yet begun to redden but the day would end differently … in a deluge of red. Ananta went to stand by the window, watching the first pink-stained rays catch the far reaches of the sky. It seemed to last longer than usual … finally there it was – the tip of the red sun peeping at him over the horizon, granting him, as it were, the last audience. He drew in a deep breath, bringing to mind the sixty-four comrades who had sworn to be by his side at this sandhi of his life.

The sun emerged in all its fullness, in all its glory, looking down at his sixty-four. He spoke for each of them: 'We swear to die. British imperialists, this day there will be no forgiveness for you, no introductions, no illusions of compassion, no mercy. Let the fires of hate and vengeance light up. The agents of British imperialism must pay for the massacre at the Jallianwala Bagh. Ma-go, give us strength and physical ability and the courage to kill the enemy.'

It was 6 a.m. There were many jobs for the day. The clock would have to be obeyed faithfully. Ananta checked the pistol at his waist, opened the door carefully and walked down the driveway to where the Baby Austin stood. He loved his little car. She was his team's 'Emden' and they changed her body paint, tyres, number plate off and on, just as the German cruiser had changed its colour, position and number of funnels. Like the Allies, the Chattogram police had been kept guessing.

The car sped through Chattogram's little roads, wound past the hill where the commissioner's bungalow stood and entered a narrow lane. Ananta parked her carefully and made his way to a tiny straw hut. He knocked thrice in a row. On a little cot, like every other day, sat Master-da – calm and serious.

'You look agitated?' Master-da observed.

'A couple of hours are all that is left. I am keeping my mind ready.'

'Do you remember the conviction with which you had told me that you would succeed in bringing back the rail company's money? Tell me are you as convinced today?'

In these last two months Master-da had asked him this question at least ten times.

'Why, Master-da? We will occupy the city. There is no power that can stop us now.'

Master-da's eyes glowed with a strange fire. He clasped Ananta's hand and spoke as if to himself, 'And what if there is a traitor in the ranks?'

This was the greatest of the biplob's enemies. The history of revolution is filled with treachery. The best – Joteen Mookerjee, Rash Bihari Basu, Vishnu Ganesh Pingle – had found their plans blighted in the bud.

'I think we have managed to set the police off on a different path.' Ananta reassured him. The rally planned for 17 April had gone off as scheduled.

'Are you absolutely convinced that there is no traitor amongst us?'

What an exquisite question. Outside the five of them no one was privy to the whole plan. If there was a traitor, how much damage could he possibly do besides give away three of four names and the particular operation that he was to take part in? But was that really Master-da's question?

'No, I have no reason to suspect any of our boys and I keep as sharp an eye upon each member of the central committee as they keep on me.'

Master-da pumped Ananta's hand vigorously and accompanied him to the door. 'When will they deliver the new car?'

'Around 9 a.m. I will go with Ambika-da.'

They exchanged smiles.

Seven a.m. and Ananta strode in through Ganesh's door. 'Hello, marshal!'

Ganesh extended a hand and led him to the table. A sketch map of Chattogram city covered most of it. Drawing up two chairs, they seated themselves and reached out for the red and blue coloured pencils. The map had already been marked extensively – the attack sites; the routes. It looked so different today. They stared at it, awestruck.

'Two years of preparation, so many rehearsals and today the curtains will rise.' Ananta was the first to break the silence.

'And let Nemesis retribute justice with wrath and retaliation.'

They went over the details one last time and then applied a match to the sheet.

Eight a.m. It was time for Lokenath Bal to come. The door opened and he walked in. Glowing skin, determination shining through, fair of speech, a beautifully well-built body, powerful arms ever ready to rise against injustice. A broad smile played on his face. He shook Ananta and Ganesh by the hand. 'There is not to reason why, there is but to do or die.' Lokenath, like all Bengali leaders, loved quoting poetry. 'Everything is ready. From my side everything will be on time.' Then he laughed, 'All for one and one for all.'

Leaving Lokenath with Ganesh, Ananta drove towards Nizam Paltan. Here he would need to be especially careful. The little houses were interspersed with narrow lanes. Any of these could have the police crouching in wait. Loosening the pistol at his waist, Ananta walked down the lane to the bamboo-and-straw hut at the end. Nirmal-da lived here alone.

Face gleaming with anticipation; he beckoned to Ananta to take a seat.

'So Nirmal-da,' Ananta laughed. 'Any chance of being a late-lateef today?'

'Forgive me, forgive me. No, brother, no. I will not be late ever again. You will see I will be there exactly on time.'

Ananta was embarrassed. Today was not the right day to be witty and in any case since that time of the railway robbery, Nirmal-da had used his own example while instructing youngsters on punctuality. Changing the topic they went over the day's programme. As Ananta rose to leave, Nirmal-da said, 'Remind the youth that it is all about Organization, Audacity and Death.'

'Be daring, be still more daring, be daring always,' Ananta added as rejoinder.

Now he would have to race back to Ganesh's shop where Ambika-da would be waiting. A gleaming Chevrolet was waiting for them at the J.N. Choudhury Company's Chevrolet showroom next to Ganesh's cloth shop. Who was it? … Either Mahendra Choudhury or Nitai who had, barely two or three days ago, brought nearly 1,200 to 1,400 rupees from home. It had been just enough for the first instalment. Sri Bireshwar Bhattacharya, who was a judge at the session's court, had agreed to stand guarantor.

The car was registered in Ambika-da's name. Ananta stepped on the accelerator. It was smooth. One barely got an indication of speed except when one happened to glance at the speedometer. The car sped towards Nizam Paltan – now at full speed, now screeching to a halt … she was perfect.

'Take the pitch-tala road towards Pahartali.'

The car hummed along the road, surfaced with coal tar and pulled up in front of the AFI armoury. A gigantic armed Pathan stood guard.

'Ambika-da, just imagine our new car in front of an armoured tank!'

'And against machine guns and cannon, our fourteen pistols and revolvers and one dozen 0.12 bore guns.'

The two laughed. 'Ambika-da, after killing the traitor, Naren Gossain, Kanai Lal went laughing to the gallows. And through his death, the fire of revolution spread. Tonight our boys will begin the writing of a new history.'

Ganesh and Nirmal-da would be making their rounds, meeting with every group. Was everyone physically and mentally well, he wondered. Their weapons, instruments and cars … were they ready according to plan? From morning to evening, things would have to be done with clock-like precision. Various group commanders would keep in touch with Ganesh, giving in their final reports. The slightest change was to be reported immediately.

Ananta had nothing to do with it. He turned the Chevrolet towards the city, dropped Ambika-da at the Congress office and then sped off towards Ganesh's house. There was Naresh on his bicycle. 'Naresh! Two questions.'

He came up to the window.

'Is everything okay? Have you personally checked every weapon in every hideout?'

'All done.' He grinned.

'Second, how is the morale in your group?'

Naresh used the thumbs up signal. 'They are betting on who will sacrifice his life first.'

Perhaps he had really nothing to ask of Naresh, but speaking with him bolstered his own courage.

'Remember Naresh, laying down our lives will never go waste. Today, we seek retribution for centuries of atyachar. We need strength, courage and morale. Make sure no one breaks down in the end. Tell them no daya, maya; not even a spot of koruna. We want cruel revenge. For Khudiram and Kanai Lal. For the women and children killed at Jallianwala Bagh.'

There was a spark in Naresh's eyes … one that would send the empire up in flames. He was ready.

He was at the base of the tila on which Ananda's house stood. It was 11 a.m. A group was waiting – Makhon, Rajat, Tegra, Ananda, Himangshu and Bidhu. They leapt up on seeing the new car: their car, their companion, their secret weapon. It was love at first sight. Some trailed their hands along the gleaming curves, some slipped inside luxuriating in the feel of the leather seats, others fiddled with the knobs. The pride on their faces raised Ananta's own morale. Ananda slipped into the driver's seat. He was to take it on a trial run, but instead of starting the engine he sat looking mildly puzzled.

'Wait,' he said and ran out. The startled group gazed after him. Within minutes he was back, running and leaping down the slope, his pillow tucked beneath his arm. Grinning sheepishly, he arranged it on the driver's seat and settled himself on top. 'Let's go,' he cocked his head at Ananta.

By now Tripura would have handed two synchronized watches to each group. He had been testing them for the last week. Saroj Bhattacharya, who was responsible for distributing the leaflets, knew where they had been hidden. But the contents remained unknown to him. The team that was to help him knew nothing of the hiding place or of the contents. The last thing on his agenda was to meet the teams before going home for lunch.

It was 1 p.m. The family had become used to the strange new indiscipline which appeared to have taken over Ananta's life – bathing when he wanted, catching a bite off and on, sleeping irregular hours. The zeal had gone out of the exercise schedule of late … it was as if a kind of lethargy had seeped in ever since the police crackdown on the supporters of Gandhi-ji. The first member of the family to come across him usually took charge of his pistol and revolver, be it Ma, Didi or Dada though it was Dada's self-appointed task to clean and lubricate the weapons. There would be little or no words exchanged. Boudi spoke little but knew what was required the moment the cloth bag was pressed into her hands. It was she who put out the cartridges in the sun and kept count. Baba and Ma had been away for several months, visiting the house on the riverbank at Double Mooring, as the doctor had prescribed it for Ma. Ananta headed towards the bathroom.

Didi was in the dining room. She looked him up and down, taking in the wet hair and fresh clothes. She returned to arranging the individual bowls of gravy, like satellites sharing the same orbit around Ananta's thala.

'We are ready.'

'For what?' She did not look up.

'Chattogram's British rule is coming to an end. Today their samadhi will be created. The IRA will occupy the city today.'

She looked up for a fraction of a second. Ananta could read her mind. These last couple of months had come as a disappointment. And then the rumours of the powdered faces; the bottles of Snow; the money wasted on restaurants and at the movie hall; Ganesh's repeated visits … what did they add up to?

'Didi, it is difficult to believe, but tonight Chattogram will fly the flag of independence in place of the Union Jack.'

Then it hit her. 'I will come along.'

'Na, that cannot happen. We are not taking our sisters along with us. This is work for the brothers. The sisters will come forward later.'

Her eyes flashed. 'Fine,' she snapped. 'I will go to Master-da.'

Didi felt he was the one pushing her away.

'No one will be able to meet Master-da today.' The words made her crumple. 'But he has sent a letter for you.'

'Where is it?'

'I am still eating!'

'Where is it?' She was using her most patient tone.

'In the moneybag.'

She brought it back; her eyes already moist from the blow to her ego. Ananta reached out and scanned the sheet of paper.

Didi,
Tonight we will go away. Today is our dying day. Perhaps we will never meet again. The revolution will lead us on to an unknown and new path today. The flag that we will leave behind with you … take care of it. The moshaal that we are lighting with the fire of revolution … let it not die out.
I congratulate you as a revolutionary.
Master-da.

She had been left out.

'Ask Master-da … compared to all the beloved brothers what is it that I lack? Just bodily strength? Doesn't he know that I am the Chattogram Balika Vibhag trainer? Boxing, knife throwing, Japani kusti, where have I fallen short? Can I not drive a car, shoot; are pistols and revolvers unknown to me? Master-da knows only too well that my bullet never misses its mark. Why this injustice? Is it just because I have been born a woman?'

How could Ananta even begin to confess that the training required for actual warfare had not been imparted to the sisters; that this decision had been taken right at the beginning? It would have broken her heart completely. She got up and left. Boudi came in to clear the thala. Ananta rinsed his mouth and took the pistol from Dada. 'Plan to leave this very night with Ma and Baba. Go away to the village. After the first round is over tonight, the British will unleash all their brutes. If they cannot get us, they will attack our homes. Master-da also feels the same way.'

He was on his way out when Didi ran up from behind and thrust a letter into his hands.

It was 2.30 p.m. Meeting at the new HQ which was Master-da's residence as of now. Nirmal-da, Ambika-da, Master-da and Ganesh were already present. There was some light banter and then the serious discussion began. Ganesh read out his plan down to the minutest of details and rehearsed verbally. Who was to be where, when and how were communications to be maintained.

Master-da had a few questions. 'Our Baby Austin will carry weapons and go with the team, attacking the club. Is the car running well? Who will drive it first? If he gets hurt who will drive it next? And what about Ananda? He drives well, there is no doubt, but compared to the size of the car he is still very small, very young.'

Every last detail was gone over. A six-cylindered car, powerful enough to rip the heaviest of doors open, was required; Lokenath[2] and his team were out that very moment, acquiring a taxi that suited the purpose. A second car would be required but sadly Heramba Bal's own Dodge was in the workshop as was Makhon's six-cylindered Essex. Hour-by-hour reports on the progress were being sent in.

The two teams that were to uproot the train lines had already been despatched to the site. They had taken up their positions and were awaiting the hour. The small teams that were to distribute the leaflets were ready and waiting, and the three small teams detailed to cut the telegraph wires had set out. Everybody's morale was up. Despite the problem with the cars it did not make sense to delay the date of action.

'Once the city has been taken, all gun shops will be attacked and emptied to arm the citizens who will come forward.' Announcements would be made over the megaphone. 'The Imperial Bank and the jail should surrender without too much fuss. And the final item on the agenda is dinner. Ananta has made an advance payment for maangsho-bhaat for sixty-four at Makleshwar Rahman's restaurant.' Ganesh ended his brief.

The meeting ended at about 4 p.m., but neither car had been repaired until then ... news came that they wouldn't be repaired before 6 or 6.30. An air of worry descended on the group.

'Not to worry,' said Ganesh, 'we will capture another taxi in time.'

Master-da looked at Ananta. 'We will fill those British mouths with ash. We will get those cars, no matter what. And if things come to such a pass, once Ananda's Chevrolet comes in from the telephone office, it will be despatched to the AFI armoury to help open the doors.'

The meeting was over. Everyone stood up. The next meeting would take place during the action. Ananta handed Master-da the letter.

> *Master-da,*
> *A revolutionary's greetings. I will not trouble you with my hurt feelings at this last moment. Your wish is my command. Bless me that I will be worthy of the responsibility you have given to me. I wish a long life for you.*
> *Didi*

Master-da smiled ruefully. 'Didi is really cross. But tell me what can I do? The future will judge us. Perhaps a day will come when the sisters will take the lead and leave us brothers far behind.'

He called for attention. That lovely deep voice, it induced a great sense of peace.

'We will lay down our unimportant lives in the cause of the motherland and jump in like braves. We will occupy the enemy's fort and fly the flag of victory. No matter how, no matter what the cost, we want the city.'

The whole house seemed to have been turned upside down. Holdalls containing bedding and three trunks lay in the middle of the floor. Dada, Didi and Boudi were busy packing. The servants had been given leave … the family was going away on holiday. Baba and Ma were back. They were sitting as if stunned out of their wits. Baba opened and shut his mouth a couple of times. Ananta briskly touched their feet and turned to his boudi.

'You have my things?'

Ma followed behind, with Baba trailing helplessly. A wave of self-importance flashed through Ananta's heart. This was a live re-enactment of *Jona o Probeer*. Drama! Drama was Ananta's lifeblood. How many times had he listened to the record at Pishemoshai's home … Probeer taking leave from his mother to go to war; asking for her blessing … a thousand times at least? Pishemoshai was the only person in Chattogram who owned a gramophone. Now Ananta was Probeer and Ma was Jona.

'What is happening today? What are you about to do? Tell me, Baba, tell me all. What will happen, what are you going to do?'

'Do not be impatient; you will get to know everything in time, in a couple of hours the whole world will know.'

'Let the world know what it will, tell me now, what is to become of you? Tell me the truth.'

'Why are you so worried? Calm down. Ki hotey paarey? Cholera, plague or TB … nothing more than that?'

'Look … I was saying …' But Baba's voice broke.

Ananta picked up his things, went into the other room and shut the door. When it opened he was standing before them dressed in khaki; stars and crossed swords gleaming on the epaulet; blue-and-silver collar tabs at his throat; cross belt and a row of medals across his chest; holsters at the waist; boot-patti and leggings; and in his hands, a golden helmet with a splendid feather. It was the uniform of a British army general.

Ma was breathing heavily. She had seen him in uniform many times but even she could see that there was something special about this one. Her eyes were drawn to the handkerchief-sized black velvet badges with the two native flags and silver embroidery around the edges … the ones she had sown through the night because Ganesh had pestered her so. The Volunteer Vahini was going to Sita Kund to help out, he had said.

Baba, who had been a silent spectator until now, said with difficulty, 'Look, are you not hurrying into things? Is the country ready? Have you thought it out? Is it correct to do something like this now?'

The kobi[3] whispered into Ananta's head:

Orey nobeen orey aamar kaancha
Orey shobooj orey obooj
Aadhmorader ghaa merey tui baacha

Rokto aalor mode mataal bhorey
Aajkey jey jaak boley boluk torey
Sakal badha helay tuchcho korey
Puchchoti tor uchchey tuley naacha.
Ay duronto ay rey aamar kaancha.

Oh my new one, oh my raw unformed one
Oh green one, oh one who does not yet understand
Strike the half dead and restore them to life.

In the drunkenness of the light of this blood-red dawn
Today, let whoever say what they will
Let every obstacle be reduced to nothing
Lift your tail and make it dance
Come my restless one, come my raw unformed one.

But there was no need to hurt Baba any further. Instead he said, 'When will it be the right time? For those that have bowed their head for two hundred years … when will the time be right for them? Bless me. Your son will die tonight for the motherland. Forget your sadness. Feel proud.'

Baba looked as if he had been struck. But he recovered quickly and said, 'My blessings for each one of you. Not death. Return victorious.'

Ananta bent to touch his feet and Ma burst into tears.

'What if I lose you forever? How will I live without you?' She could speak no more but gasped in a desperate bid to control her tears, aware that crying was an ill omen.

'Don't break down. Where will I get my courage from? Calm me. Tell me not to be afraid. Tell me to be brave. You have always helped us, so why do you hesitate now at this final moment. Smile. Laugh and say … go, go running and destroy the enemy … take your oath: Do or die.'

Dada pushed his way through and fixed the talwar to his belt.

'Boudi, Boudi, where are those cartridges … it's getting late.' Boudi had been hovering all this while in the background, the bag ready in her hand … but what else could he have said to her in farewell?

Didi handed over the pistol. 'Move forward. Let not one bullet go waste.' Ananta put the pistol away and whispered into her ear, 'These were Master-da's last words today … I have left the breech-loader at home. Use it without hesitation if required. I know your aim is never off mark.'

He bent to touch their feet one last time and Ma burst into fresh tears and clasped him to her breast. 'The badge you have sown will be my raksha kabaj,' he whispered. He crossed the uthon and turned once more to wave at them. They stared back rigid and immobile. The moment Ananta crossed the sitting room they suddenly came to life, hurrying behind him. As he got into the car, Ma cried out from the top of the steps. 'No, no, it cannot be. I bless you. Death will not be able to touch you. You will return victorious.'

The new Chevrolet was standing in the compound facing the road. Ananta started it and looked back one last time. On seeing his face she raised her hands skywards and said in tearful voice, 'My blessings. No one will be able to touch you.'

The car rolled out. His favourite lines from *Jona and Probeer* came to mind:

Akkhay kirit sheerey tabo pado dhuli
Matrinaam akkhay kabaj bukey
Shommukh shomorey morey bimuk kay korey morey

The invincible crown on my forehead is nothing but the dust of your feet
Ma's name that is the invincible shield across my breast.
Who can face me in war, who can force me to turn back?

The car rolled out of the gully and entered the wide road. He hadn't asked as to where they were going and nor had they burdened him with the details. Didi and Dada were there to look after them. After all, didn't *Anandomoth* teach that revolutionaries have no mother, no father, no home? Their only mother was the motherland.

John Younie

Steamers were a comfortable mode of travel. The Younies had embarked at Khulna on the evening of 18 April with their three daughters, Chrissie the nanny, several servants including Johur and Yakub, 100 pieces of furniture, two dogs and a cow. Milk supply, they had been warned, could be difficult in Chittagong.

John stood by himself on the deck, watching the setting sun cast its spell on the waters. They were moving up the estuary formed by the Ganges, the Brahmaputra and the Meghna at the south-west corner of the Dacca district. The main channel ran onto the Bay of Bengal as the Meghna, but to the west of it lay a great V-shaped tract – a deltoid area intersected by umpteen rivers and khals – some large some small. Dorothy was suddenly beside him. She had tiptoed up, unwilling to break the magic of the moment. 'All tightly asleep … the little bairns,' she whispered as she snuggled into the crook of his arm.

It had been one long week of hectic packing and 'redding up'. The bungalow, the drawing room in particular, had been turned into a horrible mixture of byre, threshing floor, carpenter's shop and a Whiteaway Laidlaw export department. The books, which imparted a civilized look to the room, reposed snugly in their tin-lined chests, perfumed with many camphor balls; the dismantled wall shelves turned into disconsolate planks, while pictures and rugs had simply disappeared before his eyes. It had been Dorothy who had done it all. He had leant back in his chair, figuratively patting himself for having dictated that last large judgement, while she had rushed back and forth between cases of crockery and glass fill, a lusty Elspet demanding to be fed and the blankets and clothes that he had personally intended to supervise.

The steamer crawled slowly upstream against the current, calling at little landing stages. They had reached the last one when the flame faded from the western sky and darkness descended at a single stroke. The searchlights came on, lighting up the dark sullen waters ahead, the silence broken by the churning of the paddle wheels and the monotonous refrain, ek do tin – bam mile nahivi, quaintly chanted by the native in the bows, as he cast the lead.

'They have to be built with an extremely shallow draught, you know,' John broke the silence. 'The river bed is treacherous and your Indian pilot knows that at any moment he may slip out of sixty feet of water into six. What was a ten-foot-deep channel one week may easily become a one-foot one or dry up altogether by the next. This is especially true during the rains, when the river overflows, depositing the silt it is carrying, and creating crowds of low-lying chars. They have to constantly take soundings and often, despite all these precautions, they'll barge on to a sandbank and be a whole day in getting off again.'

Despite being a big twin-decked, flat-bottomed, ungainly paddle wheeler, the steamer moved gently.

'Will we be able to take a look at your house in Barisal?'

John tightened his grip around her shoulders. 'We will sail past it early in the morning … I will point it out … it is the best one in the station and probably the best I will ever be allotted in my life. A really first-class, two-storeyed bungalow … the river barely 300 yards to the south, with the maidan – a tolerable nine-hole golf course – and a tank between them.'

Dorothy remembered. The years of separation were as if they had never been, for between them had flown voluminous letters, bridging the miles as if they never existed.

He had written:

Imagine yourself, looking out southwards at night from my upstairs verandah: across the tank in the foreground, the Bell Park and then the river. Picture a great bright Bengal moon overhead reflected in the waters of the tank and causing a great broad path of light across the ripples of the Barisal River. See also the feathery forms of casuarinas along the riverside, boldly outlined against the gleaming silver of the river. He had drawn a little sketch by the side. *And you would have said,* he had added, *isn't it beautiful and I ... yes, yes, but this is September and wouldn't you prefer sleeping to looking out upon the Barisal moon all night?*

So many times had she read the epistles and so tenderly had the words been locked away in her heart.

'The electric fans did come but until then, sleep was a fickle jade that wanted a lot of wooing,' he smiled, as if reading her thoughts.

Downstairs there had been an office room, a large dining room and drawing room with a fireplace in each, while the upstairs had two very large bedrooms with dressing rooms and a third smaller bedroom – in all John had enjoyed a compact, well-built, modern bungalow, set so as to catch the prevailing southerly breeze. The life of a grass widower in Barisal was spent mostly at work and he had summed it up thus: One bloody murder after another; I had to order the stringing up of another fellow last week; if the criminal classes of Krishnagar were bad, they are little saints compared with the local products.

'It was a lonely time for you and you hated the food.'

'Potol and lady's fingers? Who ever did come up with the idea of calling them lady's fingers? But you,' he smiled tenderly, 'living at the time in the land of plenty, wouldn't have remembered the tasteless garbage that garnishes the monsoon mourghee in the Bengal mofussil. Fortunately for me, Donovan offered to share his weekly basket of vegetables that came in from Darjeeling – a most noble collection of green peas, leeks, carrots, cabbage, French beans, broad beans, asparagus and what not. And,' said John triumphantly, 'we had ice! All thanks to Donovan ... at two annas per seer ... about two pounds approximately ... brought down from Calcutta for the club and we could help ourselves to it. Very satisfactory, what?'

The Barisal Club was a good one with three pucca tennis courts, billiards table and bridge ad lib and a decent-sized European population with nearly ten resident British families.

'But as a place, it is stiff with missions and churches,' he laughed. 'There are the Oxford Missions with three or four Oxford brothers and some fifteen, I think, Oxford sisters and a church. There are the RCs with another church and the Baptists with theirs. I had gone to the English service one Sunday and it was more like Totland Christ Church at the Isle of Wight than Ayre's Low Church with responses and psalms and what not. But very good, all the same. The Oxford sisters also run a women's hospital ...you would have been interested.'

Dorothy had got an MD from Aberdeen University for a thesis on the failure of lactation and had been looking forward to working with the tribal women. It was the only way of interacting with Indian women. Socializing between the communities was a rarity even though a number of them held senior posts and worked alongside. For John it had been limited to Major Thakur, the Punjabi civil surgeon at Barisal and his Swedish wife. His prescriptions of bed rest, a particularly foul-tasting jug soup and liquid quinine had kept him going and kept his recurrent attacks of malaria at bay.

'No solid work can be done for child welfare without the slow development of public opinion and months and months of hard work among the people by really keen and competent voluntary workers,' continued John. '... unlike that moth-eaten scheme instituted by Lady Lytton – the National Baby Week: a series of lectures, sermons, essay competitions and baby shows! The only part of the scheme for which the slightest enthusiasm had been shown was the essay competitions for which gold and silver medals had been offered. And a fat lot of good did babu so-and-so's essay, in beautiful flowery English, do to the thousands of wretched diseased infants that spawn over the alluvium.'

Johur was rigging up John's camp cot on the deck, tucking the mosquito net deftly under the mattress. It was time for Dorothy to return to the cabin. They would be up early to breakfast with Donovan, the district magistrate and collector at Barisal, before making their way to Chittagong. Chrissie was their chief worry. John hoped that the seventeen-year-old would cope, considering there would be none of the entertainment she was used to in England. The bioscope, that had been introduced late in 1928, had proved itself popular with the Aryan brother but letting Chrissie off by herself was out of the question, let alone the fact that the mere suggestion was scandalous.

Dorothy had laughed outright at his description of the help engaged by the Taylors: A cheery, red-haired young thing that plays tennis in bare legs with those little socks over the top of her tennis shoes.

Getting to be quite a middle-aged man, she had observed. And now as a father of three daughters, he couldn't agree more.

LOKENATH BAL

The afternoon of 18 April was a particularly pleasant day and many holidaymakers were out to enjoy the long weekend. Young babus, sons of wealthy men … it was evident by their outfits … walked up and down the stand looking at the taxis. The drivers called out, jostling amongst themselves: Where did the babus wish to go? Lokenath inspected the taxis. A car was selected.

'Kya naam?'

'Ahmadur Rehman, sahib. You can call me Ahmad.'[4]

'Naya gari?' Subodh Choudhury walked around, admiring the shiny new black Dodge. The driver smiled, a little shy all of a sudden. Taxi number 21929 was his pride and joy.

'My friends and I need a car for the evening. Come by sundown.'

Ahmad reported on time at the house in Patharghata. He did not seem particularly disconcerted by the fact that the babus by now were all dressed in khaki. Chittagonians had become used to seeing the Hindu youth play-acting at being soldiers, and on the lookout for people they could help.

'Lo-o-ong drive.' Makhon stressed on the 'Long'. 'Let's go for a really long drive.'

'Bhatiari tak … chalega?'

'Bahut dur. It's too far, babu-ji.'

Rajat winked rubbing his thumb and forefinger. It was settled. Nirmal-da got into the back seat and the youngsters piled in, chatting happily. Rajat sat next to the driver and set up a running conversation.

'Kon gram? And at home? … Children?'

The tarred road whizzed past beneath the wheels and soon it was the countryside that was flashing by. Above, soft puffs of clouds floated against the darkening blue of the sky.

'Foy Sagar!' Makhon pointed to the right. All heads turned and the car swerved dangerously to the right, setting up a fit of giggles. It did not matter that day, for they had the road to themselves.

The dark shape of the hills loomed to the right, and flat calm of the bay stretched out to the left. A village appeared. It had not a soul in sight.

'Fakirhat.' The driver informed them.

'What comes next?'

'Faujdarhat.'

They were climbing now through a wooded area interspersed with paddy fields.

'Ahmad-ji, stop please.'

The car rolled to a stop and the three passengers at the back stepped out to stretch their legs. The driver pulled out a beedi and took a quick look at Rajat. He nodded. They sat companionably for a while. The others were coming back. The driver put out his beedi and waited for them to get back in. They did not. Instead, they crowded around his door.

'Get out.'

The driver glanced over his shoulder, puzzled. The mouth of a pistol pointed at him. Rajat wore an apologetic smile on his face. Before the matter could sink in, powerful arms were reaching in pulling him out. Each of his soft-spoken, genteel passengers held pistols in their hands.

Lokenath dragged him into the paddy fields and pinned him down. A wad of cotton was pressed to his nose and the bottle of chloroform emptied.[5] As the man lost consciousness, they tied his legs together and his hands behind his back. Some soft cloth was wrapped around his head and face and kept in position by the rope. Lokenath looked for a suitable place where he would not be discovered easily and yet would remain out of harm's way.

Ananta Lal Singh

It was 7 p.m. On the road behind the Assam Bengal Railway office, a Chevrolet and a Baby Austin drew up side by side.

'Hello, marshal.' Ganesh craned his neck out of the window. He was in uniform, much like the one Ananta wore, except that he held a baton in his hand instead of wearing a sword at the waist, for he was the GOC and therefore a field marshal. He twirled his moustache for effect. His eyes, thought Ananta, were unusually bright.

But the news was bad: neither car had been fully repaired. The boys had been reporting every hour and then every fifteen minutes and despite goading the mechanics to hurry, not even one was close to being ready. A taxi would have to fill the gap but the teams were to move into position at 7.30.

'Move the zero hour to 10 p.m.'

Ganesh's thoughts synchronized perfectly with Ananta's. But it meant that sixty-four armed youths; dressed in uniform; ready to go would have to sit and twiddle their thumbs for another two hours. It also meant that Lokenath would have to wait around with the stolen taxi.

The teams would have to be informed. The two cars sped down to where Naresh was waiting. The Baby Austin was handed over; the new time intimated and the two marshals drove off. The road that led to the Assam Bengal Railway's general building dipped between two hills, ran along the side of the Nizam Paltan field and then split into two.

There were no municipality street lights here. The stars glittered overhead. It was a clear night and the trees cast long shadows onto the roads. On one side was a hill, on the top of which stood a sahib's bungalow. While still half a mile from the armoury, they heard the sound of a Dodge starting its engine. As it closed in, Ananta drew in a sharp breath. By the driver's side in full-dress uniform sat a British officer, his white skin gleaming pale under the headlight beam. The car drew up alongside and the young lieutenant at the wheel stepped out; opened the door for his captain and brought his white-gloved hand smartly to the peak of his cap with a click of his heel. From the rear emerged Nirmal-da, Rajat Sen and Subodh Choudhury – each one dressed according to rank.

'All has gone well at our end. Now tell us your news.' Lokenath was in no mood for small talk.

'All is well, but …'

'But what?'

'The cars that were to go to the police lines are not available. We have to arrange for one right away. We need two more hours.'

Nirmal-da became very agitated. A delay now? The small groups carrying the manila ropes, ladders, tins of petrol had already walked through the Nizam Paltan field and had taken up position near the AFI armoury. There was very little time. The others would have to be informed in a hurry. He took responsibility of informing some of the teams.

Ananta swung past Dr Jagada Biswas's home. But he had gone out, taking his car with him. Driving at top speed, Ananta dropped Ganesh off at the shop. He would send out despatch riders on cycles, while Ananta rushed to inform Master-da at the Congress office. He was maintaining contact with all the smaller teams.

'You are going to acquire a car now? We are all over the city dressed like this … two hours now? What if the first driver regains consciousness?'

'Even if he does he will not have time to report the matter. By then we would have struck. As for our boys moving around in uniform, the police are used to seeing us like this.' Ananta called over his shoulder. He was already rushing out, for Ambika-da would be waiting by now, with his instruments and petrol tins, at the designated spot close to the telephone office. And Ananda, who should have had the car by 7.50 p.m., was waiting at home to load the sledgehammers. The scheduled time of attack had been 8.05 p.m.

Ananda was waiting on the slope. He was surprised to see Ananta alone, for a second car was supposed to have followed.

'How will you go back?'

'Last-minute change of plans. Another car has to be arranged. The scheduled time for you now is 9.55 p.m.'

He ran up the wide steps cut into the hillside behind Ananda. The boy would need help with bringing down the sledgehammers that had been stowed away in his study. But he stopped himself in time. Another ten or twelve steps and he would be in the uthon.

'Ananta!'

Too late. He had been caught. Mashima's voice floated down. She must have been watching.

'Ananta, come up. Hurry.' It was an imperious command; one that could not be ignored.

Jyotsna-di (Ananda's Chhor-di) and Mashima stared. They had seen him in khaki many times but today their faces registered sheer horror.

'Ananta, Khoka said he was going away on holiday for seven days. He left wearing khaki. Where did he go?'

Ananta felt the panic rise within him. 'Is that so? Debu did not tell me anything. Why, I met him only this morning.'

Chhor-di's eyes bored their way through his head, through the falsehoods being conjured up.

'As he touched my feet he said, "Ma, don't worry, Chotkun is with you." He left without eating … today!'

It was Chotkun's birthday. The realization struck him like a bolt from the blue. The evidence was all around: the little lights in the bushes; Chhor-di's and Mashima's silk saris, their hair piled high on their heads. There must be guests within … the boys must have called her aside and made their little announcements.

'Tell me, Ananta, I can't take it any more, where did my Khoka go?'

Mashima would just have to wipe her tears and put on a façade for the sake of her guests. She would have to urge them to eat; perhaps another slice of cake, she would have to say sweetly … and hers were the best in Chattogram … knowing that her two eldest sons were leaving home perhaps never to return … she could cook and bake, all she wanted, in the days to come, but it would be in the knowledge that they would never taste her food again. A grand speech was taking shape in his head: Brave mother, heap blessings on your sons' heads; wish us all well … may we return victorious.

Instead he said, 'When he has said he will return in seven days why do you doubt him? I will find out. I will let you know tomorrow.'

He could see that she did not believe a single word. And how could she? Here he was standing dressed to the gills, all ready to pick up the younger son who had done nothing but moon about the house all evening, dressed in khaki.

'And Tun, where is he going? Why is he dressed in khaki and you, why have you come here dressed like this? Why did Tun say he would not be returning home tonight? Tell me, tell me the truth, is there any danger to your lives?' She was breaking down now.

Chhor-di turned on him aggressively, 'This is very unfair, you know. Two sons? From one family? Where are you taking them? Have you spared but a single glance at the faces of the parents?'

What could he say? Both brothers had discussed the issue and had let it be known that they were going to take part in the action. But this was quicksand; opening his mouth meant sinking in even deeper.

'Tun is still very young Ananta. At least leave him for me.' The tears were pouring freely now.

'Ananta-da, it's getting late. Come quickly.' Ananda called from down below.

'Mashima, Chhor-di, ebar aashi.' Ananta was down the steps in a flash.

The sorrow that was welling up deep within her soul clung to him and her words rang in his ears. 'Ananta, at least one, leave just one behind for me.'

Ananda was waiting in the car. 'What?' he laughed. 'Tears in your eyes? Do you not have to arrange for a car within two hours?'

In an instant he had jerked Ananta back to his senses. Together they recited Ananda's favourite lines from Kazi Nazrul:

Durgam giri, kantar moru, dustar pararbar
Longhitey hobey ratri nishithey jatrira hushiyar

High mountains, endless deserts, uncontrollable seas
Cross you will have to in the dead of the night, oh traveller be alert.

Silently in his heart Ananta swore: There shall be no Alps.

They raced to the telephone office to update Ambika-da. The news did not upset him. 'It will be all right,' he said.

Himangshu had to be picked up. He was waiting on the road that led to Ganesh's house.

'I don't like it.' He grumbled.

'Andu, we have to adapt constantly to the situation. It would be foolish to assume that it's going to be smooth sailing.'

'Tell me,' he said, 'what is to be done now?'

'That's the spirit.' Ananta got off at Ganesh's shop, handing the car over to Ananda. 'Drop Andu to the taxi stand at Lal Dighi before you join Ambika-da. Andu, bring back a taxi no matter what the cost, what the implications. There are no taxis to be had here … they are all booked for the Nikhil Bongo Karnaphuli Muslim Conference.'

'Oh, of course he will do it. Ki rey, Andu? Won't you be able to do it?'

Himangshu pulled a face at him in response.

'Remember,' said Ananta, 'impossible is a word found in the dictionary of fools.'

The five doors to the showroom that led in from the street shut every night by eight o'clock. Tonight it was no different. The showroom lights had been put out but one door, the one to the extreme right had been left open. It led to another door which opened into the main house. Haripada Mahajan stood guard today. Ananta strode in. Ganesh, Debu and Saroj Guha sat looking glum. Five double-barrelled rifles and 200 cartridges lay on the bed.

'Not working?' Ananta tried his hand. The cartridges would not fit.

'Who got these?

'Madhusudan; this one is Makhon's; Ranadhir's; Lokenath borrowed this one from Dhiren[6] and this one belongs to Krishna's kaka.'[7]

It was demoralizing … as it was, there weren't enough firearms to go around in the first place and now five were going waste. The bores had never been tested for fear of alarming the guardians, who would have then heightened security. And it was impossible to differentiate between a 0.16 and 0.12 by sight alone. All cartridges that had been bought were of 0.12 bore.

It had been nearly half an hour since Himangshu had left. Ananta went out to peer into the darkness again. Every time the headlights of a car flashed by, it would raise their hopes … surely, Himangshu would manage something.

The door opened. Swadesh Roy stood in the room looking

shell-shocked. Haripada had chosen that very moment to go for a drink of water. This was a calamity. Ananta could barely conceal the irritation on his face. He caught Ganesh's eye motioning towards the verandah.

'He usually comes at this time to chat with me … he knows I am by myself at this time of the day,' hissed Ganesh. He clearly thought Ananta was overreacting.

It was true. After all, what had he done wrong? Naresh and Debu were among the set of boys that he laughed and joked around with, and all of a sudden, he was being perceived as a nuisance. And yet here he was, staring at the rifles. 'Let's tie him up. He may be a police agent.'

Ganesh made no answer.

'Since I am not wanted here I might as well leave.' Swadesh made a move towards the door. Haripada stood hanging his head in shame.

'Quick, let's get him now.' Ananta was making hurried mental calculations: What if Swadesh went to Kotwali straightaway? No, he could not do that. He would have to get in touch with his police contact first. That man would want to meet him in person and get all the details. Then he would inform the senior police officers and then they would issue orders. By then the operation would have taken place. It was alright, Swadesh could go. He turned to Haripada. 'Cheer up,' he said. 'Everyone makes mistakes. Learn from it.'

There was no time to feel relieved, as Himangshu was not back yet. Could he not find even a horse cart? The operation had already been delayed by two hours. They would have to leave by 9.30 sharp; then another half an hour to get into position … all the other teams would be waiting. They would have to leave even if Himangshu did not make it.

'Pick up the stuff. We will march down.'

Just then a light flashed and disappeared. The bend on the road was responsible but no Himangshu appeared. The mind raced with all kinds of probabilities. The lights appeared again. It had to be just another car … it came to a stop. Himangshu was walking in. There was not a moment to lose.

'Call the driver in.'

'The babus want to discuss the money with you. Come in. They want to hire the car for the night.'

The driver came in. Ananta sized him up. He was a little younger than him. Two boys had moved quickly, blocking the doorway behind him. Taken aback, the man hesitated but then his gaze fell on the revolvers pointing towards him. Pressing a finger to his lips, Ananta motioned to him to remain silent. Pointing the revolver away, he began to swing it idly as he spoke using the Chattogram dialect.

'What is this you are looking at?'

All the driver could manage to say was, 'Haw, bau, haw, bau … yes, babu, yes, babu.'

'Arrey chinish ni? Ain kon? Aar naam janis ni? … Have you not recognized me? Who am I? Don't you know my name? Have you not heard of Ananta Singh?'

No matter what the question, all he said was 'haw bau'. He was turning pale, his arms hung uselessly by his side and his legs trembled. He was hyperventilating. He was going to fall any moment now.

'You have nothing to fear. We are not going to hurt you. You are our brother and I am sorry that I am troubling you like this. If we had known you better and could trust you, we would not be treating you like this.'

'Haw, bau.'

'Look brother, we are going for a dacoity and we need your car. But we cannot leave you in case you go to the police. That is why we have to tie you up. You understand, don't you? Please put your hands out … When we return we will let you go. You will get your car back. But do not leave until then. We are leaving a guard behind. If you move or make a noise he will shoot you.'

'Haw, bau.'

'Lie down now.' The man was ready to drop to the floor when Debu pulled out a woven reed madur for him. Everyone trooped out silently and piled into the waiting car … there was no guard being left behind.

Ananta got into the driver's seat of the Chevrolet Tourer and cursed silently. Could Himangshu not have found a more ramshackle one than this? Where was the key? There was no key. Ananta went back inside.

'Where is the key?' he asked the bound and trussed-up man.

'Nai … the two wires … just join them.'[8]

It was already 9.30. Though it coughed to life, the car still had plenty of attitude left: the clutch, brake, gear and accelerator, each with their own peculiarities. Driving fast was out of the question. At least it is a car, Ananta comforted himself. As long as it took them to the police line guardroom by 10 o'clock, they would be okay. The streets were dark, lined with tall leafy trees. Not all of Chattogram had electric lights. The ordinary citizen refrained from staying out late. Within moments, the city, barring the white man that partied late, would be fast asleep. Street lights were limited to the areas frequented by the British but they were dim. If he could stand on top of one of the hills now and look down, it would seem as if a great dark python had caught the hills in its coils.

At 9.50 p.m. they were at the big Paltan field where the sahibs played golf. It would now take them another two to three minutes to reach their destination.

Paltan Maidan occupied roughly the centre of an equilateral triangle with the police lines located at the apex to the north; the AFI headquarters and armoury at its south-western corner on the road leading from Chittagong to Pahartali; and the telephone-telegraph office occupying the south-eastern corner right in the heart of the city. On the far side of the Paltan Maidan, on the road leading from the police lines to the AFI headquarters, very close to the police lines, was a lonely tila. Perched on top, surrounded by the flaming krishnachura trees, stood the beautiful European club.

But the life seemed to be spluttering out of the car's rheumatic aching joints.

'Heart-fail!'

It had revolted intuitively at the sight of Paltan Maidan. It refused to move. There was no time to think. The boys jumped out and began to push while Ananta remained at the wheel. It gurgled and came back to life. Everyone was jumping back in when Saroj announced he had lost his revolver. It had fallen out of its holster. Fortunately, the road was completely deserted but a car could come upon them any moment, for the zila administrators all lived on this side. As Saroj scrabbled in the dust, Ananta noticed a figure on the right side of the road. They were being watched. The man stood in the shadows

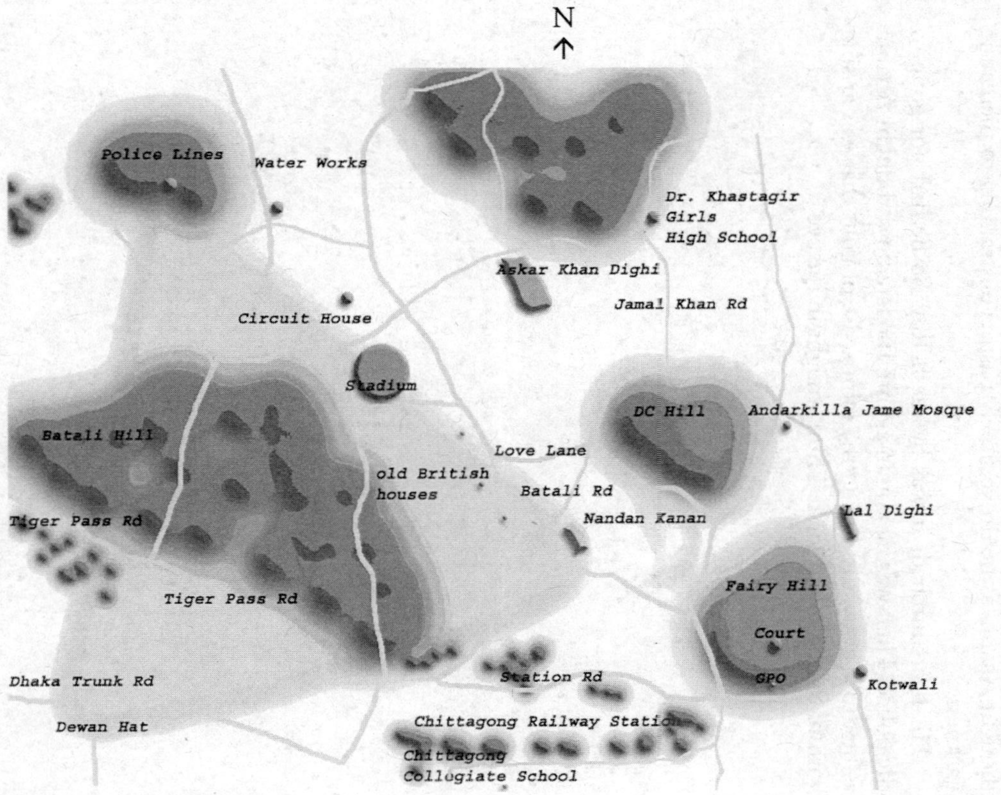
N
Police Lines
Water Works
Dr. Khastagir Girls High School
Askar Khan Dighi
Jamal Khan Rd
Circuit House
Stadium
DC Hill
Andarkilla Jame Mosque
Batali Hill
Love Lane
old British houses
Batali Rd
Nandan Kanan
Lal Dighi
Tiger Pass Rd
Tiger Pass Rd
Fairy Hill
Court
Dhaka Trunk Rd
Station Rd
GPO
Kotwali
Dewan Hat
Chittagong Railway Station
Chittagong Collegiate School

cast by the great trees of an orchard. Everyone saw him ... probably a police watcher on duty.

Impossible to create any trouble within the next five to ten minutes, thought Ananta as he drove slowly past, eyes straining to pierce the darkness.

His heart lurched. It was Swadesh Roy. So he had not gone to the police! Then was he not an agent? Too late now, thought Ananta as he drove away, dismissing the faint sense of guilt that was arising within. Swadesh had looked him straight in the eye.

TEN

Ananda Prasad Gupta

Seven figures draped in chadors waited in a Chevrolet at the bottom of the Kata-Pahar Rasta to the north of the Telephone Bhavan hill. It was an area forbidden to the general population but was drivable, as opposed to the routinely used road, which was so steep that it had been cut into steps.

At the signal, Ananda pressed down hard upon the accelerator and the car flew across the Kata-Pahar Rasta as it cut its way between two hills. The forester's bungalow stood on top of the hill to the north, looking across at the Telephone Bhavan. The car was parked in the shadows. Discarding their wrappings, the team emerged. The now khaki-clad figures raced up the hill, ducking to avoid the light that shone through the windows of Telegraph Deputy Superintendent Scott's quarters to the telegraph building on the summit. Their target was a solitary room at its eastern end. Ambika-da took position where the verandah had been walled off while Ananda slipped in. Cause minimum hurt; the words had been drilled into their heads again and again. The operator was by himself sitting at his switchboard, his back towards the door. Ananda placed the mouth of his pistol against his back and said firmly, 'Raise your hands please. There is no need to be scared. Come outside quickly.' The man had begun trembling; he was in no position to make a sound. Ananda led him by the arm to one of the chairs[1] on the verandah. 'Quiet. Face the wall and keep your hands up. Don't worry.'[2]

Ambika-da had some soft cloth soaked in chloroform ready. As the operator began to go under, Pundit-da stood guard and Ambika-da ran to take cover behind a pillar to keep watch over the southern verandah and the rooms, which would be full of night-duty workers in the telegraph section. The sounds of heavy hammers emanated from within the little room as Ananda, Biren De, Dwijen Dastidar, Niranjan Rai and Manindra Lal Guha pounded away at the switchboard and equipment.

'No shouting. Remain seated. There is no fear.' Ambika-da shouted across to the telegraph building. Not a soul stirred. They sat in their places paralysed. 'Pour the petrol.' Two minutes[3] were up and Ambika-da signalled the end. 'All clear?' he called again. Everyone had come out: the whistle was blown. Ambika-da struck a match and flung it neatly into the room. The office burst into flames.

'Telegraph office!'[4]

The boys responded to the command but by then the doors had been locked. They crashed bodily into them and the doors gave way.

'Hands up; remain still; no shouting; if you try to run I will shoot.' Ambika-da kept his finger ready on the trigger.

The room was evacuated and the work of destruction began. The match was applied and the team raced downhill. They piled quietly into the car. The sky turned red with leaping flames. A shot sounded from Mr Scott's window.[5] The Kata-Pahar Rasta echoed with the sound of two shots. Ambika-da had fired back in the direction of the sound.

Ananta Lal Singh

It was 9.55 p.m. by Ananta's watch. The car crept along the periphery of the waterworks compound. The headlights lit up the bend in the road. A figure stepped out of the shade of an enormous tree. Ananta switched off his lights and the car rolled to a stop. Master-da was a vision in white: a stiff khaddar Gandhi topee on the head; a long khaddar coat with shiny buttons; an Indian symbol, engraved onto a gleaming metal plate the size of a taka, on the right breast and the medal designed for the president of the IRA Chattogram Branch on the left; black velvet badges identifying all those taking part in the action that night on his chest and back; a white dhuti wound tightly with all pleats in place and white tennis shoes on his feet. Master-da gravely received the company's salute and addressed Ganesh, 'Shob theek? Everything all right?'

'Theek.'

A quick update followed, and bidding Master-da farewell, the company set off.

Ananta's mind tried to visualize all that was happening:

Ananda's car is now moving down the Kata-Pahar Rasta.

The Dodge is driving into the AFI headquarters. Nirmal-da would have left the car. He has led the rest of the team through the eastern corner of Paltan Maidan and is taking up position inside the AFI headquarters.

A small team is waiting for the Baby Austin in the shadows of the trees. Baby Austin 24666 is moving slowly towards the club; it is slowing down now.

Five small teams are moving by foot right now, keeping to the shadows. The final leg of their 110 yards is at its end. They will take cover behind the hedges surrounding the police barracks and wait for Ganesh to give the signal.

The road ahead turned right towards the north, hugging the boundary of the waterworks compound. Ananta stopped. It was the closest they could get without being spotted. The tila to their left was the target. The top had been levelled to accommodate the police line armoury, magazine and guardroom. Fifty to sixty yards away, a guard paced up and down: plop arm position; rifle with bayonet in place against his shoulder; crossed cartridge belts; boot-patti, khaki uniform, pugree – the very symbol of British arrogance. He faced the waterworks and kept an eye on the entire length of the road.

'Cut off safety.'

The bayonet winked wickedly, but the guardroom behind lay quiet and peaceful. The armed police contingent should be sleeping peacefully now.

'All eyes on the sentry.' They had to be up there before he could lower the rifle and point.

Keeping the pistols out of sight, Ganesh and Ananta took the slope at a run with Debu, Haripada, Saroj and Himangshu close behind. Five seconds and they were at the top; two bullets had been fired and the guard had fallen without a sound, his rifle still within his grasp. The pugree rolled to one side.

'Hato! Bhago! Jaan Bachao. Gandhi-ji ka raj aa gaya!'

Yelling at the top of their voices and firing into the air, they ran into the guardroom. No guard should get a chance to pick up his rifle. But the words Gandhi-ji ka raj had had their desired impact, being words frequently used in the army and police barracks.

'Inquilab Zindabad, Samrajyabad Dhongsho Hok ... long live revolution, down with imperialism, up with revolution, biplob dirghojibi hok.'

Six voices rent the air, creating panic amongst the sleeping policemen. Slogans and gunshots reverberated in the hills, echoing through the police lines. The guardroom[6] emptied out before their eyes, with the men, still groggy with sleep, fleeing for their lives. The slogans brought the seven small teams out of hiding and they raced uphill. Five of them were placed on patrol duty. Powerful torches flashed up and down the fields and approach roads, as hammers began to fall upon the locks of the armoury and magazine doors. The sounds trapped within the circular range of hills magnified with every echo. Within minutes, the locks were shattered and the doors flung upon.

A hush fell over the onlookers. The flashlights revealed rows and rows of muskets; Colt and Webley revolvers all stacked neatly. One voice gave a whoop of delight and then everyone joined in. Some danced in joy, some jumped up and down shouting Bande Mataram and others hugged each other in sheer joy. They were soldiers at last.

'Company fall in.' Ganesh's voice had a new spirit in it.

Two lines fell in.

Six youths, led by Tegra,[7] ran back and forth, distributing the firearms. Most were given one musket and two revolvers each. Another four distributed cartridges from the magazine. Someone pushed a revolver into his hand and minutes later Ananta found a second one being offered to him. He took both. But in the holster was the nine-shot pistol, the one that had helped capture the police lines. Ananta let it be. It would continue to occupy its rightful place.

Ganesh was calling for attention. He had found himself a raised platform. The boys stood some paces apart; muskets pointing upwards. Ganesh gave the first demonstration identifying the parts.

'Press the lever and insert the cartridge into the chamber, press the lever again, ready the striking pin, spring to strike the cartridge cap, take aim, press the trigger and the musket will fire. Now load.'

With a click, the cartridges were loaded.

'Aim.'

The muskets pointed upwards at an angle.

'Fire.'

The shots rang out as one and the Dampara Hills shuddered. The manoeuvre was practised thrice. It went off without an accident. The days spent practising upon breech-loaders had been worth it.

Now Master-da took the centre stage. 'Find the Union Jack. Burn it.'

The flag had been taken down for the night. It was retrieved and set on fire.

'Raise our flag.'

The tricolour Swadesh Pataka was raised to the sound of the bugle and a fifty-gun salute. Three rounds were fired into the night sky and the echoes lingered for many minutes before fading away. The bugle sounded a second time and the hills resonated with Bande Mataram, Inquilab Zindabad, Samrajyabad Dhongsho Hok. The Indian Republican Army had drawn its first breath.

The cheers were sounded three times and Ganesh called out. 'Take position.'

The boys surrounded the guardroom magazine and armoury.

'Lie down and keep watch along the approaches.'

Nine minutes had ticked away since the first shot had been fired.

There was one more job to be done. An Indian sipahi,[8] who was not the enemy, was lying dead. It was the white man who took advantage of the poverty of Indians to set them against their fellow men. Ananta, Debu, Haripada, Saroj and Himangshu fell in line behind Ganesh by the dead man's side. Who was this man, wondered Ananta … a Hindu or a Muslim? What caste did he belong to? Would he have joined the cause had he known about it? Ganesh took the black velvet badge with the flags off his uniform and placed it on the dead man's chest. He took a step backwards. At his command, the six saluted.

In the end what did jaat matter?

LOKENATH BAL

It was 10 p.m. A gleaming black Dodge drove in through the eastern gate, and leaving Sergeant Major J.W. Farrell's quarters to the left, took a turn into the armoury compound. Phonindra Nandi, Shanti Nag, Nitaipada Ghose, Khirod Banerjee and Probhash Bal slipped in behind the car but stuck to the shadows. The headlights were switched off and the car came to a stop. An officer jumped out to hold the door open. The sentry watched, mildly surprised at this sudden inspection. The officer, his stars gleaming in the dark, was climbing briskly up to the verandah looking him straight in the eye. Two bodyguards followed; the adjutant had arrived. As the officer reached the last step, the soldier slapped the butt of his rifle and with a click of his heel presented arms.

Lokenath removed his hand from behind his back and fired. Two other shots rang out simultaneously. Both Nirmal-da and Rajat had fired into the night. The Pathan soldiers on duty fled without a thought for their fallen colleague. One ran towards the guardroom, but a bullet picked him out and he fell screaming in the field.[9]

'Bande Mataram, Inquilab Zindabad, Samrajyabad Dhongsho Hok!' The slogans ripped through the still of the silent hours.

Lokenath walked rapidly around. The AFI armoury was a long single-storeyed building with covered verandahs along the north, west and south.

'Kon hai? Kya mangta hai?' Sergeant Major Farrell called from his verandah, dabbing a table napkin on his mouth.

'Fire. Shoot him'

Two shots rang out. Shanti Nag's breech-loader found its mark. Farrell tumbled into his garden, but the powerfully built man that he was, he managed to drag himself on his belly to where his car stood parked. He was down but he wasn't out. 'Darling,' he called in a low voice to his wife. 'Ring the police.'

The words had not gone unheard.

'Charge.'

Picking up the rifles stacked on the armoury verandah, the boys ran across, the bayonets poised for the kill.

'Cruel. That is cruel.'

'Not a hundredth of what you British have made us suffer.'

The eyes glazed over, the shock and disbelief imprinted in them forever.

'Madam, go back inside. You will be safe.' Lokenath had been watching from afar and had seen Mrs Farrell rush out. She was now standing over her dead husband's body, helpless and vulnerable. This woman ought to die like her Indian sisters at the Jallianwala Bagh … the voice in his head murmured, but instead he cried out to the steward[10] who hovered in the background, 'Take her in.' It was a sign of weakness. He turned his mind to the work at hand.

The abandoned rifles stacked on the verandah were .303 bore with ten shots. They had bayonets fitted but no cartridges. The guards had worn the cartridge belts on their persons and now they were all gone. A nuisance. Subodh brought out the heavy ropes and tied them to the handles of the armoury door. The other ends were fixed to the Dodge. Makhon stepped on the accelerator. A jerk and the doors gave way. But within was a second set of bolted iron doors – ones that opened inwards. Two enormous locks dangled before them and through the gap, stacks of ten-shot rifles[11] were visible. On the floor, beneath each rifle was a box of cartridges. Lokenath gave Rajat a nod and the two charged, their heavy powerful bodies crashing sideways into the iron. The doors burst open and Lokenath and Rajat found themselves sprawling on the floor.

'Halt!' The sentry's cry came to Lokenath's ears and he rushed out. A couple of foreigners had been attracted by the sound of firing. White faces near the gate leered at them through the dark.

'Halt!' Lokenath thundered.

'Halt?' one of the men staggered forward. He was obviously drunk and bent on investigating. 'Halt? You Bengali kutta …you dog? Halt?'

'Fire!' called Lokenath. He had recognized the voice of the AFI's adjutant, Captain Taitt. Get the bombs. Ready? Follow me. Chaaarge!'

The wine evaporated in an instant and the men melted away in the dark.

Nirmal-da was going through the contents of the armoury. Everything was as it should have been. In addition to the rifles and revolvers there were five Lewis guns … once again of 0.303 bore. He turned to Lokenath, his face glowing with contentment.

But as they knelt to open the boxes they reeled in shock.

Cullen

The Anglo-Indian railway officers and their families had been partying till late. Still groggy with rum, Sergeant Blackburn hailed a taxi outside Pahartali Club. Mr Cullen leant out of the rear window waving to him to get into the front. He was being propped upright by the two shippies who had entered harbour earlier that day.

Blackburn smiled apologetically. 'The AFI headquarters please.' His bungalow lay just within the headquarters gate. The pleasant fumes within the car formed a cocktail of their own …

'Nighty night,' sang Mr Cullen, as Blackburn got off near the gate. But Blackburn did not respond. A flashlight on the armoury verandah had caught his attention. Something was different.

'Wait,' he said breathlessly as he ran in.

'Any help?' called the shippies.

Seven or eight khaki-clad figures moved about on the verandah.

'Who is there?'

A shot sang past his ear in response.

'Naik Baghdad Shah.' Blackburn called again.

It elicited more gunshots. An electric torchlight was moving rapidly across the compound towards him.

'Run!' he called out to his companions as he bolted down the road.

As his companions took flight, Mr Cullen struggled to get out of the seat. Five or six bullets flew past his head and he lost balance. He was on the ground and rolling. Then he came to a stop beneath a hedge. A torch was being flashed over his body; the sound of a revolver going off and a shudder of agony. A bullet lodged itself in his left hip. His limbs flailed uncontrollably but then he managed to lie still. Play dead, he breathed to himself.

Two cars sped past towards Pahartali.[12] Neither stopped. Next came the sound of a terrible pounding; then the sound of two cars coming from the direction of Pahartali. The raiders were rushing past him to intercept them. There was shouting, some more firing and then a tremendous crash that deafened the night. The sound had come from the direction of the armoury.

A cyclist whistling down the road stopped; stood his cycle up against the wall of Sergeant Blackburn's bungalow and sauntered in.

Ananta Lal Singh

It was 10.10 p.m. Ambika-da's and Naresh's teams should be returning any moment. Ananta looked anxiously at his watch. The team at the AFI needed reinforcement ... he would leave as soon as the Chevrolet arrived. He glanced once more down the length of the designated approach road. Powerful torchlight beams swung along every approach. Near the bend in the road that came past the waterworks compound, a lone figure was spotted. It was striding up the road towards the police line tila.

'Hands up. Halt. Who comes there?'

The figure stood stock-still and raised its arms.

'I am Swadesh Roy.'

Ananta staggered. The one they had humiliated was here. Why had he come? But keeping Swadesh standing there just for questioning ... a stray bullet could take his life any moment, for many of the boys were still shooting into the sky at random. But they made the decision for him. The first hush that had descended upon them was replaced within seconds by shrieks of happiness.

'Swadesh has come, Swadesh has come. Swadesh Roy Ki Jai! Bande Mataram!'

There were boys racing down the slope; shouts of joy; whoops of delight. They were bringing him up. Ganesh was there right in front, arms open; now thumping him vigorously on the back; boys milling about; Swadesh looking overwhelmed. He had a musket in one hand and a bag of cartridges in the other. Confused, he stared at the revolver being held out. He looked from one hand to the other. Ananta walked up and drew him into his arms. There was a lump in his throat; it wouldn't let him speak. Instead he pulled out one of his revolvers and pressed it into his hands. He had made a mistake. Naresh and Debu had pressed for Swadesh's recruitment but he had refused as a matter of policy. There were to be no recruitments whatsoever during the last six months.

'Ki korchhilish etokhun?' Ganesh's voice was gentle as he drew him away. 'Playing your sitar?'

Swadesh looked embarrassed. The sitar was his outlet when his mind was in turmoil; Ganesh knew that. Swadesh would have heard the firing and the cheering for he lived close to the police lines. The strings would have fallen silent as he took his decision and walked out of the family hearth.

MORSEHEAD

Sergeant Morsehead had heard five or six reports in quick succession coming from the direction of the AFI armoury and two more shots immediately afterwards. From the distance he could make out khaki clad figures moving about, flashing torches. Some kind of exercise, he wondered. Captain Taitt appeared to be bending over a prostrate form on the verandah. Morsehead cycled down the road to the main gate of the armoury compound, near the Drill Hall, and propping his cycle up against the wall of Sergeant Blackburn's bungalow, walked towards the armoury. Captain Taitt pointed his revolver at him.

A soldier aimed a musket or a rifle and shone a powerful torch on him. 'Hands up.'

'Don't be a silly ass.' Morsehead wasn't in the mood.

'Hands up.'

'Alright, they are up. What's the matter?' He was still some seven yards away from them.

'That is one of them. Shoot.' Captain Taitt's English had an unmistakable Bengali overtone.

It took a fraction of a second for Morsehead to duck and run as two shots came at him simultaneously. He came into the line of sight once again at the gate and narrowly missed being shot. Not stopping to pick up his cycle he ran along the road. That man, the one that looked like Captain Taitt, he knew him by sight … it was Lokenath Bal.

He was running. He was at Piccadilly Circus. A car screeched to a stop. Captain Carter, the master of a BI ship, helped him in.

'Natives,' he gasped. '… they have the AFI armoury.'

Ananda Prasad Gupta

The Chevrolet sped through the darkness. There was complete silence inside the car. Like him, the rest of his passengers, barring Ambika-da, had no clue as to what was coming next. He had sensed their surprise as Ambika-da wagged his finger and waved him towards the Paltan grounds. So they were not going back to the Congress office to make a report to Master-da. Revolutionaries never ask questions and Ananda wasn't about to break the rule. But the questions loomed large.

The Ferari tank was coming up. Ambika-da was leaning forward into the windshield, eyes peeled. His own senses were being strained to the limit, his ears aching to pick up sounds. There it was: gunshots. His mind was still grappling with the alternatives when a faint cry caught his ear. Everyone had heard it. The car erupted with cheers of joy.

'Swadhin Bharat Ki Jai!'

Ananda stepped on the accelerator.

'Halt! Put off the light.' A voice called from the top.

Joyously Ananda leant against the horn and shouted with the others at the top of his voice: 'Bande Mataram! Inquilab Zindabad! Samrajyabad Dhongsho Hok!'

'Proceed!' The sentry called out.

The car rolled in and was greeted by joyous shouts.

'Has the Telephone Bhavan been destroyed?' Master-da was right in front.

'Burnt to ashes by now.'

'Anyone hurt?'

'No one. No one on either side.'

Master-da hugged Ambika-da. 'Khoob anondo hochchhey.'

Not just Master-da's. Happiness shone on every face. Muskets, bags of cartridges and revolvers were being handed out. Himangshu and Dada took them aside for instructions. Then they were shown their positions. Ananda gazed around, looking at the faces that were present: Tegra, Moti, Sahayram were amongst the known faces but most were completely unknown. Fakir Sen, the village boy who had camped in his study since 8 April, smiled shyly at him. Rajat-da, Naresh-da, Lokenath-da, Makhon, Bidhu-da … they were conspicuous by their absence.

It was the Baby Austin signalling. The end of the road that went past the waterworks turned left as it went out of sight. Ananda was unable to take his eyes off the bend. Then he saw them – five figures pushing a car. The horn sounded responding to the sentry's challenge. But where were the slogans? Some of the boys were running down the slope to greet them cheering, shouting 'Bande Mataram!' There was no response from the other side. Naresh-da, Bidhu-da, Tripura, Amarendra and Monoranjan were labouring up the hill, their faces grim and dark. Master-da waited by the edge.

'Why, Naresh? Why are you all so quiet? What has happened to you?'

'We have failed, Master-da.'

The words unleashed a storm in every mind.

'I do not understand. Tell me. What happened?'

'We went according to plan and entered through the many doors and windows. But the hall was empty. We rushed to the next room. That too was empty. We searched room by room. Not one sahib was to be found. A few boys and bearers were present. They started screaming in fear. I calmed them down and got to know that the sahibs had gone home at eight o'clock. It is Good Friday today.' Naresh-da winced as he spoke. His voice was sad. 'Master-da, we could not take our revenge upon the British imperialists.'

Master-da stroked his back. 'Don't let it upset you. The city is within our grasp. Revenge we will have.'

Ganesh-da and Ananta-da surrounded them. So this was the crack team that had failed. Ananda wondered what it was all about.

H.R. Wilkinson

He was being shaken awake. There was a message from the police superintendent. He had only just dozed off … this was all terribly unseemly. The manservant stood on his toes to drape the light cotton dressing gown over his shoulders. He brushed aside the gauzy fabric of the mosquito net that still clung to him coyly, unwilling to let go.

'Ten thirty, sahib.'

It wasn't all that unreasonable an hour … he had been the one to turn in early. Too early for Johnson perhaps … but his was not a home where people called in casually for a late nightcap. The district magistrate's reputation as a man of few words was well established.

The police superintendent had not come. Instead, waiting for him were two men: Sub-inspector Pratul Chandra Barua who had been sent by Johnson to inform him that the police line armoury that lay surrounded by the constables' barracks had been attacked by revolutionaries, and Mahendra De, a peon from the Telephone-Telegraph Bhavan, who carried a message from Mr Scott informing him that the telephone exchange had been burnt down by a gang of insurgents.

It sounded incredible. Wilkinson ran to get dressed, calling out instructions. Within minutes, they had crossed the Tiger Pass road that cut through the densely wooded hills towards Pahartali. Johnson, he hoped, would already be there; the armoury would have to be secured. The car was being flagged down. A group of Englishmen stood on the road near Piccadilly junction. Wilkinson recognized District Judge Lodge, Mr Wighton, Mr Farrell and Captain Taitt, the adjutant of the auxiliary force of the Assam Bengal Railways. Their wives stood to one side.

'The ladies ... take them to Mr Bliss's bungalow.'[13] Wilkinson was mortified, for Taitt's account was hair-raising. He had been to Johnson's home but the police superintendent had already left.

J.R. JOHNSON

Police Superintendent J.R. Johnson and J.C. Farmer, deputy inspector general of Bakarganj Range had given the AFI armoury a fraction of a glance as their cars zipped by. What they had seen was enough. There seemed to be no wisdom in stopping. Running before them, headed towards Pahartali, were three Europeans. Sergeant Blackburn turned out to be one of the AFI headquarters staff.

... In bed sir ... 10.30 p.m. ... cries of Bande Mataram. From verandah I see 5–6 motor cars ... 30–40 men, torches, firing ... alerted the barracks ... told each man must try do best sir ... This Sub-inspector Pratul Chandra Barua my assistant ...[14] Sub-inspector Sanjiv Chandra Nag's garbled version of natives having occupied the police lines had irritated the two officers who had settled down to their drinks hoping to call it an early night. A native wedding party! Johnson had been quick to dismiss it but the discovery of the dead telephone lines had lent some credence to the tale. It threatened to ruin a perfectly good beginning to a long weekend. Having dispatched messengers to Mr H.R. Wilkinson, the district magistrate and collector; the chief civilian authority in Chittagong, Mr Lewis; the assistant superintendent of police, and Captain Taitt, they had decided to check out the more sensitive of the two armouries first.

'The Pahartali subsidiary AFI armoury … who keeps the keys?'

Blackburn had the answer. He led them to Mr Barraclough's residence. The gunner was roused from sleep and sent with Blackburn to open up the armoury while Johnson went on to alert the Pahartali residents – Messrs Francis, Thomas, West, Provan and Tyers, and then headed back to the subsidiary armoury to draw arms.

Ananta Lal Singh

'Halt.'

The sentry's cry jerked Ananta out of his reverie. A man in uniform was walking towards them. Ambika-da's and Naresh's teams had already arrived. He was due to leave and help Nirmal-da and Lokenath.

'Halt. Who are you?' Ten guns were levelled at the man who continued to walk towards them.

'Kali. I am Kali Kinkar De.'

'Where was he coming from? Shouldn't he have been leading one of the smaller teams at the police lines?' Ananta had spoken his thoughts out loud.

'I had sent him.' Master-da explained. 'Saroj Bhattacharya had already handed the pamphlets out to the distribution teams and they would have started on the dot at eight o'clock. I sent Kali to warn Khirod Mahajan, Prafulla Mallick and Ardhendu Guha.'

So Kali had been cycling around, coordinating with the three distribution teams all this while. He came up the hill ignoring the cheers and the slogans and stood before Master-da, his head bowed. 'Master-da, I have not failed you, nor have I seized this opportunity to betray the cause or stay away from action. I am sorry I could not be back in time to play my part here.' The words poured out and in them there was anger and sorrow.

Ananta was shocked. Kali was one of the most trusted workers … he would not have required emotional blackmail to get him to do his duty. 'Really,' he muttered in a barely audible voice, 'Master-da, your embracing him now will not erase these wounds … and ones caused by words from your lips.'

Where was Ganesh? He was nowhere to be seen. It was necessary to leave for the AFI headquarters right away. Ananta strode into the guardroom. Ganesh was sitting by himself, slumped against the wall. Ananta bent over to touch his shoulder. His face was flushed, his brow burning. He said nothing. He seemed ashamed.

'It's the excitement. Rest a bit, you will feel better. I am leaving for the AFI armoury.'

He would have himself loved to have curled up in a corner for a few minutes. His shoulders were aching and his legs felt wobbly. The overenthusiastic activities of the day were telling on him now. It should have been a day of rest that preceded a night such as this one. But go he would have to, for Nirmal-da and Lokenath had only a small team by their side … but then so was the size of the enemy they were up against. The sahibs who lived in the pretty cottages that dotted the hills on that side were all armed but they would take time to organize themselves.

'Who is coming with me?' Ananta called. Tegra was the first to jump into the Chevrolet followed by Himangshu and Monoranjan. 'That's it; only three will go.' As the car rolled down the lonely stretch that ran past the clubhouse, the three youths, intoxicated by the events of the day, cheered at the top of their voices.

'Shhh.' He warned as he switched off the headlights. Who was now in control of the AFI, he wondered. Had the team succeeded … they could open fire at them by mistake. He stuck to the shadows and when about 100 yards away, he stopped. It looked as if the armoury had been taken. Sounding the horn brought back a cheerful battle cry in return. The sahibs sitting down to dinner in their homes on Batali Hill could scarcely have missed it.

Lokenath's voice called out in English, 'Who comes there?'

'General Singh and party.'

'A few men from the enemy camp are hiding along the main road. Take the side track and join us.'

Leaving the car on the road outside the main gate, they made their way down the slope, across the field towards the armoury.

'You are late.'

'Only by forty minutes.'

'A whole hour.' Lokenath was in no mood for arguments.

Ananta did not argue. He should have come earlier … by delaying, he had exposed this team to tremendous risk. There had been no need for him to wait for Naresh or Ambika-da's return. Others could have handled all that. Sheepishly he looked about the armoury. 'Heartiest Congratulations. You have done well.'

'We've got arms all right but not a single cartridge.'

He was dumbfounded. No cartridges? There were boxes that went with every firearm?

Lokenath held up belts, pouches and haversacks and grimaced.

'Are you sure? Has every nook and corner of the armoury been searched?'

'Yes, yes.' Nirmal-da was wringing his hands. 'What will happen now? So many arms; none of any use!'

Ananta had begun pacing the length of the verandah in agitation. A locked door at the southern end caught his eye.

'Why have you not broken into that room yet? Open it immediately.'

Hammers descended within seconds. The room was filled with old trunks. A couple of blows and the lids flew open. Wrapped in newspapers were cups, plates and cutlery.

'Four hundred magazine rifles, five Lewis guns … and we cannot use even one of them,' Ananta groaned inwardly.

'The other operations … did they go according to plan?' Nirmal-da was trying to take stock of the situation.

'Everything went according to plan except that it is Good Friday today and the sahibs went home early.'

'The luck of the devil is with them; any casualty on our side?'

'None.'

'And the enemy?'

'Just one.'

They had stepped down from the verandah and were walking across the field towards the road. Cars were going by, headed towards Pahartali. The sentries were calling out to each: halt; turn around; go back. The ones that didn't comply were shot at. A driver slumped over his wheel as his car rolled backwards down the hill, hit a stationary car and turned turtle.

'Let us leave,' said Ananta. 'Take what we have. Burn the rest.'

'Take all the revolvers and muskets. Break the rest.' Lokenath called.

The hammer blows began to fall and within a few minutes Lokenath called again. 'Set the armoury on fire.'

Six tins of petrol were emptied. Everyone moved away. Subodh Choudhury and Rajat Sen flung a blazing moshaal neatly into the building. Before their eyes the flames encompassed the armoury.

Lokenath drove the Dodge down to the main gate where the Chevrolet was parked. As they left the AFI compound the war cry was sounded. The flames were jumping up in an attempt to reach the sky. Every now and then a blast would take place. Bodies lay scattered. Some six or seven cars stood around uselessly.

Blinding headlights some thirty yards away stopped them on their tracks.

'Halt. Who goes there?'

'Friend.' The accent was decidedly English.

'Fire.'

Three muskets fired and while they were reloading, Ananta ran towards the car. The district magistrate's Chevrolet KA 3538 had not gone unrecognized. The driver was still in the front seat, having miraculously escaped the two bullets that went through his side of the windshield. An orderly[15] lay dead in the back seat right behind the driver. Mr Wilkinson's double-barrelled rifle and a box of cartridges lay by his side. But the magistrate was nowhere to be seen. A second car[16] with its windshield shattered stood behind; its driver was dead, as were its two European passengers.

'Where is he?' Himangshu dragged Wilkinson's driver out, shaking him like a rat. He was bleeding, unable to stand. Tegra offered to put a bullet through his head but the man was past talking.

'Where were you taking him?'

A flashlight searched the car, went over the dead Jarasandha Barua's body and then trained itself on Birman Thapa's sweat-soaked uniform and pallid countenance.

'Pahartali.'

'Liar. He is a liar. Kill him.'

Thapa was gibbering like an idiot one moment and in the next he had slumped over. A shot had grazed his chest.

'Stop.' Ananta had forced his way in. 'He is an Indian.'

Himangshu released his hold and Thapa rolled into a ditch.

It was time to return to the police lines. The AFI armoury was blazing away merrily with fire shooting into the sky like sparklers and descending in showers of shimmering stars. The trees and hills stood silhouetted against the crimson-and-gold backdrop. Chattogram's sky was on fire.

J.R. Johnson

The AFI armoury was burning. The district magistrate's car stood riddled with bullets but there was no sign of him or of the raiders. Johnson and Farmer decided on a quick recce of all the possible targets. They had with them two magazine rifles and Barraclough had drawn a Lewis gun for himself.

Finding the Imperial Bank and the Kotwali police station undisturbed, they drove down to the European Club garage. There were no sounds of firing. Johnson decided to abandon the cars and walk across the golf course.

An agitated Sanjiv Chandra Nag appeared out of the dark. 'Mr Lewis,' he said and pointed to the roof of the waterworks building.

'… informed Kotwali, sir … according to your instruction. Came back 12.30 …' he continued whispering breathlessly.

The officers headed in the direction he pointed them to.

'… Abdul Azim Khan, Yogendra Chandra Das and deputy police superintendent … constables … two muskets, cartridges … heavy firing … refuge in village over there … keeping watch over anarchists.' The breathless whispering faded into the distance. Johnson had waved him away.

Lewis and his orderly lay on their bellies keeping watch on the tila across the road. 'There are a hundred or so up there,' he said. 'The firing is coming from the direction of the reserve office.' With a pistol and a shotgun between the two of them they had rushed into the parade ground shouting: Don't shoot, we are the police, whereupon the firing had become more intense. Having spent about three quarters of an hour in a ditch they had only just managed to crawl up onto the roof.

Ananta Lal Singh

At midnight two cars crept along the Pahartali road bumping over the broken patches approaching the European Club from the west and then turned onto the 200-yard stretch of wide, beautifully maintained strip of road that led to the police lines. It looked peaceful. Both cars dipped their headlights and sounded their horns. The sentry called out. They replied using the slogans. The hill top erupted with the cries of Bande Mataram.

Ananta walked up with the others occasionally giving lung to the war cries. His legs trembled. A strange new fatigue flooded his being. He was walking with a revolver in each hand. It needed the tiniest rock now to trip up the great Ananta Lal Singh. He laughed at the thought.

Master-da was waiting. Nirmal-da briefed him.

'Not one?'

'We failed in our research.' The weight of the despair was sinking in now. It probably accounted for the fatigue. Ananta had personally taken responsibility for this part of the research … he and Ganesh.

Ganesh, who was standing right behind Master-da, looked as if he had been struck.

'We failed, Ganesh.'[17] Ananta turned wearily towards the guard-room.

The pamphlets would have all been distributed by now. The youth would be arriving by the droves in a couple of hours and there were no firearms to handout. No magazine rifles, no Lewis guns. The second stage of the operation had depended completely on the weapons captured from the enemy. The secret stash of weapons was meant only to see them through this first stage … and now all they had were sixty-four boys with outdated muskets and some revolvers. If only he could snatch a few moments of rest before the inevitable.

'Ananta-da, we have caught a man. He was pretending to be a lunatic … he must be a police watcher. What do we do with him?'

Naresh appeared not to be affected by the magnitude of the disaster. But of course! None of them knew the plan and their dependence on the firearms in the AFI armoury. They were armed. They were raring to go.

'Let's take a look at him.' Ananta followed him to the magazine section. A man[18] sat hunched over, his hands clamped by a pair of handcuffs. What was it exactly that Naresh had in mind … kill him?

'Thak,' he said. 'Once he identifies himself let him go.'

Naresh had filled him with new hope. So what if they did not find the cartridges … had they not left the armoury a blazing wreck? The enemy had no firearms either.

Light flashed. Lights streaking across the sky … towards them. A scream and the rapid staccato of gunfire. Ananta threw himself on the ground and crawled to take cover behind a choubachcha. Bullets rained down onto the field, onto the slope, striking the walls of the armoury, guardroom and magazine room. A Lewis gun was being fired from a relatively close range.

Ananta looked around anxiously. Everyone was on the ground lying side by side. The hilltop was cramped for space. The shots were coming in from the south-east.

'Aim waterworks.'

When had they climbed up to the roof of the waterworks building? Where did the Lewis gun come from? It was not something one would keep at home … the tiny armoury at the Double Mooring Jetty had two. Ananta could have kicked himself.

Muskets thundered and slogans were raised.

You have to give it to them, thought Ananta. Here they were, in a corner but ready to take on armed rebels.

J.R. Johnson

'Fire in short bursts.'

Johnson intended to make the most of the limited ammunition.

But this evoked an intensive fire from the direction of the armoury and magazine. Though most of the bullets passed over their heads several came uncomfortably close.

'Withdraw to the roof of the waterworks engineer's bungalow.'

The firing began again. But the return fire and slogan shouting showed no signs of abating. The Lewis gun had emptied out a whole drum.[19]

'They could be creeping up right now under the cover of a volley of fire,' said Farmer.

The two magazine rifles had nearly emptied themselves out.

'Keep us covered,' said Johnson as he nodded to Barraclough to follow. He would be back with reinforcements.

Ananda Prasad Gupta

The whistling of falling shells and the rumble of gunfire had gone. Breathe in breathe out, he gasped to himself. The eerie silence stung his ears. The shock was giving way to a heady sensation never experienced before. Without requiring a watch, he knew it had to be past two in the morning.

Master-da had called for attention. He was reading slowly and clearly.

'Dear soldiers of the Revolution! The great task of revolution in India has fallen on the IRA. We in Chittagong have the honour to achieve this patriotic task fulfilling the aspirations of our nation. It is a matter of great glory that today our forces have seized the strongholds of the government in Chittagong. The enemy armoury has been captured; the central telephone exchange of the town has been destroyed, external telegraph communications have been snapped, railway lines have been removed and goods trains derailed; train communications have been cut off. The enemy force has been defeated. The oppressive foreign government has ceased to exist. The national flag is flying high. It is our duty to defend it with our life and blood.

'The IRA declares today for universal information and recognition the end of predatory rule and control by the British imperial bandits on the Indian soil in Chittagong.

'Chittagong is a tiny part of India, but it is hoped and expected that the achievement of today will inspire and impel our countrymen to do likewise everywhere in India and to free our entire motherland from the unholy clutches of the British bandits before long.

'I, Surjya Sen, president of the IRA Chittagong Branch do hereby proclaim the existing council of the IRA in Chittagong to form itself into a provisional revolutionary government to carry out the following urgent tasks:

To defend and maintain the victory gained today,
To extend and intensify the armed struggle,
To suppress the enemy agent within,
To keep criminals and looters in check,
And to take further course of action, one that this provisional government will decide later.

'This provisional government expects and demands full allegiance, loyalty and active cooperation from every true son and daughter of Chittagong. And desires sympathy and active support from all the patriots and nationalists and from every person who has the well-being and liberation of India in his or her heart.

With full confidence in victory in our holy war of liberation!
No mercy to the British bandits.
Death to traitors and looters
Long live provisional revolutionary government.
Bande Mataram!'

The bugle was sounded and three rounds were fired and the slogan Bande Mataram raised thrice.

H.R. Wilkinson

That they had got away was nothing short of a miracle. Abandoning their cars and wounded colleagues they ran like never before. The white man's life was at risk … their beautiful Chittagong had turned against them. The families would have to be moved and reinforcements brought in.

A train had rushed them to the port. The steamship 'Halizones' had docked for the night. Wilkinson hurried on board to send off the telegrams.

Captain Taitt was getting the jetty armoury opened. He would round up as many men as possible including those on board the ship and catch the train back.

ELEVEN

Alexander Burnett

The myriad noises of the Indian night – that elaborate orchestra – ceased, startled by their presence. The pony, a sure-footed young thing, picked her way unaided through the dark. An owl struck a poignant note, hooting from the branches above, and the crickets picked up again, cautiously at first, furnishing the undertone before rising to a crescendo that made every blade of grass and every tree sizzle.

Alexander's sleepy brain tried to process all that had happened. His man Friday had pulled him out of bed and pushed a telegram into his hands. It contained a message from the OC, No. 2 Squadron, Surma Valley Light Horse, ordering all troopers to report to Silchar. While he had tried to fathom its meaning, he found himself being helped into his trousers and his uniform jacket – clothes that he rarely wore – and being ushered out unceremoniously. The pony had broken into a trot as soon as the syce had given him the leg-up, and the servant had come running from behind to thrust a rifle and a torch into his hands.

He switched on the flashlight and an immediate silence descended once again. The beam swung around, lighting up the little lane, as it wound through the leafy Kukicherra Tea Estate that stood in the shadow of the Lushai Hills. Now and then, there was a glint of silver in the distance. This was panther area, but Alexander took no notice, accustomed as he was to seeing tea leaves shine in the moonlight. The bullfrogs that had fallen silent picked up where they had left off and were soon accompanied by various unidentified gurgles, squeaks and shrieks. Wild jackals – the sheyaals – resumed the dulcet notes of their song. A hundred and fifty tomcats on the tiles would seem heavenly compared to this, thought Alexander as he turned the pony towards the neighbouring estate.

A car would be waiting by the broken bridge. It would take him through the fifty miles of country track to Silchar, which was the civil station of the Surma Valley in Assam. He would not make it before daylight. There was time enough to wake his friend and make him come along.

ANANTA LAL SINGH

'What will our muskets achieve against their machine guns?' Master-da was pacing up and down the verandah.

Why was he standing, wondered Ananta irritably; but then it suddenly dawned on him that so was he and so were several others.

Nirmal-da wrung his hands in despair. 'Bhai-rey-bhai, their band is playing … they are mobilizing their forces.'

Between the pair of them they were irritating him. 'What are you saying? What will they mobilize?'

'Can you not hear? The band is playing? There it is again. Listen.'

'You and your weird ideas. There is no telephone, telegraph or railway facility, the main armouries have been destroyed … it is impossible for them to mobilize any large force! Stop it.' Ananta was close to yelling. It brought Ganesh out, but he had nothing to offer either. Master-da continued to mumble to himself. What was it … what was the answer that they wanted out of him? True, the enemy was outnumbered, but it was also true that they had a few machine guns. It made sense to leave the area immediately. 'Pour the petrol,' he called.

Himangshu and another youngster splashed the petrol on the walls of the guardroom, armoury and magazine room. Hammer blows began to fall. The last job was Himangshu's. He had been especially trained for it.

'Let the prisoner go. Destroy the Lewis guns. The rest of you go down the north-east side of the hill.' Ananta barked out the orders as he went down the slope to start the Chevrolet. Ganesh's fever was beginning to worry him. The hilltop burst into flames, as was expected, but the boys set up the most hideous of screaming matches possible. He looked up in time to see a flailing human torch drop to the ground and Bidhu and Naresh racing up the slope shrieking, 'Roll, Himangshu, roll.'

He pressed on the accelerator and the car shot up the hill. How could this have happened? The boy must have splattered his clothes with the petrol. To give him his due, he was doing everything he was being told to do. The seconds lengthened before his eyes. Bidhu and Naresh were smothering the last of the flames with their bare hands. Himangshu was up and running towards him. He was in the back seat. Ganesh was suddenly beside him. Spontaneously, Ananta turned the steering wheel hard, making his way through the crowd of boys who moved aside, screwing their eyes against the beam of the headlights. He was driving cautiously, keeping a sharp lookout. Now he was creeping along the northern edge of the waterworks compound. He reached out to switch the headlights off but discovered he had already done so. The stretch of road was bad but it led towards the city where the next stage of the operations lay. No bullets came at them. The area seemed abandoned.

The car came to a stop at the bottom of the tila, close to where Himangshu lived and the boy sprang out without a word. Ananta was left with a brief impression of Ananda running after him. The primary thought in his head was to get a drink of water. He was dying of thirst. His home – they lived close to DC Hill – would be empty by now. Before the army arrived he needed that drink of water. Master-da, Nirmal-da and Ambika-da should be leading them as of this moment to Makleshwar Rahman's for dinner.

There was not a soul on the streets. They drove through the main road. As expected, the house was empty. Jibon emerged out of the back of the car. He must have got in with Ananda and Himangshu. The rooms in the house were locked, but the kitchen was open. The three of them drank glass after glass of water. There was no food anywhere; not in the kitchen, not in the dining room. Exhausted, they sank down upon the steps of the kitchen.

Forty minutes went by. Where was the army? Why wasn't the silence of Chattogram being shattered by cries of Bande Mataram and Inquilab Zindabad? Why weren't the muskets announcing their presence? The agitation was beginning to grow. One of the reasons for the exhaustion was the cumbersome uniform and all the finery. It was time to get back into a shirt and a dhuti. Ananta broke the lock that hung from the bolt on the door of his room.

An hour had gone by. They would have to look for the army. In seven minutes, they were back at the police lines. It was still a massive blaze with cartridges exploding every now and then. The boxes of gunpowder made a terrific noise. The blaze lit up the area. None of the boys were there. Hazarding a guess, they took the rough track that led to the north. It led out of the city. Keeping the headlights on, they crept carefully. Perhaps they had taken this track to seek shelter; they would surely signal.[1] Four miles went by. There was nobody in sight. Had they taken another route and gone back to the city?

Ananta turned back towards the city. It was as deserted as before. He drove along the main road down Andarkilla's Rajpath, the Basirhat police beat, jail, Kotwali, past Detective Police Deputy Inspector Sharada Babu's house to Firingee Bazaar. Nothing.

They sat by the riverside, their heads swimming. The plan was falling apart. By now the revolutionary government should have been set up in the city. It was 4.30 in the morning . . . a few crows had begun to call. The jail had to be evacuated; the Imperial Bank captured . . .

It was no longer safe to remain in the city. Abandoning the car, a sampan was hired. It was on its way to Patenga, twelve miles away. Ananta looked out at his father's second house as they passed Double Mooring: it was shrouded in darkness. The eastern sky turned red and the waters lapped red and gold. They would be safer off in an aatchala in the middle of rice fields.

The throne of Chattogram was lying vacant and the rulers had chosen bonobash – exile.

John Younie

'Beware,' whispered John. 'He seems to be under the impression that I owe him a tin of sausages.'

Donovan was cooing over dark-eyed Mary, who regarded him suspiciously. 'Her mother's mouth and her father's nose,' he declared.

Elspet, in her perambulator, beamed up at Donovan. At little over four months, she was her plump smiling self with no stranger anxiety to cast a shadow over her sunny face. Helen was not to be seen as she had run off to explore with Chrissie, the dogs in tow.

'Look at that, you blighter.' Donovan dragged John by the arm to where his gladioli from Darjeeling were flourishing, encased in wire netting three feet high. 'He has the nerve,' he turned to Dorothy, 'to boast that it was his garden that was the envy of the entire local and less competent horticulturists!' The collector drew himself up and threw out his chest. 'Now, my dear, I have it on very good authority – that is, my chaprassi's word – that your husband visited my garden everyday to gaze enviously at the said gladioli.'

'Ah, but never to forget that it was cosmos, transplanted bodily from my garden, that populated the Bell Park! Brian the district engineer,' explained John, 'was readying for an industrial and agricultural exhibition and he made two round plots: one a rockery with a flagstaff in the centre and the other with a fountain. My flowers were planted along the borders and still there were lots left – the cornflower and the antirrhinums. And in my cabbage patch …'

But Donovan who had made off with Dorothy was not listening. 'Lionel Colson,' he was saying, 'had been dragged out after dinner with an electric torch and of course it was my prized gladioli that was the decided winner … but the blasted hare trespassed on my land that night and ate right through a gladiolus, much to the vulgar pleasure of your husband … I half suspected it was him abusing my hospitality. I sat up nights with a gun,' he said meaningfully, as ribald laughter erupted from behind.

'And I wished that blessed hare a long life and a large appetite … and considering the season was closed for hares I promised to prosecute Donovan personally.' As he took his place on the verandah he observed mildly, 'I guess that explains the zareba.' Donovan shot him a furious look over the cup of tea.

'You should have seen the rohu that was caught from the tank before my house. Old Johur used to spend most of his time I can warrant, watching the anglers. It was past 6.30 p.m. one day, and I had retired upstairs for my bath when he came in to say that the biggest fish ever seen had been caught. I asked at once to see it and it turned out to be the noblest one I had laid my eyes upon – twenty-one pounds!'

'I'd love to have one of those at the end of a line,' sighed Donovan. 'They tell me the best tank is behind the jail.'

'I was sorry to learn about poor Mr Simon[2] having to abandon his trip. The old man must have been feeling the need for a little rest and quiet.' From the papers at home Dorothy had gathered that the Commission had had a pretty hectic time – with large mobs at every centre demonstrating and shouting 'Simon go back'.

'And a jolly good thing too,' added Donovan. 'For I dared not bring him ashore for fear of our local swarajists and their demonstrations ... although,' he bobbed his head, 'it would have given him a pretty good idea of the degree of civilization that prevails in these parts and how ready they are, and anxious for another large increment of self-government. I warrant he would have got more insight into the actual state of affairs during the few days of this quiet voyage than in three weeks at Calcutta, listening to the vapourings of half-baked politicians.'

'And the first question that I had decided I would recommend him to put to every villager he met in this district would be ...,' here John put up his finger as a smile trembled on his lips, 'And when did you come out of jail?' The two men burst into laughter. 'Both of us have tried this conversational gambit and in nine out of ten cases the cap fits.'

'I had dinner with Sir Charles and Lady Tegart soon after,' said Donovan, 'and got a fair idea of what happened. Mike, in addition to having to prevent the city from breaking out in mob violence – as it had done in February when the Commission had first set foot in India, had Lord Irwin on his hands. The care of all those marked and prominent people meant a great deal of extra work for him. Public appearances warranted elaborate preparatory arrangements. And the HE, though always considerate of police opinions, hated being shadowed by a watcher when he walked in the grounds of Belvedere.[3] But Mike was firm: If that chap didn't follow you about, he would be disobeying my orders and if I didn't order him to follow you about I should be neglecting my duty. The HE then expressed a wish to see a slum district of the town.'

Donovan chuckled as John let out a low whistle. 'He had heard a great deal about the terrible conditions under which the poor – particularly the poor Eurasian community – lived.'

'Perhaps he wished to verify or hoped to disprove the stories for himself.'

'Anyway, it was all terribly risky ... you know how striking a figure he makes and as Mike puts it, almost impossible to disguise as a cad. They went all the same: the viceroy, his ADC, Mike himself and one other policeman. They wore their oldest clothes and drove unescorted in a battered Ford touring car around some of the worst districts in Calcutta.'

'And was he suitably horrified?'

'Perhaps most of all by the filth of the streets and the appalling smells. He asked whether nothing could be done to remedy matters, but Mike reminded him that this was an early example of local self-government and that the swaraj-dominated corporation was the responsible body. They stopped at a particularly smelly street and HE noticed an old Muslim squatting on the ground a few yards away, gazing into space. He said to Mike, "Ask that man how he can stay here and tolerate the smell." Mike went up to the man, who ostensibly was sitting there for a breath of fresh air or to "eat-the-air", as they put it. You know Mike's extraordinary skill with Bengali. The finer nuances of the language do not escape him. "What smell?" was the response. The man was apparently mildly astonished, obviously unaware that the atmosphere was impregnated by anything less fragrant than the attar of roses. The tour was a thorough one and the viceroy came to the conclusion that even the most harrowing accounts could not compare with what he had seen.'[4]

'It is as funny a story as it is sad,' John explained to Dorothy. 'The president of the Calcutta Corporation, Mr Subhas Chandra Bose, who had been released in 1925 as an act of clemency, has been incarcerated again for holding demonstrations. He has given himself a commission in his own volunteer corps too.'

'Mike is as southern Irish as one can get,' said Donovan ruminatively. 'No one can love his country more aggressively and yet have such a deep and unquestioning loyalty to the Crown. I had a heated argument with him one day over the Black-and-Tan Regime and he quite lost it … threatened to go off and lead an Irish rebel army. "You old Shinner," Mike, I said to him, "you disloyal old devil!" Really, he had taken me aback. I had scarcely known whether to take him seriously or not. But deep down I believe that however much he believes in independence for Ireland, he desires nothing but a friendly union between her and the empire. Can such a man ever be an enemy of India's freedom? … The very idea is ludicrous.'

'I would say he loves freedom for himself as much as he does for others,' said John. Indeed there are few better constituted than he to understand what the mind of the bomb-and-pistol-wallah is blindly groping after. But he will turn his face sternly against short cuts, blazed by murder and gang robbery on the plea that they are political.'[5]

'Speaking about crime, tell me about the sausages,' said Dorothy.

The men exchanged glances. 'You know how our friend here,' John cocked an eyebrow at Donovan, 'will, after a large dinner party, wait for midnight to ask if the judge sahib has any intention of providing his guests with supper – and preferably sausages and eggs. Well, I was having the whole crowd over, for the Taylors – you know the SP and his family – were moving to Jalpaiguri and were keenly aware that I had no sausages, as I had been allowing the stores to peter out before I left for a vacation to Darjeeling. After tea that day, I had come over to ask him out for a walk and found him engaged in talking to a deputation of babus. That's when the brainwave struck and I quietly approached his old khansama who produced a tin of Walls best and promised to have it sent over without saying a word to his sahib. So about midnight when Donovan made some very pointed remarks about the desirability of providing several hungry people with supper and surely the judge sahib could not let them go home without a spot of egg and sausage, they were duly produced and greedily devoured. It was then that I proposed a vote of thanks to the collector for having so generously given us all supper. And in the coarse laughter that followed, Donovan was forced to join in …' John had not finished his story and he would not let Donovan change the topic. The juicier bit was only just coming. The cups had been refilled and the butler had left a tray with a sealed envelope behind.

'Well, since he had been hinting periodically, the thought never left my mind and I discovered that a large tin of Walls best would fit exactly inside one of Firpos ornamental cake tins. So I covered the top up with the original ornamental packing paper …'

'You did not!' Dorothy was listening open-mouthed, 'And you kept the cake for yourself?'

Nodding sagely, John continued, '… tied the whole thing up with a ribbon and got Mrs Hutchings to put it in his stocking.'

Donovan was grinning sheepishly as he held the envelope up to the light and ran the paper knife along the edge. 'I was taken in beautifully and nearly sent it on without opening it, to somebody for whom I had meant to get a Xmas present and had forgotten.' A disbelieving frown settled on his forehead and a look of shock gradually took hold.

'Well, I'll be …! The Easter Revolution has come-a-visiting.'

The message was one of many that had been sent out by the steamship 'Halizones' and routed via Fort William: SERIOUS ARMED RISING AT CHITTAGONG STOP ARMOURIES HAVE BEEN RAIDED AND TELEGRAPH CUT STOP SEND AT ONCE AT LEAST TWO COMPANIES TROOPS AND MACHINE GUNS STOP POSITION CRITICAL STOP

Alexander Burnett

The commissioner of Silchar had been flooded by telegrams from the commissioner of Chittagong, stressing the need for immediate military aid to counter the serious rioting that had broken out. A team, thirty strong, had set out immediately after breakfast, accompanied by the adjutant who was the only regular soldier present. The journey had proved uneventful until the brakes screeched, bringing the train to a halt at a point midway between Silchar and Chittagong. The train that had left a little before theirs had derailed. Making their way carefully along a stretch of improvised line past the derailed engine and trucks, they chugged ahead to enter Chittagong.

The first thing to arrest the sight was the still smoking ruins of the AFI armoury, plainly visible from where he sat in the carriage. The men jostled for a view, crowding at the windows.

The train was pulling into the station. The commissioner and other officials waited to receive them.

'... a carefully planned operation ... town taken completely by surprise.'

'... armouries looted, destroyed ... they have made off with the complete stock of rifles, all 400 of them ... not a single rifle nor musket to defend the town with; just the odd sporting gun ... An Indian dressed as an army officer called at the sergeant's residence at the AFI headquarters, was received by the wife and asked to see her husband. Quite unsuspecting, she called for him and he was promptly shot. It was the signal to the waiting insurgents to overpower the guards and transfer the entire stock of rifles and a considerable number of police muskets into the taxi cabs waiting outside. The post and telegraph office was then visited and much damage done ... by this time the alarm had been raised and the women and children moved with all speed to the safety of the ships.'

Considering the unexpectedness of the attack, the casualties had been comparatively few and the position might have been much worse had it not been for the presence of mind of an Auxiliary Force sergeant who manned a Lewis gun and used it with effect. The civilians, led by Major Baker, had worked through the night, putting out the fire at the AFI armoury and removing the ammunition out of the small magazine room, which, providentially, had been completely overlooked by the raiders.

'... after having run amok in the town for a few hours the rebels have withdrawn to the hills.'

The adjutant turned to address the Surma Valley Light Horse. 'The first task at hand is the demonstration of a show of strength. The impression that troops have arrived in force has to be created.'

Suresh De, 19 April morning, Nagarkhana Hill

A soft light spread slowly, across the eastern sky, putting out the stars one by one. They had been on the march since two o'clock the previous night, save for the little rest in a watermelon field where they had helped themselves to the fruit. Lokenath-da had announced to the young farmer on night-watch who had stumbled upon them that they were the police on the trail of a notorious group of bandits. His initial panic, on seeing so many men in khaki within his field, had been allayed, and though he refrained from pursuing the topic or accepting payment, it seemed unlikely that he had swallowed the story. He could not have possibly missed the sounds of firing that had emanated from the police lines.

A strange sense of well-being coursed through Suresh's body. The excitement of the previous evening had brought about a change. He was conscious of a new energy that was welling up from some unknown source. A tall hill was standing before them. They had been marching in single file all night, blindly following Ambika-da, cutting diagonally across the thick jungles, keeping the hills in sight. They were now veering off onto a little winding path. Then he saw it. Glittering amongst the dense foliage was a fresh water pond. It appeared almost magically; Ambika-da had led them to it unerringly and all without the aid of a compass. Why hadn't anybody thought of bringing one, wondered Suresh. Or was it because there was not an inch of land that was unknown to the leaders? The water carriers had long been emptied, and the weight of the loaded haversacks, the unwieldy muskets and the revolvers hanging from the waist had only served to sharpen the thirst. He must have been carrying at least twenty kilos? Exhilarated, the boys splashed and drank in great gulps. A tin-roofed hut stood on the edge of the cliff above but it appeared vacant. The farmers and cowherds probably used it during the afternoons. It was time to move on and climb a hill. The first one scaled wasn't good enough. A second was chosen.

The exhausted boys flung down their muskets and threw themselves to the ground. But Lokenath-da was not about to let them sleep. Groups of four or five were being assembled, instructed to find suitable places behind bushes and to keep watch along the periphery of the hill. Two teams, each comprising three sentries were to patrol the eastern and the western sides. The rest were free to nod off. But the morning sun had begun to shine and by eight o'clock sleep was no longer possible. The first job of the day was to clean and lubricate the muskets. The thok-thok khot-khot resounded among the hills, sending the birds screeching from the trees.

Not enough trees, thought Suresh squinting up at the sky. He would have liked a drink of water. The temperature had begun to rise. All these boys, he looked around; the thirst would soon be upon them. Most of the faces were new. The city lads kept to themselves and the village boys sat apart, conspicuous by their self-consciousness. Master-da, Ambika-da and Nirmal-da moved between the groups, chatting, laughing. They are trying to gauge the morale, he thought, before they disclose the next stage of the plan. It was fairly plain that the success enjoyed at the police lines was to be now followed up by guerrilla warfare. Suresh marvelled at their ingenuity … the degree of thought they had put into formulating the master plan.

Contacting Ananta Lal Singh and Ganesh Ghosh was the agenda of the day. The contact in the city who was to help out was Ardhendu Dutt. Suresh knew of him, for he was Phutu-da's classmate at the Chattogram College and lived at Sukhendu Dastidar's home as his younger brother's tutor. But Master-da had something else in mind. Manindra Lal Guha, a student of Chattogram College, was chosen: his mission was to contact either Ardhendu Dutt or Sati-da, through them establish contact with the army commanders and get back.[6]

The sleepy boys returned to their thoughts. Ardhendu Dastidar, a quiet sort but conspicuous by the raw wounds on his body, was the first to break the silence.

'As long as life lasts we should continue to fight.'

'Attack now!' said the tall, lanky sixteen-year-old,[7] resting his back against a tree trunk, chewing on a stalk of grass. This, Suresh learnt, was Quick Silver or Pulin Ghose of Goshai Danga – the fleet-footed messenger who rushed about on his bicycle through the day, carrying messages from Master-da to Ananta Lal Singh; Ananta Lal Singh's to Lokenath-da. Chattogram's police found it impossible to keep track of Pulin: now Pulin Ghose had been spotted on a sampan heading off purposefully … the message had been relayed by radio, but by the time the boat docked the bird had flown … Pulin had smelled their presence. He too came from a family that battled constantly with poverty. It made him alive to the plight of those that suffered and he volunteered with the Ram Krishna Mission, collected funds for the poor, and still found time to tend to and excel in his studies. God had poured intelligence into every nerve and fibre of his being. 'Attack the Imperial Bank,' Pulin[8] said grandly. 'And distribute the money amongst the poor.'

The armed revolution ought to hold the hands of those that are less fortunate, thought Suresh. While people in Madras survived on grass and wild plants, the Imperial Bank had continued to rake in revenue. The air was blazing, for April was a hot month. He tried to think of matters other than thirst.

'I want to remind everyone about 18 April, when our flag was raised. We have to keep it aloft.' This was Naresh Ray, the doctor and boxer, who had studied with Ganesh Ghosh's brother. It was Kartik Ghosh who had introduced him to Ananta Lal Singh.

A sudden distraction: Tripura Sen appeared, cradling in his hands a single green mango – one that he handed to Master-da. It was put away as reserve. It brought with it an instant longing for that green pool of water but it was far too dangerous to venture out in broad daylight.

Nirmal-da called for attention. He stood with one foot resting on the stump of what had once been a great tree. He had a lovely voice, and when he spoke the boys gravitated automatically towards him. 'All men were created equal. Everybody's body carries the same red blood. Then why is it that in our country such inequalities exist between the ruler and the ruled? When the ancestors of these very rulers lived in the dark ages, this calm peaceful land provided tapovans for the rishis to meditate, compose the Vedas, sing the songs of the Sama Veda and allowed educated women like Gargi and Gayatri to make a name for themselves. Sages like Vedavyas and Vashistha flourished. They were your ancestors.'

The moment Nirmal-da finished, Krishna Choudhury, who was sitting way behind everyone else, sprang to his feet and stood with his arms crossed as in Vivekananda's famous pose. 'A dependant country's sole cry is for independence. We revolutionaries will terrorize the British and install Mother India in a temple of gold …'

He was not allowed to finish, for Tegra and Mona made an appearance, faces fresh and glowing, wet hair slicking down. Where had they been? They handed over their water carriers which were filled to the brim and emptied their haversacks on to the ground: a pile of little mangoes – the green and tart kind that caused an involuntary crinkling of the eyes and filled the mouth with a rush of saliva.

'They are growing all over … and there was bel … overhanging the pool.'

'No one saw us going down or even when we were swimming … we made sure.'

The water carriers were being passed eagerly from hand to hand and glee was written all over the faces of the two rascals. Who could have the heart to scold them now?

'There are no herdsmen about …' Tegra panting from the climb reached out for the water carrier as it passed by, and peeped into it. There were a few drops left, and in that light-hearted moment of triumph, he raised the bottle to his lips without noticing Pulin's outstretched arms. A powerful arm gripped his hand and a stony cold voice spoke in his ear.

'Are you not ashamed? You have had your fill many times over and this boy who has sworn to die by your side has not had even a drop?'

Could Lokenath-da, Tegra's Shona Bhai, have humiliated him more? The blood drained from his face as Pulin grabbed eagerly at the chance to moisten his throat. Tegra was reduced to a mass of shame, a culprit caught in the act … why had he not thought of a comrade-in-arms?

'It would have been better had I just died.'

Did Tegra just say that? The words had been muttered under his breath but they had not gone unheard. Suresh caught Kali De's[9] eye: Hajaar hok … he is Loka-da's own little brother … the words remained unspoken between them.

'Not to worry. Not to worry. Tonight I am going to organize dinner for my boys.'

'What else do we need? When Ambika-da is with us we don't have to fear. He will make sure we eat tonight.' Nirmal-da was trying to lighten the atmosphere and it worked. But Tegra added in a sombre voice, 'Food we will probably eat but what about the war? When will we fight?'

It was a direct question.

Ambika-da tried to evade it. He laughed lightly. 'Look at our boys. They yearn more for a fight than for food. Fight we will, but to keep ourselves fit we have to eat. Just dying will not do. We have to kill as well.'

Bidhu Bhattacharya, the Chattogram Medical College topper and gold-medallist came to the rescue. In his Kumilla dialect he said, keeping his face poker straight, 'Haw, morum jokhon, tokhon khaiya daiya moron-ee bhalo. Ambika-da koichey, maira moroner bhalo laagi. Byass moroner age khamutto taago marumotto … yes, when I die it should be on a full tummy. Ambika-da says I am happy to die … but before I do so I would like to eat well.'

The subtle changes in Bidhu-da's voice, the expressions that had to be caught just in time, the measured laughter and the studied silence turned the mood. Everybody laughed. But there was one voice missing. It was Tegra's. His soft words did not go unheard, 'Mereyi morbo … tobey shobaar aagey morbo … Khabar jutuk na jutuk chayee shudhu juddho …I will die only after I have done with the killing but I will win the race. Food or no food, all we want is battle.'

The Nagarkhana Hill upon which they stood heard every word. The words bounced off the rocks and were picked up by the gentle breeze. They echoed again and again. 'Juddho chayee.'

Suddenly the group was activated. Gone were the thoughts of hunger, thirst and fatigue. The evening was descending fast. There was still no news of the scout.

At about 8.30 the order was given: The boys were to climb down the slope in twos. We must look like a line of ants, thought Suresh. Rajat Sen moved in front slashing at the bushes, clearing the way. He had powerful arms and was probably the strongest in the group besides Lokenath-da. A muster was ordered at the bottom: fifty-eight were present. Then began a march towards the north, scrambling through forests, over rocks and boulders. The muskets and the revolvers needed some getting used to and the boys walked carefully, trying to avoid the snake-like roots that were wont to sneak up around ankles and trip up unsuspecting hikers. With all the weight they were carrying, it would mean a nasty sprain or a broken ankle.

They would have walked nearly half a mile when the lights of the Bayezid Bostami Dargah became visible. It was the one place guaranteed to be crowded, for both Hindus and Muslims worshipped there. A whispered order to be silent passed through the line. Ambika-da turned off the path. They would not be drinking from the dargah's pond, realized Suresh. The famous pond was said to be over a thousand years old and home to the sacred tortoises and fish that lived on the puffed rice and bananas offered by the devotees. They would have to maintain a safe distance from it as well. They had reached a secluded spot. Ambika-da indicated they settle down.

'There is a second water source a little distance away,' the whisper ran down the line.

The boys were organizing themselves into small groups to go drink and wash up. Ambika-da, Master-da, Nirmal-da and Lokenath-da sat huddled together. Suresh sat by their side but could not keep himself from nodding off.

'Be ready, be ready.' Ambika-da was moving around, between the boys.

Amarendra Nandi asked for the last time, 'Does anyone else want to go to the pukur? … Anybody wants a drink?'

Some grunted sleepily. Some got up and went with him.

Bayezid Bostami was left behind. They continued their trek northwards.

'Is anyone here from Fatehabad?' Ambika-da's question was passed to the rear.

One of the village lads responded. It was Fakir Sen.[10]

'Do you know Lailar Haat?'

The boy nodded.

ANANTA LAL SINGH, 19 APRIL NIGHT

Ananta cast a hopeful glance at headmaster Aswini Kumar Bhattacharya's house. Ganesh, Makhon and he had reached Double Mooring in the afternoon and had walked along the railway line. Now that they were on the outskirts of the city, they thought it prudent to stay away from the main road and had moved onto the dirt track that led past the Collegiate School.

They peered past the gate. It would be a stroke of luck if Aswini Babu spotted them, for Ananta was certain that the fiery headmaster, even though he viewed him with a jaundiced eye, would be tremendously proud … and the news that several of his students – the stars of his school – Makhon, Ananda, Debu, Sahayram, Moti, Rajat and Mihir – were associated with the cause would probably gladden his heart. It was Makhon's presence that was making him feel bolder. It wasn't fully dark yet and surely someone would notice them and call them in. He craned his neck, checking out every nook and cranny. There was no one in the garden, nor was there anyone having tea on the verandah. A cup of tea, some biscuits! That, in the headmaster's words, would have just hit the spot. But the windows were shut tight.

The dirt track led them to the main road that took them past the Police Club, westward across the city to Sadarghat. The stretch of road was completely bereft of people. No matter which road they turned into they found it deserted. The British had gone and their Indian subordinates were lying low until orders were received.

They were below the hill where Himangshu and Ananda had been dropped off. That part seemed a little blurred to him now. He had been tired … that was all he could remember … so tired that he had not even turned around to say goodbye. A number of questions had begun to creep in. This was war. Why had he not shot Himangshu? When Ardhendu and Tarakeshwar had been burnt he had actually made such a suggestion. He would never live it down and would be grateful, a thousand times over, to Ganesh and Master-da who had stayed his hand that day. But would it be possible for anyone under these circumstances to have Himangshu treated and kept hidden? He wondered why he had sped off like that. Tiredness? Could he blame it on exhaustion? On Ganesh's fever? The faces, fifty-eight young faces, peering through the headlights … making way, without a question, for the car that was driving off … He would kick himself the rest of his life. It was his fault and his fault alone that they had been torn apart from the main body.

They were climbing the slope now keeping watch on every entrance to side lanes. If there was a message, it would be waiting in Ananda and Debu's home. Master-da must have planned to bring the army in by night. The area appeared undisturbed. Then why was his heart beating a tattoo against his ribs? He had never felt so frightened before … not even yesterday at the police lines. What was he so scared of? True, Himangshu had not come to mind until now … nor had reality hit him with full force – an operation that could have been a piece of cake had been botched. The day had been wasted … but that wasn't the problem; he knew it as soon as the house came into view.

'Ananta, at least one, leave just one behind for me.'

The words hung in the air, searing through his brain.

LOKENATH BAL, 19 APRIL NIGHT

Lokenath knocked softly on the shutters. It was nearly 2 a.m. in the morning. The shops of Lailar Haat had long closed and the people had all gone home. But a dim light flickered in one window. It would go out any moment. He knocked again. Not daring to bang harder, he kept up a soft persistent knocking. The shopkeeper was fast asleep. There was no response.

'Dukan-wallah! Dukan-wallah!'

Finally the sounds of stirring. The door opened a crack. An eye peeped out and a frightened gaze swept over the five of them. Nirmal-da kept Fakir hidden behind him.

'Don't worry. We are guards from the Panchalaish Thana.[11] We want to buy some food.'

The mud; the crumpled uniforms; the unshaven appearance. The man stared and then withdrew. The door was opened.

Lokenath stepped in. It was a bread shop but there wasn't enough bread to feed all the boys. 'What about biscuits?' he asked. 'Give us all you have.'

'Siddique, Siddique.' The shopkeeper tapped on a door at the back. 'Bring two baskets and wake Sagid.'

Two little boys emerged, groggy with sleep and helped pack the biscuits and bakarkhani bread into two large baskets. The shop had been cleaned out at a princely sum of seventeen rupees. Lokenath handed over the money and shook his head in refusal at the two Ahmed brothers who offered to carry the baskets to wherever the babus desired.

The main group had settled in a shoopoori garden near a freshwater pond. A quick meal and it was time to march. The area was too close to the Choudhury Haat station.

Half a mile across a field towards the hills, labouring under the weight of the unaccustomed baggage, the load began telling on the youths.

'But they have been exercising regularly ... they are tough,' Lokenath told himself.

No other pond had come their way but the primary concern now was to get to a safe location before dawn streaked the eastern sky. The hill with the steep face was still another half a mile away. The sounds of retching broke in on his thoughts. He had been aware that the boys had been chewing upon the green vines.

Pulin was on the ground. Writhing. Bidhu was making him stick his finger down his throat.

'He drank some of the lubricant.' Naresh said fanning him with some paper.

'Remember you are a revolutionary, Pulin. You cannot give up.' Lokenath spoke gently.

'Vomit, Pulin.' Bidhu was exhorting him.

There was little else that even two doctors could do in this wilderness. 'Your mama stays at Fatehabad doesn't he? Shall we take you to his home?'[12]

Pulin's eyes flew open. The words had come as a blow.

TWELVE

Ananta Lal Singh, 20 April morning

The sunlight inched up to his face and Ananta woke with his heart thudding. Why hadn't they been roused earlier? Had the army not come in during the night? They had all promised to keep watch and wake them the moment news came in. His companions lay fast asleep, their revolvers under their pillows. So the army had not come. His thoughts returned to the events of the previous night. His fears had been unfounded and through a fog of congratulations and blessings – Jogendramohan Meshomoshai's bear hugs, Monorama Mashima raining kisses and tears on every cheek, Chotkun bouncing up and down, Chhor-di's glowing face, Ananda's no-nonsense Thakur-Ma's blessings and Gobindo-da's open mouthed gaze, Ananta had spotted a happy and relaxed Ananda standing way behind, allowing them their share of limelight. He had mouthed Himangshu's name and Ananda had mimed that things were being taken care of, that Sukhendu Dastidar had been put in charge. They had had their dinner and gone off to sleep in Ananda's room.

Chhor-di rushed off to make tea as Ananta took a seat at the dining table. By the time the others came in, the kitchen had been galvanized into action. Aromas drifted in little clouds past the kitchen door, in accompaniment to the clinks and clatters and the sizzles. Chhor-di and Mashima would take more than a couple of minutes; the time could be put to better use. The revolvers and pistols were placed on the table and opened up. Gobindo-da hurried in with little bowls of kerosene oil and some rags which, after some dithering, were set down at the centre of the table. The look on his face said that he would have preferred if they had done their cleaning on the floor but, on a day such as this, even he held his peace. They had begun winding up, for Mashima had begun to pour out the cups of tea. Chhor-di could be seen moving towards the door balancing plates of luchis, all creamy gold and puffed.

'Maaa! Aashchhey!'

It was the scream of a child terrified beyond words.

The hair stood up along the back of the neck. A faint sour taste broke out at the back of the tongue.

At eight or nine, Chotkun was an extremely reliable little fellow and since early that morning, he had been on guard. From his vantage point he could scan nearly 200 yards of the approach road. Once the police had parked their cars, they would have another 100 yards to climb. But why were they coming here? Surely, they had enough evidence to know that Debu and Ananda would not be hanging around home. The revolvers were far from done, but snatching them up, Ananta led the others out of the back door and into the hills that formed the backdrop of the house. 'Keep walking,' he urged Ananda who was throwing anxious glances backwards. Ananda's worries were echoing in his own heart, but surely, not even the police would do anything to women and children, for Meshomoshai was not at home; in fact, they hadn't seen him that morning, for he had left early.

Ganesh had his arm around Ananda's shoulders. It was ten o'clock now and they had been waiting for nearly an hour at a spot half a mile from the house. Surely, it was safe enough now to check that all was well. They crept in silently through the back door and a single glance was enough to realize that something tremendous had taken place. Mashima and Chhor-di, through their tears, seemed aghast that they had come back.

'You have to go away … run go into hiding. Baba kay arrest korechhey …' the words were tumbling out of Mashima. '… they found Himangshu's prescription and medicines in his pocket. Ja. Ja. Don't stay a minute longer … Aamar praan bhora aashirbaad kintu tora choley ja … go away,' she sobbed.

'Maaa!' Chotkun was distressed to see his mother break down. 'Chhor-di!' he appealed but found he was being ignored. 'Dada ra to juddho korbey … they are going to war so that we can be free.' He was a little boy, scared and confused. He hugged his mother shaking her to bring her back to her senses. 'Why are you crying, Ma? Chhor-di, tui keno kaadchhis?'

Ananta bent to touch Mashima's feet but she reached past him to grab at Ananda. She clutched his head to her trembling breast as if she would never let go. All self-control had been washed away. A flood of tears broke down every defence. Chhor-di was sobbing openly as Mashima covered every inch of Ananda's face with kisses running her hands over his head, neck and chest and back as if conjuring up an invisible shield.

'Ma, why are you worrying so much? I have your blessing. I will be safe.' He cupped her face in his hands. 'My golden mother, I am so proud to have a mother like you. Will you not smile for me?'

Mashima drew him into a protective embrace and said fiercely to Ananta and Ganesh. 'You … You, are responsible for Khoka and Tun,' she began sobbing again. 'I bless you all. Tomra bechey thako … may you live.' Abruptly, she held Ananda a little way off so she could look him in the eye: 'Tell Khoka I am not angry with him … tell him your mother is a fortunate woman to have borne sons like you.' Her gaze had returned to him and her voice was stern. 'It is you … you are responsible for whatever good or bad may happen to my Khoka and Tun.'

They took the dust from Mashima and Chhor-di's feet and applied it to the heads. It was time to go.

Good, bad … in the end it is all the same for us, thought Ananta as he raised his arm in farewell.

Suresh De, 20 April morning

The morning routine of snatching a couple of hours of sleep and then rechecking the weapons had been completed. It was around noon when Ambika-da called Fakir Sen to his side. 'Go carefully home and see if you can gather some news of the city. Have the trains started moving? Have reinforcements arrived?'

Tegra jumped up. He would go with Fakir to Fatehabad, but a quick frown on Ambika-da's face shushed him.

Counting out five rupees, Ambika-da handed them over to Fakir. 'Be back by four in the afternoon and try bringing back some watermelons.'

'And some salt.' Tegra called out.

'Now tell me who is the enemy of mankind?' Master-da called for attention.

'The British.'

'Not just ordinary enemies, they are capable of unmanning mankind ... like the magician Rasputin who held the Russian monarchy in a web of illusion ... like the one Mir Jafar, the wazir of Murshidabad, found himself in. In AD 1857 the fakir[1] was reduced to a joke, the dervish turned into a monster; first Nanda Kumar was made a maharaja, then cheated and hanged; Wajid Ali Shah was deprived of his kingdom and banished to Kolkata, reduced to a nawab merely on paper. Can you find cleverer people?'

'In 1914, India was roped into a war that was not ours.' Nirmal-da took the stage. 'Without our consent we were forced into taking part. Bikaner's maharaja Ganga Singh, Sir James Meston, the Lieutenant Governor of the United Provinces of Agra and Oudh and Bengal's Sir Satyendra Prasanna Sinha took part in England's war conference and these British toadies promised aid on behalf of all of India. The common man was caught in the conspiracy and was forced to provide fifteen lakh soldiers. In 1917, 150 crore rupees and in 1918, sixty-seven crore rupees were donated to the British cause. Then the huge expenses of the war and the costs of feeding and maintaining the troops became the responsibility of the British government of India, and this dependent country was forced into accepting the orders. Food and raw materials were sent out in such quantities that the country was on the verge of declaring famine.

'Let me tell you about Annie Besant's offer of Home Rule. She was one shrewd politician. All the parties fell into her trap: Congress, Muslim League, even Bal Gangadhar Tilak, Lala Lajpat Rai and Surendranath Banerjee. The only ones that saw through it were Poona's Veer Savarkar and the Bengal revolutionaries. They said we don't need Home Rule, we do not want dominion status – we want complete independence. As the idea caught on, the Sikhs in Singapore declared independence and kept Singapore independent for seven days. Iraq came forward to help India and the Indian soldiers in Iraq formed a volunteer army. Raja Mahendra Pratap took the help of the Afghan Amir to help create an independent government on the border of India and Afghanistan.' Nirmal-da drew a breath. His eyes had sought every face, making eye contact with each one, judging the effect of his words.

'The revolution spread from Gauhati to Lahore: in 1907, Shyam Krishnavarma helped Hem Chandra Kanungo to go to Paris to learn the art of bomb making; Deputy Governor General Fraser's train was attacked; an attempt made on the life of Allen the magistrate in Dhaka; Joteen Mookerjee – Bagha Joteen – worked at smuggling in arms from Germany; newspapers like *Common Wills*, *New India*, Tilak's *Kesari* and the *Maratha* carried inflammatory news. And with the World War raging, the British feared that their golden goose had begun to flap its wings. To calm India, they promised Home Rule as soon as the War had ended. People here fell for it and the Congress and Muslim League were awash with rainbow-coloured dreams. Mahatma Gandhi rushed to the villages on a recruitment drive for British armies fighting abroad. But the Bengal revolutionaries were not fooled and the British tried to rein them in by bringing in the Bharat Raksha Rule.[2] Many were sent to jail. But at the end of the war the grand reward was the Jallianwala Bagh massacre on 13 April 1919.

'None of the promises had been kept. Instead, the Montague–Chelmsford Reform was imposed upon India. Jinnah too was disgusted. The British armed themselves with sophisticated weapons, for the Indian Arms Act was applicable to the Indians alone and not to foreigners. After the War ended, Dr Satya Pal began protesting against the version of the promised Home Rule that had been granted and a peaceful assembly was organized to protest the arrest of Kitchlew and Satya Pal without a trial. Some 20,000 people, including women and children, had gathered in the garden called Jallianwala Bagh close to the Golden Temple in Amritsar. Brigadier General Reginald Dyer, an Irishman born in Simla, brought the police and blocked the garden's only exit. Without warning, the machine guns began to fire and continued until all ammunition had been exhausted. Around 1,650 rounds were fired. People tried to escape by jumping into a well. Some 400 people died on the spot and more than 1,500 were injured.'[3]

Suresh had the words down pat. Ram Krishna-da had given him enough lessons in history. Where was he now, wondered Suresh. Here he was, in the middle of the revolution, abandoned by his mentor.

Ananda Prasad Gupta, 20 April afternoon

'They will bring many sipahis from outside and then they will burn Chattogram down to ashes. Tokhon moja bujhbey babu-ra.' The speaker directed a contemptuous jet of spittle at the ground.

'What are you saying, Mirza? You think they care? They don't fear for their lives.'

The conversation was amusing but it held no relevant content. Ananda sipped at his tea. The afternoon had been spent wandering the hills in search of as many paan-beedi shops as possible in the hope of picking up information from snatches of conversation. Their dhutis arranged in the formal malkocha pleats and shirt pockets stuffed with pencils and paper, they were agents out gathering information. Ananta-da and Ganesh-da played the role to perfection but Ananda was aware of the looks that he and Makhon drew. It was their obvious youth and city looks that went against them.

'Aapnara kara? Who are you?' The question was suddenly being directed at them.

'From the city … looking for the vidrohis … if you have information, the government will pay well.'

It bought a quick end to the chatter. Then a giggle: 'Saar, how will their news reach us? Who knows where they have gone?'

'Saar, what is the news in the city? Has the paltan arrived?' But a whisper had begun making the rounds, '… look like swadeshis.'

'On its way.' Ananta-da paid up.

As he walked past, a seedy fellow sucking his tea noisily through his front teeth grinned up at Ananda. 'Hoshiyar thakben … be on your guard.'

No one seemed to talk of having spotted a large group. Surely, the army could not be more than five to seven miles away from the city. It was well past lunch now and they had abandoned the Bayezid Bostami Road and were headed back towards the city. It was a blistering hot day with not a pond in sight. Makhon and he had not spoken all afternoon, trying to conserve the moisture in their throats but already the choking strands were winding themselves about the tonsils refusing to yield to the efforts at swallowing.

Ganesh and Ananta-da settled down for a little rest by the side of the railway tracks. They must be within half a mile of the Panchalaish Railway Station and two to three miles from the police lines, guessed Ananda. His throat was really parched now … not a pond, a tube well or even a farmer's hut in the vicinity … but in the distance, he could spy a melon patch. He stood pointing, waving, hoping someone would own up to be the proprietor. A Muslim youth stood up from amongst a group of labourers. He loped across and returned with a large fruit. The payment was made and Ananta-da used a pocket knife to slice into the crisp pink flesh. The juice was cool and refreshing. Ananda and Makhon set up a little game to see who could spit the seeds the farthest. The farmer squatted beside them, watching the competition.

'Bau.' He spoke startling them. 'Over there.'

A hundred uniformed men, rifles held in the High Port Arms position, bayonets gleaming, were marching briskly towards them.

'Run, bau. They are catching Hindus.'

It was too late. Any sudden movement would attract attention. Ganesh-da appeared not to have heard and Ananta-da gazed at the soldiers with open-mouthed fascination. Then abruptly, while still some thirty yards away, the soldiers turned left in the direction of the hills. The watermelons were consumed leisurely.

Reinforcements. The hills would be a safer bet. But Ananta-da and Ganesh-da got up and took a turn towards the city. They had to go back, realized Ananda. Where else would Master-da send word? It would have to be to his house or to Sati-da's. The appearance of the soldiers seemed to have caused a change. A heckler followed at a safe distance. His occasional taunts were drawing a crowd.

'Swadeshis … or dacoits on the run?'

'Gorment reward. Big gorment reward!'

Ananta-da and Ganesh-da quickened their pace.

LOKENATH BAL, 20 APRIL NIGHT

It was past seven. Fakir[4] had failed to return. Bidhu, who had been pacing up and down until some time back, was sitting quietly. It was strange for him to be so silent … his wild sense of humour failed to come to his rescue. It had been Dr Bidhu who had introduced and vouched for Fakir. Had the boy betrayed them? Had he gone to the police? His father must have caught him and turned him in. After all, he had remained in hiding at Debu and Ananda's house ever since his father had lodged the police complaint. Now in hindsight it appeared to have been the worst decision Ambika-da could have taken under the circumstances. Would Fakir break down under police interrogation?

They could not afford to spend another minute on the hill. The boys trooped downhill in silence. The mood had changed. They sat quietly by the side of a pond and ate the handful of flat rice moistened with curds. The nod was given and they prepared to march again.

'Why are we wandering about in the jungles and hills with no rest, no food, no bathing … what is this all about?' Naresh, Bidhu, Rajat, Debu and Tripura posed the question together. It had been on Lokenath's mind all these days but this lot had become the first to articulate it.

'What is our plan? What is our objective? We are moving further and further away from the city … We want to face the enemy. We want battle.'

The youngsters crowded around, eager to listen to the explanations. 'Juddho chayee.' There was mutiny in the air. They had all begun to question this flight to the north.

Master-da looked grave. Ordering the boys back into position, Lokenath went to confer with Master-da, Nirmal-da and Ambika-da. He personally was all for turning back and facing the enemy. With or without Ananta-da and Ganesh-da, they would forge ahead and do their best.

The decision to turn back was taken. It was already past midnight.

Ananda Prasad Gupta, 20 April night

It was dusk by the time they reached Parade Square. Ananda cast an anxious look towards the path that wound up the hill … he could tell the exact number of steps that would take him to his doorstep but the way home had now been barred. Baba! An involuntary shudder shook his frame. What had they done with him …? The morning's misery returned to hit him with full force. Ma, Chhor-di, Chotkun – they were alone up there. No, surely Baba would have found a way to get back ... there would be nothing more than detention at home. They had left the lonely stretch that went past the Government College and were on the road that circled DC Hill. Where were all the street lights and where, for that matter, was the British army? The city should have been crawling with soldiers. Ananta-da and Ganesh-da stood, gazing open-mouthed: the beautiful winding drive shaded by tall banyans, the majestic bungalow right up at the top ... it all lay in darkness. The commissioner's bungalow had been abandoned. Not even the servants had cared to stay.

Comprehension felt like a cold, wet slap. The city had been abandoned, for not enough reinforcements had arrived. Where was Master-da with the main army? The city was theirs for the taking.

Nandan Kanan lay across the road. This was a thickly populated, garrulous middle-class area where Ananta-da and Ganesh-da's names were a byword. But there was not a soul around. The streets were deserted, every door tightly shut and all lights put out. Sati-da's house stood grim and dark. But dim lights flickered through the cracks of a window next door. There were people inside ... about thirty of them. What was going on, wondered Ananda. They would all have to be from the neighbourhood, for there were no carriages or cars parked outside. Could Sati-da be in there? What if an agent was in there and recognized one of them? Makhon was given the nod and he slipped in like a cat.

Sati-da came out beaming. He was all congratulations, embracing each one, pumping their arms, gushing praises: all Chattogram was bursting with pride – the biggest thing since 1857 – pujas were being organized, prayers being offered to every household deity ... but no, he had not received word from Master-da ... and oh! Wait. Sati-da ran home and returned with a cloth bag that he pressed into Ganesh-da's hands ... some money ... 200 rupees ... every last paisa he had in the house.

It was a little before eight o'clock when they left Sati-da's home and walked the two miles through the city centre towards Rajat-da's. There was no one at the gates of the IB inspector's house in Kotwali ... no one around to stop and question the young men wandering around.

They were in Rajat-da's backyard now ... how would Binodini Mashima react? She who had been a tower of strength until now, would she have successfully held up against Ranjan Meshomoshai's undoubted anger at the betrayal? All of Rajat-da's siblings had been in on the secret ... Meshomoshai had been the only one left without an inkling. That a part of the conspiracy had been hatched in his home, against his employers; that his family had not taken his permission; that he had come to know only when the news broke and he discovered his rifle missing; his son gone – even though, to tell the truth, the last bit had turned out as much of a surprise for Mashima, for she had not been certain as to what exactly was coming. Surely, no man could take kindly to such revelations. Ananda hoped that Rajat-da had taken the rifle with him and not left it behind at the AFI armoury or the police lines. And he crossed his fingers, praying that Ranjan Meshomoshai had not charged off to make a report the moment he discovered the two missing. Makhon had gone in through the back door. Why was he taking so long? Had Meshomoshai caught him? Was Mashima not at home? A head appeared. A hand waved.

'Take your shoes off.' Ananta-da whispered.

Ananda tiptoed in. Mashima stood at the head of the stairs with a lamp, her finger pressed to her lips. She pointed to Rajat-da's room. It was one that Ananda was familiar with – one over which the revolutionaries felt a proprietary sense of ownership. It looked startlingly empty. The cupboards were bare ... all personal effects had been removed. Mashima had been expecting guests!

She was back, slightly out of breath, having carried the loaded tray up the stairs. Mashima had never permitted the servants in whenever a meeting had been in progress. Ananda touched her feet ... they all touched her feet one by one and she cupped each chin and the top of each head tenderly. Then she sat down, handed out the plates of food and listened intently to the story as they ate. Makhon had already relieved her of her worst fears: Rajat-da had survived the action on 18 April; that except for Himangshu there had been no casualties that day and that Rajat-da was with the main group.

'Stay here as long as you want but remain unseen and unheard,' she warned. 'Not even the children will be told or be allowed upstairs.' She smiled through her pain. 'They have been on their guard since the day their dada disappeared.'

Suresh De, 21 April, Badulla Hill

A sharp nudge woke Suresh. The sun was streaming down. Suresh sat up and yawned. Most of the boys were up, but he could easily have slept through the day.

'Go wash your face. It's past eight now.' Pundit-da was stretching his limbs.

Dragging himself to his feet, Suresh went to join the others – a small stream had been traced to its source and everybody was taking turns at scrubbing their faces and splashing the cool water onto their sore limbs. The eastern side of the hill was a gentle, easy climb; of course they had to choose the steep forbidding face to clamber up in the wee hours of the morning – such was their luck. Suresh returned to where the boys were reassembling and sat down cross-legged, his body limp and drained.

'Where are the watermelons?' Ambika-da's question stopped him in mid-yawn.

The watermelons? Oh! The memory of that last climb returned – falling down repeatedly, clutching at clumps of grass which gave way without warning, tumbling over each other. It had been great fun. But, he grimaced, the watermelons had gone.

'Strange.' Ambika-da's voice was on edge. 'How did you manage it? And now what will you eat? How will you preserve your strength?'

'We thought the arms were more important than watermelons.' A meek reply was heard.

'And I think both are important.' Ambika-da's voice bordered on the hysterical.

'Ambika-da,' Nirmal-da's voice was placating. '… such young boys … wandering since three days without food or water … now isn't it an achievement that they succeeded in climbing the hill? Bolo to … if they walked all the way with the melons and died … who would be eating the melons now?'

Ambika-da forced a humourless smile.

Naresh Ray, who had been sitting silently until then, got up to announce that his group had not left their melons behind and there were ten that could be shared. Ambika-da was all praise. Nirmal Lala was asked to divide them equally. Nirmal busied himself with his knife with Madhusudan Dutt helping him keep count.

Nirmal[5] was perhaps the youngest amongst them ... Bidhu Sen said he had introduced him two months before the planned action, that he was a class eight student at the Cox's Bazar High School who had run off by himself to meet Master-da at Chattogram. Nirmal had lived with him for a few days and sensed there was something afoot. Abdaar – that was the way he could get around Master-da, for the one thing he could count on was his charming and sweet little face. Master-da had been suitably amused.

How long has it been since you joined?

Two months.

What class?

Eighth.

How old are you?

Fourteen.

Baba, this is the age for you to work at your studies.

Master-da had not relented.

Nirmal had rushed back to Cox's Bazar and into Bidhu's arms insane with grief. Take me with you, he had pleaded. Bidhu had advised another meeting with Master-da but had been amazed when he learnt that Nirmal had called his classmates and handed out his books ... they made expensive gifts for one who came from a middle-class family like his! But the most surprising thing of all was that he had handed over his little suitcase, the one that he had treasured all his life. He had then left for Chattogram saying that he was leaving Cox's Bazar for good.

Once he was done, the slices were handed out. But now there was nothing left for Nirmal. The poor boy looked extremely puzzled ... he had done his math and counted the slices carefully. Madhusudan-da wore a look of incredulity. Did he make a mistake in counting? At twenty-seven[6] he was amongst one of the elders in the group, an adult – in fact one with proper work experience, having worked as a contractor in the coal mines near Jamshedpur. He was an old party worker from Beedgram and knew the leaders well. And though he came from a zamindari background, he had opted to go and find work, for he had no wish to be dependent upon his family. He had surprised everyone by landing up seventeen days before the planned action and jumping into the fray as if he had never been away. How could he have got a simple task like counting watermelon slices wrong?

But Ambika-da knew. He was up on his feet roaring with anger. 'Who is responsible for this? Who has stolen a slice? Come forward. I expect you to own up.'

'I did.' It was Tegra.

What could one do with him? Perpetually up to mischief?

'Then you must be shot. Lokenath, he is your brother. Shoot him.'

Loka-da's exasperation with Tegra was reaching its limit. 'Just because he is my brother does not mean he gets off lightly. Pronounce a judgement. If it is death, I will shoot him.' His revolver was already in his hand.[7]

This was great entertainment. But Tegra decided to complicate matters. Suddenly, he had pulled his shirt off and was standing before Ambika-da. 'Look ... I am laying my chest bare in front of you. Shoot.'

Suresh could feel the muscles of his body tensing. A cold sense of dread was creeping in. Something was going terribly wrong ... what had begun as a bit of levity ... but Master-da was now standing between them. 'Lokenath, put the revolver away.' His voice was cold.

Ambika-da was gabbling. 'Arrey baba, you have become even angrier than me. Achchha ... can I be angry with you? Can I ever let a bullet loose amongst you people? This is what you think of me, you naughty boy ... you dushtu chheley ... duronto bhaiti aamar?' He flung his arms out and clasped Tegra's rigid form to his breast. By now Tegra's face was red and furious.

'If indiscipline must be punished Lokenath, the capacity for telling the truth must also not go unrewarded.' But Master-da was speaking to everybody.

Suresh realized he had been holding his slice of water melon just below his open mouth all this while. He had not taken even one bite. The group resumed their eating. The only one that sat unmoving was Tegra. He was still in shock. Nirmal-da sat beside him stroking his back. The situation was resolved finally by Ambika-da himself.

'I have done you a great injustice.' His voice was loud enough for all to hear. 'Will you not forgive me?'

Tegra looked embarrassed.

'Look,' continued Ambika-da, 'I have not eaten yet. Will you share my slice with me?'

Ananta Lal Singh, 21 April morning

Ananta had woken early. He peered through a crack in the shutters, not daring to open them. The backyard looked undisturbed. Mashima was at the door. She came in with a tray of tea and tiptoed out again. Ananta nudged the others and turned to the tray. Mashima had arranged it as if it were a normal day. He removed the tea cosy and poured out steaming fragrant cupfuls and uncovered the plates of freshly fried luchis and spicy potatoes. His being flooded with guilt – here was Mashima brewing her finest tea for them; Lord alone knew how her own son was faring; for that matter all the young boys who had put their complete trust in him, swearing to follow him until death released them of the bond. They would have to be extremely careful with the cups and saucers; they could not afford to make the faintest 'chink'. Ananda's house had been raided the day before and though this house was secure due to Rajat's father's social standing, who knew he may well be the one to turn them in.

'Eat up,' he motioned to the others. Ganesh was picking at his food; the fever was draining him of his appetite, but this could turn out to be his last chance to eat a good meal. There was a soft knock at the door. Mashima came in to clear the plates.

'Your Meshomoshai wants to meet you. Shall I bring him up?'

The master of the household? The one whose hospitality they were enjoying? He was asking for permission?

'Yes. Yes.' Ananta sprang to his feet. 'Please. Please tell him his sons are waiting.'

The four exchanged looks. It was not that they had not met Ranjan Meshomoshai more than several times before, but on all those occasions they had been merely Rajat's friends, sons of men who were well known, good local lads pursuing their education with sincerity and no more than a few pleasantries had been exchanged. But, for the first time Meshomoshai would be meeting revolutionaries whose activities had spirited away his eldest son – a son for whom he had held great hopes … a son who he had learnt was a principal revolutionary only two days ago.

Ranjan Meshomoshai came into the room. Ananta bent low to touch his feet but was gripped firmly by the arms and prevented from completing the ritual. The tight embrace that followed, however, cleared the momentary confusion that had sparked in his heart. Rajat's father was a powerfully built man and there was little that Ananta could do but to submit. But he caught a glimpse of a face awash with tears, glowing with pride. Here was a fellow revolutionary, one he had not recognized earlier.

Meshomoshai hugged each one in turn; and no, he would not let them touch his feet, for had they not proven themselves more than his equal? He had important news. The police had announced a bounty on the head of each of his guests: Ananta and Ganesh, dead or alive, were valued at Rs 5,000/- each and Ananda and Makhon at Rs 1,000/- each. But for now he could not wait to listen to the details of the armoury raid. His face shone with simple childlike pride, especially at the part that Rajat had played. His Rajat was an all-rounder – be it his studies, be it sport … everyone knew that Rajat was in demand even when the police officers held their football matches – a teenager so sought after. Did his friends know that Rajat was a natural artist … that the quick portrait he had once sketched of Stanley Jackson during a school visit had so impressed the laat sahib that he had been prompt in offering the boy admission into art school? And now this completely new side to his son was being revealed. Few excelled in all things martial and Rajat was one of them … boxing, shooting, horse riding, driving. Through the narration, Ranjan Lal Sen's lips moved silently and Ananta knew that they were prayers, congratulatory exclamations and blessings all rolled into one.

The door burst open. It was one of Rajat's younger brothers. 'Police,' he hissed and tore down the stairs. In a flash, Ranjan Meshomoshai had pulled a table to the centre of the room and pointed to a small trapdoor which led to the attic. It had taken not more than a minute for Meshomoshai to push the table back into position and retire to his chamber. Ananda and Makhon were sent to the far corners, crouching beneath the sloping tin roof of the room, while

Ananta and Ganesh sat on the trapdoor itself; their eyes glued to the cracks. Each one held their revolvers at ready.

The sound of many people moving about: A search had already begun. The heavy tramp of boots was growing closer … they were coming up the stairs; this was it; once they were in the room how could they not help looking up.

'This way please.' Meshomoshai was leading them into the adjacent room? Poor man, this was his desperate attempt at delaying the inevitable by another minute or so.

'Aapni aagey cholun … Remain in the front please.'

Ananta knew the voice. It belonged to DIB Sachin Bhowmik who had retired from the 49 Bengal Regiment and had joined the police service. Meshomoshai was being pushed ahead as a measure of security. By choosing Rajat's home, they had pushed Meshomoshai into a corner.

They were going to come into this room any moment now … the door was kicked open and ten sipahis burst in, rifles held at ready. At the door stood Meshomoshai with Sergeant Kelly and Sachin Bhowmik crouching behind him, their revolvers digging into his back. Sweat ran in streams down Ananta's neck. This was the most humiliating scene that he had ever witnessed. Seconds ticked by … no one breathed. If the sipahis looked up, they would see the trapdoor. In case a gun battle took place, and even if they succeeded in sparing Meshomoshai, would the British spare him?

Meshomoshai was speaking … in fact he appeared to be chatting comfortably. Whatever it was that he was saying, he was succeeding in holding everyone's attention. The sipahis and officers relaxed their guard and turned to leave the room. Meshomoshai offered to see them to the door … he was playing his part with grace and elan … the ever eloquent lawyer was giving the performance of a lifetime.

Chotkun's scream of yesterday … and the quiet, whispered announcement of today: it meant only one thing – the police had caught on. They had crept up today so that none of the children on watch could spot them until it was too late

Suresh De, 21 April, Badulla Pahar

'We need two volunteers.' Master-da, Nirmal-da and Ambika-da addressed the group. 'Ones who are aware that the words pari nai … couldn't do it … are not an option. We must get in touch with Ananta and Ganesh. This is our last chance. You cannot afford to say later that you tried but couldn't do it.'

This time the volunteers would have to be chosen carefully. Two messengers had failed to return. Master-da and Nirmal-da went around visiting every individual group. Finally, it was decided that Amarendra Nandi and Diptimedha Choudhury[8] were the chosen ones. Master-da took them aside for a private conversation.

There was a strange low rumble that was growing louder.

'Air Raid! Air Raid!' Sahayram Das's, voice called out. 'Take cover! Take cover!' The aircraft flew low, circled and came back. The hillside resonated with the vibration. The aircraft moved away without bombing the area.[9]

Amarendra and Diptimedha hurried up and changed into shirts and dhutis and tucked two revolvers in at their waists. Everyone called out, wishing them luck. Ten o'clock, and they had touched Master-da's feet and set off at a run, for a bus to the city would pass through Fatikchari within the hour. Their instructions included going to the city which was some twelve to fourteen miles away; picking up information by listening to local gossip; meeting Ardhendu Guha and enlisting his help in gathering more information and locating Ananta-da and Ganesh-da; visiting the homes of Sashi Bhushan Sen, Ananda Gupta and Rajat Sen for more information and returning by seven in the evening.

It was a superhuman task, thought Suresh, but if anyone could do it, it would have to be Amarendra … he was shrewd and he was tough like tempered steel, ritually tested by fire, hand-crafted, quite literally, by Ananta Lal Singh. There could not have been many who could have boasted of facing Amarendra in the ring and not being felled by one of his blows. In his hands, the lathi spun in a blur, deflecting all that came at him; and he could race up and down the stairs, balancing on stilts six feet long, leap across from one rooftop to another … yes … he had even seen him twist a steel rod seven feet long and three inches thick into a series of five loops … Amarendra, he remembered, had won that competition. Suresh lay down on a grassy patch beneath a tree and closed his eyes. Dipti, he had met only three days ago. It was his striking good looks that first came to mind … would have to be pretty smart too if Master-da had chosen him for the mission … a good team one would say …

'Bah rey, Ambika-da! Where have your moustache and beard gone.'

Ambika-da was striding up the slope, a bunch of bananas slung across his shoulders and an earthen pot of curds in each hand. He was looking pleased with himself. The clean-shaven, freshly bathed appearance gave him a completely new look … a smaller and a younger face … it was difficult to recognize him. 'Lunch!' he called. The voice was his all right. 'Curds, flat rice and bananas … and …,' he waited for the suspense to build up 'hot khichuri for dinner!'

The excitement was infectious. Ambika-da had been plagued by the fact that his boys were going hungry … rice … that is what they needed. He had contacted relatives and friends at Fatehabad, borrowed 100 rupees and had organized some party workers in the village to cook and bring the khichuri quietly once it was dark. But, for the time being the doi, cheerey and kola would have to do. But there was something else up his sleeve. He waited until the meal was over and then like a magician played up his audience. What could it be? Roshogolla? No. Cake? No. Sandesh ? Kebabs? No. He brandished it with a flourish: it was a copy of the *Panchojanya.* The boys milled around like a swarm of bees, pouring over his shoulders as he read out the day's news: the city was crawling with soldiers after having been deserted for nearly two days; no news of an encounter with the rebels; no news of arrests. It meant Ananta Lal Singh and Ganesh Ghosh had neither been arrested, nor were they dead. It brought fresh hope to every heart … surely Amarendra would find them. Once together, they would make a formidable team. But the *Panchojanya* also revealed a darker truth: the enemy was no longer helpless; it should have been engaged earlier.

'Master-da, you need to take a decision.' Tripura Sen's voice was sombre. 'It will be unwise to wait any longer.'

Tegra had accosted Nirmal-da. 'Nirmal-da, how much longer for battle? I can't take it any more … every moment I worry that we will be attacked. It will be tonight, won't it? We will attack the enemy stronghold tonight … won't we?'

The boys were asked to gather in a semicircle. They sat cross-legged, muskets in hand.

'Brothers all.' Master-da began. 'On 18 April, before we went to battle, we had worked ourselves up mentally for war. Ours was a death programme. Today we have to take an oath once again … Jibon mrityu payer bhritto, chitto bhabonahin[10] … Life and death are underlings to be trod on while the mind is kept free from cares. I am asking everyone … now think before you speak … to ignore death and take on the powerful British army, accept death and fight. Is everyone really ready?'

Before he could complete his question, fifty-five boys gripped their muskets tighter and answered in one voice: 'We take the oath. We will fight the British. We will die. We want battle. We will kill the British and then die.'

The words shook the hill and then there was silence. Master-da stood calm and steadfast. This part had been rehearsed many times before and though he knew that Master-da was pleased, Suresh wondered if he was absolutely certain. He sneaked a look at the other faces. Were they all as convinced? Master-da's next words echoed his thoughts. He spoke slowly and deliberately.

'I am happy to see the morale … none of us wants to turn back, that I know … but there is no end to the mental preparation required. That is why I must ask you to imagine what will happen. Fifty-five muskets unequally poised against an incredible force … the fear of dying, the pain and screams of the dying, the rain of machine gunfire, streams of blood everywhere, death is an absolute certainty … I am giving you a second chance. Study your minds carefully … if anyone feels uncertain, take a decision now. Once we make a move there will be no turning back. One person's fears may at that time affect the others. Cowardice is more infectious than the bravest man's influence.'

The muskets rattled and all voices said, 'We are ready.'

Strange … Master-da was still pondering over something.

Then he said, 'I have two proposals: One, face the powerful enemy and the unequal situation and shed our blood for independence. Two, we go into hiding and when the suitable opportunity arrives, harass the enemy. Those who want to accept my second proposal do not hesitate. Go now and do your best to worry and injure the enemy.'

No one moved.

'Well then, ready for an immediate attack on the city. We need valour and courage like a lion … shahosh, bikrom and shingho bikrom.'

A strategy had to be planned: which of the targets, keeping in mind that they were by now heavily guarded, in the city would be attacked; would they enter in small groups or all together; which of the routes would be used. This time everyone was privy to the plans.

Loka-da made an observation, 'We need to know how the enemy has deployed its troops before we can deploy ours.'

Eventually, it was decided that three teams consisting of fourteen members each and one with thirteen members would be led by Lokenath-da, Ambika-da, Nirmal-da and Master-da. The soldiers of the revolution had been so divided that each team was well matched.

Two routes would be used to enter – one that went past the European Paltan Maidan, and the other past the Parade Ground. Two teams would march along each route, maintaining a distance but would remain close enough to rush to the other's aid if the need arose.

Two teams would attack the jail and two the Imperial Bank; at least one would be successful and then no matter what the results, they would congregate on Fairy Hill and fight to the last. It was to be a dramatic ending: the wake-up call that the nation needed.

It was 3 p.m. They would have to wait until Amarendra and Diptimedha returned. The sun went down but there was no sign of the two. The khichuri arrived, still steaming, in a great vessel. But the banana leaves? Those had been forgotten. The aroma of ghee; the sight of the semi-liquid yellow mix of roasted mung bean dal and rice drove many to distraction, and they plunged their hands in only to withdraw them in a hurry and cool the scalded fingers in their mouths. Salt! The volunteers had forgotten to add salt … but it scarcely mattered, for never had khichuri tasted so good. Finally, it was the turn of the watchkeepers. They were the last to eat. Amarendra and Diptimedha had still not returned.

Surjya Sen | Ambika Chakraborty | Nirmal Sen

Ananta Lal Singh | Ganesh Ghosh | Lokenath Bal

Hari Gopal Bal (Tegra) | Probhash Bal | Naresh Rai

Ardhendu Dastidar
Amarendra Nandi
Deboprasad Gupta
Rajat Sen
Jibon Ghoshal (Makhon)
Ram Krishna Biswas
Diptimedha Choudhury
Haripada Mahajan
Krishna Choudhury

Lal Mohan Sen · Monoranjan Sen · Narayan Sen

Apurva Sen (Bhola) · Tarakeshwar Dastidar (Phutu) · Kalpana Dutt

Sir Charles Tegart · John Younie

Mahatma Gandhi and Khan Abdul Ghaffar Khan, the Frontier Gandhi, at Chittaranjan Das's funeral

Charles Tegart and Lord Lytton decorate police officers and men for bravery outside Lalbazaar.

CR Das's funeral

The armoury in the AFI Headquarters

Train derailed by Chittagong rebels

Mr Wilkinson's Chevrolet with bullet holes

The Baby Austin and the taxi brought by Himangshu Bimal Sen which was driven by Ananta Lal Singh, left behind at the police lines

The Dodge taxi stolen by Lokenath Bal and his team that was used in the raid

Dead bodies of Naresh Rai (I), Tripura Sen (II) and Bidhu Bhattacharya (III) found on Jalalabad hill

Dead bodies of Hari Gopal Bal (Tegra) (IV) and Motilal Kanungo (V) found on Jalalabad Hill

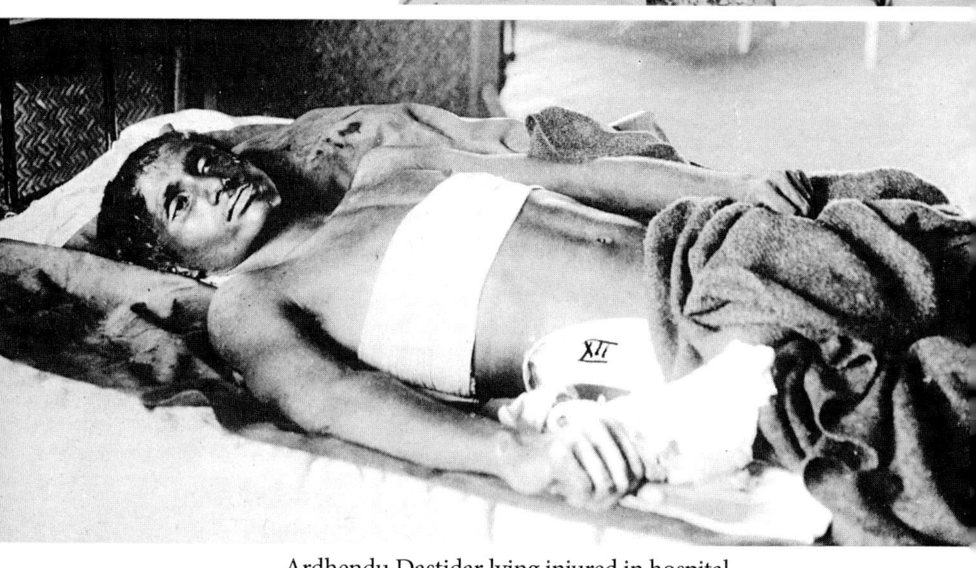

Ardhendu Dastidar lying injured in hospital

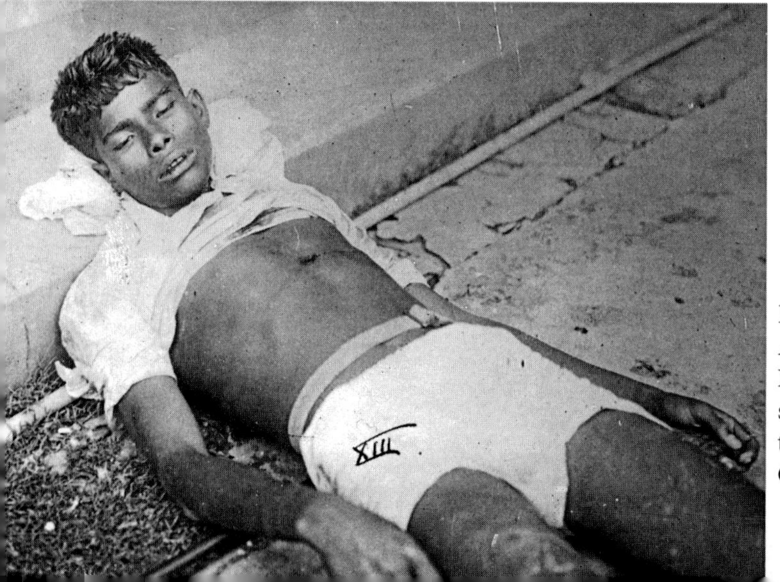

Dead body of Amarendra Nandi who was shot dead by the police in Chittagong city

21 April, 8 p.m.

'Saar. The raiders have been spotted saar.'

The effect was just what Gaffur had desired. If only he could have met the DIG instead. But Sub-inspector Siddique Dewan had insisted on accompanying him from Hatazari to Chittagong, and since it was past eight, they had gone to the residence of the police superintendent, Mr Johnson. Gaffur had bottled all the information within himself until now.

Could he, as he made his way to work that morning, have predicted that the day held such potential? He had found Sub-inspector Hem Gupta at the station with a flag, a few pieces of ammunition and a black badge. He had found them on the Nagarkhana Hill and was reporting the matter at the Hatazari Thana. Nagarkhana was a part of the range that extended northwards from the police lines to Hatazari and it meant that all the hills would have to be combed. Gaffur had, in a duty-watch kind of way, discarded his uniform, wound a lungi about his waist, planted a fez on his head, lined his eyes with surma, and set out. Making his way southwards, he had been strolling along in the hills a little to the west of the Chowdhury Hat railway station.

Mr Johnson's gaze had not wavered off his face.

'I was climbing the Badulla Pahar saar, when I see a sock, a little burnt. I also find two badges; tiny flags like the ones swadeshis use. Near the top I find watermelon shells … some not fully eaten. I didn't go any further. As I was coming down I meet peasant cutting grass while his cows drink at stream.' He wagged his head. 'Four-thirty in the afternoon saar. Waji-ud-din was his name, saar. He said be careful because fifty to sixty babus in the area … some in khaki shirts and shorts, some in white dhutis and shirts and rifles in a big pile. They had asked him what he was doing and he said he was looking for his cattle. He asked them what are you doing and they said they come from Calcutta for shikaar. He said all looked Hindu.'

Abdul Gaffur's voice was steady but there was a quivering deep inside. This information would spell great things for him.

Mr Johnson had already swung into action; messages were being sent out. The telephones had started ringing. Within a matter of minutes they were all there – District Magistrate Wilkinson, Deputy

Inspector General Farmer, Colonel Dallas Smith, the assistant superintendents of police, Mr Shooter and Mr Lewis, Captain Robinson, the commander of the Surma Valley Light Horse and Captain Taitt.

Mr Farmer and Mr Lewis were all for leaving right away but the colonel disagreed. 'It is unknown territory, one that the rebels know like the back of their hands and we have lost the opportunity of an attack at dusk. My advice would be to take them by surprise before dawn. Go by the manual: a company from the Eastern Frontier Rifles and one, Robinson, of yours; a Vickers section and four of the AFI's Lewis gun sections? By ten tonight, gentlemen!'

Word was sent to Dr Weldon to remain ready.

Mr Johnson turned to Abdul Gaffur and Siddique Dewan. They were to take a car immediately back to Chowdhury Hat and keep watch on Badulla Hill until the military train arrived.

Ananda Prasad Gupta, 21 April night, Dinesh's house

Ananda turned one last time. Binodini Mashima and Ranjan Meshomoshai were still at the door. He lifted his arm to wave and quickly looked away. After the second raid that afternoon, fortunately the police had targeted the house next door, they had all come to the conclusion that it was no longer a safe place to stay. Meshomoshai had given them money and his blessings. Mashima had wept openly.

'Perhaps we will never meet again in this lifetime … or see Rajat again … who knows if there is a life after this … but we will pray that in the next life we will have your company again.' They would be out of sight once they took the bend in the road, the one that would lead them to Firingee Bazaar. The city was crawling with soldiers, Meshomoshai had warned. Armed vehicles patrolled every street. He had not verbalized it, but each of the young men had understood that the targets that had once figured on their plans would be virtually unapproachable and they would, from now on, have to stick to the lesser used lanes, the narrow gullies and the shadows.

Ganesh-da had suggested a friend's name. Dinesh Chakraborty was also a member though Ananda had never met him. Ananta-da led the way: towards the jetty, past the Double Mooring station, skirting the banks of the Deba Lake and through a field of paddy that looked upon the Rail Class Quarters. He felt a hand press down on his shoulder and he sank to his knees, crouching down amongst the stalks. Jibon made his way across, nimble as a cat. Ten o'clock. The little colony was fast asleep. Jibon reappeared. Dinesh was with him. 'I will open the kitchen door. Be very quiet; it is one of Dada's nights off.'

Dinesh's dada was a junior employee in the railways and had been allotted a house. Taking his shoes off, Ananda crept in behind the others. No coughing, he kept telling himself and in the process, he scarcely breathed. The little, two bed-roomed house was centred around a courtyard, with a toilet on one side and a kitchen on the other.

The night would have to be passed in the kitchen … certainly not the best room in the house, for it was filthy. A warm clammy wall of air invited Ananda to cut through its thickness. The brothers did not believe in cooking and rarely ventured in. It was absolutely bare except for a pot of water that Dinesh thoughtfully left behind, before closing the door behind him. Some rather outsized mosquitoes buzzed noisily into action. The click of a latch sounded; a key turned in its lock. Dinesh, on the pretence of having used the toilet, had slipped back into bed.

No fan. Not even a tiny opening. Ananda scratched at the weals appearing rapidly all over his body. The thin cotton shirt did little to protect him. Until nine. He would have to endure this till nine in the morning ... until Dinesh's dada left for work.

THIRTEEN

Alexander Burnett, 22 April morning, Badulla Hill

Four a.m.: The military train pulled up at Chowdhury Hat. The machine guns were being positioned on the hills that looked down upon Badulla Pahar. Under the cover of continuous machine gunfire, a platoon of thirty Indian soldiers led by their Indian non-commissioned officers, were to advance up the hill and force the rebels out of hiding. In a pincer movement, Colonel Smith and Mr Farmer would close in with their two companies.

Badulla Pahar was captured at dawn. Then all hell broke loose. There was no one there. All that remained of the recent occupation were five jammed police muskets, ball cartridges, one police revolver, couple of blank cartridges and the remnants of a khichuri meal. They had given them the slip. Blackened their faces with ash. This untrained band of schoolboys!

Word was sent to the Hatazari police station in the north and Panchalaish Thana in the south. Scouts needed to be sent out immediately. Colonel Dallas Smith decided to remain near the site, setting up camp at Jharjharia Bot-tali while Mr Farmer returned with his men to the city. All roads leading in from the north needed watching. The entrances to the Imperial Bank, jail, and government and railway treasury buildings had to be sealed.

Alexander wondered how the good colonel would word his report once the initial anger had faded. Would he admit that the bunch of schoolboys had had the last laugh?

LOKENATH BAL, 22 APRIL MORNING, JALALABAD

'I know you are confused. I too cannot begin to think as to what might have befallen Amarendra and Diptimedha. But frustrations are a part of every endeavour.' Master-da addressed the boys. The sky was beginning to lighten and the little habitations in the distance had begun to show signs of life. The boys had been on the march since nine o'clock the previous night but the going had been slow. The khichuri sat heavy on their stomachs after a near fast of two days. Many had to stop several times during the march and had felt too sick to continue.

'You are tired. And so am I.' Master-da was in fact the only one who appeared completely unaffected. He moved with ease, whereas the others picked their way painfully and carefully in the dark, loaded as they were with their bags of ammunition and muskets, feeling with each step for that loose pebble, the root or a snake hole.

It was near dawn. Under no circumstances would they be making it to the city. In the distance, villagers had already begun moving about, vessels of water in hand, ready for the ritual jungle visits. A low hill stood right in front. It would have to do.

Quenching their thirst in a freshwater pool that lay at the base of the hill, Lokenath led the way up the slope. There were not enough trees, not as many as he would have liked. He stood surveying the area, disappointment etched deep on his face: the hill was too small and a railway track running from south-west to the east skirted the base of the hill about half a mile away. There were two other hills that were higher. Would making a dash for one of them be worth it? But there were more people about now: farmers carrying their ploughs, herding their cattle … it would be too risky; fifty-eight of them and carrying muskets … no, too risky. The boys were already sprawling on the ground.

A few unripe watermelons had been spotted and stolen. Master-da and Nirmal-da were slicing them but today there would not be enough to go round.[1] Tonight, Lokenath consoled himself, tonight will be the night.

John Younie, 22 April, Circuit House, Chittagong

The platform was crowded, mostly by squads of troops squatting on piles of kitbags and smoking. A liaison officer, sent by Wilkinson, whisked his suitcases into a waiting car.

'With the troopers in there, I'd reckon the Circuit House's about the safest place in town right now,' said the LO.

They were driving down the wide metalled road with the kutcha edge that skirted the Paltan Maidan. Shade trees lined it on both sides and lime-washed stones marked the culvert crossings over monsoon ditches that led into the compounds of the bungalows. In all, a well-laid British station. The pretty red-roofed Circuit House lay at the northern end of the green patch; he had been billeted there once before. A motor truck with six armed men passed them by.

'Them planters,' the LO jerked his head. 'Patrolling the city since Sunday; two hours on and one hour off – night and day! Banks, post office, docks.'[2]

The broad gravel drive curved through a compound darkened and cooled by trees. The colonnaded facade looked a dazzling white. A grizzled old bearer, white-uniformed, sashed and turbanned, came forward to lift the bags and beckoned to him. John followed him through the passages. Many of the wooden doors to the rooms had been left open as if the occupants had rushed off in a hurry.

But through the screen doors he caught sight of what was his worst nightmare: men in uniform sleeping with rifles chained to their wrists.

Slipping the old bearer a coin, John waved him away. The latch on the top of the screen door was just within his reach. Locking both sets of doors, he sat back heavily into a chair, conscious of the sudden cold sweat that had drenched his shirt. What he had just witnessed was a scene straight out of Peshawar, where blood feuds were the norm; where lived the treacherous and cruel Pathans; where Pax Britannica had given way to the barbarism of the Middle Ages. Soldiers, throughout the Khyber, slept with rifles chained to their wrists, for a British army rifle could fetch at least Rs 500/- across the border.[3] An involuntary shudder racked his frame. Little good had the practice achieved, for the Pathan night thief simply severed the wrist to which the chain was attached. What had driven the litigation-loving Bengali to turn his gentle green valley into a pocket edition of hell?

He had not been permitted into Chittagong until Colonel Dallas Smith had arrived with a 100 Gurkhas of the Eastern Frontier Rifles from Dacca. His boat had been carefully searched and the train that brought him in from Chandpur carried a military escort. But the family had not been granted permission to leave Barisal.

The old bearer was back, knocking at the door. He had a tray from which he took things and laid a single plate on a small table in the centre of the room. Then he produced the final item: a breakfast menu card stuck on a silver-plated stand.

'Sahib,' he said and waited patiently.

A knock at the door. A very pink, stout little man peered at him. 'Johnson,' he extended his hand.

John rose to greet the police superintendent.

'I hope you are being looked after all right,' he said, a trifle apologetically.

John assured him he was. 'Is it as bad as what I see?'

Johnson dropped into a chair. He leaned forward, his face strangely animated, 'This is the most amazing coup possible![4] A raiding party ... about 100 strong ... I must say the whole show was most marvellously organized down to the minute details. The attack commenced at 9.15, with one gang taking the police lines completely by surprise and another finding the Auxiliary Force armoury in a state of even greater unpreparedness. Wilkinson, Lodge and two others, alarmed by the firing at the police lines, rushed there in a car – all unarmed. They thought it was a riot over a marriage procession or something of that sort. They were fired at – four bullets piercing the windscreen and several the radiator. As they had no weapons there was nothing for them to do but to leg it for all they were worth. They got away in time to warn the people at the small armouries down at the jetties – apparently forgotten or overlooked by the raiders.'

'So they are using the AF rifles?'

Johnson shook his head. He looked up at the bearer. 'Coffee,' he said. 'No, not one was removed. They didn't have the time to get at the ammunition ... but they gutted both armouries ... Criminal unpreparedness on the part of the AFI ... two retired Punjabi sepoys on guard – a couple of decrepit ancients … Farrell, the sergeant major, was sitting, having dinner … went out to see what was happening and was shot dead. On their tail … been sighted once late last evening but Dallas seems to have lost them.' He looked thoughtful for a moment and added, 'We had them closely watched since Colson's visit in March. In fact, on 2nd April, I had revised the system. The movements of the suspects and all those capable of terrorist activities were being tabulated and the watchers were being supervised day and night. In fact the Baby Austin used in the raid was being closely watched. I had instructed that the plan be followed until 23rd April, but no watch was to be kept from 13th to 18th April to lull the suspects into thinking that the watch had been withdrawn. I had hoped,' Johnson winced as he said it, 'that it would induce them to give some clear indication about their intentions.'[5]

Wilkinson, the only other reliable source had far too much on his hands to sit down and make newcomers wise to things past and present. The club on the Pioneer Hill, across the street from the Circuit House, was rife with garbled accounts of the local gup and wild rumours. But one thing was certain: the large oil installations were safe.[6] It was clear that the affair had come as a shock to the government which had responded forthwith, promulgating an ordinance, reintroducing powers of detention. The state of uncertainty and disorganization that prevailed made him glad that Dorothy had stayed on at Donovan's. It would have driven her to fits, well not for her own sake but for the kiddies.

Ananda Prasad Gupta, 22 April

Maybe he had dozed off momentarily but Ananda was awake as soon as the door opened. He squinted painfully up at Dinesh, who stood silhouetted against the bright sunlight.

'Tell me.' His voice seemed to boom after the silence of the night. 'What do you need?'

'A bath.' Ganesh-da said, languidly stretching his arms, refusing to get up from his semi-reclining position.

'Tea and toast,' said Ananta-da.

The dhabas – little hotels in the neighbourhood – did a brisk business, making most of the bachelor status of their clients. The hot, sweet drink made Ananda feel human again. At last, the others were beginning to make sense. A city in the grip of the army … what could possibly be done with it? How could they harass the British and their army? The revolution's army had not yet entered the city … were they planning on a base in the hills and guerrilla-styled attacks? If that was indeed the plan, then Ananta-da, Ganesh-da and Lokenath-da – the three most known faces – needed to remove themselves to Kolkata. The idea that generated the most excitement was the new plan being discussed – take a British official hostage … maybe the Bengal laat sahib, perhaps the chief secretary or the chief presidency magistrate, and hold him in a house, one that had been mined. There would be guards with electric switches and revolvers and a ransom note: Leave Bharat or your officer dies.

Dinesh went out to buy lunch. Ananda slept a little. It had been decided they would leave for Kolkata in the evening. Dinesh was to bring a change of clothes, oil, soap, a safety razor, an umbrella, a ghoti – a brass water pot – and a hurricane lantern. All the articles had to look old and used; Ananta-da had stressed the fact again and again.

Suresh De, 22 April, 11 a.m., Jalalabad

The heat of the morning seemed to make every living thing wilt. By the time the discussions had come to a close, the hillside was close to burning up. This had to be the worst April that he could remember. Suresh winced and put his blistered fingers into his mouth. The musket barrel was hot; he would have to remember not to touch the metallic portions. Worst possible hill to have chosen … forget about streams, there is not even a puddle, he was grumbling silently to himself, when he spied Pundit-da's group. They were eating. Gross! A hiccup of disgust rose to his throat. Subodh Bal was actually laughing. They were sitting around in a circle – Saroj, Bon Bihari, Aswini and Sitaram. Pundit-da's four-day-old underwear, which had carried the remnants of yesterday's unsalted khichuri, formed the centre piece. A few others sauntered across to join them. Pundit-da was waving out to him. 'Sadhu rey … Come, Sadhu, come.' Suresh flashed him a grin but did not budge.

It was time for the second group of lookouts to take up their positions. Subodh left the khichuri circle and shading his brow with his hand took position behind a bush. Hemendu Dastidar, Madhusudan Dutt, Krishna Choudhury, Shanti Nag and Noni Deb went to their positions.

Suresh returned to his brooding. His saliva was turning into thick strands caking at the corner of his mouth. What would Ma be doing now? What would she say if she could see her Sadhu this way? He scraped a fingernail along the edges of his eyes. She would not have left the temple precincts these last four days, even if they closed the door on her. He could see her, her long hair open and uncombed, lying on the ground beating her breasts. If he had been starving these last couple of days, he could be more than certain that not a morsel had passed her lips. So deep was he in his picture, that he saw the priest close a door, shutting out the light that streamed from the inner sanctum and a darkness envelope both him and his mother.

Master-da and Nirmal-da were eating. He looked again carefully. They were chewing on the green skins of watermelons. With a start he realized, it was the bits they had thrown away … Master-da was eating their eto. It was sinful. Not their eto! Master-da shouldn't have contaminated himself so. Surreptitiously he touched both his earlobes, pleading silently for forgiveness. The thirst; it is all in the mind, he told himself. Shutting his eyes, he forced himself to think of the banana shoots he had chewed on yesterday. They were cool and green. The outer layers could be peeled away like an onion and who would have guessed that the inner pith held so much fluid? His head rested on his knees and he straightened up in a hurry … his nose was far too close to his armpits for his own comfort. It was good that Ma could not see him now.

There had been a scuffle. Shanti and Hemendu[7] were clambering up the slope.

'Krishna had seen them first … two naked villagers … they had nothing but their gamchhas on. They were behind a tree, looking at us and whispering.' Hemendu was gasping. 'Krishna pointed them out to me. I did not think. I ran and jumped on the two of them. Shanti was close behind me and he leapt on top of them too. We gave them a good shaking … we could have broken a couple of their bones …

they were so unbelievably skinny. They were crying, cringing ... said they hadn't meant to disturb us, they were here to collect firewood ... the children had not eaten since yesterday.'

'They looked completely harmless,' Shanti added. He was looking flustered. 'I asked them who had sent them and if they had any news of the rebels. I said we were a police party searching for the vidrohis. But the moment we loosened our hold they moved with such speed that they tumbled down the hillside as if their lives depended on it. I called out to them, offering a reward if they could bring news of the fools, but they were just intent on getting away.'

Nearly everybody had gathered around and was listening attentively. They had let the cowherd go the day before, but that was because it had been late afternoon and they would have been vacating Badulla Hill within a matter of hours ... at least, long before he could go and report to a police station, had he so wished. But this incident had taken place too early in the day. It was the extreme poverty of these villagers that was to be feared. This is what the enemy preyed upon. Of course, these could also turn out to be just ordinary villagers who would go home and mind their own business or ... A serious debate was taking place inside Suresh's head.

Master-da put an end to his train of thoughts. 'No matter how poor, the enemy's spies are our enemies. They should have been tied up.' He remained thoughtful for a moment and then said, 'It is a bad omen, not that a revolutionary should fear Saturdays and Tuesdays, but I think it is best we gear up.'

Loka-da turned to the groups and the boys sat down in little circles with the group leaders. The muskets and firearms were re-cleaned, rechecked and lubricated until the machinery worked perfectly. All screws, nuts and bolts were tightened, checked and rechecked. They went through the motions of the drills, revised the principles of throwing hand grenades and readjusted their uniforms. Would the date with destiny take place here or would it be tonight in Chattogram?

Loka-da addressed the boys. The Students' Union leader had always made the most of his gift for capturing the attention of the young ones. 'Soldiers of the revolution,' he began, 'I smell battle in the air. Our chance to vanquish this Dushshashan has come. There is no alternative but to win this battle if we do not wish to be remembered as the laughing stock. Remind yourselves: the moment and circumstance of our deaths had been determined in the very instant that we drew our first breath …'

The pep talk was cut short. The lookouts had spotted something. Subodh Roy's keen eyes had not missed the movement on the hill on the far side. A man appeared to be waving something … his shirt most probably. Mona – Monoranjan – had seen him too and pointed him out to the leaders. Suresh looked at the sky. It was approximately two o'clock. Would destiny still wait to meet them in the city?

Hem Gupta, 22 April

The taxi rattled over the six miles of kutcha road that led back from Jharjharia Bot-tali towards Chittagong. Sub-inspector Hem Gupta and Sub-inspector Mohidar Ali were hurrying back. Between them sat a nervous-looking villager who would testify that the news sent in by Sub-inspector Fazlur Rehman of the Panchalaish Thana around noon was correct. The man had more to add. The extra information was being verified right at that moment by Sub-inspector Abdur Rahim.

By 3.30 p.m. they were in Mr Johnson's room. The police superintendent was standing, the villager cowering and Hem Gupta trying to lend him courage through a vice-like grip on the scrawny arm. It was not every day that a simple villager came face-to-face with a full-blown Englishman.

'Dekho, hum bahut khush hua tumhara upar.'

'The English babu is very happy with you,' Hem Gupta whispered encouragingly into the man's ear. 'He will give you a big reward.'

'Agar tumhara pata such hua tumko sarkar bahut inam dega.' Saying this Mr Johnson reached into his pocket, pulled out a ten rupee note and thrust it into the man's hands and sprang back. He was trying not to stand too close to him for fear of intimidating him further. The man, overcome by a bout of shivering, was unable to look at the amount he had just received.

'You will get even more when the government reward comes.'

A weak smile fluttered on his lips, but still unable to raise his eyes, he whispered, 'Jo hukum … whatever the orders.'

Mr Johnson indicated that he be made to sit down. Hem Gupta led him to a bench. A peon rushed in with some water. In a while, he was calmer.

Overcoming his initial excitement, Mr Johnson adopted a kinder tone and tried looking him in the eye. 'Tum jo dekha sab such such batao … tell us truthfully what it was that you saw exactly.'

The man was ready to swoon but Johnson put up his hand. 'Jhoot mut bolo aur zyada bhi mut bolo … don't tell us lies and tell us no more than what you actually saw. Abhi batao.'

The man spoke a mix of Hindi and the Chittagong dialect. 'Ai aar hamara bandhu mili abhi dekha hitara pahar mey boitey hai … A friend and I saw them sitting on a hill.'

'How many? Kitna?'

'Ponchas shaat manoosh hoga, sahib.'

'Fifty or sixty.' Hem Gupta translated, helpfully.

'Sabka paas banduk hai?'

'Banduk …?' Hem Gupta pointed towards his own firearm.

'Haath mey aachhey aar ek jagah mey dhal korey rakha.'

'They are armed, sir.' Hem Gupta confirmed.

'Tumhara pura pata hai aur koi aadmi doosri jagah mey chhipa nahi hai … Are you sure there are no other groups hidden in the vicinity?'

'Indi oondi dekha magar chokhey nahi para … I looked around but did not see anyone else.' The man was feeling more relaxed now. His eyes never left the Englishman's face and his smile widened until his teeth hung out.

The sahib reached out and patted him, taking care not to let more than just the tips of his fingers to come in contact with his skin. 'Theek hai. Tum police kay saat jao. Ghabrao mut. Theek jagah sahib log ko deekha dena.'

What a day it had been for this pathetic creature beside him, thought Hem Gupta as he made his way to Chowdhury Hat to keep Colonel Smith and the DIG informed … a chance encounter that appeared to be a close shave with certain death was turning out to be a lucrative proposition. Ten rupees … it was unlikely that he had seen such an amount in a long time. But it was the police that could boast of the real windfall, for if anyone knew the lie of the land better, it was this creature.

Ananta Lal Singh, 22 April

Ananda sat, his lips held tightly between his teeth. Ananta scraped away at the upper lip with a razor, depriving Ananda of the silken fuzz that had been so carefully nurtured these last couple of months and admired in every glass pane or strip of mirror that came his way.

'Aashbey aashbey, baba … it will come back thicker and luxurious.'

The youngster pretended not to care.

'The trouble with you,' said Ananta, 'is this baby-soft peaches-and-cream complexion. Now remember that you are younger than you actually are … you are a school student and my sister's son, and I am a motor-car broker. Stand up now; I will tie your dhuti for you.'

Ananta wound the yards of the soft fabric skilfully around Ananda's waist securing it tightly. It would not come off while running and most of all it wouldn't reveal the two loaded pistols at the waist.

'Now no one knows they are there and neither do you. Your face must reflect what you are … a simple harmless boy unaware of the ways of the world.'

He plied a comb, coaxing a new parting out of Ananda's hair and stepped back to take in the effect.

Ganesh-da had, in the meantime, denuded his own face and taken to doing the same to Jibon's. A more youthful rounded face, burdened by large spectacles emerged. His new identity was that of a clerk, one who had begun working only the other day.

'Makhon rey, you have remained as soft as the butter your mother named you after,' Ananta-da teased, as he turned his attentions to Jibon. 'Ganesh has volunteered to be your kaka and he is a businessman. Now, the two of you walk up and down this room.'

Ananda and Jibon looked up surprised.

'Yes. Yes … perform,' said Ananta. 'I want to see if you can walk comfortably … and not scurry like two fugitives. I will have a bad back and will shuffle slightly … not too much though. All right then, let us recite our names, our father's names and the names of our villages.'

He ran his hand along the ledge of a window and examined the dirt on his fingers.

'The art of war,' he said, streaking this new acquisition along the back of his neck and behind his ears, 'is the art of deception.'

JOHN YOUNIE, 22 APRIL

'The insurgents have been spotted. They are five miles away.' The cry rang through the Circuit House. The enemy was advancing on the city. The taxis were ready at the gates.

John left for the club as soon as he had seen the troopers off. The women and children were being herded in and a division of the Assam Bengal Railway Rifles was taking up position around the premises. The band struck up a cheery tune as mothers and nursemaids soothed the little ones. Mrs Johnson, the police superintendent's wife, bustled around, organizing with a firm hand. She was a big, high-bosomed woman, with a round healthy face and a mass of curls that peeped from under her hat. Hers was a commanding presence and with Mrs Taitt by her side, the two women ensured that everyone kept calm and the children were fed. The English memsahib's adaptability! But thank God, Wilkinson had warned him against bringing the family.

A car brought Wilkinson and Johnson in from the Panchalaish Thana. It had been some years since he had last met with Wilkinson. Tall and lean, he had always cut a fine figure, one that he had worn with a faintly apologetic air. But today, the harrowed expression and the hollows beneath the eyes caught at John's heart. He shook his hand silently and led him to a chair. Wilkinson, he had learnt, had not returned home since the night of the raid.

'Three trucks and ten taxis have left via Ranger Road,' said Johnson. 'They tend to call it Rajpath nowadays.'

John pictured the route in his head … left turn onto the Bayezid Bostami Road and they would enter the hills.

'The reserve force should be boarding the train this very minute.' The hands on Johnson's wristwatch were poised to strike 4.30. 'They will be in Jalalabad in another twenty-five minutes.

'Taitt!' A flicker of exasperation flitted across Wilkinson's face. 'The man is outright obnoxious. But I was firm with him. He has to bring them back; dead or alive, but bring them back he must.'

'And he was ready with his usual answer: "I know those Bengali kuttas; I will break their teeth today,"' said Johnson wearily. 'But I was having none of his cocky attitude. Clean up before you come back, I told him.'

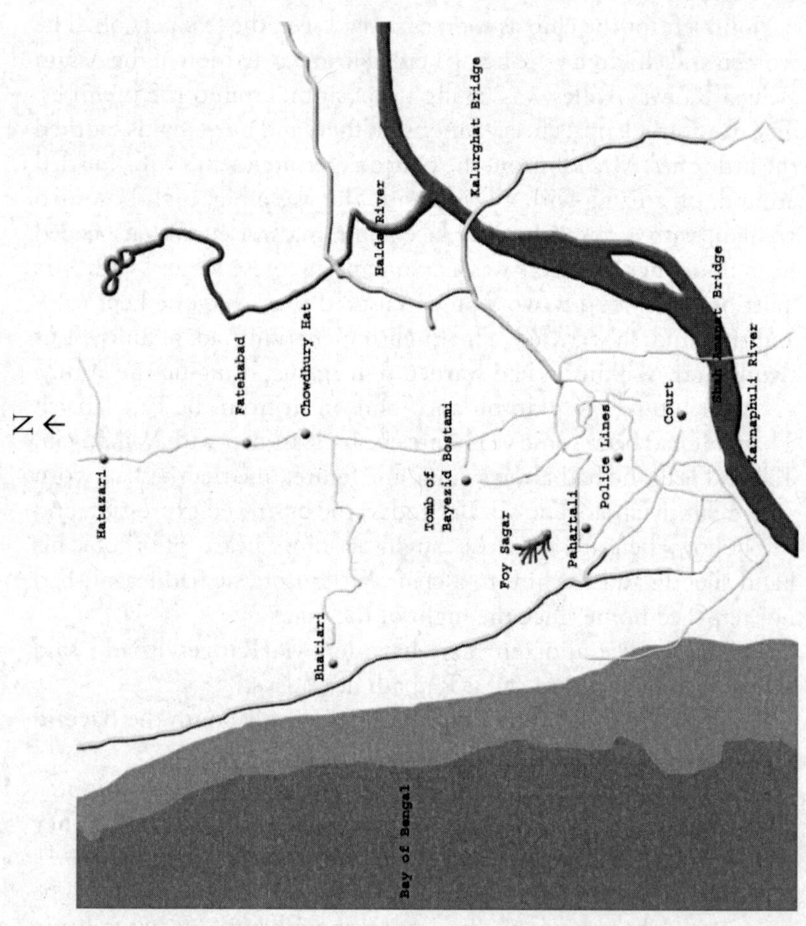
N
Hatazari
Fatehabad
Chowdhury Hat
Halda River
Kalurghat Bridge
Tomb of Bayezid Bostami
Foy Sagar
Pahartali
Police Lines
Court
Karnaphuli River
Bhatiari
Bay of Bengal

The gist of it, John gathered, was that the rebels were isolated on the top of a small hill called Jalalabad. Captain Taitt, the AFI adjutant was to lead from the front. His forces, which included the troopers, were to split into three. One unit of fifty men would crawl up the hillside, either without being seen or under the fire cover provided by their comrades, and force a surrender. Colonel Dallas Smith and Mr Farmer would take up positions to the north-east and south-west of the hill respectively, remain out of direct line of vision and prevent the rebels from escaping.

SURESH DE, 22 APRIL

For the past two-and-a-half hours, the revolutionaries had waited for a move. Eyes scanning the horizon and a sense of excitement bubbling over.

'Ambika-da.' Nirmal-da made his voice audible for all the others to listen. 'Ambika-da, now that we will probably die, does it not make you crave for a cup of hot tea and a plate of sizzling chops and cutlets?'

It made everyone laugh.

'I think my boys are more ravenous for a taste of battle than a taste of cutlets.'

'What are you saying, Ambika-da?' Bidhu-da called out. 'I could eat my cutlet and fight.'

The boys were sitting around in their groups.[8] There were eight of them, each with its own leader. The first and second were to take charge of the front line and it was the job of the third and fourth to support the first two. The fifth and sixth were positioned a little higher on the slope and were posted as lookouts. The seventh and the eighth remained on the highest part of the hill, keeping guard on all directions, ready to rush to the aid of whichever side was attacked first.

Now and then, a snatch of conversation caught Suresh's ear. There was an excited chatter taking place in low voices. He knew most of his compatriots by now at least by name.

'Is there any possibility of taking the city after wandering about the hills for four days? The enemy would have secured it by now.'

Madhusudan's voice was grave. 'Why dwell on mistakes? Raise the flag of valour on the graves of these very mistakes.'

Sahayram and Moti huddled together. They were classmates from the Collegiate School and had appeared for their matriculation examinations. Moti had Mihir Bose's father's rifle with him. Mihir had come and handed it over to him but had failed to show up. What could have happened to him and what would he say to his father? What would the police do to them?

Subodh Roy sauntered in to join the group.

'Worthless talk,' he said smugly. 'Of course the owner will be tortured.' Subodh had been asked for his father's rifle on the morning of 18 April and had removed it with a duplicate key. He had handed it over to Ganesh Ghosh by lunchtime. In the evening, he had reported to the Congress office and had discovered that he was in a group of seven, deputed to carry haversacks with cartridges, a tin of oil and a dagger.[9]

'Haldighati,' said someone. 'We are writing the script for a second Haldighati today. The British will outnumber us five to a man.'

But Tripura's group was sitting in absolute silence. Deboprasad-da had his lips pursed. Tegra had traced a message for them with his finger in the dry dust: DEATH.

A train was passing by. The faint chuff-chuff was growing louder and soon puffs of black smoke rose above the trees. The Nazir Hat branch line passed close to the hill. Then it stopped. And Suresh's heart thumped. The screeching of the brakes was audible enough. Why was it stopping when there was no station here? In fact there was no station, big or small until Chowdhury Hat, which was about two miles away? The meaning was not lost on him. It was close to five o'clock. The moment of reckoning had arrived.

A strange calm had descended on Master-da. He had been sitting a little apart from the rest. He looked across towards Loka-da who got up, from where he had been sitting with Bidhu-da, Naresh-da, Ambika-da and Nirmal-da, and ran to him. Suresh saw Master-da place an arm around his shoulders.

Lokenath Bal, 22 April

'Boloon. What is it, Master-da?'

'You can appreciate my position at this moment. At this most important juncture when we have to prove ourselves, Ananta and Ganesh are lost to us. I had counted on them to get us through these situations.' He turned to look Lokenath in the eye. 'But a new hope has arisen within me. I have you. And I know what I am saying … the responsibility that should have been shared by three people is now all yours. None of us,' he said indicating the top leadership, 'have what it takes. The lives of these boys, the honour of this venture depends entirely on you.'

It was something that Lokenath had been expecting all along: this long picnic in the hills could not have ended in any other way. And for a long time now he had suspected that the two military commanders had somehow slipped away. I will not lose, he told himself, and nor will there be a question of retreat. 'Master-da,' he said, 'give me your blessing.' Lokenath bent to take the dust of the older man's feet.

Master-da placed a hand on his head. 'Infuse our troops with your qualities – the sharpness of your mind, the belief in the power of your body. Show India the way to independence.'

A single sharp command was all it took to send his boys running to take up their respective positions. Lokenath, Master-da, Ambika-da and Nirmal-da remained at the highest point in the centre. In addition, fifty pairs of eyes scanned the base of the hill.

'Remember,' Lokenath called out, 'even the best strategy in the world will find it impossible to overcome determination.'

Then they saw them: shapes in the distance taking little running jumps and crouching amongst the paddy. Then nothing. And then another blur of movement. Naresh was the first to verbalize it: 'Many, many soldiers running towards us in broad daylight. They are either too confident or they think we are engrossed in playing cards.'

Or, thought Lokenath, their commander is afraid of the dark. He wants to wind up before any surprises can be thrown at him.

Ambika-da, who was concentrating on the numbers said, 'Looks like a trap for tigers.'

Master-da was in agreement. 'Jalalabad today is no less than a diamond mine.'

The soldiers had crossed the paddy field and had merged into the green of the jungle below.

Rajat who was at the highest point, called out in a loud whisper. 'Here they come.'

They could be seen now, darting up the slope in short bursts, taking cover behind the bushes. They were clearly visible now – short, stocky men with broad chests and powerful arms carrying rifles. Through the branches and leaves planted on the helmets one could see the faces. A Gurkha regiment had sent its men.

Conscious of his rising heartbeat, Lokenath realized that the eastern portion of the hill had been completely surrounded. A sudden commotion behind him made him turn his head. Master-da had been just in time to stop ten boys from bolting. 'Now is not the time,' he said. 'Leave the hill now and you will throw yourselves directly into their path.' He raised his voice, 'General Bal! Take charge!'

'Take positions … extended line … lie down … ready … do not fire until the command is given. The battle will begin in minutes. Let us remind ourselves of the treachery of Clive, the Jallianwala Bagh massacre, the 200 years of inhuman British rule. There is no mercy, no feelings, no forgiveness. An eye for an eye, a tooth for a tooth; we want blood. We will fight bravely and embrace death … abichalito chittey driro hastey shotrukey kothin aaghat korbo, we will break their morale … their defeat is assured … long live revolution.'

The army chanted in one voice, 'Jibon mrityu payer bhritto chitto bhabonahin.' It was a low rumble that echoed through the hill past every tree and fluttered amongst their leaves.

Suresh De, 22 April, 5.30 p.m.

A trink sounded. The enemy had fitted their bayonets.

'Nearly halfway up now.' Naresh-da's voice could be heard.

'Halt!' The word boomed across the slopes. It produced a visible effect on the crouching soldiers. Lokenath-da's voice was deep and powerful, one that would outrival any British drill sergeant's voice. 'Fire! Volley Fire!'

Suresh had been chafing all this while, with his finger on the trigger and his eye on his chosen target, for this command. The musket roared. The recoil hit him sharply along the ribs, but despite the smoke that had welled up at its mouth, he had the distinct thrill of having got his man. Volley after volley was being fired. Like him, the others had been waiting for this moment. The Gurkha army was beginning to fall apart before his eyes. Not easy to stand on a slope and fire upwards is it? He sniggered as the words flitted through his head. A Gurkha turned and ran. He ignited a stampede.

'Fire! Fire! Fire! There is no forgiveness. Destroy them all.'

Within seconds, the organized ascent had fallen into disarray. Some soldiers lay, making no attempt to move; others ran screaming for their lives, abandoning their weapons. The seconds slowed down, elongating as if with a fascination for detail. Limping, trailing their useless limbs, the enemy tumbled downwards making its way through the hail of bullets; some not even bothering to pick themselves up until they were back within the cover of the undergrowth.

Around him, the hilltop erupted with cries of triumph; pride and hate mingled into one voice: 'Ingrez die … down with the British … Long live revolution … Bande Mataram!'

Suresh had rushed with the others to the eastern edge of the hill, holding up his rifle, shaking it furiously as if it were a spear, hurling abuses. 'Why don't you fight, you British dogs? Shame on you, you British brigands, tyrants, traitors! Why are your white masters hiding? You scoundrels. You rascals. Murderers. Bloodsuckers. Down with you … you dogs. To hell with you!' The words rolled off his tongue with ease.

He could see the last of them at the far end of the paddy field jumping into the nalla where the officers waited. Heads bobbed up and down about him trying to throw the voices as far into the distance as possible. The words 'dogs' and 'British' were being enunciated with particular care. Some hugged each other. Someone began to sing '*Bolo beer cheero unnato maumo sheer*' and though many joined in, it was a tuneless effort.

'Look at them,' said Nirmal-da. 'Such powerful bodies, days of wrestling and bodybuilding invested in them, ultra-modern weapons, war experience and …' He turned to Ambika-da hugging him, 'our boys beat them.'

A bugle sounded. It drew everybody's attention, for it was the most quavering tuneless piece they had ever heard. All eyes were drawn to the nalla in the distance. And though it was nearing sunset, three

Tommies were distinctly visible beside the bugler. The body language was unmistakable: the cringing bugler, the gesticulating Tommie, the soldiers picking themselves up and limping across. They were taking up their positions again.

'Taitt.' Suresh heard Loka-da mutter.

There was some action beginning again. More men were in the formation this time. The bugle and drums sounded and the Gurkha war cry rent the air: 'Chaloho, Baroho, Maar!' A blaze of rapid fire and they emerged from the drain taking the rice field on the double.

'Positions!' Loka-da called.

Suresh lay down and took aim. Not even a span of five to seven minutes had passed since the last gun battle had ended. A British officer was running along with the front line, a second was gesticulating wildly at those in the middle. 'Swine. Rascal,' The words floated up to the hilltop. A third brought up the rear. Nearly a whole company was attempting to run up the hill, under the cover of gunfire from the nalla. The eastern sky was a deep shade of red and the glitter of the bayonets hypnotizing.

'Aashchhey.'

The call from the front line broke the spell. Master-da came up to the edge to take a look. 'Shiny weapons,' he said, 'are useful for inducing fear, but have little use in war. Remember, they are in the hands of mercenaries who are aware that they are fighting a battle that is not their own … a battle against their own people.'

The soldiers were entering the musket range. Loka-da's voice rang out. 'Fire!'

Suresh saw a line of Gurkhas go down on one knee. They took aim and their guns flashed.

'Fire!' Loka-da called again. A burst of musket fire followed Loka-da's command. 'Load! Fire!'

Return fire came up the slope again. The slopes of green Jalalabad echoed with the sound of muskets and exploding grenades.

But from their vantage point on top of the hill, concealed behind bushes, it was clear that it was their bullets that were scoring. Finding it impossible to advance, the enemy turned back again. Master-da raised the battle cry: 'Bande Mataram!' It was taken up by all who heard him.

ANANDA PRASAD GUPTA, 22 APRIL, 6.30 P.M.

Four villagers made their way down the Trunk Road, battered old umbrellas in hand and beddings rolled up in shataranjis. They were walking quickly, for it was already sundown and they had a long eight miles ahead if they were to catch the eight o'clock train from Bhatiari station. A youngster walked ahead, a hurricane lamp, as yet unlit, swinging from his hand.

An elderly figure straggling behind, sank to the ground wheezing. The youngster who had been walking ahead turned back anxiously. The lantern was lit and after a few minutes of rest, they got up again.

A bus stood by the side of the road, its khaki-clad occupants taking a tea break. They patrolled the Trunk Road, the tarmac and the dirt portions, all ninety miles of it up to Chandpur. Few lorries or buses plied this route during the day and by night it was more or less deserted.

As the four travellers approached the bus, the strains of the youngster's song floated on ahead on the night air: '*Krishno kalo tomal kalo tai to tomal bhalo.*' The Chattogram lilt lent its own comforting charm to this all-time favourite. They stopped for a bit before the bus. One held up the lantern and the elderly man craned his neck forward, a beedi trembling at his lips. Another held out the one that he had been smoking. The sallow stubbly cheeks, illuminated in the yellow light, sucked away until a glow appeared at the end. Satisfied, he drew in a lungful, holding onto it, eyes closed in bliss till the others nudged him on.

The singing was picked up again and Ananda's soulful tune lingered on the warm night breeze long after he was gone.

SURESH DE, 22 APRIL, JALALABAD

The red had gone out of the sky. It was past 6.30 and they were still waiting anxiously for the next move. Fifteen minutes passed in deafening silence. Then the bugle sounded in the nalla and the soldiers at the bottom of the hill fired a couple of rounds. All that was visible was the smoke that indicated the position of the soldiers.

The revolutionaries aimed their muskets and fired back and instantly all hell broke loose. A gunner standing high up on the south-east hill found what he was looking for – musket smoke. The machine gun fired a round upon Jalalabad.

'Enemy on the south-east hill. Aim. Ten rounds rapid fire.'

Twenty to twenty-five muskets fired back and the machine gun responded with a hail of bullets. A second machine gun on the north-east hill kicked into action. Branches flew about; pieces of bark shaved off by the onslaught came whizzing through the air. Trees grew pale by the minute, as bark was whittled off at high speed.

'No more firing.' Loka-da called in a low voice. 'All eyes focus on the hills. Look for movement. Fire only when you see movement.' He turned to Master-da. 'You need to take responsibility for the north-east side. The boys must remain alert … really alert. Nirmal-da, take charge of the south-east side. Remember, they are all hungry and very thirsty. They cannot lose their concentration now.'

The magazine belt[10] must have been taken off and a fresh one installed, for the gun on the south-east hill began to fire again. The bullets were ripping into Jalalabad, slashing it to shreds, tearing up clumps of earth where they struck. It was impossible to move. A mist hung low over the hill, one that smelt of pungent gunpowder, and the earth thundered below him. How long could they continue? Now a third machine gun, located in the nalla below, pounded into action.

'Do not move … do not raise your heads … their bullets are going waste … they will not hit you if you do not move.' Loka-da's voice came in every time there was a pause.

For Suresh in the front line, even the slightest motion was impossible. The musket barrel was growing really hot … it was impossible to touch it, let alone take aim. He had managed to pull off his shirt. That helped to hold the musket steady. Now the cartridge could no longer be forced into the chamber. He had fired no more that ten rounds since the last time he had cleaned it, but despite the smokeless black powder that was being used, it had jammed again. He would have to wait until the barrel cooled. But then again, did he dare sit up? The slightest movement seemed to be attracting gunfire. These police muskets were simply not meant for prolonged firing, he sighed.

'Keep up a controlled firing … take turns in firing … enough to let them know we are still around.' Loka-da's voice could be heard.

'Else,' Suresh completed Loka-da's meaning in his head, 'they will come up for that bayonet charge.' He was looking directly at the south-east hill. The mouth of the machine gun glowed through the mist every time it fired.

Behind the front line, the boys were taking turns. While one cleaned his musket, the other fired. He rested his head on the ground. It had been a while since his musket had packed up. There was now practically no return fire from their side. Someone shouted at him to pass him the tin of kerosene oil. It lay by his side along with the cleaning rod and the steel puff. It was of little use to him now that he was frozen in this position. He rolled the tin backwards. The endless hail of bullets was disorienting. The only things that registered were the periodic silences but of them he had lost count

'Mushkil aashan!' The triumphant cry broke through. The voice was Nirmal-da's. He guessed he was behind a bush somewhere. Something moved beside him – a figure in white dragging himself on his chest. It was Master-da holding out a freshly cleaned musket. The cartridge slid in and Suresh took aim ignoring the movement in his peripheral vision. Master-da was moving away, rapidly snaking his way across. That single red glow on the opposite hill had a mesmerizing effect. It had grown in size, looming over them.

Someone stepped across him. Tegra who had been on his right was now to his left. Horror and fascination kept his eyes glued to the small figure as it jumped up, took aim, fired and flung itself back on the ground. Tegra inched forward on his chest, jumped up and took aim again. He was still standing, when a cluster of bullets hit him. One moment he was silhouetted against the night sky, his white dhuti fluttering about his legs, and in the next he was a heap on the ground. He heard him call out, 'Master-da, bidai. Shona Bhai, aami chollam … tora chaliye ja. Britishder kachhey matha neechu korbi na.'

'Tora chaliye ja.' Tegra's last words to Loka-da, to his Shona Bhai. His words had been drowned in the gunfire but everyone had seen him fall. They knew he had bidden them farewell and encouraged them to carry on.

'Tegra has fallen … long live Tegra … long live revolution.'

Suresh turned his head to the right, to where Tegra had been. The place was occupied by Probhash Bal. But Probhash lay facing the sky, clutching his musket to his chest. There was that quick wriggling motion again and Master-da was prying the dead fingers off the weapon.

'Here' Suresh heard him say. 'Put it to good use.'

'The lever is jammed.' The voice was Bon Bihari's. Then a click; it had slid into place. The blood that had seeped in from Probhash's wounds was probably working as lubricant.

It must be well past an hour since the machine guns had taken over. Suresh got up on his knees and crawled ahead for a better view. There was Bidhu-da – Bidhu Bhattacharya – he could see him now. He was standing up and firing. He moved past Tripura Sen, who had taken cover behind a bush. He was badly wounded but still firing away.

'Keep going … it's not too long now,' Suresh heard him call out. Fellow revolutionaries he could not identify lay unmoving. These last 15 – 20 minutes seemed to be claiming more lives than before. The mouth of the machine gun glowed. A shadowy figure beside it could just be made out. Suresh went down on one knee and took careful aim. The figure appeared again, outlined against the red glow.

Bidhu-da's voice came floating across. He was still laughing.

'Arrey! Aar koto haadaabi … how many will you pump into me. Why not fire at my chest?'

Lokenath Bal, 22 April, Jalalabad

'Shona Bhai!' Lokenath had not failed to hear that cry. The battle was at such a pitch that it was impossible to get up. So much as even raising one's head got one shot, but the initial nervousness had long passed and his commands were going unheeded. Irritation and anguish flooded through him. The little one was dying, the one for whom Ma had pleaded and wept, the one who had deceived her at that last moment by changing out of uniform and then jumping out of the window when her back was turned. He could see her now smiling down at her lusty infant, clicking her tongue … it was the only sound that soothed the baby. He could remember that – imitating his mother; peering at the new little brother through the veil of hair that cascaded down from his mother's head. It was because of the clicking sound that they called him Tegra. Lokenath brushed away burning tears that had appeared unbidden. 'There is no Shona Bhai here,' he muttered. 'Learn to die like a man.'

Tripura had been hit. He had been firing away like a madman at one point and now he lay still. And now there was Deboprasad Gupta ducking behind trees, dropping to his knees. Fifteen steps! He had taken nearly fifteen steps to make it to Tripura's side. Lokenath watched in disbelief as Debu knelt, unbuttoned the battle jacket and gazed at the shattered chest with tears rolling down his face. Buttoning the jacket up, Debu stood up to give his friend a soldier's salute and made his way carefully back. It was a side to him that Lokenath had never guessed existed. Ambika-da sent word round. No more slogans to the dead … it only gave away information.

A lull in the fighting once again. Two hours had gone by since the battle had begun and vision had been reduced to grey blurred shapes. Nothing seemed to be happening and then the bugle sounded. The British were retreating. He waited, too stunned to believe it. But then came the sound … a train letting off steam … it was pulling out.

The hillside erupted with joy: Bande Mataram! Down with the British! Down with imperialism! It was unbelievable. The British had retreated.

A machine gun[11] on the north-east hill began to fire. It began to deliver the most fearsome round of all. The hillside was being torn up. Great clods of earth blew up into dust before his eyes.

'I am hit! I am hit!' The young voice belonged to fourteen-year-old Nirmal Lala who had jumped up the moment the bullet struck. All eyes were on him instantly. 'Lie down, lie down.' He lay down obediently. 'Bande Mataram,' Lokenath heard him say. Saroj Kanti Guha who lay right beside him was too shocked to move but Debu was up yet again. Through the haze of dust and smoke, Lokenath saw Debu crawl towards Nirmal. He was the youngest amongst the revolutionaries, younger than Tegra, a village boy he knew nothing about. Debu cradled his head on his lap murmuring soft comforting words, running his hands over his forehead and on his chest. Lokenath turned to his musket again. Did Nirmal register Debu's comforting presence, he wondered. Could Debu make up for the mother who was not by his side in these last moments?

With Nirmal's death, a kind of madness set in. Binod Bihari Dutt flung aside his musket and leapt up with his revolver. He was pacing before the others, 'There is no forgiveness, no forgiveness; we want blood, we want blood!'

Kali Kinkar De, whose position was beside him, kept pleading for him to lie down. It had no effect until Lokenath barked at him in a cold voice. 'Lie down right now and take your position. There is no place for madness on a battlefield.'

Bidhu's malarkey had ceased to be funny. 'Haadaaichey etokhuney haadaaichey … They have pierced me, they have pierced me … Naresh chollam … tomarey receive korum … waiting to receive you.' Naresh went crazy. He jumped up only to become the next victim.

There was a continuous motion about them: bullets bringing in a rush of hot air, in which swirled fragments of wood and bark. A youngster, within Lokenath's line of vision convulsed and lay still.

'Orey, tor ki holo rey?'

'Lokenath-da, I am hit.' He was a handsome well-built youth, one that did not fall prey to fear easily.

'Pick up your musket. Fire up your revolutionary spirit. It's nothing but a piece of wood.' Lokenath's reassurance worked like magic. It no longer mattered whether they got off the hill alive – that machine gun on the north-east hill had to be put out. 'Fire. Fire. Fire. Do not stop firing. Silence that gun.' Lokenath dragged himself closer to the edge. The flash of the machine gun had grown smaller. It had moved out of the musket range.

A bullet sliced through Binod Bihari Dutt's scapula. He was soaked instantly in blood. But Binod did not die. He continued firing. Let life go if it had to be done but that enemy machine gun had to be put out …

'Ambika-da has fallen … we want revenge.' He craned his head backwards for a glimpse. Ardhendu who had moved up was immediately behind him. He lay clutching his abdomen and through his fingers, Lokenath saw the unmistakable sheen of bowels. The bandages and the sticking plaster, the raw burn wounds, the gleam of intestines. Bile rose in Lokenath's throat. His chest was near bursting … if only he could have had a sip of water. The water carriers were all empty by now.

'Loka-da, I have a green mango.' Quick Silver Pulin, who lay beside him, chin glued to his musket, called out. Pulin's admiration for him was no secret. Being held in awe was the one thing all youth leaders took in their stride. Lokenath shook his head. 'Hold onto it. We will share it.'

The machine gun paused. The cartridge belt was being changed. It was time to put that mango to use. He turned his head and called out to Pulin. The boy arched his back and froze in the act, caught in the sudden burst of fire. Lokenath stared in horror as the convulsing form struck the ground and a mangled hand reached out to him. For the first time that evening the tears came streaming down. Laying his musket aside he dragged himself across. With great care, so that Pulin would feel no pain, he opened the bloodied fist. Making no attempt to wipe it clean, Lokenath looked directly into the young boy's eyes as he bit into the precious mango.

Ananda Prasad Gupta, 22 April

'Four third-class tickets; Number 3, Up Mail.'

Two bright spots of colour rose to Ananda's cheeks as he paid for the tickets to Laksham Junction. The request for tickets to Kumilla had brought the stationmaster to the window. He had stared, as the clerk curtly announced that there was no provision for tickets from Bhatiari to Kumilla. One would have to buy a ticket all the way to Laksham. It was close to eight. The train was at the platform. Ananda nodded, keeping his gaze level and held out the money. It was his pale skin that was attracting this unwarranted attention. Turning, he hurried towards the platform trying not to break into a run.

Ananta-da and Ganesh-da took in the near-empty compartment at a glance and decided to settle down somewhere in the middle. Drawing their shawls about their faces, they appeared to drift off to sleep as the train clacked over the rails. Ananda kept an eye on the doors at both ends. Asvini Ghose – the nameplate had been pinned onto the uniform – the stationmaster had left him decidedly uncomfortable.

The dark of the night rushed by, interspersed by the little lights of the villages as the train gathered speed. He was very alive to the changes in pace, glancing nervously as it slowed at the little stations, letting in the calls of the vendors. Miles sped by. The image of the stationmaster faded.

Suresh De, 22 April

Something loomed beside him, pressing down on his chest; his throat felt dry; his eyes refused to focus in the cocoon of haze that surrounded him. All he remembered was the pain. And the familiar smell of gunpowder.

His name was being called. The voice faded.

He was lying on the earth, now suddenly and violently awake, heart thudding, ears ringing. His face was burning and there was that jabbing pain again. Against a ringing silence, his name was being called.

Twigs were being snapped, thorns being torn from his clothes.

'Shaapey bor … Blessings in a curse!' the words came clearly through. He was being dragged. He rolled over, unresisting. His name was being called repeatedly. Now there was Shanti Nag's face framed by the starriest sky he could ever remember. It was coming back now.

'Get up,we need to get to a safe place.'

It was out of the question. Movement was out of the question. 'Shoot me.' Suresh mouthed the words with difficulty, pointing towards his chest with … not with his right hand for that seemed to have disappeared … parted company quite painlessly.

Shanti sat unmoving. Was he not aware that a noose hung about his neck? A white man's blood was on his hands. But now he had his arms firmly about Suresh's chest, dragging him to a clearing on the slope. Suresh was rolling down the hill, sometimes slowly with Shanti protecting his face, his hand guiding the motion and sometimes almost as if he was out of control. They had reached the bottom of the hill. He was lying against the trunk of a great tree.

Panic was setting in. He could smell it in the air. There was nobody in sight: Master-da, Loka-da, the rest of them. It was reasonable for Shanti to panic, for he was not from Chattogram. He would be completely lost now. So was Suresh, except that he didn't care. Shanti had gone off. He could hear him calling. He could hear the desperation in his voice. Comprehension seeped in. They had given him up for dead and had gone. Only Shanti had remained behind and had got delayed, trying to carry him downhill … that explained the thorny bush … they had obviously tumbled. Now he too had gone.

Shanti was back. He was holding his water carrier to Suresh's lips. The water was fresh and cool and it seemed to flow directly into his limbs, invigorating them with the strength he had never thought would come back. Suresh pulled himself up into a sitting posture. He could have sworn that Shanti's eyes were about to pop. The water had worked wonders.

'The British have gone.'

For Suresh, at that moment, it mattered little.

'Master-da, Lokenath-da – they have all gone. We need to go.'

With Shanti's arms supporting him, he stood up. His right arm and hand, they were all there – hanging heavy and lifeless, swathed in cotton and bandages.

'I have signalled with my flash light, even climbed up a tree and called. But there is no response. I found a pool, it had a little stream running into it, I followed it for a bit but there was nobody there.' Shanti was beginning to gabble. The relief in his voice evident: now that there was someone to talk to.

They took a couple of steps. The dressing was soaked through with blood. Shanti added more bandages over the layers.

'There must be heavy patrolling in the area. We need to be getting along. Hold this.'

He positioned the musket butt under Suresh's left shoulder. Through all this, Shanti had clung to his musket. The revolvers? he wondered idly. A glance told him that they hung both at his waist and Shanti's. With Shanti's arm around his waist, Suresh was suddenly overcome by the urge to get away from the area as quickly as possible. It was so dark that visibility was limited to a couple of feet. And with the area completely unknown, what if they came across someone … the blood and the dirt, the weapons, the injury …

They walked for a while and then Shanti broke the silence. 'I am sorry,' he said, 'I don't think you will use this arm again.'

'What happened in the end?'

'The machine gun suddenly stopped firing and about ten or fifteen minutes later we heard a whistle, their train was leaving. It was exactly eight o'clock. It was incredible. We've won, Suresh! But so many are dead … ten are dead. We examined all of them again and again. There was so much of blood; the ground had turned to slush at places. Master-da asked us to collect all the firearms and shoot those we thought would not make it through the night. All those lessons in first aid and I could not help any of them. I checked again and again to see if they were breathing … But there was something different about you. I could not leave you behind … Ambika-da is still alive but they could not bring him down. He was conscious enough to tell Master-da to remove the money from his pocket. Motilal Kanungo was breathing but not responding. Subodh Roy had been keeping an eye on him since he was shot, gave him the last of his water hoping to ease his pain, hoping to see him dead before we left but … And Ardhendu Dastidar … his abdomen has been blown open but he had been firing till the last. Master-da left a revolver with him in case of … well in case some wild animals came by. Lokenath-da called us all. He asked us to fall in and pay our respects to the dead. Then we turned to leave. Binod Choudhury [12] – he has a neck wound, and Binod Bihari Dutt – they both had to be helped. I went back to take one last look at you.'

They had been walking for some time now, restricting the use of the flashlight to a minimum. A large hill loomed up ahead. They were back where they had started.

John Younie

It was soon after dark that the jubilant planters returned. Johnson and Wilkinson had left to do the rounds of the thanas where news was expected. The ladies crowded around, silent with expectation, as Alexander Burnett came by to reassure them that all was well. John Younie gathered the impression that they had been accompanied by some forty Gurkhas. The atmosphere in the club turned festive with much cheering – Mrs Johnson's voice carrying through the room.

'The Mussalman led us up a mile-long sandy-bottomed ravine leading into the hills. He pointed to a low range of hills about 300 yards away and said they were up there. Scarcely had he spoken, when a perfect hail of bullets whistled over our heads.' He paused for effect. 'We lost no time in taking cover and replying. To get within more effective range, we crept up the nalla and opened fire again at roughly 200 yards. The rebels could be clearly seen moving about in the scrub jungle … easy targets, but it was then that we discovered that in our hurry we had left the tripod for our Hotchkiss machine gun behind.'

There was a cry of dismay and a loud sniff from Mrs J as Burnett hastened to make amends. Young Mrs Taitt stared at the carpet with her lips pursed.

'An attempt was made to hold the gun in position by hand but the heat of the barrel stopped us from doing so for more than a few rounds at a time. After maintaining heavy fire for nearly an hour, we decided to advance – which without the cover of machine gunfire was risky, but we managed to cross the stretch of open dhan khet and occupy the insurgents' positions. They had retreated further into the hills but we had them at closer range now and a steady battle was kept up until dusk when it was decided to withdraw and return to Chittagong. A force of the Eastern Frontier Rifles, 200 strong, was to assist us, but they failed to show up.[13] We couldn't wait for them, for we had to be back for our patrolling duties and besides, it was pointless to try and follow them into the jungle.' Burnett clicked his tongue '… a splendid opportunity missed as they were cornered in a bottlenecked valley with one outlet to the sea.'

John pushed past the ladies and went up to shake Burnett's hand. 'Should have been able to pursue the operation to a more satisfactory conclusion but … no fault of the SVLH. You lot have done an excellent job.'

The two men stepped out onto the verandah.

'The rebels appear to have been drilling for months under the guise of athletic associations under the supervision of a Sikh,[14] reputed to be an expert in frontier warfare and a deserter from the army. Captain Taitt was of the opinion that had they been armed with .303 rifles and ammunition, nothing could have prevented their occupying Chittagong and terrorizing the whole district. But,' Alexander flashed a cheeky grin as he turned to leave. 'Their shooting must have been pretty wild as our total number of casualties consists of one man shot through the wrist.'

A great pity, thought John. From the descriptions it seemed apparent that the tila had been selected and arranged as a fortified ammunition dump for months without being detected … if only there had been a sufficient force, they could have completely surrounded the little tila and the entire hornet's nest could have been exterminated. Where had Dallas Smith and his hundred disappeared to … and all that talk of bringing in aeroplanes, regulars and a detachment of Gurkhas from Shillong? As far as he could see, it was all talk. Why the hell couldn't they bring down a couple of hundred Gurkhas from Shillong; after all, they were the fellows who were in the Abor[15] show and were used to this kind of jungle fighting. Three is to one … the army manual's instructions were pretty clear on this point: take on one enemy company with three of your own. Why had they then sent seventy men against the hundred raiders?[16] The show is being managed with a surprising lack of ineffectiveness, if not ineptitude. The gang will now succeed in making their escape and some may try to double back and commit some outrage here.

He settled down in an armchair, having resolved to keep the families company that night. There was something to say for them. For the rebels, or rather the schoolboys and their master, had achieved complete success in their objectives in the town and then, undeterred by the unexpected arrival on the scene of a Lewis gun, did not forthwith proceed to scatter into hiding but marched off into the hills, still a united disciplined force, one which, as soon as the forces of authority came in touch with them, had made a united and determined effort to annihilate them.

The correct facts would take time to be uncovered but meanwhile the planters appeared to have thoroughly enjoyed the little skirmish. They would get paid of course … he made a quick mental calculation, deducting the money order charges and the annual SVLH membership subscription. It would leave them with nine rupees of the original fourteen in hand. The government had it in for all of them these days …

FOURTEEN

Ananda Prasad Gupta, 23 April, Feni Station

'Cha Cha Heni Heni.'

The calls were floating in now. Ananda was dimly aware of the lights flashing onto his face. It was well past midnight – probably one o' clock; they were pulling up at Feni station. They were nearly sixty miles from Chattogram now.

The train came to a halt. Ananda sat up. The rest were still dozing or appeared fast asleep.

'Bhatiari to Laksham, Bhatiari to Laksham.'

Two police officers and about ten constables had boarded the train checking tickets at random. All sleep vanished in seconds though Ananta-da and Ganesh-da continued to doze. They adjusted their positions to more comfortable ones but Ananda knew they had repositioned their weapons. He exchanged a quick glance with Makhon and quickly made sure that he could pull out his own in an instant if required. The police party was coming closer. His heart beating wildly, he wondered what Ananta-da and Ganesh-da were planning to do. Would they try and fool the police or would they begin shooting straight away? Neither of them was making any eye contact … what were they thinking?

'Bhatiari to Laksham?'

Ananta-da yawned and produced the tickets.

The sipahis had rifles slung over their shoulders and batons in their hands.

Sub-inspector Jatindra Mohan Rai examined them and handed them to the Inspector Abdul Mohammad Fazal Wasid. They were looking at the ticket numbers.

'Name?' The havaldar barked.

'Mahim Chandra Sen,' Ananta-da identified himself. 'My nephew,' he pointed to Ananda.

Ganesh-da and Makhon identified themselves as the Guhas. 'Family business,' he said briefly.

'Guhas and Sens? Boddi and Kayast?' The sub-inspector smirked. 'Can't be related.'

'Where to? Kumilla? Then why the tickets to Laksham? Home address?'

'Abhaya Ashram Feni Bazaar.' Ananta-da said weakly.

'Never seen you there … been there six months.' The sub-inspector took a sudden decision. 'Off,' he said. 'Off the train now.'

Ganesh-da fell at the inspector's feet. 'Daroga Babu,' he whimpered. 'We have done nothing wrong. We have not withheld any information. It is all a mistake. Saar, if you order it … they will listen. Have pity on us; we fear the police.'

It was clear the inspector felt sympathetic. He glanced at the sub-inspector who in turn shot the havaldar a look.

'Look,' began the inspector, 'I don't really want to harass you but we all work for a living. If the Bhatiari stationmaster had not sent us a telegram and the ticket numbers given to the guard not matched, we would not have been forced into this unpleasant task. Come. Don't worry. We will take a statement – a jabaan-bandi – and let you go.'

Ananta Lal Singh, 23 April, Feni Station

How had the stationmaster guessed? Was every traveller supposed to know that tickets from Bhatiari to Kumilla were not sold? Or was it Ananda's face? It did belong to the refined upper class, but then again, would such a boy be associated with terrorists? Ananta lurched as he stepped down. There were several helping hands … amongst them those of J.B. Ferera's. The name plate blazed before his eyes.

'Oh! You are an Anglo. Great piece of work …' Ananta muttered to himself as he shot a silent look, pregnant with suffering, in the guard's direction. He was the one that had kept an eye on their compartment and pointed it out to the police. 'And your colleague … what a super little sleuth … but obviously not as clever as he thinks he is for the police are still chatting away with us instead of gunning us down.'

Ananta walked hunched over like a sick old man, his head trembling ever so slightly. They were being led away from the engine. This train was blocking the escape route to the north. A barbed-wire fence ran alongside the platform blocking the southern side. Making a run for it would mean running along the tracks and getting gunned down in the process. They had walked the complete length of the train. A coughing fit forced him to the ground and in those few moments he had loosened the automatic pistol and the Webley revolver at his waist. Ananda and Makhon helped him up and requested for some water. They were so scared; it was showing on their faces. How could boys like these be a part of a dreaded gang? Jatin Babu, the sub-inspector, was all kindness. He was Haran's – Shourindra Mohan Choudhury's – mama; had he any clue that his nephew had been a part of the teams that disrupted the rail lines on the night of 18 April?

They took some time at the water fountain. On the tracks beyond the one on which the Number 3, Up Mail stood, was another train – its engine headed towards Chattogram. It was full of armed Gurkha soldiers.[1] There was no hope of escape.

They were being marched into the Assistant Stationmaster Pulin Bihari Majumdar's room. The little room choked with people – the police, two ticket collectors Prafulla Pathak and Abdul Hakim and the signaller Lal Mia; nobody wanted to miss out on the action.

The inspector took the assistant stationmaster's chair right beside the entrance door and sat with his back to the window. The sub-inspector perched on the table in front, his legs dangling, with Ganesh, Makhon, Ananda, Ananta and a constable cooped up between him and a set of almirahs that lined the wall at the back. The constables that could not fit in the room milled about on the outside crowding the door, peering through the window. Ganesh was asked to open up the bedding, which he did. He then requested to be allowed to go and relieve himself. The good-natured inspector instructed the havaldar and two constables to take him out.

'Koi, baba?' Ananta whined. 'You have checked all our baggage; now finish with the jabaan-bandi.'

The inspector looked faintly embarrassed. 'A body search is part of our routine. Let us get over with it and you can go.'

A constable stepped up. Makhon was right in front, close to the door. It was now or never; better dead than be taken alive. DANGEROUS AND ARMED CHITTAGONG REVOLUTIONARIES ARRESTED. The headlines flashed before him. The constable's hands were reaching out for Makhon's waist; all eyes riveted on them; the moment that every magician waits for. It was over in a fraction of a second: the constable behind him had been shot in the thigh; he was up on the table growling jaan bachao … run for your lives; another constable shot in the leg; the light put out by a third bullet, the tiny room miraculously emptying. The one thing that had registered, through the gunpowder fumes, was the sight of Ananda running out with the crowd. Could there be a policeman waiting for him by the door? Ananta took a flying leap from the table to a spot outside the door. The sub-inspector was standing about five arm-lengths to his left, his face frozen in alarm. Was he about to shoot? There was no time to think. Ananta fired the pistol and ran. He had lost sight of Ananda.

The person he was following seemed to be headed towards the tracks leading eastwards. It didn't seem to be either Ananda or Makhon. Was it just another railway employee fleeing in panic? There were agitated people coming up behind him: more employees or the police? Ananta made a quick diversion to the south. In his panic he had forgotten the barbed wire fence that ran along the length of the station.

Ananda Prasad Gupta, 23 April

Ananda was running, the blood pounding in his ears, each ragged breath burning its way through his chest and nostrils. There was shouting … they were chasing him. Where was he? And where were the others? The comfort of tarmac beneath his feet … he had wandered onto the Trunk Road. Mica glistened up at him through the dark; miles of dark stretched on either side … standing paddy, he guessed. He must be quite far from the station now … there were no more voices following him. One voice penetrated, through the buzz that the new silence had induced. It was Makhon's.

'Wait.' He called again. How long had he been following him?

Makhon ran up the last few steps and sat down heavily. 'Can't any more.' There was a shiver in his voice.

Ananda's hands felt wet. He let go of Makhon's arm and turned his flashlight on. There was blood. Too much, he thought. Makhon was bleeding copiously; it poured down his forehead, streaking his face, down his neck, soaking his shirt; he was so pale, so cold. Gingerly Ananda parted his hair and recoiled in horror. A laceration extended all the way down his scalp, the edges curling outwards, revealing the pale pink gleam of tissues and the sickening white of bone. He waited to catch his breath.

'But how?'

'A lathi … the constable behind the almirah.'

The almirah? But Makhon had been closest to the door and amongst the first to leave the room, even before the smell of gunpowder had set off that coughing fit. Ananda was rubbing Makhon's hands now and alternately trying to press his handkerchief down on the wound and jumping away as if it were hot coals. His hand grew gradually steadier and Makhon calmer.

With Makhon leaning against him Ananda led the way to a pool of water. The blood was washed away and the head bound as best as possible. They sat down for some time. It was difficult to gauge direction in the dark. Had they been running towards Kumilla or were they closer to Chattogram now? There were no lights, no signs of habitation close by. Nor were there any signs of either Ganesh-da or Ananta-da. Had they managed to escape? Were they alive?

'What constable? What almirah?'

'I heard a shot behind me and ran out. But Ananta-da had been left behind inside. He would need backup. I thought there would be a crossfire situation and we would end up shooting ourselves so I ran back inside and took cover behind the almirah. The light had gone out. I did not see the constable on the floor, hiding behind the almirah. As I crouched he hit me on the head … twice … and grabbed one of my revolvers. But I ran out before he could shoot me.'

Ananda hugged his friend in relief. Makhon was lucky to have got away alive. He had thought of the others, while he, Ananda, had fled in panic.

It was nearly 3 a.m. now, they guessed. That they were on the Feni Trunk Road was obvious. They set off in the direction they hoped was east.

Shadows seemed to jump out, as if cohorts of policemen lay in hiding, waiting for two young lads to come their way. They pressed down as gently as possible with each step, for the sounds of their own feet transformed themselves into several footfalls. Lone soldiers appearing to be on guard turned out to be innocuous palms. The boys watched and dodged their way down the road.

What if Ananta-da and Ganesh-da were somewhere close by? How would they even know that Ananda Prasad Gupta and Jibon Ghoshal had gone by? Calling them by name would be giving themselves away. Sing; that was the answer; sing as loudly as possible; surely their voices would not go unrecognized.

Ananda and Makhon walked quickly down the road belting out the verses, at the top of their lungs, without a thought for melody. The eastern sky was taking on a lighter hue; it would be dawn soon. There had been no time to plan, for they had walked most of the night, hoping to catch up with Ganesh-da or Ananta-da. They would have to take to the hills soon.

It was light enough now to make out the figure of a man some 200 yards in front. He was walking away from them briskly but who could be out at this hour? Nervously, they peeped over their shoulders. Police parties were known to do this. The man up ahead seemed to slow his pace. The boys slowed down watching him intently. Then, in what seemed to be a deliberate attempt to close the gap, the man sat down by the side of the road. He got up after a while and began to walk again. The boys shadowed him, always maintaining a safe distance. He would soon turn off on to a side road. They would have to be careful until then.

The man settled down under a tree. His chador was draped over his head and shoulders, his face completely covered. It was quite obvious now he was waiting for them to go past and that was when he would begin to tail them.

The boys exchanged glances. The man appeared to be resting, pretending as if he didn't realize that they stood so close.

'Hands up.'

Fingers were ready on the triggers, the revolvers pointing directly at the man's chest.

The apparition raised its arms without protest.

'Who are you?'

'Srijukto – The honourable – Ganesh Ghosh.' The form convulsed with laughter.

The boys all but literally dove into his chest. Ganesh-da's body burned with fever.

Ananda turned angrily on him. 'And where have you been all this while? How did you get out of the station?'

'A neat little getaway.' He laughed. 'I kept insisting that I could not defile the station compound but they would not take me beyond the tracks. I had to finally squat there itself. The havaldar and the sipahis were trying to look away discreetly when I heard the shots. The next thing they knew was that they were staring down the mouths of two revolvers. They knew what was best for them … and you?' He was looking at Makhon's bandaged head.

Makhon stalled as if he were trying to think of the best way to explain. The story did not sound as great as the first time round. 'It was pretty foolish of me,' he agreed.

Ananta Lal Singh, 23 April

The barbed wire clung tenaciously and his hands were of little use, for both held weapons. A good hard yank succeeded in freeing most of the clothing. Sticky warmth trickled down a leg, but clamouring for attention was the gate – the gate used by the third-class passengers; it had stood right beside him all this while, waiting to be opened. In no more than a couple of seconds Ananta was outside the station compound, striding towards the dimly outlined residential area. Never in his life had he experienced the kind of energy that coursed through his veins at this very moment. There was a sensation of soaring within, that promised to lend him wings. His stomach churned without warning. His feet were slipping, sliding in wet mud. His arms jerked helplessly; it was impossible to maintain his balance, with both his hands occupied as they were: fingers at the ready on the triggers.

The injustice of it all was too much to bear, for it had been no more than two seconds ago that he was standing entangled in barbed wire. And now he was up to his neck in slush, hands raised above his head. He had completely missed the freshly built hut by the side of the road and the pit that had been dug to help churn sticky mud for the plaster. Could anyone have transited from such emotional highs to depths as low as this, in such little time? Ananta flailed his arms against the strong suction maintained by the thick mud.

Fortunately, there was no one to see him as he crawled out – a spectre emerging from its miry lair. The one thing he was certain of by now was that there was nobody chasing him. He made his way back through the fields to the railway track. He was now about 300 yards away from the station. It did not look as if there was much happening there. Perhaps the others had got away safely.

Crossing the tracks, he made off towards the north. He would have to reach the hills by first light. There was no dearth of water, for the fields were criss-crossed by irrigation channels. He crossed them all, splashing his way through muddy pools, running streams and wide canals. He had walked most of the night. It was perhaps safe to stop now. Sitting down beside a pool he washed the mud that caked his torso and limbs and bound a wound that bled persistently. The firearms needed to be cleaned. That was more important. The little 0.450-bore pistol could fire nine times in one go but one shot had already been used on the sub-inspector and of the six that had been in the revolver, five had already been fired. He rummaged through the bag of spares but there was nothing there, for he had divided the ammunition between Ananda and Makhon. So now he was dependent on the pistol. Carefully, he began cleaning it out. There was something wrong; his blood began to run cold; the ejector spring had broken.

AMBIKA CHAKRABORTY, 23 APRIL, JALALABAD

It was the moaning that first broke through his consciousness. A light rain pattering down had roused him. The night was icy cold, pitch dark and the silence hard on the ears. His eyelids would not open. He struggled with them, scraping at the congealed blood that glued them together. He was lying out in the open. Was the battle over? There was that moan again. Someone was in pain. The memories came rushing back. Surjya Babu had knelt by his side and wished him goodbye. He had said that he was leaving with the boys. Did he remember to give the money to Surjya Babu? His hand went to his shirt pocket. It was empty. He had about 100 to 150 rupees in there. He must have. Where were all the British soldiers? Why hadn't they taken him away or killed him? Where was the revolver? He had a distinct memory of a voice that told him that there was a revolver and a musket being left behind for him. Subodh … It had been Subodh Roy's voice. Or was it Bon Bihari's? It was too much to remember. The boy had seemed unwilling to let him be.

Ah! Here was the revolver. Ambika groped at it with his fingers but why was he not able to raise his arm? He was too weak; his arm had become very heavy … oho, someone had bandaged it with great care. He would have to leave quickly now. As he struggled to sit up, the darkness that surrounded him was set into motion. It whirled about him like cyclone, threatening to tear his head from its moorings. Ambika clutched at his face. What was this? A hard object stuck to the middle of his forehead? He squeezed the skin around it and tugged gently. There, it was out. His forehead had begun streaming. He wiped his eye and examined the object. It was a bullet.

That sound, the moan. Somebody was alive. Where was the voice coming from?

'Ambika-da,' it said. 'Ambika-da, are you alive?' The voice belonged to Ardhendu Dastidar. Ambika struggled to his feet. His head was reeling; his body shaking violently; but he needed to be on his feet.

'Yes. Yes. I am alive. Where are you? How are you? Get up … try to get up. We have to get off the hill.'

Ardhendu appeared, dragging himself with the help of his musket. The tall slight figure was bent over, clutching his abdomen. He was bare-bodied. They moved to the north-east edge of the hill. The distance, not even ten yards, took them all of fifteen minutes and with it all of the boy's strength. He fell crashing to the ground. 'Ambika-da,' he gasped, 'I cannot go further … my body will not let me.'

Ambika stood for a few moments. If he tried to kneel beside Ardhendu, it was unlikely that he would stand up again.

'Go, Ambika-da.' Ardhendu pleaded. 'Tell Master-da that I remember his words … liberty or death.'

His heart was on the point of bursting. His lips trembling, he whispered, 'Bhai, I will tell Master-da about you … May you live long … Long live the revolution.'

He stretched a leg out to place his foot on the slope … but his head would not help balance his body. He began to roll. The gravel was loose and treacherous, hastening his descent and ripping into his clothes and flesh. Jalalabad: a mother. Upon her breast many of those that had become closer than brothers had found a place to rest their heads. She would surely have place for him – for one more child too tired to keep his eyes open.

A small bush spread out its branches and its thorns reached out to him. He had stopped rolling. He lay quietly, examining the situation. His body was quite whole … not smashed to bits as he had expected. But he was still some distance from the base. In an hour it would be light … there was still time for escape. He could not risk standing up again on such a steep slope. It would be better to drag himself on his chest.

Suresh De, 23 April

It was the tightness in his chest that would not let the air in … Suresh became aware that he had been running. The sight of Jalalabad Hill had struck terror in his heart. How like a demoness she had drawn them back, lusting after the share of blood she had been cheated of. He did not know how and for how long, but he had managed to keep up with Shanti.

The dense woods were becoming sparse now, glimpses of the sky more frequent. Soon the ground beneath their feet began to harden. He heaved a sigh of relief; they had ventured onto a well-used path. Far into the distance, lights appeared. They twinkled like a small cluster of stars. It was Shanti's belief that it was there that they would be safe. Keeping the lights in sight, the boys kept moving.

It was a small village, still fast asleep. They crept down the little lanes. The poorest of the poor appeared to live there – people who could only afford a little thresh for their roofs and were barely capable of covering themselves. Who amongst them could afford to be sympathetic? Did they care that the British that ruled the land fed off them or know that their fellow Indians, who were better off than they were, could only bring them trouble?

Keenly aware of their appearance, Suresh and Shanti looked for a hut on the outskirts. Two strangers in bloodied khaki carrying four revolvers and a musket would be enough to drive anybody hysterical. They would have to contain the panic before it spread through the village. If reason did not work, force would have to.

The owner responded to the repeated knocking and stood transfixed. His mouth was opening slowly as an uncontrollable scream was welling up from within when a sharp rebuke from Shanti jerked him back to his senses. Suresh started immediately on an entreating note: their lives depended on him; he had nothing to fear. Would he not save the lives of two swadeshis on the run? It seemed like ages before the man moved a muscle. All this while he had remained partially concealed behind the door. He now held it open, still not having said a word.

Shanti helped Suresh to the floor, as the owner lit an oil lamp and cleared a little space for them. He sat on his haunches staring at them. Now it seemed that he was stunned at his good fortune: heroes at his doorstep. Abruptly he rose, brought a clay pot from a corner and set it before them. It had the remainders of the rice he had cooked the previous day and soaked in water. Shanti reached out for some of the fermenting mixture and placed it into Suresh's mouth. It was the first mouthful that he tasted since that last khichuri meal on Badulla Hill. The panta-bhaat was amrit. The man was not finished yet. He brought out a handful of dried fish. The two boys ate their fill, but in their hearts they knew that man had emptied his complete stock of food. He would go hungry that day. The oil in the little lamp had burned off, and their eyes would not remain open but their host was still full of questions.

He was shaking them awake. It was a little before dawn. They would have to go. A change of clothes was desperately required but all their host had to offer was the lungi that he wore every year on Id. It was well worn but whole. This he handed to Shanti. There was nothing else barring the frayed lungi that he had on. He sat glumly as Suresh stared at him with beseeching eyes. Anything would do. He had to get out of that blood-stained uniform. After some agonizing moments, the man brought another clay pot from the corner. It held his stash of tatters – the ones he was saving to make a kantha.

'It will do.'

Two vests, so threadbare that they barely held together, were tucked in at the waist where the lungi was knotted. But try as they might, the revolvers could not be hidden.

'Leave them with me, babu, I will keep them safe for you.' He had removed the soiled dressings from Suresh's arm and had replaced them with some torn cloth.

Two Muslim village lads left before the cock crowed. The last hour had been spent in prayer until the chosen Koranic verses could be recited fluently. Suresh turned to take one last look at his host.

'You are one of us now,' he whispered.

Ananda Prasad Gupta, 23 April

Ananda kept his arm firmly around Makhon's waist. He had begun to lean heavily against him, tiring him out in the process. They had been walking now for several hours and had entered the dense forests of the hill tracts. In their excitement, they had lost count of the number of times they had fallen down and dragged themselves through barbed-wire fences. Through the night, every time he had brushed against Ganesh-da, he had felt the heat his body gave off and smelt the fever on his breath. On the other hand, Makhon, who clung to him, had grown colder and clammier and his teeth had chattered in bouts. With dawn breaking, Ananda took in, for the first time, the appearances of his companions. Ganesh-da, puffy and flushed, with red-rimmed eyes. His face was speckled with what looked like mosquito bites. Makhon had gone a nasty leaden colour. Gruesome blood clots had congealed about his head, streaking his forehead and neck. The boy appeared on the verge of collapse. It made him forget the thirst that clawed at his throat.

They made their way slowly till they came across a little pond. The first mouthful of the amber-coloured water made his stomach contract. Then he noticed the rotting vegetation. There was little choice; it would have to do. Drinking in great gulps he filled his belly before washing his face and hands and sank to the ground beside Makhon. Ganesh-da sat, examining his arms thoughtfully. Little blisters filled with a cloudy grey fluid had appeared on top of some of the lesions. Little black crusts had begun to form on some, but between them a fresh crop had made its appearance. They didn't hold his attention for long and soon he was chivvying them up the slopes.

The daylight was growing stronger and they climbed steadily for the next three hours. In all, they would have been a good fourteen or fifteen miles away from Feni and now all of them were struggling. They could go no further … the decision was a unanimous one. If they did not find some food quickly enough, the only choice left would be to lie down and let their bodies rot in the wilderness.

A movement caught their eye. They were being watched. A woodcutter crouched in the undergrowth. Ganesh-da approached him, asking for help. He pointed to a group of huts nestled in the woods.

The chief was finding it difficult to tear his eyes off Makhon. At last he spoke … it was a dialect of Bengali. 'Dakaat na ki?'

'No not dacoits … just harmless villagers … lost travellers.' Ganesh-da hastened to reassure him. Pointing towards Jibon, he had indicated that he needed help. 'Tripped against the roots of a tree … very hurt.' The pox that covered Ganesh-da's body somehow lent credence to his tale.

They were asked to sit down and instructions issued to a manservant. In a while a thala piled high with steaming hot rice … the grains thick and coarse … three semi-ripe bananas and a pot of water was placed before them.

Ananda and Makhon watched as Ganesh-da mashed the bananas with his fingers and used it to help roll portions of rice into balls and popped them deftly into his mouth. They followed, pretending it was nothing new and it turned out to be a fine meal – one for which they were profusely grateful. Leaving the little hamlet, they decided to abandon the Kumilla plan and go to Kolkata instead. But they would need to make a visit to Sylhet first, for that was where Ananda's mashi, his mother's sister, Sumati Majumdar, lived. They could always depend on her to lend them enough money to get to Kolkata.

Hem Gupta, 23 April

Fifty men from the Eastern Frontier Rifles took their position at the base of the hill while Sub-inspector Hem Gupta and his men approached the Jalalabad Hill from the back. There seemed to be no sign of activity but it was wise to take cover behind bushes and make a quick run for the next one further up the slope. The hill had been completely wrecked. Who would have said it had not been a giant plough at work through the night? The trees that had continued to stand looked pale as ghosts, with their bark all flayed off.

There was a faint sound. The men froze, their weapons poised. There it was again – a faint moaning. Hem Gupta emerged from his cover, spotted a wounded youth lying at the edge and rushed to his side. He appeared to have been shot through the back and the bullet had probably passed through the abdomen, for he was drenched in blood. He was asking for water. The sub-inspector held his bottle to his lips.

'Who are you? What is your name?'

'Ardhendu Shekhar Dastidar.'

The youth's body bore wounds, some of which were raw and some partially healed. He would have to be moved to hospital soon if he was to be taken alive. Ten bodies lay along the slopes. The soil had turned dark where they lay. Some of the bodies were so badly mutilated and torn up that they were unrecognizable. Hem Gupta realized that he had been unconsciously trying to fit the forms into the one that haunted him. Was he relieved that none of the bodies resembled that of Rajat the footballer? He was amongst those that were being watched … perhaps he had got away. Hem Gupta was surprised by his own emotions. Did he really care? He was being called … another one was alive … groaning only when roused. Once he managed to mumble his name … Motilal Kanungo. An all-clear signal was made: the area was safe.

The armoured train had arrived. Dr Weldon, DIG Farmer, Col Dallas Smith, Mr Lewis, and several others came up the slope. The top brass was disappointed. They had hoped to take more revolutionaries alive. After the battle against the presumed 100 raiders, a tiny bunch of dead bodies was in fact a liability – one that would whip up a frenzy of emotions and patriotic fervour. The bodies could not be taken back to the city or handed over to the families.

Dr Weldon and his team examined Ardhendu Dastidar, gave him some first aid and removed him to the armoured train. Motilal Kanungo was pronounced beyond help. He was given a shot of morphia to ease the pain until his heart gave out. The rest were declared dead.

Hem Gupta began the strip-search, examining the contents of their pockets and bags. Some of the dead had been well known local lads … some he had never set eyes upon. Here was Hari Gopal – the youngest of the Bal household, constantly courting trouble … where was that brother of his, that youth icon? Hem Gupta felt a tug in his heart. Hari Gopal Bal – Tegra – look at him now, so young, so vulnerable, so innocent in a simple cotton shirt and dhuti, hair tousled, face smudged with earth. What was he doing among this bunch of boys in khaki playing at being soldiers? A couple of faces looked familiar … Chattogram was a small town. He stopped by one that was very familiar: Pulin Bikash Ghose. A brief impression of a fleeing form and the faint echo of a laugh … he shook his head as if trying to dispel the emotions rising within. This was madness, taking on an empire's forces! Beyond a doubt, this was Ananta Lal Singh's band. Here lay another youngster, perhaps even younger than Hari Gopal – this one he had never seen before. What were the ringleaders up to now? These unknown faces had obviously been recruited from outside Chattogram, ones that the police would never have known existed. Some of the bodies were so mangled that identification was going to prove near impossible. Now, here was a well-known face: Dr Bidhu Bhushan Bhattacharya, the gold medallist of the Chattogram Medical College. What a waste of a life. Beside him lay his best friend and college mate, Dr Naresh Ray, with his wealthy background, pampered upbringing, medical degree … The constables had pulled out a sheet of paper from Naresh Ray's pocket. The contents were sufficient to freeze the marrow of every white man standing there.

It was a map of the European Club … barely 300 yards from the police lines, that lovely little clubhouse with its krishnachura-shaded driveway, the one that the elite amongst the whites frequented … perfect to the last detail. It had been breached, its sanctity violated.

He watched the shadows chase across Mr Farmer's face. The details in Naresh Ray's map were too graphic for comfort. Every entrance and exit was marked, with additional notes; the almirahs and their positions had been carefully noted; the exact arrangement of the billiards table and the chairs ... Could it be possible that there was a traitor amongst the staff? Were revolutionaries moving undetected in areas meant for Europeans only?

Another piece of paper had been found. It held a handwritten message: If anybody tells you that an act of armed resistance even if offered by ten men only, even if offered by men armed with stones, any and every such man who tells that such an act of resistance is premature, imprudent or dangerous shall at once be spurned and spat at; for remark you thus and recollect that somehow somewhere, and by somebody, a beginning must be made and that the first act of resistance is always and shall always be premature, imprudent, unwise and dangerous.

'Lalor. James Finton Lalor.' Mr Lewis murmured. 'The Irish revolutionary ... handwriting to go for analysis.'

It was near noon when Mr Johnson arrived with a photographer and a fingerprinting expert. He rushed to the side of the only one who could remotely be called alive. Motilal was jerked into consciousness. A statement had to be got out of him before he died. But he was too far gone. They bent over him, trying to catch the meaning of his groans.

'Ananta Lal Singh said that not enough Englishmen have been killed.'

Lokenath Bal, 23 April

'Loka-da, khetey hobey ... we have to eat.'

It was typical of Ranadhir to come to the point directly. Lokenath looked wearily at the exhausted band. Apathy had got the better of them. The sun was high and yet none of them had bothered to move to the shade. Die like a man: his last words to the little one spoken less than twelve hours ago. It was time to follow his own advice and be a man. There were lives he was still responsible for.

Ranadhir crouched by his side, scrutinizing his face. 'If we don't eat we will lose all our strength.' The boy spoke earnestly.

'Tai … Is that so?' A smile eased its way through the creases on his forehead. The boy was no older than Tegra. Kobiraj Jayanta Dasgupta had a flourishing practice prescribing traditional Indian drugs. Here was his little son … the matriculation exams were over … did he hope to become a doctor, following in his father's footsteps? It appeared to be the family's chosen profession, for his cousin was already a captain in the Indian Medical Service.

'Cholo.' Kali Chakraborty, alias Pundit, having struggled to his feet, held out an arm. He pulled him to his feet. Had it not been for him, they would never have found their way amongst the maze of hills. They had lost Master-da and his group sometime during the night. Rajat waved cheekily at him and turned on his side. The morning light; the hunger pangs – nothing troubled him. Nor did Debu or Mona stir.

Lokenath's muscles protested as he gingerly set foot on the sloping path. The gravel slipped beneath the boot soles, forcing him to break into a run. A narrow footpath snaked past the hill. He crouched down by Pundit's side taking cover behind the trunk of a great tree, revolvers held ready. Minutes ticked by but not a soul came by. The sunlit mango groves, striped with light and shade, lay still and quiet. Lokenath peered down the lane lined with tall ancient trees. The light rain of the previous night had washed the dust off and the leaves glistened black and green. The fruit had begun to plump and ripen.

'Neither man nor beast in sight.' Lokenath was annoyed. He sat down heavily and loosened the strings of his boot.

'Shhh.' Pundit warned and pointed. In the distance, a lone figure had materialized. He was walking purposefully down the lane, unaware that two khaki-clad figures waited to pounce on him.

'Forgive me, brother. I did not mean to scare you. Just come with us up this hill. We need your help.'

Prodded by the revolvers, the man acquiesced reluctantly. How would he react to the sight of a bunch of armed youths, all dressed for battle? Lokenath maintained a firm grip on the man's arm. 'We are lost … we are swadeshis.' He kept up a conversation, trying to comfort the man. Seeing them, the boys rushed up. Despite their bizarre battle-stained appearance, the morning light revealed pleasant-faced young lads.

'We have not eaten for a long while now. You will have to exchange clothes with one of us and give us directions to the local haat.'

Without a word, the man stripped off his vest and lungi and clambered into the shirt and shorts that Pundit handed over to him. The news of the battle had been doing its rounds since the previous evening: The swadeshis had declared war.

Ananta Lal Singh, 23 April

His eyelids refused to open against the glare of the sun. His body was stiff and sore and his throat parched. The blue sky reeled above him and little white flashes streaked behind his eyelids. Eight o'clock, he guessed. The useless weapons, the panic, the mad dash for the hills … it was all coming back.

He was amazed he had fallen asleep at all. Disconsolately, he examined the blisters on his feet. The wound in the leg had stopped oozing, but a sense of isolation was creeping in. The others had gone. The weapons were now no more than a burden. And if he was caught, the police would boast of having apprehended an armed and dangerous revolutionary. Buoyed by his own sense of humour he began to draft the new script for the day. The clothing and the weapons would have to go. Burying them in a pit under a bush, he stood up a new man. The mud and blood were gone. He was stark naked except for a filthy strip wound around his middle, tucked into which was a twenty-rupee note – the last of his money. An idiot: that was to be his new identity – naked and crazed, giggling and gesturing, weeping or chattering.

He made his way downhill through the jungles, play-acting all the while regardless of whether anyone was in sight. There were times when he was struck dumb and times when he lost his hearing. Rice fields, farmlands, more jungles and stretches of land lying fallow … the thirst was upon him now and his head had begun to spin. He had come upon a barren stretch with not a tree in sight. Should he collapse now, this blazing sun would suck the fluids from his body; he, Ananta Lal Singh, would lie here forever – a shrivelled mummy, his life's work undone. The thought sent a surge through his limbs. The wild grass that he was trying to chew barely wet his tongue; he searched among the blades for juicier stalks. A partially eaten green mango lay in a clump of grass. There was no mango tree in the vicinity. Someone must have tossed it here … it was eto but the uneaten portion was turgid and fresh, triggering a flow of saliva. Without further thought, he chewed on the unformed flesh sucking frantically at the seed. The skin gave way to the bitter insides.

The sour tartness wet the insides of his mouth and throat. Smacking his lips he walked on, careful not to venture too close to the road … the Trunk Road. A lone woman tilled her land in the distance. Ananta approached her whining and grovelling – a crazy mute and obviously thirsty. She came forward with a small watermelon, probably her own lunch, and held her vessel of water over his cupped hands. Ananta demolished the melon as he watched her at work. Should he confide in her? A couple of men were making their way towards the field. Thinking the better of it, he left in a hurry.

It was past noon. The sun blazed down mercilessly and now some urchins had begun to tail him. They tittered and flung stones. The deaf and dumb act proved a real handicap. Some bigger boys joined in. Ananta could only cringe in response. He could not shout, nor call for help. Even a mock charge had the possibility of giving away his sanity. Tears welled up as a large stone found its mark. Was there not one child among this lot that would even try and protest? They followed him for nearly a mile before tiring of the game. Relieved, he dropped to his knees at the first pool of water that appeared. It was putrid.

He was close to the railway tracks now. It was the new line that had been laid from Feni to Bilonia. He continued to follow it. A large house on the bank of a dighi appeared in the distance. His tormentors had driven all thoughts of food from his mind, but now the pangs of hunger had returned with a vengeance.

A high wall enclosed a large compound. Voices could be heard, possibly a group of young children. Ananta squatted by the side of the dighi. The embankment had been bricked and plastered, probably by the owner of the big house. It was obviously a private reservoir. He finished drinking and then made his way to the house. It was nearly two o'clock in the afternoon. There were no adults in sight, only a group of four or five startled boys. They came forward to investigate, and suddenly out of nowhere there were nearly fifteen of them, taunting, leering, pulling faces. Ananta's heart lurched: not the same monster again. He pointed to his mouth and to his stomach. It only produced jeers. Some ordered him to leave outright. Ananta held his head pretending that he was dizzy and sank to the ground. It touched not one chord of sympathy. They did not have the courage to approach him but aimed punches and kicks from a distance. But surely, the racket they were creating would produce an adult – one who would either show a little mercy or drive him away.

'Ki korchhish ... what are you doing? Why do you harass him?' A young girl, one really no more than a child, pushed her way to the front. Her eyes, large and wary, remained fixed on his face. He touched his lips with all his fingertips as if putting an invisible ball of food in. She remained mesmerized for a few minutes before pushing her way back through the throng. Her appearance had been effective, for a silence now hung over the yard. She was back with some food bundled in a banana leaf but was too afraid to come any closer. She put it down and moved away, waving her hands, indicating that he pick it up and leave. This wide-eyed child was a vision in her simple cotton sari, her hair hanging in braids – a picture of compassion, an epitome of all the wonderful maternal instincts that go into the making of a woman. Some of the boys yelled out the instructions and Ananta picked up the bundle and limped his way to the banks of the dighi. The children were following him, as was the little girl. She maintained a safe distance. The bundle held a generous helping of rice, dal and vegetables cooked with medium-sized prawns. Neither pulao nor mutton curry, nothing could have made a more sumptuous meal. He gobbled down the food sometimes using his left hand and at times his right. The children doubled up with laughter. Sometimes he pretended to examine the food as if trying to decide what to eat next stealing all the while quiet glances at the girl whose mood alternated between sombre to childish delight, infected by the devilish glee of her companions.

The meal over, he made his way down the road play-acting for the benefit of those that followed. He turned to look back one last time. She was still there amongst the rest of them.[2]

Hem Gupta, 23 April, Jalalabad

Not enough Englishmen had been killed?

Hem Gupta stared at the DIG in disbelief. Did he actually draw so much of meaning from those agonized sounds? He personally had not been able to make anything out of it. The only time Motilal appeared to be making any sense was when he tried to indicate his unwillingness to respond … could the boy, even in this agony, still enjoy such a macabre sense of humour? The British officers conferred amongst themselves while he stood to one side awaiting orders.

The photographer set about his work, first taking pictures of individual corpses, then with their shirts pulled up exposing the injuries. The dead were then lined up and photographed in groups of three.

The AB Railway was sending in the firewood. Hem Gupta was to oversee the digging of a pit which would then be layered with wood. Individual pyres out in the open would mean risking a forest fire. These boys were Hindus, like himself. They would be leaving the world without the benefit of prayers, without the knowledge of their families. Most of the afternoon had been spent in making an inventory of items that had been seized: forty-three police muskets, bags of cartridges that had not been fired, empties that had been collected from the site, revolver cartridges, a pistol with an ivory handle and a sword. A document had been retrieved from Tripura Sen's pocket, from which it was apparent that they had modelled their revolution along the lines of the Easter Revolution in Ireland.

It was late evening before the bodies were placed in the pit. More wood was added and the petrol cans emptied. The lead actors of the British war effort bared their heads, and the Gurkhas stood to attention – the mouth of their rifle barrels positioned on the left toe, both hands on the rifle butt, chins down, staring steadfastly at their buttons. The darkening sky turned a dull red with the crackling blaze and Hem Gupta held his head low. Not every eye, he suspected, was dry. He could feel the photographer's eyes boring through his skull. He knew. It was an inkling that bound them, one that would trouble them the rest of their lives: Motilal Kanungo's heart had still been beating as he was dragged into the pit.

Ambika Chakraborty, 23 April

Booming commands in English voices, the tramp of many feet – the armed police had moved about him all day. Crouching under a bush, too terrified to even turn on his side, Ambika had had to manually peel his eyelids apart to view the goings-on on the hilltop. The Indian constables had waved the white flag, signalling that it was safe for the British to ascend. He hoped the boy, Ardhendu, had succeeded in hiding from them.

A red glow on the hilltop was growing into a blaze. A funeral pyre! Great orange tongues reached up, licking the darkening horizon, showering golden sparks into the forest below. Blood had been spilled for the great mother: Ambika clung to the earth in prayer.

The leaves rustled behind him and dry twigs snapped. A man in khaki was headed his way. He stopped at the sight of the revolver aimed at his chest.

'Drop the spear.'

The weapon fell clattering from his hands.

'Forgive me.' Ambika apologized. 'I will not shoot you. You are my brother, not my enemy.' He put away the revolver. 'The British are the enemy – yours and mine. You are my brother.'

The chowkidar stood rooted to the spot.

'A friend of mine is very badly injured. Please go look for him.' Ambika held out a fistful of coins. 'The police will have gone by now.' His fingers trembled open. 'He must be somewhere on that slope.' The man knelt and closed Ambika's fingers about the coins and held his hand. 'I am a poor Muslim. I work because I am a slave to my stomach but I cannot take your money. I will look for your friend.'

'But before you go, help me move to another spot.' The man grasped him by the waist and hoisted him to his feet. They lurched slowly to the bank of the khal. 'I will be back in half an hour,' he said and leaping nimbly across the uneven ground, disappeared from view.

Ambika dragged himself to his feet and stumbled across to a banana grove. From here he would be able to keep watch. Would the man return alone? Half an hour, then an hour went by. He pulled out his revolver. It would have to serve him in case the man brought the police along. But the cartridges had all been fired. There was no sense in taking any further risk. He reached for a banana leaf and wrapping the revolver securely in it, lowered himself into the waters of the khal. The water was surprisingly cold for the time of the year, or perhaps it appeared so because of the amount of blood he had lost. But the khals and rivulets were as much home to him as the hill tracts of Chittagong. Darkness had set in. With the revolver raised above the surface of the water, he made his way to the far bank. Hoisting himself up, he discarded his blood-stained clothes. Fatehabad, a village he knew like the back of his hand, was a few miles away.

It was close to 8 p.m. when he pushed Dr Bagla Chakraborty's door open. The good doctor turned ashen at the sight of the near-naked man. He had recognized him instantly even though the beard and moustache had gone. So he had heard all the news! Ambika was certain that the 5,000-rupee reward on his head had had tongues wagging in the village.

'Look, Ambika Babu,' the doctor took a firm stand. 'I am a family man. If the police get to know, there will be no end to my troubles. Pray forgive me … you may please come'.[3]

'There are no police on my trail as of the moment but I desperately need some first aid, after which I will leave immediately.'

The rear door had swung open. Doctor Chakraborty's brother had walked in. 'Ambika-da!' he gasped. Turning to the doctor, he made up his mind for him. 'Dada, you stitch him up; I am going to get some clothes … don't worry Ambika-da,' he called over his shoulder. 'I have some money saved.'

Ananda Prasad Gupta, 23 April

Sounds of singing and the beating of a drum could be heard. The village that lay across the field was decorated with lights. Lanterns hung from trees. The tune, the beat – a devotional song; it was a kirtan in progress.

They had spent the day resting in the forest and had moved out when it became dark and had, since then, been following the railway tracks, hoping to cover the eight miles that would take them to the nearest railway station. Every house that came along the way had been approached. Most had turned them away, barring the master of one house who had generously poured a little flat rice into the shirt fronts that they held bunched up. The station was still many miles away.

Where there was a puja, there would be proshaad … everyone was entitled to food from which the gods themselves had partaken. Ganesh-da craned his neck and was looking about. Realizing what he was looking for, Ananda kept an eye out for someone who looked like the local heavyweight, someone they could entreat to give them some proshaad. The villagers were all caught up in the ecstasy of the moment. Some were dancing to the beat of the khol, some sat deep in meditation. No one seemed in a hurry to end the revelry and the proshaad would not be shared until then.

'Where is the puja?' whispered Makhon. 'If it is over, they can begin handing out the proshaad to those who want to leave.'

Ganesh-da was making his way towards an elderly man. He appeared to be in charge. A polite request was made. He gave no indication of having heard. Ganesh-da waited for a while and then asked again. Ananda tried his luck. The local honcho appeared to have no time for strangers. But this was also probably their last chance to eat.

'Dada! Dada!'

The plaintive voices eventually caught his notice but the look he flashed had no sympathy or kindness. An arrogant suspicious face, thought Ananda – probably suffers from bad moods all hours of the day … rather like that notorious pundit of '*Hing Ting Chhat*'.

'Babu ra … you babus, where are you from?'

Despite their ragged and dishevelled condition, they had been addressed as babu. Ganesh-da fabricated a fascinating account of their supposed birthplace.

'What brings you here?'

A polite answer was given but it resulted in a stream of questions. It was clear the interrogation would be a never-ending one. For a while Ganesh-da fielded the questions with dexterity but it had to be brought to an end. Digging for worms should not, after all, bring one face-to-face with a snake. Ganesh-da reminded him of the principal purpose. Could they please have some proshaad and be allowed to continue on their way?

The irritation on the man's face was evident. Why this demand for proshaad even before the kirtan had ended? 'But you have not answered my question. What is your profession?'

'We work as washermen,' said Ganesh-da.

His eyes flashed dark with suspicion. The men he had thought of as gentlemen had turned out to be washermen. A crowd had gathered. Who are these men? Where are they from? The questions seemed to fly at them. That the simple act of asking for proshaad would throw them into such a situation had been inconceivable. The sweat began pouring down Ananda's neck. The crowd was increasing as were the numbers of questions. Perhaps they had taken them to be bahurupias or dakaats.

'OK, tell us which way is north?'

What was this? Until now they had been coming up with completely imaginary answers. How could they answer a question such as this one? The elements were against them. The sky was overcast and in the dark east, west, north and south had all merged into one.

'Which way is north? Why are you quiet? Answer me.' The interrogator leant towards Ananda, intent on making a discovery.

Not answering the question would look bad and guesswork could prove dangerous. Why had they entered this village at all? Ananda began to curse himself. The proshaad that now lay in store could prevent them from leaving with their bones intact. Suddenly, for no good reason he pointed to one side. Even as he raised his hand he knew he had pointed to the wrong side. The suspicion harboured by the interrogators spread like lightning through the crowd. The murmuring became ominous.

Ganesh-da seized control. Fury playing on his face, he barked at the crowd. 'Are we thieves or dacoits? You have started talking like lawyers. We come from a village far away. Is it possible to figure out directions in a new place? Let us have you in our village on a night as dark as this and I'll see how many answers you come up with.' Turning on his heel, he stormed away walking rapidly to increase the distance from the crowd. Ananda and Makhon lost no time in following suit. Looking nervously over his shoulder, Ananda was relieved to see that Ganesh-da's outburst had had its desired effect. He let out a sigh. Never would he go, seeking an easy meal amongst a crowd.

The night had deepened. They had passed several villages. The sound of travellers' footsteps did not go unnoticed in regions like this. It brought the villagers out of their doors.

'Who are you? Name? Which village? ... Where are you going?'

Questions were thrown at them all along the way. These were people who would not let any unknown person pass without first satisfying their curiosity.

They had reached the station. It was nearly ten o'clock. A market close by was still open. With the money left over from buying the tickets, Ganesh-da bought himself a bundle of beedis and a lungi and a fez for each of them. Heading for the rice fields, they changed into their new costumes.

The Feni incident had led to a state of high alert all along the Assam Bengal Railway lines. As the train slowed down at stations, teams of policemen entered each compartment and subjected every traveller to scrutiny. The new costumes helped. Pulling at their beedis they chatted comfortably with the other passengers in the third-class compartment. Soon they had become one with their fellow travellers – simple village folk going about their business.

A policeman standing on the platform came up to the window. His eyes lingered on Ananda's face. Then suddenly bringing his lips right next to his ears hissed, 'Are you really a Muslim?' His heart leapt up hammering loudly against his chest. He could barely keep his voice steady. 'Why, can you not see? Here is my chacha beside me.'

The policeman stared at Ganesh-da. 'You are his chacha?'

Ganesh-da seemed more intent on his beedi. He gave a grunt.

The train began to roll and Ananda closed his eyes against the wave of nausea that engulfed him.

Ananta Lal Singh, 23 April

The rivulets would lead him to the Gumti; the Gumti would take him to Kumilla. Ananta raised himself from the waters of the nalla and removed the notes held carefully between his teeth. The sun was close to setting. A destination? A destination had not yet been decided upon. He would need a boat to take him to Kumilla.

A lone fisherman sat upon the banks, whiling away his time. Did he look like a man to be trusted? Ananta loped towards him, whining and pointing to his mouth. He wasn't really hungry but he needed to make contact. The man turned out to be a kindly sort and without hesitation indicated that he should follow. They walked silently until he was ushered into a hut. All of a sudden, he was surrounded by the family: men, women, wide-eyed children. They all gathered around. A large plate was pushed before him. It was piled high with food. The family jostled with each other for a better view. It was feeding time at the zoo.

'Looks like a student,' observed one.

'The hair had been freshly cropped.'

'Strong? What do you say? Worth twelve rupees of labour?'

Ananta forced himself to eat.

A wrinkled old man peered at him for a while before breaking his silence. 'Say what you will … doesn't look mad to me. CID? Who knows?'

It was fun, but staying any longer could become dangerous. A fit appeared to grab hold of him. Beginning with his hands, the jerking spread slowly through his body. Ananta stood up abruptly and walked out. The fisherman ran behind for a while. He seemed a kind man. Ananta considered confiding in him. But after the conversation that had just taken place in his house, he thought better of it.

The Bilonia bazaar would have to be crossed. There was little choice. Until now he had avoided all crowded places. But darkness was on his side and the streets had emptied. People had gone home after the day's buying and selling. Ananta was able to make his way through without attracting attention. He was now close to the railway tracks. About 500 yards away, figures moved around a bonfire. The flames leapt into the air. In another couple of minutes it would become too dark to move without the help of a flashlight. A bugle sounded. He was in the middle of a cantonment. He would have to make it to the hills while visibility lasted.

LOKENATH BAL, 23 APRIL

They were engrossed in making a meal of bananas, flat rice and jaggery.

'Which is the nearest village?'

The Muslim pointed into the distance. 'Kattali village … three miles.'

They were near the sea! Lokenath stared open-mouthed at the Muslim who had resumed his eating, without realizing the effect it had had on his companions.

'Bhai,' Lokenath nudged him. 'Will you take us there?' He knew Zamindar Pranhari Das's son Suren. Despite the fact that father and son were ardent Congress supporters, Lokenath and Suren had bonded over music. In fact, it had been Suren's rendition of '*Bande Mataram*' sung to Rabindranath Tagore's tune that had held scores of people spellbound at a recent concert. Suren had given up his job to join Gandhi-ji's Ashahjog Aandolan in 1922 and had since then not gone back to work. He now concentrated on running a music school – the Arjya Samaj Music Academy. Surely, he wouldn't turn them away. The zamindar had quite a fierce reputation – one that had driven the little fishing village to revolt sometime back. It had been with great difficulty that the household had escaped the villagers' wrath. But Suren would be there … it would be all right.

Suren was not at home. At 11 p.m. when the band of khaki-clad boys carrying firearms trooped into the courtyard, Pranhari Babu came rushing out in alarm, as the terror-stricken household cowered indoors. But within moments all was clear. Here were the victorious soldiers of Jalalabad, at their doorstep. It was a matter of honour … a matter of great pride that they had chosen this home. The women got down to work, chattering shrilly. The kitchen doors were thrown open, lamps lit and the larders emptied to cook a hurried meal. The younger men of the house helped the boys wash up, pouring out pitchers of water onto extended hands while others brought out the stocks of sal leaf platters that had been left over from the last communal meal that had been held in the zamindar's house.

Pranhari Babu was supervising the distribution of fresh shirts and dhutis. He turned to Lokenath. 'Change … I will have your uniforms destroyed.'

The shoes and socks were left in a pile along with firearms. The boys had begun sitting down in two rows. Lokenath found his place and sat down cross-legged on the floor. He wriggled his toes – it had been such relief to splash them with water. A young man rushed along the line, pouring cool water into the earthenware pots that had been placed in front of them. A young boy followed, depositing a pinch of salt and a wedge of lemon on each platter. Behind him came a man with a metal bucket, ladling out their first real meal in days.

As the boys took their leave, Pranhari Babu thrust a wad of notes into his hands. 'You will need this. God be with you.' Not one eye remained dry, as the household showered them with blessings. It made him wonder at the misgivings that had tortured him through the day.

They had reached the banks of the river. They were now two miles east of the Double Mooring jetty. 'Those of you who will be safe at home, either your own or a friend's or relative's … here take some of the money.' They would have to break up. A group moving about in the villages was bound to attract attention. Lokenath handed out the notes. 'Move in twos or alone. Hand over the firearms … you are innocent … you don't know anything.'

Debu, Rajat, Mona, Subodh Choudhury and Phonindra Nandi collected the muskets and revolvers.

'Keep an ear out. Master-da will send word … come at once.' Lokenath saw Pundit, Ranadhir, Sahayram and Saroj Guha off. He turned to Swadesh. 'The police have no clue that you are involved with us … here …' He held out some money.

'I am not going back.' Swadesh was firm. There would be no arguing.

'Loka-da, lets go to my village home in Koyepara.' Rajat turned to the Muslim guide. 'Will you be able to help us cross?'

'Bau, I will have to get my mama. If you let me go, I will fetch him within the hour. You hide in that boat.'

Could they trust him? Lokenath remained silent for a couple of minutes. 'We will wait,' he said.

FIFTEEN

Ananta Lal Singh, 24 April

A crow sat high up, announcing the morning. A rosy blush filtered through dark branches. A wave of pain swept through Ananta's cold and stiff body. As he tried to move, the blanket of earth that had covered him all night cracked and fell apart, sending a fine spray up his nostrils. He had dug himself in against the chill of the night. A fox had kept vigil, howling occasionally. He could sleep some more … a lot more. But the morning mist was clearing and he was by now in dire need of help.

A farmer leading a cow walked past him. A few minutes later, another went by. They were taking their cows to the pastures. In the distance, a pair of oxen, invigorated by the morning air, rounded the corner at a fast clip. The owner followed, a plough resting on his shoulders. The man went past, appearing not to have seen him. Ananta took a long look at his retreating back and decided to take his chance. He sprinted after him.

'Brother, spare me a glance.'

The man pretended not to have heard.

'Look at my condition. Look at the terrible state I am in.'

'What happened?' The voice was gruff. It was a response, even though the man had not bothered to look at him.

'Look brother, I am a swadeshi. I fought with the police … shot a few of them.' Ananta switched quickly to the local dialect.

The words did not affect the man's pace. Ananta kept up.

Suddenly he barked, 'Why? Why did you shoot the police?'

'For our country. They have been terrorizing our people, killing innocents.'

There was no response.

'Give me a minute. Please.' Ananta pleaded. 'I will tell you everything.'

It made no difference. The oxen walked on steadily and the owner followed. Only a slight nod of the head indicated that Ananta should follow.

They had reached the fields. Motioning him to a side, the man busied himself. Ananta squatted, watching the man till his fields without a care in the world. A bugle sounded.

'Bilonia. Troops of the maharaja of Tripura.'

The information startled Ananta. Troops sent by the maharaja of Tripura? He pleaded with the farmer, the distress in his voice now evident. 'Bhai, take me home. Please. Before they see me.'

The man seemed unperturbed. He waved him aside and continued with his work. Ananta went back to his place and sat down. But now he had begun to feel physically ill. His gut had worked itself into knots and he would have thrown up had the arrival of another young man not distracted him. The farmer handed the plough over and motioned to Ananta. They kept up a quick pace and were soon at the man's hut. Wordlessly, he handed Ananta a clean shirt and a dhuti and pointed to an empty room.

He lay quietly on the floor for hours. At last an elderly woman opened the door, pushed a plate of dry flat rice and jaggery and a pot of water before him and waited till he began to eat. This was the fare of the simple Bengali villager. Ananta chewed each mouthful, painfully washing it down with water amused by his own soft city habits. Where in these outskirts was the ghee that would pop each flake into a crunchy melt-in-the-mouth delicacy or the creamy yoghurt to soften it with? The plate lasted him a long while and he then retreated back into his corner.

The daylight had gone. It was past dusk, the moment the cows recognized as homecoming time. Ananta's host stepped into the room, his hand cupped around a flickering flame. He put the little oil lamp down and settled himself on the floor. He was ready for a talk: where would Ananta go; how would he get to Kumilla; would the Chowdhury Hat Road be the best one to follow; how much money did he have? Ananta handed all his money over. His host would decide when and how he was to leave.

Ambika Chakraborty, 24 April

'Ei shaala, kaun hai rey? Kahan sey aata hai?' A couple of inebriated policemen called out from the distance. Ambika was standing by himself at the Dewanji ghat. He would need a boatman to ferry him across the Halda to Noapara.

'I had gone to Fatehabad to attend a dinner invitation,' he called back. 'I am going home now.'

'Ja ja bhag, shaala.'

A lone fisherman was checking his net by the light of a flickering lamp. He came across, warily eyeing the policemen. Ambika handed him eight annas. The man was pleased.

Nibaran De, of Sharada village in the Noapara Thana area, was a sympathizer. But what if he wasn't home? Perhaps his neighbour would let him in … no matter how, he would have to make it to one refuge or the other before first light. Thanking the fisherman, he made his way down the dirt track. But the fear of the tiger brings on the dusk even quicker and the pale cold light of dawn picked out the lock that hung from Nibaran's door. The neighbour was up, smoking his beedi at the doorstep but, at the sight of him, hurried back inside. There was no refuge to be had here. There was no choice. Ambika took to his heels. Much as it would distress her, his father's sister – his pishima – would have to accommodate him.

Deyapara was the next village and as he burst in, it was her that he first encountered. His elderly aunt backed away hurriedly, sitting down heavily onto the ground, open-mouthed with horror. When sound did emerge from those toothless gums it was a wail of anguish. She rocked back and forth beating her chest as strands of stringy grey and oily white, which was all that was left of her hair, flapped forwards and back.

'You cannot drive me away like … like some sort of evil spirit.'

The words came in a torrent of abuse. 'Ey ki shorbonash! Why have you come? Why do you want to eat my son?' Her howling brought the household running. It was something that Ambika had been totally unprepared for but he had to seize charge.

'Stop screaming.' He snapped at his aunt. 'If you know what is good for you, keep calm. I am here for a day and I intend to stay. You will have to make sure I am safe. If you act funny,' his voice grew cold and dangerous, 'I will tell the police that you have been helping the revolutionaries for many months now … I will drag you all down with me. Let us see if that precious son of yours can hold on to that government post after that.'

Sanity returned. Pishemoshai held him by the arm drawing him indoors. 'Now be quiet. I am here. You will be safe.' Pishima readjusted her dishevelled sari to waddle in after him, commiserating over his wounds. 'My poor child, how long have you gone hungry?' She called to her son. 'Go get him a bucket of water and a change of clothes.'

A high-grade fever with rigor had set in by evening, but there was no way out. It was dark outside and he would have to leave. Pishima and Pishemoshai heaped blessings on his head and showed him the door. Were the wounds infected or was it the prolonged submersion in the waters of the khal? Ambika stumbled along the way, unable to think clearly.

He was standing outside a palm-leaf hut, begging to be let in. An old bearded man peered out into the dark and then came rushing to prop him up. 'You are alive, my child, my Ambika! We thought we had lost you. Come, come you are home now. You are safe.'

'Amjad Chacha?' Ambika mumbled weakly. He had made his way like a homing pigeon.

Here Ambika stayed till 6 May, until he was well again. Amjad Chacha's son set out in search of Master-da. One day, he brought news and Ambika handed him a letter: *Master-da, I did not die. I am alive and well. Contact me. Shaathi.*

John Younie, 24 April

The bearer set down the supper tray. A late edition had been brought out by the *Statesman*. John had decided to eat by himself, for the planters were all out on patrol.

> NINE KILLED IN BATTLE WITH ARMED RAIDERS
> **Troops open heavy fire on Chittagong fugitives**
> **Flight into Jungle**
> **Police shot in a train in arresting suspects**

Retreat into the jungle – raiders leave ammunition and guns before flight … (from our own correspondent) Chittagong April 23

The raiders casualties believed to be twelve, all sons of prominent citizens, well to do businessmen, none among the attacking forces … The troops opened heavy fire from the hilltops and maintained it until dark when the rebels retreated into the jungle. This being very dense the troops returned leaving pickets. This morning a patrol recruited from the railway battalion searched and found nine dead and three seriously wounded…

House Search by police. Noakhali April 22

The police searched the house of Mr Haran Chandra Ghose Chowdhury, President of the local Civil Disobedience Committees early this morning and arrested Kesavlal Ghose a first year student of Feni College… in connection with the Chittagong outrage

Police shot on Station.

Revolver attack by four passengers… a police sub inspector, two constables, ticket collector and a chaukidar were shot by four passengers from Bhatiari at Feni on the Eastern Bengal Railway on Tuesday night in connection with the Chittagong outrage… inspector removed to Chittagong by the next train … the constables to the local hospital… Sixteen people arrested at Feni following home searches believed to be in connection with the Chittagong riots…

12 Reported Killed.

Troops pursuing rebels in the jungle...
another detachment arrived today ...
suspected areas being strongly guarded ...
40 taxi cabs requisitioned for emergency...

John drew up a sheet of paper. No one in Chittagong had time for idle chatter but Donovan, enjoying Dorothy's company at Barisal, most certainly did.

Circuit House, Chittagong 24.4.30
...You will have read in the Statesman of the Feni outrage. It was all due to the incredible negligence of the inspector. He had arrested four suspects and brought them in into the assistant stationmaster's room and did not search them – can you believe it? Then one of them asked if he might go out to pumpship and as soon as he was led out he whipped out a couple of automatics and started a rough house. Needless to say, all four got away. There have been several house searches here and today they got one youth. He crawled into a culvert in the bazaar and fired at Johnson and the others. Johnson let him have it and when the corpse was dug out they found on him one revolver and one automatic. I suspect that probably quite a number of the gang either have slipped back to the jungle or else after the raid was over, nipped home to hide and if possible keep in touch with developments in Chittagong.

It appears that one part of the scheme miscarried which had for its object the whole scale shooting up of the sahibs at the club ... You know the club, with the long flight of steps leading up to it ... their intention was to wait and shoot up the sahibs as they all came down the steps to their cars.

It has been a thoroughly bad show from the first to the last and I can see that there is going to be a lot of dirty linen washed and much mutual recrimination when the inevitable enquiry is held ...

Yours very sincerely,
J. Younie

There was plenty of the dirty linen, he had mentioned, already on display. A.R. Leishman, president of the Chittagong Chamber of Commerce, had been in a fine temper when he had dropped in for a visit. A terrorist organization, he had said unctuously, appears to have existed for some months under the very noses of the local authorities, and no action appeared to have been taken to repress their meetings or to search their houses till well after the raids. He was demanding the stationing of regular troops, the holding of vigorous searches and an immediate enquiry. I have written, he had said, to the chief secretary of the government of Bengal saying if the civil authorities had no inkling of the condition which produced this outbreak, an early explanation from the government was due to the citizens of Chittagong. If the civil authorities were in possession of any information which might justifiably demand methods of precaution, we are entitled to ask why no warning of any sort was given to the commanding officer and adjutant of the AFI Battalion of the AB Railway.[1]

It boggles the mind, he said, especially if you stop to consider that the attacks were carried through with military precision and obviously after much drill and rehearsal. How could they possibly have missed it?

From the little titbits that John had picked up it appeared that Lieutenant General C.J. Deverell, the officiating chief of army staff had taken serious note of the intelligence lapse and had asked the general officer commanding-in-chief, Eastern Command, to enquire whether prior information of a possible raid in Chittagong had been communicated to the headquarters, Presidency and Assam district. On learning that the answer was an unqualified no, he had written to the home ministry.[2]

And they were right; nobody could afford to run the risk of a similar lack of liaison occurring elsewhere.

Lokenath Bal, 25 April

Binoy-da[3] led the way walking rapidly through the dark. 'Master-da and Nirmal-da are at my house. They arrived this morning. The rest have gone home.'

Binoy, Jogesh and Gobindo were responsible first-rankers who had been reserved for the second phase of the operation. They were in their mid-twenties and had been awaiting their turn eagerly. When Lokenath and his band of six arrived at Rajat's village home, they had been contacted by Binoy-da within hours.

'Where have they been until now?'

'In Jhunku's[4] village home at Noapara. Fortunately, his parents were in the city. The old caretaker, Jashti-da, had let them in. That old man is so shrewd that he required no explanations … he had heard that his little dada-babu had run away from home with a rifle and that a battle had been fought with the British. Any fool could put two and two together. Jashti-da gave them the little he had in the house … his own stock of cheerey, and was enterprising enough to arrange for a change of clothes for the twenty of them. Master-da ordered the boys, not in the police eye, to return home. Jhunku wept and pleaded with Nirmal-da. But he was firm.'

Lokenath nodded. Jhunku was one of Nirmal-da's recruits.

'But both Nirmal-da and Master-da were certain that his father, Ratul Babu, will be able to pull some strings at court and keep his son from being investigated. After all, Moti had taken Mihir Bose's father's rifle and as far as we know Mihir has not been arrested. Master-da impressed upon Jhunku that even if he did get arrested he was to be strong enough to withstand every torture possible and not blurt out names or details. Binod Bihari Dutt has been taken to his sister's house in Fatehabad. Kali De, who took on the responsibility, will make his way home thereafter. But Lokenath,' Binoy-da looked him in the eye. 'I am being honest. It will be too dangerous for us to keep you. Yours is too known a face … and your colouring … bhai, it attracts too much of attention.'

'What did Master-da do with the weapons?

'Made bundles of five each and sent them off to various places. What did you do?'

Lokenath pursed his lips. 'We wrapped them carefully and sank them in a pukur.'[5]

Binoy-da's eyebrows arched upwards in horror. 'It's all right.' Lokenath said. We remember the spot.

The boy on guard duty announced the arrival of Lokenath's team.

Master-da and Nirmal-da rushed downstairs to greet them. Binoy-da's house had become the field headquarters. Master-da was in agreement: Lokenath would have to be shifted out for the sake of security.

The sentry announced the arrival of Mahendra Choudhury. 'He is running our intelligence agency,' explained Nirmal-da. 'Send him up.'

The boy had participated in the armoury raid and at Jalalabad, but was again one about whom Lokenath knew little. Master-da, Ambika-da and Nirmal-da had brought in a number of unknown faces from the far-flung villages.

Mahendra began to speak in a breathless sort of way … an intense kind of lad, thought Lokenath.

'Ambika-da was not to be found on Jalalabad … Ardhendu Dastidar is in hospital … Union Merchant Association and Sadarghat Club have been raided. Bad news – Amarendra Nandi has been shot dead in the city; Himangshu and Sukhendu were arrested the day after the raid and Sahayram Das and Subodh Roy yesterday.' He continued ignoring the look of horror on the faces. 'Relatives are being arrested and tortured …' He grimaced. 'One boy, I don't know who, has confessed. The city has been armed to the teeth,' he looked meaningfully at Master-da and Nirmal-da. 'Mr Lowman is coming to visit. Oh! And the Feni encounter … the revolutionaries shot their way out.'

'Where is Ananta-da?' One of the younger lot piped up.

Master-da rose. Placing his arm around Mahendra's shoulders, he led him out of the room. Lokenath watched as Master-da placed his mouth right next to Mahendra's ear. It was a piece of advice he gave all his trusted boys: give information on a need-to-know basis only. Mahendra slipped a note from out of his shoe. 'Sati-da sent this for you.'

Lokenath leant across to Nirmal-da. 'Did Mahendra not go home?' he whispered. Nirmal-da shook his head. 'He stole all that he could on that last day and has sworn never to go back again. In any case, there is a price on his head.' He laughed. 'The boy is a moron-paagol – bent on giving his life for the country. Biren De and two others are helping him. We have given him the code name Zamindar.'

Binoy-da came up to Lokenath. With him was another fresh-faced youngster, one he had got a little familiar with during the sojourn in the hills. 'Go home with him and stay indoors during the day ... while that white skin of yours serves you on many occasions, in villages like these, it is your enemy.'

Lokenath left with the quiet young lad. They walked through the village streets, sticking to the shadows. They were home a little before dawn.

'Please sit.' The boy left him in a room on the ground floor and ran upstairs. Lokenath waited, feeling a little uncomfortable. He was a little desperate to wash and freshen up. An hour went by and then another fifteen minutes. It would be light soon. What if someone walked in? He went to the bottom of the stairs and called. There was no response. Had something gone wrong? He yelled out at the top of his voice and waited. Footsteps came pattering down the stairs but he could tell it was not the boy's. A grown man appeared. He held the boy's revolvers in his hands.

'Here,' he said. 'Take them. My nephew no longer wishes to speak with you. Forgive us; we are a simple family that needs no trouble. You know that the police are out to get you. We most respectfully request that you don't stay in this house. You may come now.'

Stunned, Lokenath stammered, 'I would like to talk to him before I go.' What had happened to that confident youth that had fought by his side? One hour with his uncle had confused him.

'That is not possible.'

'Well then, you will simply have to put up with me until it is dark and safe for me to leave ... or else if they see me leaving from your house ...' The unspoken words had their desired effect. The uncle got up and left.

It was not that he was neglected the rest of the day, for he managed a bath and was served a full meal but it became a great learning experience: family elders held great power over the minds of the youth. That night he slipped out after dark and made his way to Nirmal-da's mamar-bari.

Ananta Lal Singh, 27 April

The farmer, Suren, led Ananta through a little-used route that wound its way through the hills. A police barricade stood before them. It was time to put on the mute act. He was proud of his dexterity with dialects but this was not the time to put it to test. The police went through their questions and Suren fielded them adroitly. They were let into Choddo Gram. Kumilla was another twenty miles away and buses ran every hour.

As luck would have it, three of the buses that plied the route had broken down that day and the fourth, though headed towards Kumilla, was not accepting passengers, for it was on its way to have a broken spring repaired. After much pleading and bargaining, a deal was struck for a generous payment. The driver would take the two of them along. But the bus was not scheduled to leave until another two hours. Ananta would have to remain out of sight. Suren's cousin kept shop in Choddo Gram and it was there that the pair headed.

He waited by himself in a room while the cousins caught up with each other. The minutes ticked by. Suren emerged after a while and they made their way back to the bus station. The driver was waiting, revving his engine impatiently. Ananta swung himself up. His companion did not board the bus. He remained where he was.

A defiant shake of the head was all that was forthcoming. Why had he changed his mind so suddenly?

The bus had begun to roll.

'Give me some money,' signalled Ananta, the pleading in his eyes turning to panic.

The farmer upturned both his hands in a gesture that said there was none left. The bus was speeding now. It was embarrassing, to say the least. How would he now pay the driver? And what had happened at the cousin's house? The man he had trusted so completely during the last three days … could he have turned against him in a matter of hours? Had the cousins tipped the police off? It was too late now. Ananta sat staring at the countryside that was flashing by. He should be ready to jump if the bus was stopped en route.

Kumilla was now no more than a couple of miles away. At last Ananta ventured to make conversation as best as he could in the local dialect. Did the driver know the advocate Kamini Dutt? Everybody, it seemed, knew Kamini Babu. Ananta's heart was at peace. If he could make it to the Dutt household all his worries would be taken care of.

KALPANA DUTT

Dinner was over and the lights put out at last. May had arrived, bringing with it two months of summer vacations. Tired out with the end-of-term revelry, the girls had turned in for the night and the last of the restless movements had come to an end. The dormitory echoed the soft regular sounds of breathing. But Kalpana lay wide awake. 'Perhaps he does not want me … he doesn't think me to be good enough.' She turned on her side and shut her eyes.

Never in their wildest dreams would her father, a loyal government servant, or her grandfather, who held the British title of Rai Bahadur, have guessed what it was that was tormenting her. Their pampered darling lived independently in Kolkata as a second-year BSc Chemistry student at Bethune College. Never would they have imagined that a daughter of Chattogram's famous Duttagupta household could have stolen out of the security of the girl's hostel, made her way in the dark through the streets of Kolkata to the shadier parts of the town, seeking an audience with two wanted terrorists, reiterating that she was trustworthy and she was determined. And what would the terrorists in that pokey little underground have made of a tall, willowy, unusually pretty girl at their doorstep? Hers was too known a face and she came from too well known a family … a family of wealthy British loyalists.

It had been days since Kalpana had met with Purnendu Dastidar and Kebla-da. Why had she not heard from them? Was Master-da not to be traced since the revolution or was he still hell-bent on having nothing to do with women and girls?

'Who will give me the revolutionary's dikkha?' she sighed, brushing the flimsy veil of the mosquito netting aside. Her fingers moved reassuringly against the metal trunk that safeguarded her most precious possessions. She got out of bed as gently as possible, taking care not to make the slightest sound.

It was 1 a.m. She lit a small kerosene lamp, turning down the wick to keep the flame as low as possible. Opening the trunk, she removed the framed picture and set it upon the study table. The flickering glow lit up the serene face of the dark skinned goddess, making her tongue look redder than ever. A glance around the room assured her that the girls were sound asleep. The metal blade of the dagger caught the light as she fumbled with the buttons of her blouse. Kalpana held her breath as the wicked tip sliced through the tender skin. The ruby droplet trembled on the pale skin of the breast.

'Ma-go,' the words came softly. 'I will give my life for independence … this I promise. With you as witness I give myself the dikkha.'[6]

NOTES

CHAPTER 1

1. Now within the Indian state of Jharkhand.
2. Lord Lytton I served as viceroy from 1876 to 1880. On 1 January 1877, the Delhi Durbar was held and Queen Victoria was proclaimed empress of India.
3. Lord Lytton II served as governor of Bengal from 1922 to 1927 and was succeeded by Sir Stanley Jackson.
4. Bengal Criminal Law Amendment Act.
5. *Chittagong Armoury Raiders – Reminiscences,* Kalpana Dutt
6. Ashahjog Aandolan.
7. The Bengal Technical College is now a part of Jadavpur University.
8. The incident is dated to 10 April 1906. Joteen Mookerjee had by then wed Indubala. Their firstborn, a son, had recently passed away after an epidemic of cholera.

CHAPTER 2

1. The Dum Dum Aerodrome at Kolkata had been completed under the supervision of the assistant magistrate and SDO of Barrackpore and Dum Dum, John Younie, in November 1920. It became one of the most important aerial junctions in the route to the East with two Handley Page machines, holding twenty passengers, flying daily.
2. Outram Institute within Fort William was formerly Fort House which housed the governor general until Government House, also known as Governor's House or Raj Bhavan, was completed in 1803.

3. Adapted from http://www.flightglobal.com/pdfarchive/view/1929/1929%20-%200480.html
4. Sir Charles Augustus Tegart, known as Gus to the family, earned a number of nicknames while in India, the most popular one being Mike.
5. Sir Stanley Jackson served in the Royal Lancaster Regiment of Militia in the Second Boer War and was transferred to the West Yorkshire Regiment as a Lieutenant Colonel in 1914. In 1915, he was elected member of parliament representing Howdenshire (Yorkshire) until he resigned in 1926. He served as financial secretary to the War Office during the years 1922–1923. In 1927, he was appointed governor of Bengal.
6. Most probably a 1927 model 519 B or a series two 510 Fiat Tourer, this car was later damaged in a bomb blast; refer photograph.
7. Kyd Street has been renamed Dr M.D. Ishaque Road. The property Number 2 Kyd Street, is today a condominium complex housing the MLA Hostel.
8. David Petrie was then director of criminal intelligence in India. He was appointed head of MI5 by Churchill just before World War II.
9. Bengal Youth Assembly or yuva sammelan.
10. A discussion as to whether Damodar Chapekar is the first martyr is inevitable. One must however keep in mind that Mangal Pande and others, who lost their lives during the first uprising of 1857 were sentenced to death for mutiny under the army law.
11. Member of the Royal Victorian Order.
12. Document marked secret and signed by Sir Charles Tegart. Source: University of Cambridge.
13. C.R. Das (b. 5 Nov 1870, d. 16 June 1925): Started his career with the successful defence of Aurobindo Ghose in the 1909 Alipore Bomb Case. In December 1922, a faction of the Indian National Congress unhappy with Gandhi-ji's suspension of all civil resistance after the Chauri Chaura incident formed the Congress Khilafat Swaraj Party with Das as the president and Motilal Nehru as one of the secretaries. Other prominent members were Huseyn Shaheed Suhravardi, Subhas Chandra Bose and Vithalbhai Patel, whose younger brother – Vallabhbhai

– remained with the No Changers who had accepted Gandhiji's proposal. With C.R. Das's death and Nehru's return to the mainstream Congress, the Swaraj Party lost its steam. Before his death C.R. Das gifted his house and lands to the nation on which Chittaranjan Seva Sadan – a women's hospital was built.

CHAPTER 3

1. British Midnapore.
2. From 17 November 1921 to 17 March 1922 Edward, the Prince of Wales, toured India. During the visit he inaugurated the Victoria Memorial Hall. But protests erupted all over India culminating in the Chauri Chaura incident when Gandhi withdrew the call for agitation.
3. Field Marshal, Ganesh Ghosh, *Chattogram Yuva-Vidroha 1930–34 Aalokmela*, p. 82.
4. Shaheed Nirmal Sen, 29 July 1925. See *Chattogram Yuva-Vidroha 1930–34 Aalokmela*, p. 77.
5. 10 November 1925.

CHAPTER 4

1. Kuldip Nayar, *Without Fear,* page 96. Bhagat Singh and Batukeshwar Dutt continued the hunger strike even after Jatin's death maintaining it for 116 days. On 5 October 1929, Bhagat Singh's father had his way and convinced them to give up the fast. They had surpassed the ninety-seven-day world record set by an Irish revolutionary.

CHAPTER 5

1. Chittopriya had been found dead and Jyotish Pal wounded.
2. He remained director until 1931 and was succeeded by H. Williamson. Petrie served with Tegart later in Palestine.
3. Dr Ganguli, who was among the treating physicians, records that Magistrate Kilby along with Tegart and Denham had Joteen Mookerjee admitted at about 11 p.m. on 9 September.

Joteen thanked the magistrate and said: 'Remember, I alone am responsible for all that has been done in Bengal till now… they are mere boys (speaking of his companions) … see that they are acquitted.' Then he vomited and exclaimed: 'Strange; still so much blood left? …Fortunately, every drop of it has been shed in the worship of the Mother. It can never end in failure.'

The operation was a success and the next morning he greeted the British officers cheerfully. Tegart asked whether he could do anything else. After the officers left, Joteen Mookerjee tore off his bandages and stitches while in full possession of his lucidity… He passed away with a smile.

On receiving Lord Hardinge's cable announcing the death of Joteen Mookerjee, Lord Chamberlain had cabled back saying: I PRESUME THAT EVERY PRECAUTION HAS BEEN TAKEN TO PREVENT DISCLOSURE THROUGH THE PRESS.

Taken from *Bagha Jatin – Life and Times of Jatindranath Mukherjee* by Prithwindra Mukherjee.

4. 'My father – Tejendranath – was six when he saw, at Benares, in January 1915, on getting off the carriage, JNM my grandfather – make a sign and a sahib (probably disguised as an Indian) come forward and carry their luggage upstairs. JNM told him: Now you know exactly where I am.

   'That was Tegart. That was shortly before the 21 February armed rising organized by Rasbehari Bose (Rash Bihari Basu) under JNM's leadership; the two leaders often met at Benares. Both Tegart and JNM were fond of disguises and kept an eye on each other.' Prithwindra Mukherjee (grandson of Joteen Mookerjee).

CHAPTER 6

1. Rabindranath Tagore.
2. The Red Sea.
3. The Mediterranean Sea.
4. In a telegram to J.M. Sengupta on 7 March 1930, Jawaharlal Nehru wrote: if Chittagong does not elect within the time allotted the AICC elections will take place without them. AICC Papers, G 120/1929, *Do And Die,* page 43, Manini Chatterjee.

5. Later Lord Justice Rowlatt.
6. He received the CIE in 1917 and joined Royal Flying Corps in France. Sir Charles Tegart Collection at the Middle East Centre, St Antony's College, Oxford.

CHAPTER 7

1. *Memoirs of an Indian Policeman:* Mechhua Bazaar Bomb Case, Kathleen Francis Tegart.
2. Police records quoted in *Agnigarbha Chattogram* by Ananta Lal Singh.
3. The Rowlatt Act had been repealed in 1922.
4. Rai Bhupendranath Chatterji Bahadur, special superintendent of police, Intelligence Branch. The death is recorded in the diary of Sir Charles Tegart and quoted in the *Memoirs of an Indian Policeman* by Kathleen Francis Tegart. Sir Charles Tegart fought for pensions for his officers and men and for their widows. It is unfair, he said, that when an ICS man dies his widow is entitled to a pension but not so a policeman's widow. In addition, he fought for better pay and housing for all ranks, saying it was the only way to attract the good people to the service.

   Nadia district's Ananta Hari Mitra, Chattogram's Sukhendu Dutt, Dhaka's Birendra Chatterji, Chattogram's Pramod Ranjan Choudhury and seven others were caught on 28 May1926 in association with the murder. Hari Narayan Chandra or Hari-da, who led that group, used to conduct classes in bomb manufacturing for his group and had permitted the Chittagong lads, including Ananta Lal Singh and Ganesh Ghosh during their days in Calcutta in the 1923–1924 period, to attend his lecture demonstrations. He taught them to make picric acid, picric powder, guncotton, potassium cyanide, prussic gas and prussic acid; how to light a bomb with carbon disulphuride and yellow phosphorous. While the youngsters were kept busy manufacturing explosives, Hari-da tested his handmade grenade shells. In September 1926, Pramod Ranjan Choudhury and Ananta Hari Mitra were hanged within the precincts of the jail. Dhruv, Ananta Chakraborty and Hari-da were sent to the Burma Jail to serve a life sentence.

5. Sir Charles Tegart had received his knighthood at the New Years Honours of 1926. In May 1937, he received the KCIE – Knight Commander of the Indian Empire, at the Coronation Honours following the coronation of King George VI and Queen Elizabeth.

Chapter 9

1. Rabindranath Tagore.
2. There is some controversy as to whether Lokenath Bal was a member of the core group. However, from Lokenath Bal's own writings (quoted in *Chattogram Yuva-Vidroha 1930–34 Aalokmela*) it is evident that he was engaged in scouting for a suitable car at 3 p.m. that day.
3. Rabindranath Tagore.
4. Deposition of Ahmadur Rehman. *Yuva-Vidroha*, part I, Ananta Lal Singh.
5. Too much had been used, which caused him facial burns. That same night Tazu Mia (PW 29) was returning along the road from his father-in-law's house when between Faujdarhat and Fakirhat he heard someone groaning in a field by the roadside. He found Ahmadur Rehman lying beside a patch of jungle. He had superficial burns on his face and his taxi was nowhere to be found. Tazu Mia fetched a taxi from Idagaon and took him to the General Hospital. At about 3.45 a.m., the sub-divisional officer came to the hospital and recorded his statement.
6. Dhirendra Lal Dastidar was from a small zamindar family and though he was very close to Lokenath and fond of the entire group, he had been left out. His wealthy background had gone against him. The family rifle had been frequently borrowed for shikaar and on that day Lokenath and Ganesh had borrowed in addition two swords and one stick gun. Dhiren had no clue as to why they were being taken. The rifle remained behind in Ganesh's room and Dhiren was arrested. He spent two years in jail quite happily with his friends. Though he was freed, he was held back as a detenue for many years. Eventually, he landed in

Rangoon, converted to Sikhism and took on the name Ranjit Singh. He continued to remain in touch with his friends.

7. Krishna Choudhury's kaka, Manindra Lal Choudhury, was a lawyer at court. The rifle had been taken from his almirah. Nothing in the almirah had been disturbed, not even the box. The rifle was not found missing until 22 April. On 23 April, Manindra Babu reported the loss to the Kotwali and also the fact that his nephew was missing. Krishna went into hiding after the Battle of Jalalabad and lived with the Chakma tribe. He returned to take part in the cricket ground encounter and was hanged along with Himangshu Chakraborty.
8. Deposition of Abdul Rashid, who was employed as driver of taxi number 20469 by its owner Fajlur Rehman of Agrabad. On the evening of 18 April he and his assistant Sultan Ahmed were waiting at the taxi stand near Lal Dighi when at about 8.30 or 9 p.m., a Hindu youth whom he did not know before came up and, engaging the taxi, asked him to drive on. He was about to take his assistant with him but the passenger objected saying there would be no room for him as there would be others coming. Under the direction of his passenger, Abdul drove to Sadarghat Road and was ordered to stop opposite a house on the left-hand side of the road about 200 paces from Ezekiel's shop. The passenger entered this house and after a little while came out and asked the driver to come inside. He went in. A man dressed in khaki uniform (shorts, tunic and topee) levelled a pistol at him and ordered him to keep quiet. They took him to a small room inside the house and binding his hands and feet, left him lying on the floor. Then they pointed their pistols at his chest and asked if he recognized any of them. Terror-stricken, he shook his head. As they went off they warned him that they were leaving a guard to watch him and shoot him if he made the slightest sound. He next heard them starting up his car.

   Janab Abdul Mia had not given out Ananta Lal Singh's name despite the fact that he had identified himself. The next morning he had got up and instead of making a report to the police had gone quietly home. How many sympathizers we have … how many support us silently … we have no count.

In fact there is more in the judgment report:

> ... At the AFI headquarters Mr Lewis went inside leaving Abdul Rashid to wait in the car but as Mr Lewis was long in returning he got tired of waiting and went home.

It was something that was just not done those days. One could not even think of behaving like this with an Englishman ... let alone Mr Lewis who was Chattogram's assistant police superintendent at the time. He later became the battalion commander of the Eastern Frontier Rifles. And a poor ordinary taxi driver left the sahib high and dry! *Yuva-Vidroha,* part I, Ananta Lal Singh.

CHAPTER 10

1. *Chattogram Bidroher Kahini*, Ananda Gupta
2. During the trial, the police had taken the operator to meet Ananda Gupta to facilitate identification in court. But the operator stuck to his story. 'He became unconscious and did not see what happened. He shouted, he says but nobody came, so he went to the basha of the telegraph lineman Janab Ali.' Judgment of the Chittagong Armoury Raid case.
3. Police report: The photographs Ex XXXV taken by the SDO Telegraphs (PW 48) and the enlargement (Ex CLXX) by PW 4 show more fully and forcibly than any witness can describe the extent of the damage that was done. The telephone switchboard and all the connected apparatus were reduced to a smouldering wreck. Curiously enough, the fire-blackened dial of the clock, which hung on the wall behind the switchboard, with its hands arrested at 9.50 p.m. offers its own silent testimony to the time at which the outrage was committed.
4. Shaheed Surya Sen Bhavan publication: Biplobi Neta Ambika Chakraborty, author Dwijen Dastidar.
5. Mr Horn had fired Mr Scott's rifle... Ananta Lal Singh.

   W.D. Horn's deposition: 'Soon after 10 p.m., on the way back from the deputy superintendent's quarters I heard the commotion in the telephone department. Through the windows on the eastern side I could see five to six men that seemed to be Bengalis, hammering away at the boards. It looked as if they were intent on destroying everything. I called out, "Who is there?" But there was no reply. I thought I saw one of them look at me. A shot was fired. I ran back to the deputy superintendent and reported the matter. He ran out with his rifle immediately but by then a huge fire had broken out at the telephone exchange.' *Chattogram Bidroher Kahini*, Ananda Gupta.

6. Amongst those in the guardroom, one injured man ran all the way home while several others went off to the city and did not return before three or four days. Constable Jaykaran had a similar story to tell during the trial: 'Roused by the report of guns, he got up and was stretching out his hand for his rifle when he was shot in the left buttock, whereupon he leapt from the verandah and ran for cover to the jungle, west of the doctor's quarters.'

   The barracks had emptied out as well. Constable Sital Prasad Dubey, who was sleeping in the number 1 barrack, was likewise awakened by the firing ...as he approached the magazine, the revolutionaries turned their torchlights upon him and fired. The bullet hit him on the left hand, whereupon he ran back to the police hospital where he lurked all night until 8 a.m.

   Two guards that changed their minds and made their way back, probably to collect intelligence, were caught, handcuffed and locked up in one of the barracks. *Chattogram Bidroher Kahini*, Ananda Gupta.

7. Tegra was put in charge of distributing firearms from the armouries. *Chittagong Armoury Raiders – Reminiscences*, Kalpana Dutt.

   Tegra and Bidhu went to the European club. *Biplobi Mahanayak Surjya Sen O Chattogram Yuva-Vidroha 1930–34.*

8. During the trial it was learnt that he was Ramani Chakraborty.
9. Gholam Jhilani was admitted to the Pahartali Railway Hospital the next day by the chief medical officer of the Assam Bengal Railway, Mr Weldon.
10. Abdul Sovan slipped out of the back door, ran to the Chittagong Railway Station and reported to a disbelieving assistant stationmaster on duty who informed the sub-inspector in charge

of the railway police only when he realized his phone had gone dead. Abdul Sovan was sent with a written message to Major Baker, the traffic manager. By the time Baker reached, the AFI armoury was on fire.

11. The Auxiliary Force had been created to put down Indian regiments that revolted. The AFI armoury had some 400 magazine rifles and 200–300 muskets. There were five Lewis guns at the AFI armoury as opposed to the two at the police lines. The slow-loading muskets meant for the Indians, fired one bullet at a time, which travelled no more than 200 yards. The magazine rifle meant to be used only by the British could accommodate ten cartridges at a time and fire rapidly. The barrel of the magazine rifle had been so designed that the powerful cartridges would emerge as nickel-coated lead bullets capable of travelling up to 1,000 yards.

    In those days four companies formed a battalion. Each company was drawn from different regiments – three Indian and one British. The British company was meant to keep watch over their Indian mates, making it difficult for them to conspire.

12. Police Superintendent Johnson and DIG Farmer checking out Sub-inspector Sanjiv Chandra Nag's news. *Do And Die,* Manini Chatterjee.
13. Mr Bliss was the agent of the Assam Bengal Railway and the most prominent of civilians in Chittagong.
14. Deposition of Sanjiv Chandra Nag: 'My name is Sanjiv Chandra Nag. I am a sub-inspector of the reserve forces at the police lines. Last night I went to bed at 10 p.m. Around 10.30 p.m. gunshots and cries of Bande Mataram woke me. From my verandah I could see 5 or 6 motorcars standing in front of the armoury. Nearly 30–40 men, torches in hand, had collected. They were firing. I realized that the revolutionaries had attacked the armoury. I ran towards the barracks alerting the others. Each man must try and do his best. With my assistant, Sub-inspector Pratul Chandra Barua, I ran to the police superintendent's bungalow. The DIG was notified. Then, as instructed, I went to alert the police station at Kotwali. The message was passed to the deputy superintendent and the detective police inspector. At 12.30

a.m. with Abdul Azim Khan, Yogendra Chandra Das and the deputy police superintendent, a few constables, two muskets and cartridges we went towards the lines. The revolutionaries were engaged in heavy firing. Unable to approach them, we took refuge in a village to the south of the armoury. We kept watch over the anarchists.' *Chattogram Bidroher Kahini*, Ananda Gupta.

15. There were six people killed that night according to Dr Weldon's deposition: the AFI sentry; Sergeant Major Farrell; a car with a dead man in the driver's seat, a dead man in the back and the body of an Anglo-Indian lying on the running board; Jarasandha Barua, the district magistrate's orderly.
16. Captain Taitt had escaped without a scratch.
17. The newly constructed magazine room with the ammunition was a small room at the opposite end of the building from the armoury, at the east end of the south verandah. *Do And Die*, p. 96, Manini Chatterjee.
18. 'In the busti, Azim met Constable Jogendra Ghose who handed him a pair of handcuffs, saying that the raiders had captured him and handcuffed him with them. He was returning to the barracks about 10.30 p.m. …at the wooden bridge in the front of the magazine when he was challenged and on hearing shouts of Bande Mataram threw his tunic and pugree behind him. Fifteen to twenty people variously dressed and armed with pistols and torchlights surrounded him. To the suggestion that he was a policeman he replied with a vehement denial. They seized him, handcuffed him and threatened to kill him if he made the slightest noise. As he sat imprisoned in the magazine room, he heard the sounds of firing and orders to load and reload. Later on when all the noise had ceased, he ventured out and finding the raiders gone, slipped the handcuff off his right wrist and ran… the witness has demonstrated before us the Houdini-like facility with which he can slip his hands out of locked handcuffs.' From the judgment of the Chittagong Armoury Raid.
19. To the revolutionaries' 300 to 400 bullets they had returned some 141 rounds from their machine guns and magazine rifles.

CHAPTER 11

1. 'The sad part was that they had seen us and thinking we were the enemy had lain down in the fields. How could they even think that the British would drive so slowly with headlights on through areas where revolutionaries were known to be moving about?' *Yuva-Vidroha part I*, Ananta Lal Singh.
2. The Simon Commission arrived in India in February 1928, to widespread demonstrations, and visited Calcutta around Christmas of that year.
3. Viceregal House in Calcutta, today houses the National Library of India. It is said to have been acquired by Warren Hastings. The house was sold to Major Tolly in the 1780s. From 1854 to 1911 it housed a series of lieutenant governors until the capital moved to Delhi. The governor of Bengal then moved to Governor's House, the modern day Raj Bhavan, while Belvedere was maintained to receive the viceroy during his visits to Calcutta.
4. *Memoirs of an Indian Policeman,* p. 198, Kathleen Francis Tegart.
5. *Memoirs of an Indian Policeman* by Kathleen Francis Tegart. The conversation ascribed to Donovan and John Younie had taken place between two unnamed friends. But Donovan and Sir Charles Tegart had been close friends and remained so till the end of their lives.
6. *Yuva-Vidroha, part I*, by Ananta Lal Singh: Manindra Lal Guha, who had taken part in the Telephone Bhavan action the previous day, did not return and a few months later appeared for his BA finals and passed.
7. Quoted in *Chattogram Bidroher Kahini,* Ananda Gupta.
8. Pulin and Binod Dutt had introduced their classmate Kali De in 1927. They were all a part of the Sadarghat Club. *Youth vs Raj*, Sona Roy.
9. Story related by Kali De to Ananta Lal Singh. *Yuva-Vidroha, part I,* Ananta Lal Singh.
10. *Muktir Sopon Jalalabad*, Suresh De.
11. *Chattogram Bidroher Kahini*, Ananda Gupta: The shopkeeper's deposition.

12. *Chattogram Bidroher Kahini*, Ananda Gupta.

CHAPTER 12

1. Referring to Bahadur Shah Zafar, the last Mughal emperor.
2. Defence of India Act.
3. *Without Fear* by Kuldip Nayar.
4. Fakir Chandra Sen had wandered about from one relative's house to another before he was arrested. The boy had been in hiding in Ananda Prasad Gupta's house for some days, since the police complaint made by his father, and had no idea of the planned action. On the morning of 18 April Naresh Ray had told him to report to the Congress office after sunset. Sahayram Das had come for him; given him the uniform, and they had both driven down to the Congress office in the Baby Austin. Fakir had worn his shirt and dhuti over the uniform. At the Congress office Ambika Chakraborty informed him that Sahayram was to be his group leader. 110 *Youth vs Raj*, Sona Roy, p. 108.
5. *Chattogram Bidroher Kahini*, Ananda Gupta.
6. *Chattogram Bidroher Kahini*, Ananda Gupta.
7. *Muktir Sopon Jalalabad,* Suresh De.
8. *Muktir Sopon Jalalabad,* Suresh De.
9. *Muktir Sopon Jalalabad,* Suresh De.
10. Rabindranath Tagore.

CHAPTER 13

1. Quoting from Subodh Roy's unpublished memoir *Do And Die,* Manini Chatterjee.
2. Alexander Burnett Papers.
3. Younie Papers, p. 182.
4. Quoted from *Political trouble in India 1917–1930,* H.W. Hale. The rest of Johnson's words have been taken from Younie Papers.
5. *Agnigarbha Chattogram: Quotes from police records*, Ananta Lal Singh.
6. *The Argus* (Melbourne, Vic.: 1848–1954), Monday 21 April 1930, p. 9.

7. This is Suresh De's version. Ananta Lal Singh says it was Nirmal Sen who had interviewed the villagers.
8. *1st group*: Suresh De (Sadhu), Dwijen Dastidar (went to telephone exchange), Niranjan Rai, Shaileshwar Chakraborty, Jiten Dasgupta, Binod Choudhury; *2nd group*: Krishna Choudhury, Binod Bihari Dutt, Saroj Guha, Kali Kinkar De, Madhusudan Dutt, Noni Gopal Deb, Malin Ghose; *3rd group*: Khirod Banerjee, Hemendu Dastidar, Kalipada Chakraborty (Pundit), Ardhendu Dastidar, Ranadhir Dasgupta; *4th group*: Sahayram Das, Motilal Kanungo (Moti), Bidhu Bhushan Bhattacharya (Bidhu-da), Narayan Sen, Pulin Bikash Ghose, Naresh Ray; *5th group*: Mahendra Choudhury, Nirmal Lala, Birendra Kishore De, Vijay Sen, Nitaipada Ghose; *6th group*: Shanti Nag, Aswini Choudhury, Bon Bihari Dutt, Sashank Dutt, Subodh Bal; *7th group*: Phonindra Nandi (Phoni), Haripada Mahajan, Bhabatosh Bhattacharya, Sudhangshu Bimal Bose, Subodh Choudhury, Subodh Roy (Jhunku), Bidhu Sen; *8th group*: Tripura Sen, Monoranjan Sen (Mona), Deboprasad Gupta (Debu), Hari Gopal Bal (Tegra), Rajat Sen, Swadesh Roy, Probhash Bal, Sitaram Biswas.
9. *Do And Die*, p. 77, Manini Chatterjee.
10. Each belt carried 250 bullets.
11. A Vicker's gun section had taken position spewing close to 350 bullets per minute.
12. Interviewed by Sachidananda Mohanty.
13. From Captain Taitt's deposition: 'I sent a team from the Surma Valley Light Horse Vahini to take position on the crest of another hillock, 50 to 60 yards away. The rest were sent to occupy another about 100 yards away, while I maintained my position in between. The firing was resumed and kept up till darkness fell at 6.45 p.m., for the zila magistrate had ordered that the soldiers were to return to Chattogram before evening set in … I met with Col Dallas Smith who had arrived by the armoured train. I gave him a full report. The rebels were still firing at us. The colonel had a division with Lewis guns sent in. Five rounds were fired and that brought an end to the battle. It was nearly 7.15 by then. I remained with Colonel Dallas Smith until 9.30 or 10 o'clock and then returned to Chattogram.'

Sub-inspector Hem Gupta's deposition varies slightly: 'At 4 p.m. we had all left. With us were soldiers from Surma Valley Light Horse and the Eastern Frontier Rifles led by Captain Taitt and Captain Robertson. By 4.30 to 4.45 we had reached Jharjharia Bot-tali. Mr Farmer was waiting. He had with him soldiers from the Eastern Frontier Rifles … We went past a masjid towards Jalalabad. Captain Taitt divided the men into groups. Captain Taitt and I, accompanied by four soldiers from the Surma Valley Light Horse and four from the Eastern Frontier Rifles, formed a group. We had reached the base of a densely wooded hill when a voice cried: "Halt." Then almost immediately we were fired upon. We ran and took cover in a drain and fired back. We could hear the rebels shout Bande Mataram. The firing continued for nearly two hours. It was fast and furious during the first hour but petered down in the second. The stray odd round continued to be fired for a while. It was getting dark and we returned the way we had come. The armoured train had arrived. Colonel Dallas Smith, ASP Mr Lewis and a few Gurkhas from the Eastern Frontier Rifles were waiting. They had Lewis guns. They climbed a hill and began firing upon the Jalalabad hill. While we took refuge beside the armoured train, the Surma Valley Light Horse and others returned to Chattogram … After firing a couple of rounds from the Lewis guns there were no more sounds to be heard from the rebels. Colonel Smith and Mr Lewis returned to the armoured train. We waited until 11.30 p.m. before returning to Chattogram.'

In the Judgment of the Chittagong Armoury Raid, Mr Younie records: '… Capt Taitt withdrew his men and sent them back to Chittagong by 7 p.m. While the fire was on, Mr Farmer's party with their Lewis gun had taken cover behind a hill to the south of that occupied by the raiders but could not open fire as he could see nobody on account of the intervening jungle … Col Dallas Smith sent Mr Lewis with a small party and a Lewis gun to the top of the hill on the left side of the defile leading to Jalalabad hill … It was nearly dark. The raiders' guns were still flashing. Mr Lewis aimed the rifles and machine guns at those flashes. They then advanced to another hill further on and fired again until the raiders' fire completely died away …Col Dallas Smith and the whole force went back to Chittagong which they reached about 11p.m. Only sub-inspectors Abdul Gaffur and Siddique Dewan remained overnight at Jharjharia Bot-tali.'

The various depositions given by the British camp describing the Battle of Jalalabad contradict each other, leading the reader to favour the version given by the revolutionaries.

14. Alexander Burnett is referring to Ananta Lal Singh, mistaking him for a Sikh, for both Sikhs and Rajputs share the title Singh. At times like these there is no end to the number of rumours that abound.
15. The Abors of modern-day Arunachal Pradesh were first discovered by the British in 1826. In 1911, the British assistant political officer, Mr Williamson, his colleague Dr Gregorson and their party were murdered while touring the Tibetan border area. It resulted in a punitive expedition by the British Indian army.
16. This particular observation about sending seventy against a hundred when the army manuals clearly states a ratio of 3:1 is not John Younie's but that of Ananta Lal Singh. The rest has been drawn from the Younie Papers.

CHAPTER 14

1. This train was carrying the Tripura state troops belonging to the maharaja of Agartala and was headed towards Bilonia to counter the revolutionaries. The police had been waiting at Feni station to welcome them when the telegram from the Bhatiari stationmaster arrived.
2. The last few years of Ananta Lal Singh's life had to be spent once again in jail. He had been convicted for a dacoity conducted in independent India. Once again, he chose to defend himself and raised the money for the expenses by publishing his account of the revolution in a popular Bengali magazine. This story had elicited a response and a young woman had come to meet him in jail, claiming to be the girl he had written about. Ananta Lal Singh passed away before the case could be concluded. Though he maintained his innocence till the end, it is well known that

he had been obsessed with the unification of Bengal – a passion shared by many, including Sarat Chandra Bose who had not only contributed to the fund but had written about it openly in his last editorial, minutes before he passed away.

3. Bengalis avoid using the words 'go' or 'going', 'I will be back' is preferred to 'I am going', 'you may come' actually means 'you may go', etc.

CHAPTER 15

1. Letter from the chairman, Chittagong Branch, European Association, to the political secretary, Government of Bengal dated 1 May 1930, in GOI Home Poll File No. 336/1930. Quoted in *Do And Die*, Manini Chatterjee.
2. Note attached to copy of Letter No. 57869/163/G dated 13 June 1930 from the general officer commanding-in-chief, Eastern Command, to the chief of general staff, Army Headquarters, Simla, in GOI Home Poll File No. 4/9/31.
3. Binoy Sen.
4. Subodh Roy.
5. These were retrieved by Shanti Chakraborty of the Anushilan Party who later switched to Master-da's group.
6. Master-da and his boys had long abandoned this practice of drawing blood for the dikkha (initiation), but Kalpana did not know that.

GLOSSARY OF BENGALI WORDS AND EXPRESSIONS

Aag	Hindi word for fire
Aaggey	(Hindi aagya) beg permission
Aamader chokhey dhulo diye palalo kothaye. Achchha dekhbo – palabi kothaye? Dhora ki porbi na?	Fooled us, has he? Let us see – where will you run? Will you not be caught?
Aamar praan bhora aashirbaad	I bless you with all my soul
Aanchal	(Hindi pallu) the long free end of the sari
Aandolan	movement
Aatchala	a hut, the roof of which is assembled by putting together eight mats.
Abdaar	to exercise a loved one's right to make demands
Abeer	red-coloured powder used during the festival of Holi
Abritti	recitation
Ahimsa	the doctrine of doing no harm
Ain Amanya	non-cooperation movement
Akhara	gymnasium
Allah ho Akbar	(Arabic) God is great
Almirah	(Arabic) cupboard
Aalok	light
Aalta	a red dye applied to the rim of women's feet
Amar	immortal
Amavasya	new moon

Amrit	sacred elixir
Anna	a coin. Sixteen annas make a rupee.
Attar	a perfume extracted from roses
Atyachar	torture
Atyachari	the one who tortures
Baas	that's all
Baba	father or son
Babu	a gentleman belonging to the educated middleclass equivalent to the English Esquire. It is often tagged onto names as a measure of respect. The term was extended to Indian government servants, all of whom were drawn from the middle class.
Bagaan-bari	a large bungalow surrounded by large gardens
Bagh	tiger
Bahurupia	con-men who assume many disguises
Balika	girl
Bande Mataram	(Hindi Vande Mataram) prayer to the motherland, a song by Bankim Chandra Chattopadhyay
Basha	a temporary residence
Bau	the word babu being pronounced in the Chittagong dialect
Bazaar	market. The term was used by the British to denote the Indian quarters.
Beedi	hand-made cigarettes filled with tobacco flakes and wrapped in leaves of East Indian Ebony tree
Beel	natural waterbody
Bel	Bengal quince
Bhaat	steamed rice
Bhadralok	civilized middle class
Bhagya	fortune
Bhai	brother
Bhai-rey-bhai	brother-o-brother
Bharatvarsh	the land of Bharat or Hindustan or India.

	The country gets its name from the legendary King Bharat. The Arabs named Bharatvarsh the land of Hind or Hindustan as it lay across the river Sindh, a name they mispronounced as Hind and called its people the Hindu. The British in turn mispronounced Hind as Ind and called the river Indus and the land India.
Bharatvarshi	people of the land of Bharat
Bhojali	dagger
Bhojali	Gurkha dagger
Bhojon	(Hindi bhojan) feast, in common parlance, it means the act of eating
Bhoy	fear
Bhrahmacharya	bachelorhood
Bigha	a measure of land
Bijoya	(Hindi vijaya) victory
Bikrom	(Hindi vikram) valour
Biplob	revolution
Boloon	Please speak.
Bon	(Hindi van) forest
Bor-da	eldest brother
Boudi	elder brother's wife
Bundobust	preparations
Burkha	a long dress worn by Muslim women which covers them from head to foot and has a piece of net before the eyes.
Burra	(Hindi) for big or senior
Busti	settlement
Cha	(Hindi chai) tea
Chacha	Hindi word for father's younger brother
Chai	Hindi word for tea
Chandal	one of the lowest castes who carry out the last funeral rituals.
Chandan	sandalwood
Chaprassi	a low-grade employee who runs errands and does odd jobs.

Char	sandbank
Cheerey	flat rice; dry and hard; needs to be soaked or fried before it can be eaten.
Chhoi	a small covered area with one opening on the deck of a boat
Chhokra	little rascal – a term both derogatory and yet implying fondness at the same time
Chik	reed curtains
Chol	let us go
Chot-potey	quick-footed
Choubachcha	a small water-storage tank
Chowki	low wooden stool
Crore	hundred lakhs or ten million
Da	abbreviation for dada
Dada Babu	Dada
Dada	elder brother. The term is extended to men and boys older in age or in stature (as the son of the master of the house) as a measure of respect.
Dadi	Hindi word for paternal grandmother. The term is used to address ladies of one's grandmother's age.
Dakaat	dacoit. Like the highwaymen who looted coaches on the highway, dacoits loot travellers and raid homes.
Dal	lentils
Danda-beri	the assembly of shackles and wooden or iron rods used to bind dangerous convicts
Daroga	head of a police station
Daya	mercy
Debota	(Hindi devta) god
Dekhli	did you see?
Dera	camp
Deshpran	the life of the nation
Devi	the term refers to a goddess but is also tagged on to the names of women as a measure of respect.

Dhaba	roadside food stall
Dhan khet	rice fields
Dhoop	(Hindi agarbatti) joss sticks
Dhuti	(Hindi dhoti) a long piece of fabric wound around the waist and legs by Hindu men
Di	abbreviation for didi
Didi	elder sister. The term is extended to women and girls older in age or in stature (as in the daughter of the master of the house) as a measure of respect.
Didimoni	Didi
Dighi	reservoir
Dikkha	initiation
Durbar	court. The term refers to the court held by British royals in India.
Duronto	hyperactive
Durry	coarse cotton mats like a shataranji
Dushshashan	one of the evil brothers from the legend Mahabharata
Dushtu	naughty
Ejlash	raised platform, the place where the judge will sit
Eto	(Hindi jootha) contaminated by another mouth
Ferari	absconders on the run
Firingee	(Hindi Firangee) refers to a person of European origin. It is derived from the word Frank.
Gaj	thirty-six inches or one yard
Gamchha	a thin red-coloured fabric, usually checked, used as a towel or a wipe
Ghee	clarified butter
Ghomta	the edge of a sari draped over a woman's head as a veil
Ghrina	hate
Gita	sacred Hindu book
Godha	a canal with sides made permanent with bricks and cement

Golmal	trouble
Gup	gossip
Haat	village markets
Hajat-ghar	lock-up room
Hartal	Hindi word meaning strike
Hato Bhago! Jaan Bachao	Move Run! Save your lives.
Hilsa	a type of salmon
Hoi-hoi-roi-roi	a medley of cheerful boisterous chatter, including singing and dancing with loud cheering
Ingrez	Englishman
Jaat	a combination of caste; race; religion
Jaithaima	jaithamoshai's wife
Jaithamoshai	father's elder brother
Jamadar	Indian office bearer, usually in charge of keys
Jamadarni	Indian office bearer, usually in charge of keys
Japani kusti	the Japanese style of wrestling
Jatra	a play performed in an open area
Ji	added on to the names of older men or women as a measure of respect. The use is popular among north Indians.
Ji	used as a suffix with north Indian names as a mark of respect
Joy	(Hindi jai) hail
Juddho	war
Kaka	father's younger brother. The term is used to address men younger than one's father.
Kakima	kaka's wife
Kala Pani	black waters or the Ocean
Kalchand	Shiva
Kali Bari	temple of Kali
Kansha	bell metal
Kantha	a light highly decorated cotton quilt made of several layers of fine muslin, stitched with a running stitch called the kantha stitch

Kartik	Hindu month corresponding to mid-October to mid-November
Kaun hai	Hindi words meaning who is there?
Khaddar	coarse hand-spun cotton cloth
Khal	canal
Khalaas	finish. The word is an Arabic word used popularly throughout India.
Khansama	Urdu word for chef
Khela	play
Khichuri	a semi-solid preparation of rice and lentils. The recipe was adapted by the British to make kedgeree.
Khoi	soft puffed rice
Khoka	little boy, used as a term of endearment
Khol	drum
Khoob anondo hochchhey	I am experiencing tremendous happiness
Khunti	a metal spatula
Ki hotey paarey	what can happen?
Ki korchhilish etokhun	what were you doing till now?
Kirtan	devotional song
Kobi	poet. The word in this text refers to Rabindranath Tagore unless otherwise specified.
Kokil	Indian cuckoo
Kon hai? Kya mangta hai	Who is there? What do you want?
Korobi	oleander
Koruna	compassion
Kotha	house of ill repute
Kukri	curved dagger used by the Gurkhas
Kusti	wrestling
Kutcha	Hindi word for temporary or raw. Antonym pucca
Kutchery	court
Lajja	shame
Lakh (lac)	one hundred thousand

Lathi	wooden rods
Lokkhi	Laxmi, the goddess of wealth and prosperity
Lomba	tall
Luchi	light puffy fried Indian bread
Lungi	a length of cloth wrapped around the waist and legs; commonly worn by Muslim men
Ma	mother or daughter; used also when referring to the mother goddess
Machaan	elevated seat, platform
Madur	a woven mat
Maidan	field
Majhi	boatman
Mali	gardener
Mama	mother's brother
Mamar-bari	mama's home
Mamima	mama's wife
Mantra	chant
Masala	Hindi word for spice
Mashima	mother's sister. The term is used to address ladies of one's mother's age.
Maya	illusion
Meherbani	Urdu for much obliged
Mej-da	an older brother but second in line after the eldest
Meshomoshai	mashima's husband
Mon	(Hindi mun; English maund) forty seers to a mon
Moori	crisp puffed rice
Moshai	an abbreviated version of Mohashoy – a formal way of addressing men instead of the relatively informal babu
Moshai	tagged on to the names of gentlemen as a measure of respect
Mourghee	chicken
Mukti Aadesh-nama	release order
Murga	chicken or more specifically a cock
Mushaira	a singing competition

Nalla	open drain
Namastey	the traditional Hindu salutation with folded hands: I salute the god within you.
Natok	(Hindi natak) drama
Nazar-bandi	a captive who has to remain within sight of the police or under house arrest
Neem	Azadirachta indica, a medicinal plant
Nikumma	Urdu word for good-for-nothing
Nouko	small boat
Paagol	(Hindi paagal or pugla) insane
Pallu	see aanchal
Paltan	platoon
Panja	hand
Panta-bhaat	boiled rice soaked overnight until it ferments
Pari nai	couldn't do it
Peyey boshbey	will take you for granted
Phalar	a light refreshment of fruit, sweets and curds
Phool	flower
Pishemoshai	pishima's husband
Pishima	father's sister
Porotha	(Hindi paratha) fried Indian bread
Potol	pointed gourd; *Trichosanthes dioica*
Pradeep	a little earthenware oil lamp
Pronam	taking the dust off an elder's feet as a mark of respect and applying it to one's head
Proshaad	(Hindi prasad) food shared by the gods and the devotees
Pugla	Hindi word for mad or insane; see paagol
Pukur	reservoir; pond
Pul	bridge
Purna swaraj	complete independence
Purnima	full moon
Purut	(Hindi purohit) priest; respectfully referred to as purut-moshai
Raag	or raga – the principles on which Indian classical music is based
Rajmistri	mason

Raksha kabaj	protective shield
Riyaz	voice training; singing practice
Rohu	a type of carp
Roop	appearance; beauty
Sadhu	see sanyasi
Sajna Danta	drumstick pods
Samadhi	memorial built over the ashes of the dead
Samiti	association
Sandesh	a sweet made of cottage cheese
Sandhi	the crossover period
Sanyas	relinquishing the material world
Sanyasi	one who has relinquished the material world
Seer	a measure of weight, a little less than a kilogram
Sej-da	an older brother but third in line after the eldest
Shaala	(Hindi sala) wife's brother; also used as an abuse
Shaathi	companion
Shahbaash	well done
Shahosh	courage
Shakti	strength; a name for the mother goddess
Shashan	(Hindi shamshan) funeral ground
Shataranji	a coarse cotton mat
Sheedur	(Hindi sindoor) vermilion worn in the parting of the hair as a symbol of marriage
Shikaar	hunt
Shikkha	education
Shinduk	strong boxes made of metal or wood
Shingho bikrom	lion-like courage
Shishu	infant
Shoontki	dried fish, a favourite amongst the people of East Bengal
Shoopoori	(Hindi supari) betel nut
Shorbonash	(Hindi sarvanash) calamity
Sipahi	sepoy

Sraddha ceremony	prayers held for the dead
Sraddha	religious ceremony held for the dead
Surahi	A clay pot used to cool and store water
Swadeshi	revolutionary
Swadhin	free
Talwar	sword
Teerth	pilgrimage
Thakur	god
Thakur-Dada (Dadu)	paternal grandfather. The term is used to address men of one's grandfather's age.
Thakur-Ma	paternal grandmother. The term is used to address ladies of one's grandmother's age.
Thala	metal platter
Thamo	stop
Tikka gharry	horse drawn cart also known as the Tumtum
Tila	hillock
Tui	you, the version used with extreme familiarity as opposed to tumi which is less formal and aapni which is formal
Tumasha	show
Ude-thakur	Oriya Brahmins are noted for their simplicity and country bumpkin ways. The term is used by Bengalis to describe a simple person.
Upasana griha	prayer room used by members of the Brahmo Samaj
Uthon	courtyard
Vakalatnama	power of attorney given to a lawyer to represent his client in court
Vibhag	division
Vidrohi	revolutionist
Zila	district

Pronunciation

ch as in the Hindi word chamcha
chch as in the Hindi word bachcha
chh as in the Hindi word chhatri

Places

British names	**Indian names**
India	Bharat; Bharatvarsh; Hindustan
Calcutta	Kolkata
Midnapore	Medinipur
Alipore	Alipur
Comilla	Kumilla
Burdwan	Barddhaman
Dacca	Dhaka
Chandernagore	Chandannagar
Cawnpore	Kanpur
Hooghly	Hugli
Bombay	Mumbai

BIBLIOGRAPHY

Bibliography of published works

Ananta Lal Singh: *Agnigarbha Chattogram* (Bidyodoy Library Pvt Ltd, 1968)

Ananta Lal Singh: *Yuva-Vidroha part I* (Sen & Company, Calcutta, 1968)

Ananta Lal Singh: *Surjya Sener Swapna o Sadhana* (Publisher Baj Kishore Mandal, Vishwavani Prakashini)

Ananta Lal Singh: *Keo Boley Biplobi, Keo Boley Dakaat* (Publisher Rabin Bal, Shaivya Pustakalay)

Ananta Lal Singh: *Mahanayak Surjya Sen Chattogram Biplob Pratham Khanda* (Publisher Mayukh Basu, 19 Shyama Charan De Street, Calcutta, 1976)

Ananta Lal Singh: *Aami Sheyee May* (Publisher Braj Kishore Mandal, Vishwavani Prakashini)

Ananda Prasad Gupta: *Chattogram Bidroher Kahini* (Published by Girin Chaktaborty, Purabi Publishers Limited, 1948)

Suresh De: *Muktir Sopon Jalalabad* (Publisher Pratap Kumar Roy, Aaj Kal Publishers Ltd, Calcutta 2001)

Charu Bikash Dutt: *Chattogram Astragar Loonthon* (Sri Charu Bikash Dutt, Paschim Bongo Pradeshik Rashtriya Samiti)

Malcolm Kennedy: *The Diaries of Captain Malcolm Duncan Kennedy, 1917–1946*

Ganesh Ghosh: *Biplobi Surjya Sen* (Biplob Teerth Chattogram Smriti Sansthan Prakashan, Shaheed Surya Sen Bhavan)

Biplobi Neta Ambika Chakraborty (Biplob Teerth Chattogram Smriti Sansthan Prakashan, Shaheed Surya Sen Bhavan)

Biplobi Mahanayak Surjya Sen O Chattogram Yuva-Vidroha 1930–34

(Biplob Teerth Chattogram Smriti Sansthan Prakashan, Shaheed Surya Sen Bhavan)

Chattogram Yuva-Vidroha 1930–34 Aalokmela (Biplob Teerth Chattogram Smriti Sansthan Prakashan, Shaheed Surya Sen Bhavan)

Kalpana Dutt: *Chittagong Armoury Raiders – Reminiscences* (1979, People's Publishing House Private Limited)

Hemanta Kumar Sarkar: *Revolutionaries of Bengal: Their methods and ideals* by *Biplobi Ganesh Ghosh* (Biplob Teerth Chattogram Smriti Sansthan Prakashan, Shaheed Surya Sen Bhavan)

Manini Chatterjee: *Do And Die – The Chittagong Uprising 1930–1934* (Penguin Books India, 1999)

Sona Roy: *Youth vs Raj – Bengal 1920 –1925* (Das Gupta & Company Private Ltd)

I. Mallikarjuna Sharma: *In Retrospect, Volume 3, East India, Part II, Bengal, Assam and Orissa – Sagas of heroism and sacrifice of Indian Revolutionaries* (Mrs I. Balamani for Ravi Sasi Enterprises 2001)

Kuldip Nayar: *Without Fear* (Harper Collins Publishers, 2007)

Sumit Sarkar: *Modern India 1885–1947* (Macmillan India Limited)

S.P.P.K. Naidu: *The British Prison system in Andaman*

Prithwindra Mukherjee: *Bagha Jatin – Life and Times of Jatindranath Mukherjee* (National Book Trust, India)

Bibliography of Unpublished Works

Younie Papers (British Library Archives)

Burnett Papers (British Library Archives)

Tegart Papers (University of Cambridge Archives)

Memoirs of an Indian Policeman by Kathleen Francis Tegart (University of Cambridge Archives)

Official Records

Judgment of the Special Tribunal in Chittagong Armoury Raid Case No. 1 of 1930 (The Emperor vs Subodh Chandra Biswas and Others)

Judgment of the Special Tribunal in Chittagong Armoury Raid

Supplementary Case (The Emperor vs Ambika Charan Chakrabarty, Hemendu Bikash Dastidar and Saroj Kanti Guha) of 1933

Judgement of the Special Tribunal in the Chittagong Second Supplementary Armoury Raid Case (the Emperor vs Surjya Sen, Tarakeshwar Dastidar and Kalpana Dutt)

Judgement of the Court of the Commissioners appointed under the Criminal Law Ammendment Act, 1926, for the trial of Dinesh Chandra Mazumdar. Sec. 307 IPC, Secs 3,4 and 5 Explosive Substance Act & c.

Judgement. (Emperor vs Dr Narain Roy and Others)

Muzzaffarpur Bomb Outrage, 1906-8 Notes on Outrages, Compiled in 1917, J.C. Nixon, ICS

Alipore Conspiracy Case, 1906-8 Notes on Outrages, Compiled in 1917, J.C. Nixon, ICS

Murder of Narendranath Gossain, 1906-8 Notes on Outrages, Compiled in 1917, J.C. Nixon, ICS

Terrorism in India, A Speech – delivered before the Society, Sir Charles Tegart, CSI, CIE, MVO (The Royal Empire Society – formerly The Royal Colonial Society)

Newspapers

The Courier Mail, National Library of Australia http://nla.gov.au/nla.news

The Argus (Melbourne, Vic.), National Library of Australia http://nla.gov.au/nla.news

The Canberra Times, National Library of Australia http://nla.gov.au/nla.news

Journals

Obituary Lt Col NS Simpson, *British Medical Journal*, December 27, 1930

Notes For Sir Charles Augustus Tegart, Tegart Treeclimbers, www.tegart.com

Obituary Stanley Jackson, http://www.cricinfo.com/england/content/player/15463.html

PEOPLE TELLING THE STORY

Ananda Prasad Gupta
Ram Krishna Biswas
Lady Kathleen Tegart
Sir Charles Tegart
Ananta Lal Singh
Suresh De
John Younie
Lokenath Bal
H.R. Wilkinson
Alexander Burnett
Hem Gupta
Ramani Majumdar
Ambika Charan Chakraborty
Kalpana Dutt
Morsehead
Cullen
Premlata
Kundaprabha
Dorothy Younie
Biren De
Pritilata Waddadar
Haripada Bhattacharya
Kali Kinkar De
Angus Kennedy
Mahendra Choudhury
Brajen Sen
J.R. Johnson

WHO'S WHO

INDIAN CAMP

Abani Mukherji: Part of the Joteen Mookerjee team that was involved in the Indo-German conspiracy during WW I. He went to Japan to establish contacts.

Abdul Ghaffar Khan: The leader of the Pathans; known as Frontier Gandhi; also called Badshah Khan by the Pathans.

Abdul Hakim: Ticket collector at Feni railway station.

Abdul Majid: Police officer who saw the Hindus in the Suluk Bahar House

Abdur Sattar (1917–76): A Muslim youth who sheltered Surjya Sen and the revolutionaries many times in his house during the second phase of the revolution and arranged for shelters in the homes of Muslim families; was arrested in 1934 under the Bengal Ordinance; released in 1937; lived on in Chattogram after partition.

Afsar-ud-din: Was introduced by his classmate Ananta Lal Singh in 1918; he was not keen on having Ganesh Ghosh – a fellow classmate – in the group. Ananta Lal Singh had finally introduced Ganesh Ghosh the next year.

Ahmadur Rehman: A taxi driver whose car was taken by Lokenath Bal's team and used for the raid on the AFI armoury.

Ajit Biswas: Was introduced by Tarakeshwar Dastidar to Ram Krishna Biswas.

Akhil Chandra Dutt: The barrister from Kumilla who helped Ananta Lal Singh escape to Kolkata after the raid; also was among the team of defence lawyers in the CAR Case.

Amarendra Nandi: A student of Chattogram College; became a sanyasi; joined the revolution reluctantly; became a member of the Sadarghat Club and a part of the Volunteer Vahini; was a part of the European Club attack team on the night of the CAR; was sent from Badulla Pahar along with Diptimedha Choudhury to contact Ananta Lal Singh and Ganesh Ghosh; was shot dead in Chittagong city on 24 April 1930.

Ambika Charan Chakraborty (b. 28 September 1892, d. 5 March 1962): One among the leaders in group formed in 1918; helped carry the AB Railway dacoity loot to Calcutta; consumed spurious cyanide along with Surjya Sen during the Nagarkhana Hill battle and was arrested, charged and acquitted in the Suluk Bahar Arms Case; rearrested under the Bengal Ordinance in 1924 and released in 1928; was one of the five leaders in the CAR; led the telephone bhavan and telegraph exchange wrecking team on the night of 18 April; escaped despite being injured in the Jalalabad encounter; was arrested in October 1930; sent for trial with Saroj Kanti Guha and Hemendu Bikash Dastidar in the Supplementary CAR Case and was initially sentenced to death on 10 February 1933; sentence was reduced to transportation for life after an appeal and he was sent to the Andamans; released in 1946; joined the Communist Party; died in a road accident in Kolkata.

Amjad Chacha: A Muslim farmer who looked after Ambika Chakraborty when he escaped from the battle site on Jalalabad.

Amulya Acharya (1917–99): Was arrested in 1935 for murdering the police agent Paresh Gupta; was sentenced to hard labour for ten years; settled in Kolkata after independence and partition.

Amulya Biswas: Was incarcerated in Chittagong Jail for revolutionary activities; tried to help Surjya Sen escape from jail by contacting Sailesh Ray.

Amulya Mukherji: Member of the Anushilan Party; helped Lokenath in Kumilla.

Ananda Prasad Gupta (pronounced Anondo in Bengali; called Tun by the family) (b. 1914, d. 8 December 2005): Came from an anglicized Brahmo family; was a student of the Municipal School and Collegiate School, took his matriculation exams before the CAR and found out later that he had passed; came away with Ananta Lal Singh, Ganesh Ghosh and Jibon Ghoshal who were taking the burnt Himangshu Bimal Sen from the police lines to a safe place in the city and as a result was separated from the main group; took part in the Feni encounter; had chickenpox by the time he reached Kolkata; went into hiding in Chandannagar along with Ananta Lal Singh, Ganesh Ghosh and Jibon Ghoshal; was shot in the leg and arrested during the Chandannagar encounter and brought back for trial to Chattogram; sentenced to transportation for life to the Andamans where the inappropriate use of morphine prescribed by the jail doctor turned him into an addict; continued to be in the Andamans through the period in which the Japanese remained in occupation, i.e., 23 March 1942 to 7 October 1945; was released in 1946 when the British regained possession; brought to his cousins' – George and Biju Patnaik – home in Ananda Bhavan, Cuttack; moved back to the hospital attached with Calcutta Medical College on account of his ill health; interned in Siuri where he met his would-be wife Sunanda; sued the British government for his morphine addiction and won his case; was on his way to Germany for treatment when a medical emergency forced him to disembark in the UK; settled in the UK; passed away on 8 December 2005 in London.

Ananta Chakraborty: On 10 November 1925 he, along with Pramod Ranjan Choudhury and Rakhal De helped Surjya Sen escape from a police raid on the house in Shobhabazaar before they were themselves arrested; attacked and killed Rai Bahadur Bhupen Chatterji during a meeting at Alipore Central Jail; was arrested and tried along with Nadia's Ananta Hari Mitra, Chattogram's Sukhendu Dutt, Dhaka's Birendra Chatterji, Chattogram's Pramod Ranjan Choudhury and seven others; he and Hari Narayan Chandra were sent to the Burma Jail to serve a life sentence.

Ananta Hari Mitra (b. 1906, hanged September 1926): Belonged to Nadia district; attacked and killed Rai Bahadur Bhupen Chatterji during a meeting at Alipore Central Jail; was arrested and tried along with Chattogram's Sukhendu Dutt, Dhaka's Birendra Chatterji, Chattogram's Pramod Ranjan Choudhury, Ananta Chakraborty and seven others; was hanged along with Pramod Ranjan Choudhury.

Ananta Lal Singh (pronounced Ononto in Bengali) (b. 1901, d. 25 January 1979): Took part in the Paraikora dacoity; took part in an attempt to kill Sir Charles Tegart; led the AB Railway dacoity in December 1923 and escaped from the Nagarkhana battle site; was arrested by Sub-inspector Prafulla Roy but was acquitted; was rearrested on 1 October 1924 under the Bengal Ordinance and held until 1928; was one of the five leaders in the CAR; led the police line attack on the night of 18 April 1930; was separated from the main group on the night of 18 April 1930; took part in the Feni encounter on 22 April 1930; went into hiding in Kolkata and then in Chandannagar; surrendered to the police on 28 June 1930; took part in the Dynamite Conspiracy while in jail; was sentenced to transportation for life and sent to the Andamans; took part in the second hunger strike in the Cellular Jail; repatriated in 1938 and released in 1946; joined the Communist Party; dreamt and plotted towards an united Bengal until the end of his life; was arrested for supposedly masterminding a successive spate of robberies, ostensibly a fund-collection drive for the unification of Bengal; fought his own case; was released from jail, on account of ill health, a few months before his death; he was never convicted.

Anil Bandhu Das (1915–94): Was influenced by his classmates Krishna Choudhury and Ardhendu Guha and guided by Ananta Lal Singh and Ganesh Ghosh; he stole chemicals and money from his father's pharmaceutical shop and passed them on to the revolutionaries; ran away and went into hiding when the theft was discovered; was arrested in June 1930 in connection with the CAR Case; confessed and then retracted his statement; sentenced to hard labour for three years at Borstal Jail; rearrested immediately afterwards under the Bengal Ordinance; passed his matriculation while in jail.

Anil Kumar De (b. 1914): Joined the second phase of the revolution; went to Kolkata to help Indumati Singh gather materials for manufacturing landmines; helped in the Dynamite Conspiracy; was arrested in 1933 and held without trial until 1936; settled in Kolkata after independence and partition.

Anil Kumar Rakshit (1915–79): Joined Surjya Sen's group in 1929; was granted bail in CAR Case; was arrested in connection with the Dynamite Conspiracy Case on 3 June 1931 and sentenced to hard labour; rearrested under the Bengal Ordinance as soon as his time was up; spent a total of eight years in jail; joined the Communist Party; settled in Kolkata after independence and partition.

Anuja Sen: Belonged to the Jugantar Party; was killed in the Dalhousie Square bomb blast while trying to assassinate Sir Charles Tegart.

Anukul Mukherji: He helped Ananta Lal Singh buy weapons in Kolkata.

Anurup Sen: A Chattogram man and a senior graduate teacher of Burul High School in 24 Parganas; he was amongst the leaders who formed the party with Surjya Sen, Nagen Sen – Julu-da, Ambika Chakraborty and Charu Bikash Dutta in 1918 when Ananta Lal Singh first joined. He was arrested in the Dakshineshwar Bomb case in 1925 and interned in Moynaguri village where he contracted cholera and died in 1926.

Apurva Sen (Bhola): A Saroatali boy; was introduced by Tarakeshwar Dastidar to Ram Krishna Biswas and the group; was a good singer; lived with his doting dadas and boudis and used the opportunity to donate several gold ornaments to the cause; took part in the Dynamite Conspiracy and worked with Kali Kinkar De and Premlata; succeeded in escaping with Kali Kinkar when the police investigating the Dynamite Conspiracy raided Kali Kinkar's home; was shot dead in the Dhalghat raid; he was seventeen when he died.

Arati Rakshit (later Singh) (b. 1919): Was introduced to Kalpana Dutt and Ardhendu Guha while still a schoolgirl; at first took charge of the groups seditious materials; later Kalpana left a trunk filled with bottles of acid in her care; her elder brother Anil Rakshit was out on bail in the CAR Case and was involved in the Dynamite Conspiracy and was sentenced to hard labour; she was placed under house arrest in April 1935 and released on 1 October 1935.

Ardhendu Dutt (1906–96): Joined Surjya Sen's group in 1922; was introduced by Tarakeshwar Dastidar to Ram Krishna Biswas; took care of the weapons from 1924 to 1928 when the party leaders were in jail; introduced his classmate Tarakeshwar Dastidar to Ananta Lal Singh; had taken Ananta Lal Singh to meet Surjya Sen when his wife had died; did not take part in the CAR or the Battle of Jalalabad as he had been reserved for the second phase of the revolution; was employed as the residential tutor of Sukhendu

Bikash Dastidar's younger brother; helped the absconders in the second phase; was arrested in September 1930 under the Bengal Ordinance for eight years; his parents were arrested and sentenced to hard labour in 1934 for sheltering absconders; settled in independent India.

Ardhendu Guha (Shishu) (b. 1912): Son of a Congressman; was introduced by Ananta Lal Singh to Surjya Sen in 1929; was in the pamphlets distribution team in the CAR; arrived at Ganesh Ghosh's shop to join up with the army on the night of 18 April but finding no one there returned home; was arrested within a couple of hours and taken to jail; granted bail in the CAR Case; led the Dynamite Conspiracy and was arrested in connection with it on 4 June 1931; was sentenced to hard labour and released in 1938; opened a photography studio in Chattogram with the help of Sarat Chandra Bose – his studio displayed the photographs of the revolutionaries on the walls; was rearrested at the start of World War II under the Defence of India Act and released in 1941; after Ananta Lal Singh's and Ganesh Ghosh's release in 1946, Ardhendu's wife Nivedita carried two army revolvers for them to Kolkata; after partition Ardhendu Guha settled in Kolkata and opened a photography studio in College Street. It became a meeting point for Surjya Sen's group; Ganesh Ghosh was made president and the Biplob Teerth Chattogram Smriti Sanstha was founded in 1970 and Ardhendu Guha became its secretary; in 1987 they built the Surya Sen Bhavan.

Ardhendu Shekhar Dastidar: Homeopathy student and a devotee of Shri Ramkrishna; lived at the Congress office with Surjya Sen; was the younger brother of Purnendu Dastidar; was burnt along with Tarakeshwar Dastidar while making explosives; was mortally injured in the Battle of Jalalabad and was removed to hospital where he was interrogated before he passed away.

Arun Dastidar (Tulu) (1915–2000): The son of a Port Trust officer and not in the police eye; helped in the second phase of the revolution; hid a trunk of acid and gunpowder in his house; carried out research on the areas to be mined; was arrested in May 1932 and held without trial for four years; took part in the Bharat Chhoro Aandolan in 1942; passed away in 2000.

Ashu Ranjan De (b. 1914): Was introduced by Sukhendu Bikash Dutt in 1929; lived on the banks of the Askar Khan Dighi and helped in the Dynamite Conspiracy; was arrested in June 1931; was acquitted but made to leave Chattogram; arrested from Kolkata on 7 December 1933 under the Bengal Ordinance and moved between jails until he was finally interned in his own home on the banks of Askar Khan Dighi in 1937; released in 1938; settled in independent India.

Ashutosh Bhattacharya: Brother of Bhabatosh Bhattacharya; was set free in the CAR Case because of lack of evidence.

Aswini Choudhury (1912–40): Was a part of the Telephone Bhavan wrecking team on the night of the CAR; took part in the Battle of Jalalabad; returned home and was arrested in connection with the CAR Case; acquitted and rearrested immediately under the Bengal Ordinance until 1937; suffered a head injury while in jail which cost him his sight; he died three years later.

Aswini Guha: This twenty-five-year-old was arrested in April 1931 on the charge of helping absconders; moved around to many jails; finally declared mad and sent to the asylum at Ranchi where he died in 1934.

Aswini Kumar Bhattacharya: Headmaster, Collegiate School.

Badal: A member of the Bengal Volunteers, Sudhir Gupta of BBD trio was involved in the shoot-out at Writers' Building and was said to be the one who killed Colonel N.S. Simpson.

Bankim Chandra Chattopadhyay: Author of *Anandomoth* and the song '*Bande Mataram*'.

Barindra Ghose: (Barin) Was the younger brother of Aurobindo Ghose and the founder of the Bengal movement.

B.C. Roy (Dr): Mayor of Calcutta.

Beni Choudhury and Dhiren Das: The local guides who had brought Kali Kinkar De and Tarakeshwar Dastidar from the Amiable Shelter at Habilash Dwip to the rendezvous spot by the pukur on the night of the Gairala encounter when Surjya Sen was arrested.

Benoy Krishna Basu: A member of the Bengal Volunteers; killed Mr Lowman at the Dacca Mitford Hospital; committed suicide after the attack on Writers' Building as part of the BBD trio, which claimed Colonel Simpson's life.

Benu Ghoshal (1917–90): Younger brother of Jibon Ghoshal; was introduced at the behest of Ananta Lal Singh by Ardhendu Guha in 1931; helped Kalpana Dutt in the Dynamite Conspiracy after Ardhendu Guha was held back in jail; funded the revolutionaries with money without his father's knowledge; researched areas that were to be mined; was arrested and held for three years.

Bhabatosh Bhattacharya (1913–48): Was the son of Bipin Bhattacharya, the Hindu priest at the Sadarghat Kali Bari; took part in the CAR and the Battle of Jalalabad; his brother Ashutosh was arrested; after eight months of remaining in hiding he left with Haripada Mahajan and went to Burma; was helped by Haripada Mahajan's family contacts; was joined by Sudhangshu Basu some four years later. Burma was occupied by the Japanese in 1942, the British fled and Haripada Mahajan died the same year. In 1945 the British retook Burma and offered to help the Indians in Burma return home and Bhabatosh and Sudhangshu availed the opportunity; the family took a while to recognize them and in a few days they were taken to jail. However, the situation was no longer conducive to carry out a trial and they were released.

Bhola Nath Chatterji: Was a part of the Indo-German conspiracy during WWI.

Bhola: See Apurva Sen.

Bhupen Dutt (Bhupendra Kumar Dutt) (b. 8 October 1894, d. 29 December 1979): Led the Kolkata team of Jugantar; took charge of Ananta Lal Singh, Ganesh Ghosh, Ananda Prasad Gupta and Jibon Ghoshal in Kolkata and moved them to Chandannagar; was arrested in 1930 and kept in jail for eight years; elected as an MP in Pakistan, before serving as an MLA; returned to India in 1962; wrote the biography of Joteen Mookerjee.

Bidhu Bhushan Bhattacharya (Bidhu): A youth from Kumilla who graduated from Chittagong Medical College with a gold medal; took part in the CAR; was in the team that had gone to attack the European Club; died at Jalalabad.

Bidhu Bhushan Sen (1910–93): Was a Saroatali High School student and was introduced by Tarakeshwar Dastidar to Surjya Sen who gave him the responsibility of the Cox's Bazar group of revolutionaries; he introduced Nirmal Lala, the youngest martyr of the Battle of

Jalalabad; was a part of the police line attack team on the night of the CAR; took part in the Battle of Jalalabad; since he was not known to the police he was sent back to Cox's Bazar; he was arrested and brought to Chattogram Jail but was released for lack of evidence; went into hiding and got back in touch with Surjya Sen; helped Ardhendu Guha keep in touch with Surjya Sen during the Dynamite Conspiracy; was arrested again under the Bengal Ordinance and held without trial; joined the Communist Party and settled in East Pakistan which later became Bangladesh.

Bimal Dasgupta: He and Jatijiban Ghose of the Bengal Volunteers murdered James Peddie, district magistrate of Medinipur on 7 April 1931. Kanai Bhattacharya pretended to be Bimal Dasgupta and shot dead R.R. Garlick, district and sessions judge of Alipore and then committed suicide. Bimal was arrested when he tried shooting Mr Villiers on 29 October 1931.

Bina Das: A student of the Diocesan College who shot at Sir Stanley Jackson during a convocation ceremony in 1932.

Binod Bihari Choudhury (b. 1911): Took part in the police line attack on the night of the CAR; took part and was injured in the Battle of Jalalabad; went into hiding in Dhaka; was arrested on 18 August 1933 but as there was no evidence to connect him to the CAR or the other cases he was detained under the Bengal Ordinance until 1938; got a law degree while in jail; joined the Congress; was personal secretary to Nellie Sengupta; settled in Chattogram which became first a part of East Pakistan and is now a part of Bangladesh.

Binod Bihari Dutt (1908–98): Introduced by Kalipada Chakraborty in 1926 while he was still a schoolboy; was a part of the police line attack team on the night of the CAR; took part and was grievously injured in the Battle of Jalalabad and was taken to his sister's house in Fatehabad by Kali Kinkar De; regained his health and contacted Surjya Sen within two months; carried a reward of Rs 1,000/- on his head; was with Tarakeshwar Dastidar (Phutu) when they were chased by Sub-inspector Sashank Bhattacharya whom Tarakeshwar eventually killed ... according to *Chattogram Yuva-Vidroha 1930–34 Aalokmela*, published by Biplob Teerth Chattogram Smriti Sansthan Prakashan, Shaheed Surya Sen Bhavan. (However, Ananta Lal Singh says it was Biren De who was with Tarakeshwar Dastidar during the incident and gives the date as 31 March 31.) Surjya Sen made him the head of the Noakhali zila; was a part of original plan in which he and a few others would lob hand bombs at the crowd and give Haripada the chance to enter the ring that surrounded Ahsanulla – this plan however failed; guided Sailesh Ray in the murder of the police superintendent of Kumilla, Mr Ellison; became the IRA leader after Tarakeshwar Dastidar; masterminded the cricket ground attack of 7 January 1934 as a protest against the sentences pronounced for Surjya Sen and Tarakeshwar Dastidar.

Binodini Sen (1894–1986): Mother of Rajat Sen; donated her ornaments and money for the cause; allowed the youngsters to take her husband's rifle and practise shooting; permitted the leaders to use the rooms upstairs for their meetings while she remained on guard; permitted Rajat to take away his father's rifle two or three days before the CAR; the rifle was discovered at the armoury which led to her husband's arrest; gave refuge to Ananta Lal Singh, Ganesh Ghosh, Ananda Prasad Gupta and Jibon Ghoshal on the night of 20 April 1930; had received Rajat and his companions on the night of 6 May 1930, the house had been raided that night and Rajat, Deboprasad, Swadesh and Monoranjan killed at the Kalarpol encounter; six months later Ananta Lal Singh had sent her a letter through Ardhendu Guha requesting her help in the Dynamite Conspiracy and she permitted Ardhendu Guha, Kalpana Dutt and Apurva Sen to use her house for manufacturing explosives; it was on her property that Kalpana Dutt fired a revolver for the first time; kept the three revolvers Surjya Sen had sent through Ardhendu Guha in safe keeping until they could be smuggled into jail; kept the trunk filled with bottles of acid that Kalpana had brought from Kolkata; gave Kalpana refuge the day she was chased by the police, but Kalpana had been arrested later that evening while trying to make her way back to Kattali village; then she lost touch with the revolutionaries and moved to Kolkata after independence and partition.

Binoy Kumar Sen (Binoy-da) (b. 1905): Participated in the AB Railway strike led by Deshpriya Jatindra Mohan Sengupta in 1921; took responsibility of the Raozan district, Noapara and Koyepara areas from 1924 to 1928 when the leaders were jailed under the Bengal Ordinance; taught in Koyepara School; did not take part in the CAR or the Battle of Jalalabad as he had been one of the first-rankers reserved for the second phase; his home became Surjya Sen's headquarters in the period immediately following the Battle of Jalalabad; with Ardhendu Dutt, Manindra Majumdar, Sachindra Prasad Sen, he moved between the villages and districts, building up teams and coordinating plans for guerrilla warfare; arrested on 30 October 1931; released in 1938; joined the Communist Party; lived on in Chattogram after independence and partition.

Bipin Bhattacharya: The purut at the Sadarghat Kali Bari and the father of Bhabatosh and Ashutosh.

Bipin Bihari Ghosh: Ganesh Ghosh's father.

Biren De: See Birendra Krishna De.

Biren Duttagupta: Shot Shamsul Alam.

Birendra Krishna De (Biren De) (b. 1908, accidentally shot dead March 1931): Part of the Telephone Bhavan wrecking team on the night of the CAR; took part in the Battle of Jalalabad; was with Tarakeshwar Dastidar (Phutu) when they were chased by Sub-inspector Sashank Bhattacharya whom Tarakeshwar eventually killed. (*Chattogram Yuva-Vidroha 1930–34 Aalokmela*, published by Biplob Teerth Chattogram Smriti Sansthan Prakashan, Shaheed Surya Sen Bhavan, says it was Binod Bihari Dutt and the date was 31 May 1931.) Biren took Surjya Sen to secret meetings; was accidentally shot during a firing practice which led to his death; was looked after by a notorious dacoit, Gagan Ghose, until he passed away and was buried on the banks of the Srimati River.

Bireshwar Roy (1913–91): Was introduced by Kalipada Chakraborty in 1927; was responsible for keeping the arms safe after the CAR and the Battle of Jalalabad; took part in the first failed attempt on the AB Railway Institute, Pahartali, led by Shaileshwar Chakraborty; took part in the second attempt on the AB Railway Institute, Pahartali, led by Pritilata Waddadar; was arrested in 1933 and held without trial until 1938; settled in Kolkata in independent India.

B.K. Banerjee: Of the Hindustan Republication Association; plotted the assassination of Tegart in 1927.

Bon Bihari Dutt (1911–94): Joined Surjya Sen's group in 1926; organized the music session in the field to draw crowds away from the Congress office the day Tarakeshwar Dastidar and Ardhendu Shekhar Dastidar had been burnt in an explosion and were being evacuated; was a part of the police line attack team on the night of the CAR; took part in the Battle of Jalalabad; was arrested in May but released within two months for lack of evidence; was arrested in September 1930 under the Bengal Ordinance and held without trial; passed his BA exams from within jail; joined the Communist Party after release; settled in Kolkata and worked in the Calcutta Corporation after independence and partition.

Brajendra Sen (Brajen) (1904–88): Was the contact in Gairala village who had fixed up the home of Niranjan and Khirodprabha Biswas for the next four days; he was Zamindar Netra Sen's younger brother; he was arrested along with Surjya Sen on 16 February 1933 and identified his brother as the traitor; was satisfied that justice had been done when news arrived that Netra Sen had been beheaded; was sentenced to four years of hard labour; released in 1938; settled in Chattogram and was jailed for six years by the Government of East Pakistan.

Brajendralal Choudhury (b. 1917, committed suicide in jail in 1934): Was responsible for finding shelters for the revolutionaries and for Surjya Sen; was arrested on 7 February 1933; was unable to withstand the torture in jail and committed suicide.

Chandra Shekhar-da: Gave the Chittagong boys swimming lessons.

Chandrashekhar De: Had been involved in the Rajabazaar Bomb case; he had then reformed and tried to get Ananta Lal Singh to confess about the Paraikora dacoity.

Charu Bikash Dutt (b. 1895): Was amongst the first-ranker leaders along with Surjya Sen in 1918; he broke away from Surjya Sen's group and joined Anushilan; was arrested under the Bengal Ordinance in 1932 and was released in 1938; joined the Congress party.

Chittaranjan Das or C.R. Das (Deshbandhu): Started his career with the successful defence of Aurobindo Ghose in the 1909 Alipore Bomb Case. In December 1922, a faction of the Indian National Congress, unhappy with Gandhi-ji's suspension of all civil resistance after the Chauri Chaura incident, formed the Congress Khilafat Swarajya Party with Das as the president and Motilal Nehru as one of the secretaries. Other prominent members were Huseyn Shaheed Suhrawardy, Subhas Chandra Bose and Vithalbhai Patel, whose younger brother – Vallabhbhai – remained with the No Changers who had accepted Gandhi-ji's proposal. With C.R. Das's death and Nehru's return to the mainstream Congress, the Swaraj Party lost its steam. Before his death, C.R. Das gifted his house and lands to the nation on which Chittaranjan Seva Sadan – a women's hospital was built.

Dalil Rehman: Surjya Sen's student who carried Surjya Sen's letters to his wife; carried the AB Railway dacoity loot to Kolkata along with Ambika Chakraborty.

Deben De (Khoka): Took part in the first attempt to kill Sir Charles Tegart in Kolkata; came away from Kolkata with Ananta Lal Singh; stayed in the Suluk Bahar house and took part in AB Railway dacoity; escaped after the battle on Nagarkhana Hill; was arrested under the Bengal Ordinance of 1930; died in a motor accident in independent India.

Deboprasad Gupta (called Debu by his friends, Khoka by his parents and Dada by Ananda Prasad Gupta): Second-year student of Chattogram College; involved with manufacturing explosives; the study room used by the two brothers had been converted into a lab; their home provided shelters for revolutionaries on the run and the woods behind their house served as a training ground to practise firing; was a part of the police line attack team on the night of 18 April 1930 according to *Chattogram Yuva-Vidroha 1930 –34 Aalokmela*, published by Biplob Teerth Chattogram Smriti Sansthan Prakashan, Shaheed Surya Sen Bhavan, but according to Ananta Lal Singh, he was a part of the European Club attack team; took part in the Battle of Jalalabad; preferred to commit suicide instead of surrendering in the Kalarpol encounter; regretted he had been unable to kill Mr Lowman even as he lay dying.

Deenbandhu Majumdar: Kali Kinkar De's mama; took part in the first failed attempt on the AB Railway Institute at Pahartali.

Dhiren Das: A revolutionary who was supposed to help Ananta Lal Singh and the boys escape from jail after the Dynamite Conspiracy.

He was supposed to wait at an appointed site with a truck to drive them to the river front.

Dhirendra Lal Dastidar (Dhiren): Had lent his rifle for the CAR, which had been left behind at Ganesh Ghosh's house. Though Dhiren had not participated in the actual armoury raid and the subsequent encounters, he had been arrested and kept in jail for two years; he was acquitted for lack of evidence; eventually settled in Burma having taken up the Sikh faith and assumed the name Ranjit Singh.

Dhirendralal Barua: A schoolboy from Jeshtapur village who was arrested in 1931 for helping the absconders; he died after a beating in Chittagong Jail.

Dinesh Chakraborty (b. 1912): Was involved in distributing pamphlets on the night of the CAR; hid Ananta Lal Singh, Ganesh Ghosh, Ananda Prasad Gupta and Jibon Ghoshal in his brother's house in the Railway Quarters in Chittagong on the night of 21 April 1930 and helped them leave for Kolkata; was responsible for sending news that the raid had been successful to pamphlet distribution teams waiting in the city both times during the first unsuccessful raid on the AB Railway Institute at Pahartali led by Shaileshwar Chakraborty and the second successful raid led by Pritilata Waddadar; arrested in November 1932 and held under the Bengal Ordinance until 1938.

Dinesh Chandra Majumdar: Of the Jugantar Party; attempted to assassinate Sir Charles Tegart in Dalhousie Square by throwing bombs at his car.

Dinesh Dasgupta (b. 1911): Joined the group while still a student in the Chattogram Municipal School but became actively involved in the second phase when he helped the absconders by arranging for money and shelters; when Sachindra Prasad Sengupta (Maan-da) the area in-charge for Chattogram city went into hiding, Dinesh took over the responsibility; he had arranged for the Dhalghat shelter; was arrested after the raid on Dhalghat and was sentenced to four years of hard labour; was sentenced to an additional year of hard labour for having disobeyed jail rules and sent to the Cellular Jail in the Andamans; participated in the hunger strike of 1932; released in 1938; joined the Congress Socialist Party and later the Lok Dal; spent his last years looking after the welfare of the tribes of Bengal.

Dinesh Gupta: Of the Bengal Volunteers; was the lone survivor of the BBD trio. He was sentenced to execution by Judge Garlick.

Diptimedha Choudhury (b. 1914): Took part in the CAR; was sent from Badulla Pahar along with Amarendra Nandi to contact Ananta Lal Singh and Ganesh Ghosh but by the time they had returned, the revolutionary army had moved on and as a result they lost touch; he was arrested and served for five years as a political prisoner.

Dr Bagla Chakraborty: A doctor who treated Ambika Chakraborty after Jalalabad.

Dr G.S. Bose: Lecturer on abnormal psychology at Calcutta University gave expert comments in Gopi Nath Saha's case.

Dr Jagada Ranjan Biswas: The doctor who treated Ram Krishna Biswas, Ardhendu Dastidar and Tarakeshwar Dastidar for burn injuries. Ananta Lal Singh refers to him on one occasion as as Dr Jagada Sarkar.

Dr Narain Chandra Roy: Came in to treat Ananta Lal Singh in Chandannagar; manufactured bombs; was arrested and given transportation for life; carried a trunk filled with study material for the boys in the Cellular Jail in Andamans.

Durgadas Dutt Gupta, Rai Bahadur: Kalpana Dutt's grandfather.

Durgakripa Biswas: Ram Krishna's father.

Dwijendranath Dastidar (Dwijen; Shonkhu) (1911–82): Was a student of Chattogram College when he was introduced to Surjya Sen by Kalipada Chakraborty in 1929; was a part of the telegraph and telephone office wrecking team on the night of the CAR; took part in the Battle of Jalalabad; since he was not a known revolutionist in the eyes of the police he left for Kolkata and passed his IA from Vidyasagar College; was arrested in May 1932 under the Bengal Ordinance; released in 1938; joined the Forward Block; died in independent India.

Fakir Chandra Sen (Bengali records say Sengupta) (1915–93): Was recruited by Bidhu Bhattacharya in 1928; was part of the police line attack team on the night of the CAR; was sent from the hills to collect news in Fatehabad and was unable to return; was arrested within a few days; confessed initially but retracted his statement later; was punched in the nose by B.J. Shooter; sent to Andamans but granted clemency; released in 1938; passed his BA from the Kanungo-para College; settled in Kolkata after independence and partition and worked in the Calcutta Corporation.

Fakir Rai Choudhury (Jibendra) (1915–93): Belonged to a wealthy family and was the famous football player of Collegiate School; joined the revolution in the second phase and helped by keeping contraband items in his house and supporting the group with money; was arrested in 1933 and held for five years.

Fazlur Rehman: Jail warder who tried to help Surjya Sen escape from Chittagong Jail.

Gagan Ghose: The bandit who looked after Biren De till he died.

Gamma: See Prafulla Das.

Gandhi: Also called Malang Baba, Mahatma or Bapu.

Ganesh Ghosh (b. 22 June 1900, d. 22 December 1992): Introduced to Surjya Sen in 1919 by Ananta Lal Singh; took part in the Ashahjog Aandolan; was arrested in the 1923 Maniktala Bomb Case but was acquitted; arrested on 1 October 1924 under the Bengal Ordinance and released in 1928; was one of the five leaders in the CAR; led the police line attack on the night of 18 April 1930; was separated from the main group on the night of 18 April 1930; took part in the Feni encounter on 22 April 1930; went into hiding in Kolkata and then in Chandannagar; surrendered to the police on 28 June 1930; took part in the Dynamite Conspiracy; sentenced to transportation for life and was sent to the Andamans; released in 1946; joined the Communist Party and was arrested because the party was at the time considered an illegal one and served nearly ten years in jail in both colonial and independent India; was elected to the Lok Sabha in 1967; became president of the Biplob Teerth Chattogram Smriti; oversaw the building of Shaheed Surya Sen Bhavan in 1987.

Girish Ghose: The unbelieving playwright who became a devotee of Ramkrishna Paramahansa and his wife Sri Ma.

Gobindo: A first-ranker who had been reserved for the second phase of the operation; helped the revolutionaries after the Battle of Jalalabad.

Gobindo-da: The manservant in Ananda Prasad Gupta's home.

Golab Babu (Gulab Singh): Ananta Lal Singh's father.

Gopi Nath Saha (Gopi): Killed Earnest Day mistaking him to be Sir Charles Tegart and was hanged.

Haralal Choudhury (1908–98): Joined Surjya Sen while still a student in Saroatali School; introduced Sukumar Bhowmik, Shourindra Dutt Choudhury and Sailesh Ray; headed the Mir Sarai, Kumilla and Feni zilas; distributed pamphlets outside Chattogram on the night of the CAR; accompanied Lokenath from Chattogram to Kumilla; was arrested in 1932 under the Bengal Ordinance; passed his BA and law exams while in jail; released in 1938; taught in various schools in both colonial and independent India; settled in independent India.

Haran (Shourindra Mohan Choudhury): Part of Railway line 1 wrecking team; his mama was the sub-inspector who tried to search Ananta Lal Singh, Ganesh Ghosh, Jibon Ghoshal and Ananda Prasad Gupta at the Feni railway station, was shot and yet refused to identify Ananta Lal Singh in the police line-up.

Harendralal Chakraborty: Took part in the attack on the cricket ground on 7 January 1934 led by Krishna Choudhury – a protest against the sentence passed on Surjya Sen; he was severely wounded during the encounter and arrested; hanged on 5 June 1934 in Midnapore Jail along with Krishna Choudhury.

Hari Gopal Bal (Tegra): Lokenath Bal's youngest brother; Ananda Prasad Gupta's classmate; he took part in the CAR and died in the Battle of Jalalabad.

Hari Narayan Chandra (Hari-da): Taught the young revolutionaries bomb making; was incriminated in the murder of Rai Bahadur Bhupen Chatterji during a meeting at Alipore Central Jail; was arrested and tried along with Nadia's Ananta Hari Mitra, Chattogram's Sukhendu Dutt, Dhaka's Birendra Chatterji, Chattogram's Pramod Ranjan Choudhury and seven others; he and Ananta Chakraborty were sent to the Burma Jail to serve a life sentence.

Haripada Bhattacharya (1914–93): Was a student of Saroatali High School; single-handedly killed Khan Bahadur Ahsanulla on 30 August 1931; underwent severe torture and was blinded in one eye; was tried by a judge and jury and was declared free to go; the case was sent to the high court which sentenced Haripada to the Andamans; released in 1946 along with Ananta Lal Singh, Ganesh Ghosh and the others; settled in Siliguri in independent India .

Haripada Mahajan: The son of a wealthy family; was a part of the police line attack team on the night of the CAR; took part in the Battle of Jalalabad; waited in hiding for eight months for Surjya Sen to send him a call, then left for Burma together with Bhabatosh Bhattacharya; fell ill and died in 1942 while still in Burma.

Helfferich: The contact in Batavia who was involved in the Indo-German conspiracy hatched during WW I.

Hemendu Bikash Dastidar (1914–74): Was a student of the Chattogram Municipal High School and was in class 9 when he joined Surjya Sen's group; had picked a fight with Karunamoy over the debate topic 'The pen is mightier than the sword'; was a part of the police line attack team on the night of the CAR; took part in the Battle of Jalalabad; went into hiding and used the alias Boro-khoka, was arrested on 28 August 1932 while coming out of the mess at 130, Maniktala Street; was tried along with Ambika Chakraborty and Saroj Kanti Guha in the Supplementary Armoury Raid Case Trial and was acquitted; was rearrested immediately under the Bengal Ordinance; was released in 1938; settled in Chattogram which became a part of East Pakistan and then Bangladesh.

Heramba Bal: His Dodge could not be used for the CAR; was arrested and tried but was acquitted for lack of evidence.

Himangshu Bhowmik (Raja): Who killed a traitor.

Himangshu Bimal Chakraborty: Took part in the attack on the cricket ground on 7 January 1934 led by Krishna Choudhury – a protest against the sentence passed on Surjya Sen; he was severely wounded during the encounter and died in hospital.

Himangshu Bimal Sen (Andu): Ananda Prasad Gupta's classmate; kept watch on Inspector Sharada Bhattacharya's house; took part in the CAR and suffered fatal burns that night.

Horen Sen: Ram Krishna's friend.

Hriday Ranjan Das: Was Madhusudan Guha's father's godown manager; he had taken charge of the trunk that Madhusudan (who was then out on bail in the CAR Case) had smuggled into the godown; accompanied by Robi Sen, dressed in a sari, had visited Pritilata Waddadar's father and taken one of his properties on rent for the Dynamite Conspiracy; after Madhusudan was arrested in the Dynamite Conspiracy, Hriday opened the trunk and discovered the landmines; he was in the process of burying them when he was caught by the police; was sentenced for five years of hard labour at the Andamans; settled in Chattogram and passed away in 1997.

Indumati Singh (modified later to Sinha) (b. 1900, d. 5 May 1967): Elder sister of Ananta Lal Singh and Nand Lal Singh; was connected with the revolutionaries since 1923; built up a women's group in 1928 and offered them physical education, training in martial arts and weapons training; put herself in charge of the fund collection drive to pay for the CAR case; helped in the Dynamite Conspiracy; was arrested in Kumilla after the murder of Judge Stevens in 1932 and detained without trial for the next five years at Hijli; was a practising homeopath before she was jailed; passed her matriculation exams while in jail.

Jadu Gopal Mukherji: Member of the Indo-German conspiracy hatched during WW I.

Jagadish Roy: Brother of Kalarpol martyr Swadesh Roy.

Jaitra Mohan Das: Haripada Mahajan's uncle.

Jashoda Ranjan Pal (1900–28): Served as lance naik of the 49 Bengal Regiment in the First World War; was amongst the first-rankers who joined Surjya Sen's group in 1918; was responsible for weapons training; moved to Kolkata with a job in the customs office at Maniktala and worked with the Jugantar group helping to manufacture bombs; met Ananta Lal Singh and Ganesh Ghosh once again in Kolkata after the Paraikora dacoity; was associated with Gopi Nath Saha who murdered Earnest Day in January 1924; arrested in the Maniktala bomb conspiracy in 1924; sentenced for seven years to Dhaka Central Jail where he contracted tuberculosis and died in 1928.

Jatindra Mohan Sengupta (shortened to J.M. Sengupta or J.M. Sen; also referred to as Deshpriya): Defended Santosh-da, Surjya Sen and Ambika-da in the Suluk Bahar case; Premananda's case for the murder of Sub-inspector Prafulla Roy.

Jatindranath Das: Jatin Das of the Anushilan Party who worked with Bhagat Singh.

Jibon Ghoshal (Makhon) (b. 1910, killed 1 September 1930): A year senior to Ananda Prasad Gupta in school; forged his father's signature to withdraw money for the revolution, lent the family Essex to transport the burn victims – Tarakeshwar Dastidar and Ardhendu Shekhar Dastidar; drove the Dodge to the AFI armoury for the raid; came away with Ananta Lal Singh, Ganesh Ghosh and Ananda Prasad Gupta who were taking the burnt Himangshu Bimal Sen from the police lines to a safe place in the city and as a result was separated from the main group; took part in the Feni encounter; had chickenpox by the time he reached Kolkata; went into hiding in Chandannagar along with Ananta Lal Singh, Ganesh Ghosh and Ananda Prasad Gupta; was killed during the Chandannagar encounter on 1 September 1930.

Jitendra Mohan Dasgupta (Jiten Das): Payaj Kanti Choudhury and Pulin Ghose's classmate; took part in the CAR; died in the Battle of Jalalabad.

Jitendra Nath Lahiri: Part of the Indo-German conspiracy which was hatched during WW I.

J.K. Ghoshal: Jibon Ghoshal's father's elder brother; represented the revolutionaries at court.

Jogendramohan Gupta: Father of Deboprasad and Ananda Prasad Gupta.

Jogesh Majumdar (Jayadrath): Had been responsible for keeping Kali Kinkar safe; worked at the AB Railway Institute at Pahartali and had taken the responsibility of providing the signal for the attack during both the first failed attempt and the second successful attack.

Jogesh: A responsible first-ranker who had been reserved for the second phase of the operation.

Joteen Mookerjee (Bagha Joteen; Joteendra Nath Mookerjee; Jatindra Nath Mukherjee) (b. 7 December 1879, d. 10 September 1915): Part of the Indo-German conspiracy hatched during WW I.

Julu-da: See Nagendranath Sen.

Jyoti Prasad Gupta (called Chotkun by the family): Deboprasad and Ananda Prasad Gupta's youngest brother.

Jyotish Bhowmik (Jyotish-da): Who sent books to Ananta Lal Singh at Alipore Central Jail.

Jyotish Ghose: Accompanied Subhas Chandra Bose, Deshpriya Jatindra Mohan Sengupta, and Nripen Banerjee to Chattogram for the Congress Assembly of May 1929. Ananta Lal Singh had met him in Kolkata soon after the Paraikora dacoity in 1923. He remembers him as someone who read copiously. He is possibly the same person who inspired Gopi Nath Saha to kill Tegart.

Jyotsna-di: Ananda's Chhor-di.

Kali Kinkar De (Kali or Kali Kinkar) (b. 1910, d. 4 September 1989): Recruited when he was in class 9 by his juniors from school – Pulin Ghose and Binod Bihari Dutt who took him to Kalipada Chakraborty and Surjya Sen in 1928; was a part of the police line attack team but had been sent off by Surjya Sen to inform the pamphlet distribution teams about the change in timings and as a result arrived after the police lines had been taken on the night of the CAR; took part in the Battle of Jalalabad; after the battle he left the wounded Binod Bihari Dutt in the care of his sister at Fatehabad and went home where he found his parents had arranged a match for him; married Premlata; took part in the Dynamite Conspiracy but succeeded in evading arrest; took part in both the first failed attempt and the second successful attack led by Pritilata Waddadar on the AB Railway Institute at Pahartali; carried a reward of Rs 1,000/- on his head; was arrested in December 1933; shared a cell with Sudhindra Dasgupta at Chittagong Jail; sentenced to transportation for life at the Andamans; his wife Premlata committed suicide when she learnt of his sentence; described the last hours of Surjya Sen's life to the inmates of the Cellular Jail in the Andamans; released in 1945; settled in Chattogram which became a part of East Pakistan and later Bangladesh.

Kali Prasanna Choudhury: Ram Krishna Biswas's brother-in-law.

Kalicharan Ghose: The author of *Rolls of Honour*; looked after Ananda Prasad Gupta and Jibon Ghoshal in Kolkata.

Kalipada Chakraborty (Kali or Pundit) (1908–92): Joined Surjya Sen's group in 1923; was a Sanskrit scholar which earned him the name Pundit; was a part of the Telephone Bhavan wrecking team on the night of the CAR; took part in the Battle of Jalalabad; went with

Ram Krishna Biswas to assassinate Mr Craig but killed Inspector Tarini Mukherji instead on 1 December 1930; was arrested and received a sentence of transportation for life and was sent to the Andamans; released in 1946; joined the Communist Party; lived in Chattogram even after partition.

Kalpana Dutt (actually Kalpana Dutt Gupta but had shortened her surname to Dutt; called Bhulu by family; code name Rama) (b. 1913, d. 8 February 1995): Assisted in the Dynamite Conspiracy; absconded to join Surjya Sen's group but was arrested; absconded again while out on bail; escaped from the Gairala encounter; maintained meticulous notes on the preparation of explosives; was involved in the plot to kill District Magistrate H.S. Hands; was arrested after the Gohira encounter; tried along with Surjya Sen and Tarakeshwar Dastidar; sent to Hijli Jail; Rabindranath Tagore wrote to the governor requesting Kalpana's release in 1938; Reverend C.F. Andrews met the governor requesting her release as did Mahatma Gandhi; released in 1939; joined the Communist Party; married the Communist Party leader P.C. Joshi in 1943.

Kalyani Das: The elder sister of Bina Das; started the Girl Student Societies.

Kamala Banerjee (later Mukherji) (b. 1914): Member of Jugantar; helped Kalpana Dutt during the Dynamite Conspiracy; was arrested towards the end of 1931 under the Bengal Ordinance; released in 1938.

Kamal-ud-din (b. 1910); Son of a farmer; joined Surjya Sen's group in 1930; realizing that Ardhendu Guha, who was then out on bail, was meeting Surjya Sen in Sharat De's house and that the village had been surrounded by the army and the police, Kamal-ud-din rushed with the warning and took them into his own house and hid them inside the women's quarter, thus saving them that day as Muslim homes were seldom searched; joined the Communist Party and lived in Chattogram after partition.

Kamini Dutt of Kumilla: Advocate who represented a revolutionary in the CAR trial.

Kanailal Dutta: Chandannagar lad who was a part of Barin Ghose's team; killed the traitor Narendra Nath Gossain within the jail premises and was hanged for the crime.

Kanchanlata: The Christian lady who acted as hostess to Ananta Lal Singh, Ganesh Ghosh, Ananda Prasad Gupta and Jibon Ghoshal in Khidirpur.

Kazi Nazrul Islam: A poet famous for his spirited verses that encouraged the fight for freedom; settled in independent India after partition; was declared the national poet of Bangladesh.

Kebla-da: See Monoranjan Rai.

Khirod Mahajan: Was in the pamphlet distribution team

Khirod Banerjee (1912–48): Lived in the Pahartali Railway Quarters; joined Surjya Sen's group in 1929; researched the AFI armoury before the CAR; was a part of the AFI armoury attack team on the night of the CAR; took part in the Battle of Jalalabad; was advised by Surjya Sen to leave Chattogram since he was not familiar with the local dialect; was arrested from Canning in 1935; was detained without trial for three years; died of tuberculosis in 1948.

Khirodprabha Biswas (1888–1996): The landlady at the Gairala shelter who looked after Surjya Sen, Kalpana Dutt, Shanti Chakraborty, Manilal Dutt and Brajen Sen; was arrested after the encounter on 16 February 1933 along with Surjya Sen and Brajen Sen; released in 1938; settled in Kolkata after independence and partition.

Khoka-da: See Monoranjan Dasgupta

Khoka Sen: Ram Krishna Biswas's friend.

Khoka: See Deben De.

Khoka: See Deboprasad Gupta.

Khudiram Bose: Threw a bomb at what he thought was Mr Kingsford's carriage and ended up killing Mrs and Ms Kennedy in April 1908. He was a part of Barin Ghose's team.

Kiran Sen (1915–98): Joined the revolution in its second phase; beheaded the traitor Zamindar Netra Sen on 9 January 1934, three days before Surjya Sen was hanged; he was helped by Rabindra Nandi; went into hiding in Rangoon; arrested from Rangoon and held without trial until 1938; his role in the murder was a well-kept secret until independence; settled in independent India.

Kobi Nabinchandra Sen: An ICS officer who was penalized for writing in favour of independence.

Kobi: The Kobi and Gurudev are references to the poet Rabindranath Tagore.

Kobiraj Jayanta Dasgupta: Ranadhir Dasgupta's father.

Krishna Choudhury (b. 1912, hanged 5 June 1934): Was a part of the group that beat up Karunamoy for announcing the debate on the topic 'the pen is mightier than the sword'; had taken his uncle's rifle for the CAR and his uncle, who was a lawyer, had reported the loss of the rifle and the fact that his nephew was missing; took part in the CAR; participated in the Battle of Jalalabad after which his family sent him out of Chittagong to hide amongst the Chakma tribes; returned after two years and led the attack on the cricket ground on 7 January 1934 – a protest against the sentence passed on Surjya Sen; he was severely wounded during the encounter and arrested; hanged on 5 June 1934 in Midnapore Jail.

Kundaprabha Sengupta (Kunda; code name: Kobi) (1917–90): Introduced by Mahendra Choudhury; sheltered Surjya Sen in her home in Sripur; kept the revolutionaries' writings hidden in her home; was arrested for being in possession of seditious writings and sentenced in 1934 to six months of hard labour; rearrested again under Shantrashbad Virodhi Aain until March 1935.

Lady Macbeth: Code name for hostess at Jeshtapur shelter – Kutir.

Lal Mia: The signaller at Feni railway station.

Lal Mohan Sen: The son of a wealthy family; recruited by Ananda Prasad Gupta; led the Railway line 1 wrecking team; confessed during the CAR case and was the last to retract his statement; was said to have beaten up a convict overseer in the Chittagong Jail which led to a search of the jail; was sent to the Andamans and released in August 1945; returned to his home in Sandwip Island; was killed within three or four days of his return, while trying to stop a communal riot.

Lala Lajpat Rai: A senior Congress leader who died as a result of police brutality.

Lecturer: See Mani Dutt.

Lokenath Bal (called Shona-bhai by his younger brothers and sisters, Lokenath-da or Loka-da by his young friends) (b. 8 March 1908, d. 1964): Was the Students Union secretary; led the AFI raid team on 18 April 1930; was battle commander at Jalalabad, led his team out of the hills and met up with Surjya Sen's team; was arrested during the Chandannagar encounter; was awarded transportation for life and sent to the Andamans; released in 1946; joined the Radical Democratic Party and later the Congress party; served as deputy commissioner of the Calcutta Corporation; died suddenly of a heart attack.

Madhusudan Dutt: Kept the party alive during the time the leaders were arrested under the 1924 Bengal Ordinance; worked as a contractor in Jamshedpur and sent his savings to the party; returned to Chattogram a few days before the raid and took part in the CAR; died at Jalalabad at the age of twenty-four.

Madhusudan Guha (Madhu): Was arrested in connection with the CAR case and released on bail; helped in the Dynamite Conspiracy; acquitted for lack of evidence.

Mahendra Choudhury (code name Zamindar, known to Kundaprabha as Mani-da) (1912–88): Was a class 9 student at the Chattogram Municipal High School when he joined Surjya Sen's group in 1929; had woken Suresh De by throwing roshogollas and then climbing up to his window; took part in the armoury raid; took part in the Battle of Jalalabad; led the intelligence department of the revolutionaries; brought back the news of Nirmal Sen's death at Dhalghat; took part in the first failed attempt on the AB Railway Institute, Pahartali; took part in the second attempt on the AB Railway Institute, Pahartali, led by Pritilata Waddadar; tried to have Special Superintendent Nalini Majumdar killed but the plan did not work out; was arrested in December 1933 and detained without trial until 1937; joined the Congress party; settled in Kolkata after independence and partition.

Mahendra Lal Biswas: Sixty-year-old Mahendra Lal had offered Surjya Sen and the revolutionaries his home as a secure shelter after they returned from the Battle of Jalalabad; was arrested in 1935; had protested against the torture in the jail and died within a few days.

Maklas Rehman: Worked at the AB Railway workshop; had been Ananta Lal Singh's neighbour nearly ten years ago and had seen him at AB Railway dacoity site.

Makleshwar Rahman: Was waiting to provide dinner for the revolutionaries at his restaurant on the night of the armoury raid.

Malin Bikash Ghose: Took part in the CAR and in the Battle of Jalalabad; was arrested but was set free after the trial due to lack of evidence.

Manilal Dutt (Mani Dutt, code name Lecturer) (1915–92): Was introduced by Tarakeshwar Dastidar and Ram Krishna Biswas after the CAR; lived as a residential tutor in Dhalghat and took Surjya Sen and Pritilata from the Dhalghat encounter site to the shelter in Jeshtapur village; followed Surjya Sen's instructions and went into hiding; met Kalpana Dutt in Pritilata's house; helped Kalpana escape from the Gairala encounter by hiding amongst a stack of rice sheaves for a day before making it to safety; was involved in the plot to kill District Magistrate H.S. Hands; was arrested in 1933 for being in possession of a revolver and sentenced to hard labour at the Andamans; was released in 1945; settled in Kolkata after independence and partition.

Manindra Lal Guha (1909–77): Was a student of BA at Chattogram College; took part in wrecking the Telephone Exchange according to Manini Chatterjee in *Do And Die* but according to *Chattogram Yuva-Vidroha 1930–34 Aalokmela* he had taken part in the police line attack; absconded on the 19 April 1930 when he was sent back from the hills to contact Ananta Lal Singh and Ganesh Ghosh; was arrested on 25 December 1931 under the Bengal Ordinance and detained until 1938; he settled in Chattogram which became a part of East Pakistan and later Bangladesh.

Manindra Majumdar (b. 1904): Was Surjya Sen's deputy in Sripur and Haola; he was not amongst the ones that the police had an eye on; was a first-ranker whom Surjya Sen had reserved for the second phase; his home on the banks of the Karnaphuli was surrounded by coconut and betel nut palms and it was converted into a secret meeting place; during the time Ardhendu Guha was out on bail and working on the Dynamite Conspiracy, he would meet Surjya Sen at Manindra Majumdar's home; the garden served as the studio in which revolutionaries due to leave for their last action were photographed; was a skilled sailor, helped Surjya Sen and Nirmal-da cross the Karnaphuli by night for the secret meetings and was mentioned as the one who would wait with the sampan during the proposed jail break; Ananta Lal Singh and Ganesh

Ghosh's plan to kill Mr Craig had been discussed in this shelter and Ram Krishna Biswas and Kalipada Chakraborty detailed; arrested in May 1931 and held without trial until 1938; settled in independent India.

Maulvi Abdulla: a Congress party worker who accompanied Ananta Lal Singh to Kolkata.

Maulvi Makleshwar Rehman: The Kumilla zila Congress secretary who helped Ananta Lal Singh escape to Kolkata.

Mihir Bose: Lent his father's rifle for the CAR but did not take part himself.

Mir Ahmad Ali (1915–73): Joined Surjya Sen's group while still a schoolboy and introduced several Muslim boys to the group; sheltered Surjya Sen and Nirmal-da in his own home; was extremely keen on taking part in the action but he did not get the opportunity; was arrested in November 1933 but his mother continued to shelter revolutionaries; was released in 1938; settled in Kolkata after independence and partition.

Mona: See Monoranjan Sen.

Monorama: Mother of Jyotsna, Deboprasad, Ananda Prasad and Jyoti Prasad, wife of Jogendramohan Gupta (called Rama by her husband).

Monoranjan Dasgupta (called Khoka-da by Kalpana Dutt): Joined Tarakeshwar Dastidar, Kalpana Dutt and Sudhindra Dasgupta at Gohira shelter the night before the encounter; was killed in the dawn encounter on 19 May 1933.

Monoranjan De: Arranged for the Gohira shelter and led the way; sounded the warning that the house had been surrounded; arrested on the day of the Gohira encounter and sentenced to four years of hard labour.

Monoranjan Rai (Kebla-da); (1909–92): Was introduced by Tarakeshwar Dastidar in 1926; went into hiding in Kolkata after the CAR; introduced Pritilata Waddadar and Kalpana Dutt to Surjya Sen; took bombs across to Surjya Sen and helped in the Dynamite Conspiracy; was arrested in November 1930 and held without trial for seven years; joined the Communist Party and took part in the Shramik Aandolan; was elected thrice to the West Bengal Vidhan Sabha.

Monoranjan Sen (Mona): First-year intermediate student of Chattogram College; was part of the European Club attack team on the night of the armoury raid; took part in the Battle of Jalalabad; preferred to commit suicide instead of surrendering in the Kalarpol encounter; his father, Rajan Sen, an elderly man and a pleader of Chattogram court was kicked to death by Sergeant Kelly in the retaliation that followed the assassination of Khan Bahadur Ahsanulla.

Motilal Kanungo (Moti): Ananda Prasad Gupta's classmate; took part in the CAR; died in the Battle of Jalalabad.

Motilal Nehru: A Congressman and the father of Jawaharlal Nehru.

Mr Peters: A European who sold weapons to Ananta Lal Singh.

Mrinalini Sen (b. 1917): Sister of Rajat Sen; lived with her parents in the Firingee Bazaar area; joined the Volunteer Vahini for girls in 1929 during the Congress Assembly in Chattogram; she and her mother, Binodini Sen, helped Kalpana Dutt and Ardhendu Guha during the Dynamite Conspiracy; kept guard with her mother when meetings were conducted in their house; was placed under house arrest in 1932; settled in Kolkata with her parents after independence and partition.

Nagendranath Sen (Nagen Sen; Julu-da): Served with the 49 Bengal Regiment in the First World War; was posted to Mesopotamia; amongst the first-rank leaders in 1918; taught the revolutionists the use of weapons; led the Paraikora dacoity along with Nirmal Sen; attempted to murder Tegart twice; was arrested on 27 March 1925 under the Bengal Ordinance, was released in 1928; married in 1928 and moved away from the revolution; helped Ananta Lal Singh hide in Kolkata after the CAR and the Feni encounter; was arrested under the Ordinance and remained in jail from 26 September 1930 to 1938.

Nand Lal Singh (modified later to Sinha) (b. 7 February 1902, d. 27 July 1987): Son of Golab Singh and Rajkumari Devi; Ananta Lal Singh's older brother and Indumati Singh's younger brother; joined Surjya Sen's group in 1918; joined the Pahartali Railway Workshop as an apprentice and joined in the strike demanding better wages and benefits for the workers; married in 1925; stopped work as an active revolutionary but continued to help his brother and supported the movement; was arrested along with his father after the CAR; received hard labour of two years for his part in the CAR; was rearrested under the Bengal Ordinance as soon as his term was over and was released in 1935; harassed by the government after the disappearance of Neta-ji Subhas Chandra Bose in 1941; was awarded the Tamrapatra in recognition of services in the cause for freedom in 1975.

Narain Chandra Roy (Doctor): Looked after Ananta Lal Singh in Chandannagar; manufactured bombs used in Dalhousie Square bomb blast which targeted Sir Charles Tegart; sentenced to transportation for life to the Andamans; took with him trunks full of books to educate the youngsters serving their time in the Andamans.

Narayan Sen (Anath Rai) (1912–56): Was a part of the police line attack team; took part in the Battle of Jalalabad; went into hiding for the next eighteen years living in disguise under the noses of the police in Kolkata.

Naren Das: Was in the pamphlet distribution team after Pritilata successfully carried out the Pahartali Club raid.

Naren Dutt: Kamini Dutt's youngest brother and the owner of Bengal Immunity Ltd.

Narendranath Bhattacharya (C. Martin, M.N. Roy): Part of the Indo-German conspiracy during WW I.

Naresh Ray: Was a youth from Mymensingh who graduated from Chittagong Medical College; was Bidhu Bhattacharya's best friend; took part in the CAR; was in the team that had gone to attack the European Club; died at Jalalabad.

Nawab Mincha: Was the youngest Muslim revolutionary and was introduced by Maulvi Mir Ahmad; lured the police agent Paresh Gupta to a place where he was murdered by Amulya Acharya; was sentenced to two years of hard labour.

Nayantara Devi: Was Ram Krishna Biswas's mother.

Nepal Dastidar (1911–94): Helped the absconders during the second phase of the revolution; took responsibility of the weapons; was arrested in 1934 and sentenced to hard labour at the Borstal Jail; released in 1937; took part in the Bharat Chhoro Aandolan; lived in Chattogram and took part in Bangladesh's independence movement.

Netra Sen: Zamindar of Gairala village who betrayed Surjya Sen, and the older brother of Brajen Sen. Was beheaded by Kiran Sen.

Nibaran Ghose (1915–98): Was introduced by Kalipada Chakraborty; helped Kalpana carry nitric acid from Kolkata to Chittagong; laid the landmines in the Dynamite Conspiracy and was arrested while carrying explosives after a night's work on 3 June 1931; was sentenced to hard labour and released in 1938; lived in Chattogram which became a part of East Pakistan and then Bangladesh.

Niranjan Rai (b. 1914): Was a part of the Telephone Bhavan wrecking team on the night of the CAR; took part in the Battle of Jalalabad; returned to his village home and was not arrested for he was never seen as a suspect by the police; left for Rangoon sometime later and lived there until his death.

Niranjan Sengupta: Ganesh Ghosh's friend from Anushilan who spent time with Surjya Sen in jail; was arrested in the Mechhua Bazaar case.

Nirendralal Bhattacharya: A schoolboy from Saroatali High School; was arrested in 1933 on the charge of carrying messages; committed suicide after two years in Hijli Jail.

Nirmal Lala: Fourteen-year-old from Cox's Bazar; took part in CAR; the youngest martyr of Jalalabad; was introduced by Bidhu Bhushan Sen; was unknown to most people which included his colleagues; when he was hit, his compatriots had called to Surjya Sen saying a little boy has fallen; the photograph of his dead body was identified as that of Sudhangshu Bose's by Sudhangshu's father and uncle while Sudhangshu escaped to Burma.

Nirmal Sen (b. 1900, killed 13 June 1932): Led Paraikora dacoity along with Julu-da; stayed in the Suluk Bahar house but missed taking part in the AB Railway dacoity; was arrested under the BCLA in 1925 and was released on 27 November 1926; was one of the five leaders in the CAR; led the AFI raid team on the night of 18 April 1930; took part in Jalalabad; was killed in the Dhalghat encounter.

Nirmal Sen: A revolutionary from the city. Not the Nirmal Sen who was amongst the leaders.

Nishi Chandra De: Kali Kinkar De's kaka; lived in a two-storeyed mud house surrounded by fruit trees close to a large pukur; worked at the AB Railway workshop at Pahartali; had iron bombshells cast at the workshop and turned his house into a factory where he manufactured landmines to be used in the Dynamite Conspiracy; his house was raided by a large contingent of armed police led by Mr Hicks, Khan Sahib Ahsanulla and DIG Wright on 3 June 1931; of the five revolutionaries who were at work inside, Kali Kinkar De and Apurva Sen succeeded in breaking through the cordon and escaping while Nishi De, Ardhendu Guha, Sushil Sen and Prafulla Mallick were arrested; Nishi De was acquitted by the special tribunal; lived in Chattogram after partition.

Nitaipada Ghose (Nitai) (1914–72): His father worked in the AB Railway; lived close to the AFI and with four companions walked to the site of attack on the night of the CAR; took part in the Battle of Jalalabad; returned to Jessore on Surjya Sen's instructions; was arrested in May 1930 in connection with the CAR Case; was acquitted for lack of evidence; rearrested immediately under the Bengal Ordinance and detained for the next five years.

Nityananda Gopal: The witness who had given an accurate description of Gopi Nath Saha to the police.

Nityaranjan Sen: Took part in the attack on the cricket ground on 7 January 1934 led by Krishna Choudhury – a protest against the sentence passed on Surjya Sen; flung a bomb which exploded close to Police Superintendent Cleary; he was killed during the encounter.

Nivedita Choudhury (later Guha) (b. 1920): Was influenced by her uncle Sudhindra Das and hid the groups' seditious literature in her house; arranged for shelters for Kalpana Dutt and other absconders; was placed under house arrest from 30 October 1932 to February 1933; married Ardhendu Guha in 1943; joined the Communist Party; travelled on two occasions with her children, carrying arms to Kolkata for Ananta Lal Singh and Ganesh Ghosh who had just been released.

Noni Das: Helped Kalpana in Dynamite Conspiracy case once Ardhendu Guha was held back in jail.

Noni Dutt (Noni-da): Advocate Kamini Dutt's son.

Noni Gopal Deb (Noni) (1913–86): His father worked with the AB Railway and Noni lived with his father at Double Mooring; he was a class 10 student when he took part in the police line attack on the night of the CAR; took part in the Battle of Jalalabad; returned to Kumilla; was arrested in May 1930, tried in the CAR case and was acquitted; was rearrested immediately under the Bengal Ordinance and released in 1938; settled in Agartala in independent India.

N.R. Dasgupta: A lawyer who represented the revolutionaries at court.

Nripa Gopal: Was involved in the fight with Karunamoy over the topic of the school debate 'the pen is mightier than the sword'.

Nripen Banerjee: A senior politician; the vice principal of Chittagong Government College and related to Suhashini Ganguli (Putu-di); attended the Congress Assembly in Chittagong in 1929; investigated the riots along with Deshpriya Jatindra Mohan Sengupta after the assassination of Khan Bahadur Ahsanulla.

Nripen: Plotted the assassination of Tegart along with Gopi Nath Saha.

Panchanon Babu: Helped out with shopping at Chandannagar.

Pannalal Sen (b. 1901): Took part in the first failed attempt on the AB Railway Institute at Pahartali; took part in the second successful attempt led by Pritilata on the AB Railway Institute at Pahartali; worked at Ram Chandra Singh's soda water shop on the banks of the Lal Dighi and maintained a liaison with the jail staff to help Surjya Sen escape from jail; was arrested on 15 July 1933 under the Bengal Ordinance and was released in 1938; settled in Assam in independent India.

Payaj Kanti Choudhury: Had resisted joining the revolution but had personally sought out Kali Kinkar De after the names of the martyrs of the Battle of Jalalabad was made known. Two of his classmates, Pulin Ghose and Jiten Das, figured in that list; assumed responsibility for distributing pamphlets during the first failed attempt on the AB Railway Institute at Pahartali; distributed pamphlets after the second successful attempt led by Pritilata on the AB Railway Institute at Pahartali; died after an interrogation by Captain Stevenson of MIO.

Phonindra Nandi (Phoni) (1911–40 in jail): Amarendra Nandi's cousin; was in the AFI raid team on the night of the CAR; took part in the Battle of Jalalabad; had gone with Rajat, Debu, Swadesh, Mona and Subodh to attack a club in the city but was arrested just before the Kalarpol encounter; took part in the Dynamite Conspiracy while in jail; received life sentence and was sent to Andamans where he contracted tuberculosis; was brought back to Alipore Central Jail but despite Sarat Chandra Bose's attempts, he was denied release and proper medical treatment; died in Alipore Central Jail in 1940.

Prabhat Ranjan Dutt (1914–78): Introduced by Ram Krishna Biswas; his home served as a weapons store; helped Kalpana in the Dynamite Conspiracy once Ardhendu was held back in jail; helped lay the mines; was arrested and sent to the Midnapore Jail; helped Dinesh Majumdar escape from Midnapore Jail; was rearrested under the Bengal Ordinance as soon as his time was up and moved to Hijli; was released in 1937 and settled in Calcutta in independent India.

Prafulla Babu: Taught young revolutionaries swimming.

Prafulla Pathak: Ticket collector at Feni railway station.

Prafulla Ranjan Das (Gamma) (b. 1915): Was a part of the first failed attempt on AB Railway Institute at Pahartali led by Shaileshwar Chakraborty; was a part of the second attack on the AB Railway Institute at Pahartali led by Pritilata Waddadar; was arrested on 12 March 1933 under the Bengal Ordinance and released in 1938.

Prafulla Ranjan Mallick (b. 1911): Introduced by Kali Kinkar De; was a member of the pamphlets distribution team on the night of the CAR; retrieved the weapons hidden in a pukur in the forests by Surjya Sen's group; laid the landmines and was arrested on 4 June 1931 from the house of Kali Kinkar De in connection with the Dynamite Conspiracy Case; sentenced to hard labour; released in 1937; lived in Chattogram until his death.

Pramod Dasgupta: Laid the landmines in the Dynamite Conspiracy.

Pramod Ranjan Choudhury (b. 1900, hanged September 1926): Introduced Ananta Lal Singh to Surjya Sen and was amongst the first-rankers in the group formed in 1918; moved to Anushilan along with Charu Bikash Dutt; was a part of the dacoity in Chattogram's Noapara zila; while arrests were being carried out under the Bengal Ordinance of 1924, he escaped with Surjya Sen to Kolkata; on 10

November 1925 he, along with Ananta Chakraborty and Rakhal De, helped Surjya Sen escape from a police raid on the house in Shobhabazaar before they were themselves arrested; murdered Rai Bahadur Bhupen Chatterji during a meeting at Alipore Central Jail and was tried along with Chattogram's Sukhendu Dutt, Dhaka's Birendra Chatterji, Ananta Hari Mitra and others; was hanged along with Ananta Hari Mitra.

Pranhari Das: Zamindar of Kattali village, father of musician Suren Das, gave refuge to Lokenath's group after the Battle of Jalalabad.

Prasanna Talukdar (b. 1889): Landlord at the Gohira village shelter; brother of Purno Talukdar who was killed in the encounter; was injured in the encounter and arrested; sentenced to three years of hard labour; lived in Chattogram after partition.

Prashant Dasgupta (1917–2000): Was introduced in the second phase of the revolution by Dhiren De (most probably Biren De), who had returned from the Battle of Jalalabad; arranged for shelters for the absconders; placed under house arrest in 1933 and later made to leave Chattogram; settled in independent India.

Pratul Babu: Old-time revolutionary who was excluded from Surjya Sen's group.

Pratul Bhattacharya: An Anushilan Party member and Ganesh Ghosh's friend.

Pravin-da: Old-time revolutionary who was excluded from Surjya Sen's group.

Premananda Dutt: Responded to C.R. Das's call and left his job to take part in the Ashahjog Aandolan for which he was arrested; supported the AB Railway workers' strike in 1921; was introduced by Ananta Lal Singh to the revolutionary group; took part in the Paraikora dacoity; betrayed Ananta Lal Singh and then regretting the action murdered Sub-inspector Prafulla Roy; was acquitted but rearrested under the Bengal Ordinance; eventually lost his mind and was sent to the asylum in Ranchi where he died.

Premlata: Kali Kinkar De's first wife whom he called Priti; she took part in the Dynamite Conspiracy; learnt how to fire a revolver but was sent back after Kalpana Dutt's arrest; committed suicide when she learnt her husband had been sentenced for life to the Andamans.

Pritilata Waddadar (code name Rani) (b. 5 May 1911, committed suicide 24 September 1932): One of her father's properties was used for manufacturing explosives for the Dynamite Conspiracy; was present at Dhalghat the day it was raided on 13 June 1932; became headmistress of Nandan Kanan High School after the Dhalghat encounter; successfully led the attack on the AB Railway Institute at Pahartali on 24 September 1932 and committed suicide immediately afterwards.

Probhash Bal: Lokenath and Tegra's seventeen-year-old cousin; was recruited by Kalipada Chakraborty and forced to give up smoking; took part in the CAR and went for the raid on the AFI armoury; died at Jalalabad.

Prodyot Bhattacharya: The juvenile involved in the murder of District Magistrate Douglas of Midnapore; was hanged at Midnapore Central Jail on 13 January 1933.

Pulin Bihari Majumdar: Assistant stationmaster at Feni railway station.

Pulin Ghose: Known as Quick Silver the messenger; recruited Kali Kinkar De; took part in the CAR; drank lubricant out of desperation while trekking through the hills; held out a green mango as he lay dying at Jalalabad – one that he had saved for Lokenath.

Pundit: See Kalipada Chakraborty.

Purnendu Dastidar: Ardhendu Shekhar Dastidar's elder brother; along with Renu Rai and Kamala Banerjee, helped Kalpana Dutt procure nitric acid in Kolkata.

Purno Talukdar: Fifty-year-old landlord at the Gohira village shelter, killed during the encounter on 19 May 1933.

Pushpo Kuntala Devi (Pushpo Boudi): Surjya Sen's wife.

Rabindra Nandi (Khoka) (b. 1916): Accompanied Kiran Sen on the mission to kill Zamindar Netra Sen who had betrayed Surjya Sen; was arrested in 1934 under the Bengal Ordinance; sentenced to two years of hard labour for disobeying jail rules; released in 1938; settled in independent India.

Rabindra Narayan Sen (Robi Sen) (1910–80): A youth from Saroatali village who worked as a driver for Jibon Ghoshal's father; was a skilled electrician and a member of the Sadarghat Club; was recruited by Ardhendu Guha as per Ananta Lal Singh's instructions;

supervised the electrical connections in the landmines; was a fresh-faced lad and, dressed in a sari, had accompanied Hriday Das and approached Pritilata Waddadar's father to take one of his properties on rent; he was to wait at the appointed site with a truck on the day of the proposed jail break; was arrested in connection with the Dynamite Conspiracy and sentenced to hard labour for seven years; settled in independent India.

Rajan Sen (called Rajani Sen in *Chattogram Yuva-Vidroha 1930–34 Aalokmela*): Kalarpol Shaheed Monoranjan Sen's sixty-year-old father; a pleader of the Chittagong court; he was kicked to death in his own house by Sergeant Kelly during the riots that followed Khan Bahadur Ahsanulla's murder.

Rajani Biswas: Ananta Lal Singh's neighbour and advocate who advised him not to resist a search; represented the revolutionaries at court in the CAR case.

Rajat Sen: First-year intermediate student of Chittagong College; a good footballer who used to play with the police teams; a good artist – Sir Stanley Jackson had once offered to recommend him for admission to art college; nearly as powerfully built as Lokenath Bal; his house served as a training centre; was a part of the AFI raid team on the night of the CAR; took part in the Battle of Jalalabad; preferred to commit suicide instead of surrendering in the Kalarpol encounter.

Rajen Das: A man as old as Surjya Sen, who harangued him for not doing enough work and got frightened when Ananta Lal Singh put him through a test at night.

Rajendra Kumar Dasgupta (Rajen Das) (b. 1903): Stayed in the Suluk Bahar house and took part in the AB Railway dacoity; during the Nagarkhana Hill battle he consumed the same spurious cyanide that Surjya Sen and Ambika Chakraborty had consumed; regained consciousness at night and found himself lying in an obscure part of the hill; went home and went into hiding; was arrested on 16 February 1925 under the Bengal Ordinance; lost his mental balance after being tortured in jail and was released on 25 September 1928.

Rakhal De (b. 1901): A friend of Surjya Sen's students Sukumar Biswas and Dalil Rehman; was arrested, along with Ananta Chakrborty and Pramod Ranjan Choudhury, on 10 November 1925 from the Shobhabazaar shelter after helping Surjya Sen escape; prosecuted in the Dakshineshwar Bomb Case; was given life transportation for the murder of Rai Bahadur Bhupen Chatterji and moved between several jails, spending twelve years in the Andamans before securing his release in 1936; joined the Congress and led the Bhudaan Aandolan; settled in independent India.

Rakhal Sakha Basak: Took part in the Dynamite Conspiracy; gunpowder was made at his home.

Ram Krishna Biswas (called Ledu by the family): Younger brother of Sitaram Biswas who took part in the CAR and the Battle of Jalalabad; was introduced to Surjya Sen by Tarakeshwar Dastidar; mentored Suresh De; made and put up revolutionary posters in the city; suffered serious burns while manufacturing percussion caps just before the armoury raid; went with Kalipada Chakraborty to assassinate Mr Craig on 1 December 1930 but killed Inspector Tarini Mukherji by mistake; motivated Pritilata Waddadar who came to meet him in jail; was hanged at Alipore Central Jail on 4 August 1931.

Ram Krishna Chakraborty: Minor boy who was arrested on 13 June 1932 along with his mother, Savitri Devi – the landlady at Dhalghat; was sentenced to four years of hard labour and moved to Midnapore Central Jail where he was made to work the oil mills; denied permission to meet his mother despite having contracted tuberculosis; died in jail in 1934.

Ramani Nath Banerjee (1914–2001): Was introduced by Ardhendu Guha; was responsible for planting two motor car batteries and connecting the lead wires to the landmines under the court building; was arrested in 1932 and placed under house arrest first in his Chattogram home and later in his ancestral home in Dhaka.

Ramen Bhowmik: Under the guidance of Saroj Kanti Guha, he shot L.G. Durno, district magistrate of Dhaka.

Ranadhir Dasgupta (1915–88): Had brought his father's rifle for the raid; participated in the police line attack on the night of the CAR; took part in the Battle of Jalalabad; was arrested and tried in the CAR Case; was given transportation for life but granted clemency; resisted his father's attempt to appeal and reopen the case; took part in the second hunger strike in the Cellular Jail; was released in December 1938; joined the Communist Party; settled in Kolkata after partition.

Ranjan Lal Sen: The father of Rajat Sen, a lawyer by profession.

Rash Bihari Basu: A journalist implicated in the attack on Lord Hardinge; escaped to Japan from where he continued fuelling the revolution.

Rashik Nandi: Amarendra Nandi's father.

Ratneshwar Sheel (b. 1917): Was introduced by Binod Bihari Dutt in the second phase of the revolution; was arrested from his home in Durgapur and sentenced to hard labour under the Indian Arms Act on 6 September 1935; joined the Communist Party and settled in independent India.

Robi Sen: See Rabindra Narayan Sen.

Rohini Barua (b. 1915): Was a Buddhist by religion; believed in achieving freedom for India; was harassed by police while they were picking up suspicious youths but since there was no evidence against him, he was held without trial as a detenue; was moved from jail to jail and finally interned in a village under the Gwaland Thana. He was being constantly called to the thana and being harassed by the daroga. On 15 June 1935, Rohini drew a talwar and slew the daroga inside the thana; there was no evidence of his guilt but Rohini insisted on confessing and refused the advice to apply for an appeal. He was hanged on 15 December 1935 at the Faridpore Jail.

Sachin Sanyal (Sachindranath Sanyal) (1873–1942): Founder member of the Hindustan Republican Association, which after 1928 became the Hindustan Socialist Republican Association; was extensively involved in the Ghadr conspiracy and went into hiding in 1915; was tried and sentenced in the Kakori Conspiracy Case in 1925 and sent to the Cellular Jail in the Andamans; wrote his book *Bandi Jibon* – A Captive Life; died while in the Gorakhpur Jail.

Sachin Sen: Ram Krishna's friend.

Sachindra Prasad Sen (Maan-da) (1909–80): Lived in Saroatali village; son of a Congressman who involved him in the Ashahjog Aandolan of 1922; was a BA student in Chattogram College; carried weapons for Ananta Lal Singh from Kolkata in 1929; after the CAR and the

Battle of Jalalabad his house became a secret meeting place for the leaders; took part in the Dynamite Conspiracy and was made the area in-charge for Chattogram city; went into hiding, was arrested in December 1932 from Kumilla and detained under the Bengal Ordinance until 1938; settled in independent India.

Sahayram Das (1913–91): Was recruited by classmates Sukhendu Bikash Dutt and Motilal Kanungo; was in the same class as Ananda Prasad Gupta; took part in the CAR; took part in the Battle of Jalalabad; returned home but was handed over to the police by his own uncle; took part in the Dynamite Conspiracy; sang Bande Mataram in court the day Motilal Nehru died; transported for life to the Andamans; released in 1946; joined the Communist Party.

Sailendra Nath Ghose: The president of the Indian National Congress of America who threatened to have Gandhi replaced in case he backed down during the negotiations with the British.

Sailesh Ray (b. 1911): A new member of the Chittagong group introduced by Haralal Choudhury; was guided by Binod Bihari Dutt and carried out the murder of the police superintendent of Kumilla, Mr Ellison, on 29 July 1932; was caught outside Chittagong Jail while trying to arrange for Surjya Sen's escape; was sentenced for seven years to the Andamans under the Indian Arms Act on 25 May 1933; took part in the thirty-eight-day hunger strike while in the Cellular Jail; was released in 1940 and rearrested because of World War II; lived for a while in East Pakistan and then moved to independent India.

Sampad Choudhury: This nineteen-year-old was arrested in 1933 for helping absconders; died in 1934 while still in prison.

Sanjiv Dutt: Kamini Dutt's youngest son who lived in Shyambazaar, Kolkata.

Santosh-da: Led the group that carried out the Shankharitola post office dacoity.

Sarat Chandra Bose (b. 6 September 1889, d. 20 February 1950): The barrister who came to defend Ananta Lal Singh; also the older brother of Subhas Chandra Bose; brought four freshly made hand grenades packed with TNT and 2,000 rupees to Chattogram for Surjya Sen; helped rehabilitate some of the revolutionaries when they were released from jail; worked for reunification of Bengal and was the first to donate money into the fund being raised by Ananta Lal Singh; in a signed editorial to be published in *The Nation* written half an hour before his death he appealed to the people of India and Pakistan: *That East Bengal as a distinct and separate State should join the Indian Union and that the people of India and Pakistan should bring pressure to bear upon their respective Governments to bring it about as soon as possible.* He further appealed to the Bengalis, both Hindu and Muslim, to abjure the cult of violence, restore sobriety and sanity, re-establish communal harmony; not look either Delhi way or Karachi way for the light would not come from there. *Be guided by the light within* was his last request to the Bengalis.

Saroj Bhattacharya: Was on the pamphlet distribution team on the night of the CAR.

Saroj Kanti Guha (1912–85): Was introduced by Ananta Lal Singh; stole jewellery worth Rs 1,000/- that was being readied for a wedding in the family and handed it to Ananta Lal Singh; was sent as a trainer for Indumati Singh's physical education classes for girls; was a part of the police line attack team on the night of the CAR; took part in the Battle of Jalalabad; went into hiding and under Surjya Sen's directions, masterminded the attempt on Mr Durno's life; was arrested on 3 August 1932 from the district of Noakhali; was tried along with Ambika Chakraborty in the Supplementary Armoury Raid Case Trial which began on 2 January 1933; sentenced to transportation for life to the Andamans; joined the Communist Party on release and settled in West Bengal in independent India.

Sarojini and Nalini Pal: The two sisters belonged to a wealthy family from Fatehabad and studied at Bethune College in Kolkata; they carried a trunk filled with twenty pounds of acid, on Kalpana's behalf, from Kolkata to Chattogram.

Sashank Dutt: Was an intermediate student at Chattogram College; took part in the CAR; died in the Battle of Jalalabad.

Sashank Mohan Choudhury (Madan) (b. 1919): Knew that Sailesh Ray, the tutor who lived in his house, had kept a suitcase with contraband goods in the study room; was seen moving the suitcase out of the house the night Sailesh Ray was arrested; was arrested and sentenced to three years of hard labour at the Borstal Jail.

Sashi Bhushan Sen (most probably Sati-da): Amarendra Nandi and Diptimedha Choudhury were supposed to go from Badulla Hill and try to get in touch with Sashi Bhushan Sen for news about Ananta Lal Singh and Ganesh Ghosh.

Sasmal B.N.: A barrister styled as the pride of Midnapore; argued on behalf of Ananta Lal Singh, Ganesh Ghosh and Lokenath Bal during the conclusion of the case.

Sati-da: See Sashi Bhushan Sen.

Satish Chandra De: Suresh De's older brother.

Satish Pakrashi: An Anushilan Party member; also Ganesh Ghosh's friend; was arrested in the Mechhua Bazaar Case along with Niranjan Sengupta.

Savitri Chakraborty (b. 1887): Hostess at Dhalghat who along with her daughter, Snehalata, and son, Ram Krishna, looked after Surjya Sen, Nirmal Sen, Apurva Sen and Pritilata Waddadar; was arrested after the raid on 13 June 1932 in which Nirmal Sen, Apurva Sen and Captain Cameron were killed and her house blown apart; her daughter turned Crown witness; her son died of tuberculosis while in jail; she refused to confess despite the torture; was not accepted by her relatives after she was released and lived as a destitute.

S.C. Mukherji: Represented the revolutionaries at court.

Shaileshwar Chakraborty: A youth originally from Cox's Bazar who was a BA student in Kumilla; took part in the CAR and the Battle of Jalalabad; was a part of the original plan to kill Khan Bahadur Ahsanulla – he and some others were to lob hand bombs at the crowd and give Haripada the chance to enter the ring that surrounded Ahsanulla, but that day the plan failed and Haripada single-handedly shot the Khan Bahadur on 30 August 1931; led the first failed attempt on AB Railway Institute at Pahartali on10 August 1932 and committed suicide that night; was given a hurried burial by his colleagues; he was nineteen years old when he died.

Shaileshwar: Was responsible for distributing leaflets on the night of 18 April 1930.

Shankar: Had come to inform Ananta Lal Singh when Ram Krishna got burnt; was responsible for making the Dui thaiya dui anna

– two rupees two annas–statement which became a joke in the group; was a part of the railway line 2 wrecking team.

Shanti Bhushan Nag (1912–72): Was a Chattogram Municipal High School student and joined Surjya Sen's group in 1928; was a part of the AFI raid team in the CAR, his bullet struck Sergeant Major J.W. Farrell; took part in the Battle of Jalalabad; helped Suresh De escape from the Jalalabad battle site and took him to his family home in Dhaka; was arrested in May 1930 from his own home in Kumilla; was acquitted for lack of evidence but rearrested immediately under the Bengal Ordinance and kept in jail for the next six years; settled in Agartala in independent India.

Shanti Chakraborty (1914–43): Joined Anushilan Party as a student of class 8 in 1930; was involved in the picketing of a liquor shop when he got beaten up by a police sergeant; retrieved the firearms that were hidden by Lokenath's team in a pukur after the Battle of Jalalabad and handed them over to the Anushilan Party leaders; got in touch with the CAR absconders in 1932 and joined Masterda's group; took part in the first failed attempt on the AB Railway Institute at Pahartali; took part in the second successful attempt led by Pritilata on the AB Railway Institute at Pahartali; was called Doordeshi Dada or Shanti-da by Kalpana; was injured while escaping from the Gairala village raid; was arrested in 1934, tried under the Indian Arms Act and sentenced to hard labour in the Andamans Cellular Jail; joined the Communist Party on release; became ill and died in Chattogram Hospital.

Shanti Ranjan Sen (1915–94): Was on the pamphlet distribution team during the first failed attempt on the AB Railway Institute at Pahartali; distributed the pamphlets during the second successful attempt led by Pritilata on the AB Railway Institute at Pahartali; was involved in a plot to kill H.S. Hands together with Kalpana Dutt and Manilal Dutt; was arrested on 24 September 1933; released in 1938; joined the Communist Party; settled in independent India.

Sharat Chandra Chattopadhyay (Chatterji): A celebrated author of Bengal who wrote *Pather Dabi*, a work that the revolutionaries read copiously.

Sharat Chandra Chattopadhyay: Howrah Zila Congress president.

Sharat Kanungo (Naingta) (b. 1915): Belonged to a wealthy family and was not looked at with suspicion by the police; his house was used for nearly a year during the Dynamite Conspiracy; was arrested in December 1931 and held for five years.

Shashadhar Acharya: Member of the Jugantar party in Kolkata and a worker in Eastern Railway, Howrah Department; took the responsibility of looking after four revolutionists on the run – Ananta Lal Singh, Ganesh Ghosh, Ananda Prasad Gupta and Jibon Ghoshal; pretended to be married to Suhashini Ganguli and took a house in Chandannagar where the revolutionists were put up; was arrested on 1 September 1930; was tortured severely but could not be formally punished because the crime had been committed in the French-occupied Chandannagar; he was held instead under the Bengal Ordinance for several years.

Shourindra Mohan Dutt Choudhury (called Dutt Rai by *Chattogram Yuva-Vidroha 1930–34 Aalokmela*) (1910–88): Was in Lal Mohan Sen's group that wrecked one of the railway lines on the night of the CAR; was arrested in May 1930 in connection with the CAR Case; was acquitted for lack of evidence; rearrested immediately afterwards under the Bengal Ordinance and was released in 1938; settled in Agartala in independent India.

Sitangshu Sarkar: The medical student who looked after Ananda Gupta and Jibon Ghoshal in Kolkata.

Sitaram Biswas (b. 1912): Ram Krishna Biswas's brother; took part in the police line attack on the night of the CAR; participated in the Battle of Jalalabad; went into hiding after Ram Krishna was hanged; was arrested in March 1933 but could not be tried due to lack of evidence and was detained under the Bengal Ordinance until 1938; settled in Delhi in independent India.

S.K. Basu: A lawyer who represented the revolutionists in the CAR Case.

Sripati Choudhury; (b. 1912): Was the son of a wealthy businessman; stole money from his father and gave it for the CAR; went into hiding in Akyab; was not able to make it back in time for the CAR; arrested on 27 April 1930 and released on bail; was acquitted due to lack of evidence; rearrested immediately under the Bengal Ordinance; released in 1937.

Srish Bose: Lawyer from Chandannagar who represented revolutionaries. Was christened Verbose by John Younie.

Subhas Chandra Bose (later known as Neta-ji): Younger brother of Sarat Chandra Bose, the barrister.

Subodh Bal (b. 1911, d. 25 December 1984): Joined Surjya Sen's group in 1929 while he was a first-year student in Chattogram College; was a part of the police line attack team on the night of the CAR; took part in the Battle of Jalalabad; returned home after the battles and was arrested within a few days; released on bail; was acquitted for lack of evidence in the CAR Case but was rearrested immediately under the Bengal Ordinance and detained until 1938; settled in Kolkata after independence and partition.

Subodh Chandra Biswas: Shouted slogans when Ananta Lal Singh was brought to jail; was the first name in the case – Chittagong Armoury Raid Case No. 1 1930 – The Emperor vs Subodh Chandra Biswas and Others; was a part of the Dynamite Conspiracy; was acquitted for lack of evidence.

Subodh Chandra Roy (Subodh Roy or Jhunku) (b. 1915): Son of the prominent lawyer Ratul Kumar Roy and cousin of Kalpana Dutt; recruited by Nirmal Sen in 1927 at the age of eleven; his father complained to the police that his son had taken his rifle without permission and was missing; took part in the police line attack on the night of the CAR; participated in the Battle of Jalalabad – describes the initial scene as: *When I saw the Gurkhas with bayonets, I thought of shooting myself, then I thought I would not see my mother again* (see p. 112 of *Do And Die* by Manini Chatterjee); led Surjya Sen's group to his village home where they rested before dispersing; was arrested when he reached his home in the city; shouted slogans when Ananta Lal Singh was brought to jail; sentenced to hard labour in the Andamans but granted clemency on account of his age; released in 1938; joined the Communist Party; settled in independent India.

Subodh Choudhury (1910–72): Recruited as a Congress member by Tripura Sen and was hurt in the fighting during the Congress meeting on 21 September 1929 and taken to hospital; was visited by Ananta Lal Singh, Ganesh Ghosh and Lokenath Bal; his home in the Railway Quarters was given as a correspondence address to the Mechhua Bazaar conspirators and was raided; brought dhutis to help cover Tarakeshwar Dastidar and Ardhendu Shekhar Dastidar while Ananta Lal Singh was driving around with them waiting for a shelter to be fixed; studied the AFI armoury; was a part of the AFI armoury raid team on the night of the CAR; took part in the Battle of Jalalabad; had gone with Rajat, Debu, Swadesh, Mona and Phonindra to attack a club in the city but was arrested just before the Kalarpol encounter; took part in the Dynamite Conspiracy while in jail; received a life sentence and was sent to Andamans; released in 1946; joined the Communist Party; was elected to the Vidhan Sabha three times.

Subodh Mitra (1911–91): Was introduced while still a schoolboy at Feni by Haralal Choudhury; was a part of the Railway line 1 wrecking team led by Lal Mohan Sen; returned home to Feni that night; was arrested in May 1930 and tried in connection with the CAR Case; was acquitted for lack of evidence but rearrested immediately under the Bengal Ordinance; released in 1937; settled in independent India.

Sudhangshu Bimal Bose (1912–88): Joined the group in 1928; was a member of the Sadarghat Club; was a part of the police line attack team on the night of the CAR; took part in the Battle of Jalalabad; his father and uncle went to court and identified the photograph of Nirmal Lala's dead body as that of Sudhangshu's; after about four years he went to Burma and joined up with Haripada Mahajan and Bhabatosh Bhattacharya; Burma was occupied by the Japanese in 1942 and the British fled, Haripada Mahajan died the same year; in 1945 the British retook Burma and offered to help the Indians in Burma return home. Bhabatosh and Sudhangshu took the opportunity; the families took a while to recognize them and in a few days they were taken to jail; however the situation was no longer conducive to carry out a trial and they were released; settled in Chattogram which became a part of East Pakistan and later a part of Bangladesh.

Sudhindra Nath Das (Sudhindra) (1911–94): Joined Surjya Sen's group while a schoolboy; in the second phase of the revolution he helped with arranging shelters and collecting funds for the CAR absconders; was arrested in the Gohira village encounter along with Tarakeshwar Dastidar and Kalpana Dutt; shared the cell with Kali Kinkar De and replied to the letters Premlata sent; was sentenced to four years of hard labour; released in 1938; rearrested in 1942 for participating in the Bharat Chhoro Aandolan; settled in independent India.

Suhashini Ganguli (Putu-di) (1907–65): Ex-student of Bethune College in Kolkata; member of the Jugantar party; pretended to be Acharya's wife at Chandannagar and looked after Ananta Lal Singh, Ganesh Ghosh, Jibon Ghoshal, Ananda Prasad Gupta and Lokenath Bal; was arrested in the Chandannagar encounter; was arrested in 1942 for participating in the Bharat Chhoro Aandolan; arrested in 1948 for being a member of the Communist Party which was seen as an illegal party.

Sukhendu Bikash Dastidar (1913–78): His younger brother's residential tutor was Ardhendu Dutt who was also involved in the revolution; looked after Himangshu when he was burnt on the night of the CAR; was responsible for distributing pamphlets on the night of the CAR; returned after the distribution and waited near Ganesh Ghosh's shop to join the victorious revolutionaries and eventually went home disappointed; was arrested on the morning of 19 April 1930 while still in possession of the pamphlets; shouted slogans when Ananta Lal Singh was brought to jail; was a proficient sampan sailor and was named as one who would help sail the sampan across the river during the planned jail break from Chittagong Jail; was given transportation for life and sent to the Andamans but granted clemency; released in 1946 and joined the Communist Party; settled in East Pakistan which eventually became Bangladesh.

Sukhendu Bikash Dutt (1906–68): Part of Surjya Sen's group; left Bengal to build up the organization in Bihar and had been arrested in the Deogarh Conspiracy; sentenced to hard labour for five years and was then detained in jail under the Bengal Ordinance; tried to help Surjya Sen escape from jail; released in 1938; joined the Congress.

Sukhendu Bikash Dutt: Ananda Gupta's classmate who had been stabbed during the September 1929 elections in Chattogram.

Sukhendu Dutt: Along with Dhaka's Birendra Chatterji, Chattogram's Pramod Ranjan Choudhury, Nadia's Ananta Hari Mitra and seven others attacked and killed Rai Bahadur Bhupen Chatterji during a meeting at Alipore Central Jail; was tried but not hanged. He may or may not be the same Sukhendu Bikash Dutt who was arrested in the Deogarh Conspiracy Case and tried to help Master-da escape from jail.

Sukumar Bhowmik (b. 1913): Part of railway line 1 wrecking team led by Lal Mohan Sen on the night of the CAR; arrested in June 1930; was set free after the CAR trial for lack of evidence; was rearrested under the Bengal Ordinance and released in 1938; settled in Agartala in independent India.

Sukumar Biswas: The nephew of Ananta Lal Singh's old colleague and brother-in-arms Premananda; one of Surjya Sen's students who had carried letters from Surjya Sen to his wife; had a restaurant in Kolkata; probably the one who betrayed Ananta Lal Singh to Tegart.

Sukumar Kanungo: Came into contact with the revolutionaries while they were in hiding after the Battle of Jalalabad. Was accidentally shot dead in 1931, during a weapons training session and was given a quiet burial in the hills.

Sumati Majumdar: Ananda Gupta's aunt who gave him and Jibon Ghoshal money to escape to Kolkata.

Sunil De: Part of railway line 2 wrecking team.

Suren: The farmer who had provided Ananta Lal Singh refuge.

Suresh Banik (code name Pathik): His home was a shelter called Tapovan; was arrested for sheltering absconders; was sentenced to hard labour in Dhaka Central Jail where he contracted smallpox and was placed in an isolation cell where he died.

Suresh Chandra De (Sadhu) (b. 1911, d. 21 May 1990): Was a student of class 9 in the Municipal High School when Kalipada Chakraborty introduced him to Surjya Sen; mentored by Ram Krishna Biswas; was a part of the police line raid team on the night of the CAR; injured in the Battle of Jalalabad; had a bullet in his arm and succeeded in escaping with the help of Shanti Nag; went into hiding in his family home at Dhaka; was arrested in January 1933 and held without trial for four years; settled in Jamshedpur in independent India; the boy who had no shoes during his youth founded Sreeleathers in 1952.

Surjya Sen (Surya Sen) (b. 22 March 1894, hanged 12 January 1934): Son of Rajmoni Sen and Sashibala Devi of Noapara village.

Sushil Dasgupta (1911–87): Was with Surjya Sen, Kalpana Dutt, Mani Dutt, Shanti Chakraborty and Brajen Sen in the shelter at Gairala village when it was raided; succeeded in escaping; arrested on 15 August 1933 and held without trial until 1938; settled in independent India.

Sushil Kumar De (Sushil De) (b. 1908, d. 29 June 2000): Introduced by classmate Sarada Seel in 1923; was caught while learning to fire a revolver and arrested in 1928; was a part of the railway line wrecking team led by Upen Bhattacharya on the night of the CAR; returned to Chattogram that very night to join up with Surjya Sen and the revolutionaries but not finding them there went back to the village; was arrested but released after two months due to lack of evidence; helped the absconders and arranged to move them between secure shelters; was a part of the original plan to kill Khan Bahadur Ahsanulla – he and others were to lob hand bombs at the crowd and give Haripada the chance to enter the ring that surrounded the target; was part of the first failed attempt on AB Railway Institute at Pahartali led by Shaileshwar Chakraborty; had found the Jeshtapur shelter which Surjya Sen had named Kutir; was part of the second attack on the AB Railway Institute at Pahartali led by Pritilata Waddadar; was arrested in September 1933 under the Arms Act and sentenced to seven years in the Andamans; protested against the treatment meted out to political prisoners; released in 1939 but was barred from entering Chattogram; joined the Communist Party in Kolkata and participated in the Shramik Aandolan; was rearrested in 1940, when WW II broke out, under the Defence of India Act and released in 1942; settled in Chattogram but was imprisoned by the Government of East Pakistan; moved to Agartala in independent India.

Sushil Sen: Was arrested and tried in the Dynamite Conspiracy Case.

Swadesh Roy: Member of Sadarghat Club; a contractor by profession; was not invited to join the revolution and had been rebuffed several times but still went to join them voluntarily on the night of 18 April 1930 when he heard the firing at the police lines; took part in the Battle of Jalalabad; preferred to commit suicide instead of surrendering in the Kalarpol encounter.

Taracharan Baba: The sadhu who visited Chittagong.

Tarakeshwar Dastidar (Phutu) (b. 1904, hanged 12 January 1934): Became a part of the movement in 1924 when the leaders had all been arrested under the Bengal Ordinance; was introduced by Ardhendu Dutt to Ananta Lal Singh in 1928; introduced Ram Krishna Biswas; looked after Ram Krishna Biswas when he was burnt while making explosives; was a chemistry student at Chattogram College and was involved in manufacturing explosives; was burnt along with Ardhendu Shekhar Dastidar during an explosion in the Congress office before the raid and as a result could not take part in the CAR or in the Jalalabad encounter; took part in the Dynamite Conspiracy; he and Biren De were chased by Detective Inspector Sashank Bhattacharya. Tarakeshwar killed him near Barma village; became the IRA leader after Surjya Sen's capture; surrendered at the Gohira village encounter on 18 May 1933; was hanged along with Surjya Sen in Chittagong Jail.

Tegra: See Hari Gopal Bal.

Tripura Sen: Was made a lieutenant in the Volunteer Vahini during the Congress Assembly in Chittagong; was responsible for making sure all watches were synchronized on the night of the CAR; was a part of the team that went to attack the European Club; died at Jalalabad.

Umesh Singh: Ananta Lal Singh's cousin in Tripura, who helped acquire arms.

Upen Bhattacharya (1899–1965): Stayed in the Suluk Bahar house and took part in the AB Railway dacoity in December 1923; escaped from the Nagarkhana Hill battle site; was arrested in the Maniktala Bomb Case and released just before the Chittagong Armoury Raid; he was keen on taking part and was mentioned in the mobilization list found in Ganesh Ghosh's home after the raid; was a part of the railway line 2 wrecking team and the telegraph line disruption team; returned to the city on 19 April 1930 to take part in the second phase but finding nobody he returned home; was arrested in a few days but was allowed to go within three months because of lack of evidence; maintained contact with Surjya Sen;

was arrested in 1932 and held without trial for six years; settled in East Pakistan which became Bangladesh.

Basanta Kumar Bandopadhyay: A resident of Gondolpara, Chandannagar, who helped Ananta Lal Singh, Ganesh Ghosh, Jibon Ghoshal and Ananda Prasad Gupta enter Chandannagar.

Vasant Majumdar: One of Kumilla's richest zamindars who helped Ananta Lal Singh escape to Kolkata after the CAR.

Vijay Krishna Aich (b. 1913): Joined Surjya Sen's group in 1929; led the railway line 2 wrecking team; walked back to Chattogram to join up with the army but finding them gone went back into the village; was arrested a month later and released due to lack of evidence; rearrested in September 1930 under the Bengal Ordinance and spent six years in various jails; settled in Kolkata after independence and partition and worked in the New Secretariat Building.

Vijay Krishna Sen (mentioned in *Chattogram Yuva-Vidroha 1930–34 Aalokmela*) (b. 1911, d. 7 May 1992): Was a part of the police line attack team on the night of the CAR; took part in the Battle of Jalalabad; was not in the police eye and was able to return home safely; was arrested under the Bengal Ordinance in 1932 and detained without trial until 1938; settled in Agartala in independent India.

Vijay Kumar Sen: Took part in the CAR; participated in the Battle of Jalalabad and is mentioned as a member of group number 5 in Suresh De's list in *Muktir Sopon Jalalabad*; was in jail when Ananda Prasad Gupta was brought to Chattogram Jail and had been granted bail – mentioned in Ananda Gupta's list and in Ananta Lal Singh's list; tried in the CAR Case: acquitted for lack of evidence.

British Camp

Ahsanulla (Khan Sahib): Arrested Ambika Chakraborty from Potiya; present at the Kalarpol encounter; killed by Haripada Bhattacharya after a football match.

Ali Pande (sub-inspector): Took part in the Kalarpol encounter.

Ali Rahim: The vice president of the Union Board who was a witness in the Kalarpol encounter.

Azim Abdul (sub-inspector): Launched a hunt for Tegra, Tripura and Bidhu on 25 March 1930; hunted for Ram Krishna after a case was registered on his name under the Explosive Substances Act; took part in the Kalarpol encounter.

Baker (major): Traffic manager during the time of the armoury attacks; became OC of the local unit of the AFI and led the attack on Chittagong as part of revenge for Ahsanulla's murder.

Banerjee Bimalpada: Chinsura police inspector who gave evidence in the Chandannagar case.

Barraclough: The gunner who fired a Lewis gun from the roof of the waterworks building on to the police lines.

Bartley F.D.: Police officer who accompanied Tegart to Chandannagar; analysed the Dalhousie Square Bomb Case.

Barua Jarasandha: District Magistrate Wilkinson's orderly who died on 18 April 1930.

Barua P.K.: Beat constable at Kalarpol.

Barua Pratul Chandra (sub-inspector): Was sent by Johnson to inform Wilkinson of the attack on the police lines.

Bennet: The handwriting expert.

Bhattacharya Sashank (detective inspector): Killed by Tarakeshwar Dastidar at the Barma village encounter.

Bhattacharya Sharada (IB inspector): Warned Jogendramohan Gupta that his sons Deboprasad and Ananda Prasad were mixing with undesirable company; was threatened by Ananta Lal Singh, Ganesh Ghosh, Lokenath Bal, Jibon Ghoshal and Naresh Ray and warned against picking on their group of boys; tried to influence Sarada Seel, Monoranjan Sen and Bhabatosh Bhattacharya into becoming informers; was cross-examined by J.K. Ghoshal and Sarat Chandra Bose during the trial.

Bhowmik Rohini (sub-inspector): Tried to influence Sarada Seel into becoming an informer and took him to Inspector Sharada Bhattacharya's house; was present at the Kalarpol encounter.

Bhowmik Sachin: DIB officer who raided Rajat Sen's home.

Bikash Sukhendu: Public prosecutor's assistant in the CAR Case.

Blackburn (sergeant): Who discovered the AFI armoury being raided and ran towards Pahartali; was picked up by Police Superintendent Johnson.

Bliss: Agent of the Assam Bengal Railway and the most prominent of civilians in Chittagong.

Bloomfield: European warder who helped smuggle explosives and material into jail for the Dynamite Conspiracy.

Bose Monoranjan (sub-inspector): Went with Cameron to Dhalghat.

Buckland (lieutenant colonel): Posted to Chittagong to maintain peace and order.

Burke: Taitt's successor at the AFI.

Burman Braj Bihari (DSP): Police officer who led the Nagarkhana Hill battle.

Burnett Alexander: Tea planter and trooper in the SVLH who took part in the Battle of Jalalabad.

Burt: Superintendent of Narayangunj River Police.

Cameron (captain of the2/8 Gurkha Regiment): Was killed at the Dhalghat raid by Nirmal Sen.

Cassells: John Younie's first boss in India who was shot and injured by a revolutionist.

Chatterji Basanta Kumar: Deputy superintendent in Kolkata; a bomb had been thrown in his house in November 1914 during a meeting in which Tegart was present; was killed by terrorists in 1916.

Chatterji Bhupendranath (Rai Bahadur): Special superintendent of police, Intelligence Branch, in Kolkata, killed by the inmates of Alipore Jail during an official visit in 1926.

Chatterji Srigyan (Gyan Babu): Jail superintendent and doctor.

Chaudhury Lalit Mohan (beat constable): At Kalarpol.

Chrissie: The nanny who worked for the Younies.

Cleary M.F. (superintendent of police, Chittagong): At cricket ground encounter.

Colson Lionel H.: Judged Donovan's gladioli as the best flowers in Barisal, deputy inspector general, Intelligence Bureau, West Bengal; practised shooting with Tegart on the rooftop; visited Chittagong in March 1930 and warned the police about an upcoming revolutionary uprising; interviewed Ananta Lal Singh on his surrender; succeeded Tegart as police commissioner of Bengal.

Costello: Chief Justice in 1929; was twice president of the Bengal Flying Club. He was later a member of the tribunal that tried the sensational Bhawal Sanyasi Case.

Craig: Succeeded Lowman as IG Police and was Ram Krishna's target, but Inspector Tarini Mukherji was shot instead by mistake.

Cullen: A civilian in Chittagong

Cumming (Mrs): Her husband was in charge of the steamer service.

Das Jogendra (sub-inspector): Present at Kalarpol.

Das S.R.: The advocate general who had facilitated the meeting between Tegart and Gandhi in 1925.

Day Earnest: Businessman killed by Gopi Nath Saha.

De Chandra Kumar (constable): Gave a statement in the Amarendra Nandi case.

De Umesh Chandra (DIB sub-inspector): Caught Sailesh Ray outside Chittagong Jail.

Denham Godfrey Charles: Sir Charles Tegart's colleague in the police service.

Deverell C.J. (lieutenant general): The officiating chief of army staff at the time of the CAR.

Dewan Siddique (sub-inspector): Had accompanied Gaffur to the residence of Mr Johnson to give news of the presence of the raiders on Badulla Hill; another of Rajat Sen's football buddies; Khan Bahadur Ahsanulla's blue-eyed boy and captain of the football team; attacked Haripada Bhattacharya after the murder of Ahsanulla.

Dey Prasanna K.: Kalarpol beat constable.

Donovan John: District magistrate and collector of Barisal; John Younie left his family with Donovan when he first came to Chittagong; congratulated Younie on the birth of his son; was on the terrorist hit list and was sent back to Britain; was a good friend of Sir Charles Tegart.

Durno L.G.: Was then the collector at Krishnanagar; when district magistrate of Dhaka, he was shot by Ramen Bhowmik who had been guided by Saroj Kanti Guha.

Dutt Som: Jail superintendent at Hijli Central Jail.

Ellison: Police superintendent of Kumilla; was killed by Sailesh Ray.

Emery: Oecken's successor at the Imperial Bank; Burma golf champion in 1929.

Eric Hodson: The police superintendent of Dhaka; was shot and injured at the Dacca Mitford Hospital grounds in the same incident in which Lowman was killed.

Farmer J.C.: Was deputed to the IARO and made responsible for raising a Bengali regiment during WW I; was deputy inspector general, Bakarganj range, during the armoury raid; was with Police Superintendent Johnson on the roof of the waterworks building on the night of 18 April 1930; took part in the Battle of Jalalabad; was a part of the Kalarpol encounter.

Farrell (sergeant major): Was shot dead during the AFI armoury raid.

Farrell: A civilian in Chittagong; was amongst the civilians who met Mr Wilkinson at the Piccadilly Junction on the night of 18 April 1930; had dinner with John Younie and Ricardo Richardson in January 1932.

Ferera J.B.: the Anglo-Indian guard on the train to Feni who pointed out Ananta Lal Singh, Ganesh Ghosh, Ananda Prasad Gupta and Jibon Ghoshal to the police at Feni railway station.

Finney: A police officer who went to Chandannagar with Tegart.

Francis: Civilian who helped douse the fire at the AFI.

Fullerton (vice admiral): On board the *Effingham*.

Gaffur Abdul: A peasant who gave information about swadeshis being present on Jalalabad Hill.

Garlick R.R.: District and sessions judge of Alipore court who tried the Dalhousie Square Bomb Case; sentenced Dinesh Gupta of BBD trio to death for the murder of Col Simpson; was assassinated in his court. A letter signed as Bimal Dasgupta accused him of the unjust hanging of Dinesh Gupta but the actual killer was Kanai Bhattacharya.

Gascoigne Julian: ADC to Stanley Jackson.

Ghose Asvini: The stationmaster who informed the police that four suspicious youths had boarded the train to Laksham on the night of 22 April 1930.

Ghose Heramba (inspector): Was present at Kalarpol.

Ghose Jogendra (constable): Was held by the revolutionaries at the police lines on the night of 18 April 1930 and was released just before the armoury was set on fire.

Goldfrap: The colonel of the Mahrattas commanding the military forces posted to Chittagong.

Gordon A.G. (DIG): Succeeded Farmer.

Gupta Dhirendra Mohan: Deputy magistrate involved in the Kalarpol case.

Gupta Hem (sub-inspector): Rajat Sen's football buddy; escorted the informer, who had news of the presence of revolutionaries in Jalalabad, to Chittagong to meet Mr Johnson; present at the Battle of Jalalabad and helped with the cremation the next day; present at Kalarpol and gave an eyewitness account at court.

Gupta Jogendra (DIB inspector): Kept an eye on Kalpana Dutt.

Haig H.G.: Home member of the Government of India in 1933.

Hailey Malcolm: Governor of Punjab, 1924–28; governor of UP, 1928–30.

Hallet M.G.: Home secretary in 1933.

Halliday Frank: Police commissioner of Bengal before Tegart.

Hands H.S.: District magistrate, Chittagong, who eventually saw the capture of Surjya Sen; a golf blue; had pressed for a fine of Rs 80,000/-.

Haq Abdul (Khan Bahadur): The Muslim member of the CAR Case tribunal (with Younie).

Hardinge Lord: Viceroy of India, 1910–16.

Hemmins: Witnessed the Dalhousie Square bomb blast.

Hicks V.W.F.: Became superintendent of police in Chittagong after Mr Wright committed suicide.

Hicks W.B.: Additional police superintendent; superintendent and jail super; later special superintendent. His initials have been mentioned as W.B. or W.V. Possibly he is the same V.W.F. Hicks who succeeded Mr Wright and petitioned the courts in the Supplementary Armoury Raid Case Trial as quoted in *Mahanayak Surjya Sen Chattogram Biplob Pratham Khand,* p. 180, by Ananta Lal Singh.

Hicks: Reached Pahartali club raid site led by Pritilata.

Hoare Samuel: Secretary of State for India.

Ila Devi: Princess, the eldest daughter of the Maharani of Cooch Bihar.

Irwin: Viceroy of India, 1926–31.

Jackson Julia: Wife of Stanley Jackson.

Jackson Stanley Francis (Jackers): Governor of Bengal from 1927 to 1932.

Janvrin: A police officer who went to Chandannagar with Tegart.

Johnson Jean: Wife of Police Superintendent J.R. Johnson.

Johnson J.R.: Police superintendent of Chittagong during the armoury raid.

Johnstone: A police officer who went to Chandannagar with Tegart.

Johur: John Younie's butler.

Kapur (major): New civil surgeon posted to Chittagong; John Younie and Captain Taitt seconded his membership to the club.

Keen (major): The officer commanding the 1/9 Royal Jats that carried out the Gohira encounter in which Kalpana Dutt and Tarakeshwar Dastidar were captured.

Kelly (sergeant): Raided Rajat Sen's home; kicked Kalarpol Shaheed Monoranjan Sen's old father to death.

Kemm: Collector and district magistrate of Chittagong who succeeded Wilkinson.

Kennedy Angus (of 2/8 Gurkhas): Posted to Chittagong; went to investigate the Pahartali Railway Institute bomb attack site, the one that had been led by Pritilata.

Keywood (sergeant): Went with Tegart to Chandannagar; gave evidence in court.

Khan Subah: Sir Charles Augustus Tegart's driver.

Khatri Kesh Bahadur (rifleman of 2/9 Gurkhas): Caught Brajen Sen.

Khatri Man Bahadur (rifleman of 2/9 Gurkhas): Caught Surjya Sen.

Khatri Nar Singh (lance naik of 2/9 Gurkhas): Caught Brajen Sen.

Kishori Babu (inspector of police): Let Lokenath go at the railway station.

Kumar Babu: Who took Ananta Lal Singh into the IB office at 13, Lord Sinha Street.

Le Brocq: A police officer who went to Chandannagar with Tegart.

Leishman A.R.: the president of the Chittagong Chamber of Commerce.

Leonard: Officer of the Mahratta Regiment posted to Chittagong; south India golf champion.

Lewis (ASP): Took charge of the revolutionaries on their way from Chittagong Jail to court and back, was part of the Battle of Jalalabad, the Kalarpol encounter and the vengeance wreaked upon Chittagong following the Ahsanulla murder.

Lodge: The district and sessions judge at Chittagong during the armoury raids; he was succeeded by John Younie. He was later a member of the tribunal that tried the sensational Bhawal Sanyasi Case.
Lowman Francis John: Inspector general of police who interviewed Ananta Lal Singh after his surrender; was assassinated by Benoy Krishna Basu on the grounds of Dacca Mitford Hospital.
Lytton (Lord): Governor of Bengal before Sir Stanley Jackson.
MacDonald Ramsay: Prime minister of Britain.
Maitra: Dr Sheldon's second-in-command of bomb disposal.
Majumdar Nalini (Rai Bahadur): Special superintendent no. 3 of the Intelligence Branch; was a distant relative of Sukumar Biswas, the nephew of Premananda, and tried to influence him to betray Ananta Lal Singh; Ananta Lal Singh was brought to his office when he surrendered; escaped an attempt on his life during his daughter's wedding by refusing to come out of his room.
Majumdar Pulin Bihari: Assistant stationmaster of Feni; witnessed the interrogation of Ananta Lal Singh, Ganesh Ghosh, Jibon Ghoshal and Ananda Prasad Gupta and their subsequent escape.
Majumdar Ramani (sub-inspector): Took notes during the Congress Assembly in May 1929.
Martin (Mrs): Congratulated Younie on the birth of his son.
Matilal (havaldar): Led entire Potiya detachment of thirty-five sipahis for Gairala encounter in which Surjya Sen was captured.
McDonald (inspector of police): Present during Kalarpol; wounded in the AB Railway Institute Pahartali raid carried out by Pritilata Waddadar.
McKinty: Police officer at Kolkata who went to Chandannagar with Tegart; later intelligence chief of Bengal police.
Mills: Special Branch officer at Kolkata.
Minto (Lord): Viceroy of India, 1905–10.
Monk: Built the bridge over the Karnaphuli.
Mookerjee Rajendranath (Sir): Patron of the Bengal Flying Club who hosted the inauguration lunch.
Moore Arthur: Supported the establishment of the Bengal Club.
Morsehead (sergeant): Who went into the AFI armoury on the night of the CAR and thought Lokenath Bal was Captain Taitt; narrowly missed being shot.

Mukherji Tarini (inspector): Mistaken for IG Police Craig and shot by Ram Krishna Biswas at the Chandpur railway station.

Nag Sanjiv Chandra: The sub-inspector of the reserve forces at the police lines who informed Johnson and Farmer of the attack; met Johnson, Farmer and Barraclough as they walked across the maidan to the waterworks building; the same line babu whose son had taken Ananta Lal Singh and Ganesh Ghosh on a tour of the police lines.

Nangle: Officer of Eastern Frontier Rifles who took part in the attack on Chittagong as revenge for Ahsanulla's murder.

Nelson: Commissioner of Chittagong who investigated the riots that followed the assassination of Khan Bahadur Ahsanulla.

Nixon John: ICS officer who shared the chummery with Sir Charles Tegart.

Oecken: Played golf with John Younie.

Peddie James: District magistrate of Midnapore who was murdered by Bimal Dasgupta.

Petrie David: Director of Criminal Intelligence in India. He was appointed head of MI5 by Churchill just before World War II.

Polly: Played golf with John Younie.

Prentice William (Sir): Chief secretary; later Home member of the executive council of the Government of Bengal.

Provan: A civilian who helped douse the fire at the AFI.

R (Mrs): Wife of Ricardo Richardson.

Rahim Abdur (sub-inspector): Verified information about the presence of revolutionaries on Jalalabad Hill; took part in the Kalarpol encounter.

Rai Jatindra Mohan (sub-inspector) (Jatin Babu): Caught Ananta Lal Singh, Ganesh Ghosh, Ananda Prasad Gupta and Jibon Ghoshal at Feni; Haran's mama; was wounded by Ananta Lal Singh.

Rai S.N. (SDO): Came to visit Ananta Lal Singh in Chittagong Jail.

Ramsbotham: Congratulated Younie on the birth of his son.

Rand: Poona's plague commissioner.

Rankin John (Sir): Chief Justice.

Rehman Fazlur (sub-inspector): Of the Panchalaish Thana; was present at Kalarpol.

Reid: Commissioner of Chittagong who succeeded Nelson.

Reid: Chief secretary.
Richardson Ricardo: Head of the National Bank.
Robinson (captain): Commander of the Surma Valley Light Horse.
Rochfort: Played golf with John Younie.
Roxburg: Chief presidency magistrate.
Roy Prafulla (sub-inspector): Who arrested Ananta Lal Singh in 1924; was murdered by Premananda.
Sarkar Bhujang (inspector): Failed to recognize Ananta Lal Singh as he drove out of the intelligence office at 13, Lord Sinha Street.
Satish Chandra Rai Bahadur: Ananta Lal Singh's father's friend before whom Prafulla Roy gave his dying declaration.
Sattar Abdul (Khan Bahadur): Public prosecutor in the CAR Case.
Scott: The telegraph deputy superintendent who ran out with his rifle as soon as he heard of the attack on the Telephone Bhavan and Telegraph Exchange.
Sen Amarendra Nath (A.N. Sen): Who took over the post of judge at Krishnanagar from John Younie; tried the Dynamite Conspiracy Case.
Sen Manmatha (Rai Bahadur) (Deputy Superintendent of Police): who offered the deal to Ananta Lal Singh, Ganesh Ghosh and Lokenath Bal – there would be no hanging if they permitted the case to proceed and did not indulge in any more conspiracies.
Sharpe W. McC.: President of the tribunal who, with his colleagues R.K. Ghose and Khondakar Ali Taib, tried Surjya Sen, Tarakeshwar Dastidar and Kalpana Dutt.
Sheldon: Chief inspector of explosives.
Shooter B.J.: ASP at Chittagong; present at the Battle of Jalalabad; instrumental in wrecking vengeance upon Chittagong after the assassination of Khan Bahadur Ahsanulla; committed suicide on 23 January 1932.
Simpson N.S. (colonel): Ex-IMS, inspector general of prisons; was murdered by the BBD trio.
Smith Dallas (colonel): In Eastern Frontier Rifles.
Sovan Abdul: Sergeant Major J.W. Farrell's butler.
Spears: A mercantile marine officer who witnessed the Dalhousie Square bomb blast.
Spencer: Police officer who went to Chandannagar with Tegart.

Springfield (additional superintendent of police): Was in charge of the Intelligence Branch in Chittagong when Surjya Sen was caught; struck Surjya Sen on the chest with his revolver.

Stephenson Hugh: Governor of Bengal in 1925.

Stevens C.B.J.: District magistrate and collector at Kumilla who was shot dead by Shanti and Suniti.

Stevenson (captain): The military intelligence officer (MIO) posted to Chittagong: responsible for Payaj Kanti Choudhury's death; assumed full control of jail on the day of Surjya Sen and Tarakeshwar Dastidar's hanging.

Stork H.C. (judge): Was judge in Chittagong in 1923–24; tried the Suluk Bahar Arms Collection Case; with N.K. Bose and L.B. Das as part of the tribunal pronounced Dinesh Majumdar guilty; was president of the tribunal that tried Dr Narain Roy and, with his colleagues Ashutosh Ghose and Adiluzzaman Khan, found him and one Dr B.C. Bose to be the most culpable.

Suhrawardy Hassan (lieutenant colonel): Knighted for saving the life of Sir Stanley Jackson during the Calcutta University convocation of 1931.

Taitt (captain): the adjutant of the auxiliary force of the Assam Bengal Railways during the armoury raids.

Taylor: Police officer.

Tegart Charles Augustus (b. 5 October 1881, d. 6 April 1946): Started service as an assistant superintendent of police of Patna city; moved to Calcutta in 1906, as acting deputy commissioner; was posted in 1913 as deputy commissioner to the political branch of the Bengal CID which by then had been renamed the Intelligence Branch; granted a commission in the Army Service Corps in 1917 to serve in the War but was recalled to India to give evidence before the Rowlatt Committee; received the CIE later that year and joined Royal Flying Corps in France; remained behind with the army of occupation for nearly a year before being seconded for special intelligence duties in Britain; served as police commissioner of Bengal from 1923 to 15 December 1931; served on the council of the Secretary of State for India till 1937; was made a KCIE during the coronation honours in May 1937; refused the appointment as inspector general of police in Palestine and agreed to work in a freelance capacity with

Sir David Petrie; reorganized the CID, created the Rural Mounted Police force, the barbed-wire entanglement in the form of a fence running the length of the frontier road with an electrified detector wire throughout and concrete pillboxes placed at strategic points along the fence – the Tegart Wall and the Tegart Forts; returned to Britain and personally appealed to the Irish to support Britain in WW II; accepted a job in the ministry of supply and worked along with Sir John Nixon during the War; took charge of the ministry of food's anti-black-market campaign during the War and found himself disgusted at the low standards of honesty generally prevailing in the country; created an intelligence bureau and selected his own personal staff which included Lionel Colson and targeted the big conspiracies that were robbing the nation of food; went on sick leave some weeks after VE Day, suffered the first of a series of heart attacks which eventually proved fatal, still looked forward to complete recovery and resigned two months before his death only because the bureau could not be left without a head.

Tegart Edward: Sir Charles' Augustus Tegart's brother.

Tegart Kathleen Francis: Wife of Police Commissioner Sir Charles Augustus Tegart.

Tegart Robert: Sir Charles' Augustus Tegart's brother.

Thapa Birman: District Magistrate Wilkinson's driver.

Thomas: A civilian who helped douse the fire at the AFI.

Todd R.D. (sergeant of the Calcutta Mounted Police): Gave evidence on the Chandannagar case in court.

Tyers: A civilian who helped douse the fire at the AFI.

Victor Sassoon: Gifted a gypsy moth to the Bengal Flying Club.

Villiers Edward: President, European Association, India; shot at by Bimal Dasgupta.

Wasid Abdul Mohammad Fazal (Inspector): Police inspector who caught Ananta Lal Singh, Ganesh Ghosh, Jibon Ghoshal and Ananda Prasad Gupta at Feni railway station.

Waterworth: Police officer who went to Chandannagar with Tegart.

Waumsley T.H.: Captain of the 2/9 Gurkhas; captured Surjya Sen.

Weale: Police officer who went to Chandannagar with Tegart.

Wedgewood Benn: Secretary of State for India.

Weldon (Dr): Civil surgeon of Chittagong.

West: A civilian who helped douse the fire at the AFI.
White: Head of the PWD.
Wighton: A civilian in Chittagong.
Wigram Kenneth: Chief of general staff of the British Indian Army.
Wilkinson H.R.: Collector and district magistrate of Chittagong during the CAR.
Williams A.deC.: District and sessions judge of Chittagong who succeeded John Younie; tried Ambika Chakraborty.
Williamson H.: Intelligence Bureau chief in 1933.
Willingdon Freeman-Thomas, 1st Marquess of Willingdon: Viceroy of India, 18 April 1931–18 April 1936; Lord Irwin's successor to the post of viceroy of India.
Woods (major): Helped Colonel Buckland maintain order in Chittagong after the CAR.
Wright (police superintendent): Who relieved Johnson; committed suicide soon thereafter.
Wright: The European warder who helped smuggle explosives and material into jail for the Dynamite Conspiracy.
Yates (captain of Assam Rifles): Was a part of the attack on Chittagong as part of revenge for Ahsanulla's murder.
Younie Dorothy: Wife of John Younie and a doctor by profession.
Younie Elspet Margaret: Daughter of John and Dorothy Younie.
Younie Helen: Daughter of John and Dorothy Younie.
Younie John (5 April 1893–9 Sept 42): District and sessions judge of Chittagong and the president of the tribunal trying the CAR Case; posted to Darjeeling where he tried the Lebong Case; posted as district and sessions judge of Jessore, Sylhet and Assam; decided to retire from India and settle in Scotland in 1937 but found it difficult to find employment and agreed to return to India to complete the remaining two years of his Indian service; was posted as additional district and sessions judge of 24 Parganas, Alipore, Calcutta in 1939; district and sessions judge, Komilla and Dhaka in 1941; became secretary, judicial department and remembrancer of legal affairs, Kolkata, in 1942; died in Kolkata of dengue fever after a full day at work.
Younie Mary: Daughter of John and Dorothy Younie.

TIMELINE:

9 September 1915: Battle of Balasore. Joteen Mookerjee is martyred.

1919: Jallianwala Bagh massacre in Amritsar.

1921: Gandhi's Non-cooperation Movement

1919–1924: Khilafat Movement – a pan-Islamic movement is launched by the Ottomans. Gandhi supports the movement in India.

1923: Charles Tegart accepts the post of police commissioner of Bengal.

1923: Paraikora dacoity takes place.

December 1923: AB Railway dacoity followed by the Nagarkhana Hill battle. Surjya Sen and Ambika Chakraborty are arrested from the site and charged with the Suluk Bahar House Collection of Arms Case and the Nagarkhana Hill Battle Case. Ananta Lal Singh escapes. He is charged with the AB Railway Dacoity Case.

12 January 1924: Gopi Nath Saha shoots Earnest Day in Calcutta mistaking him for Tegart.

Early 1924: Ananta Lal Singh is arrested by sub-inspector Prafulla Roy.

24 May 1924: Chattogram sub-inspector Prafulla Roy is murdered by Premananda.

1924: Surjya Sen, Ambika Chakraborty and Ananta Lal Singh are acquitted.

1 October 1924: The Secret Ordinance comes into affect. Ananta Lal Singh, Ganesh Ghosh and Ambika Chakraborty are amongst those (Subhas Bose in Kolkata is also amongst the lot) that are picked up from home and thrown into jail. Nirmal Sen is arrested in July 1925.

25 June 1925: Gandhi and Tegart hold a private meeting.
1926: Tegart receives knighthood.
8 October 1926: Surjya Sen is arrested and moved around between jails on the west coast of India.
1928: Surjya Sen, Ambika Charan Chakraborty, Nirmal Sen, Ananta Lal Singh, Ganesh Ghosh and Charu Bikash Dutt are released from jail.
30 October 1928: Protest march against the Simon Commission in Lahore.
17 November 1928: Lala Lajpat Rai dies after being beaten up by Superintendent of Police J.A. Scott during the protest march of 30 October 1928.
17 December 1928: Murder of Deputy Superintendent of Police J.P. Saunders.
29 December 1928: The 44th session of the Indian National Congress is held.
2 February 1929: Sir Stanley Jackson inaugurates the Bengal Flying Club.
February 1929: A Congress committee is formed in Chattogram with Mohim Chandra Das as president and Surjya Sen as secretary. A Youth Congress is formed with Ganesh Ghosh as secretary; a Students' Union with Lokenath Bal as secretary. Ananta Lal Singh is appointed instructor to various gymnasiums.
8 April 1929: Bhagat Singh and Batukeshwar Dutt throw harmless bombs in the Central Legislative Assembly.
April 1929: Tegarts and Jacksons holiday in Darjeeling. Tegarts go to Britain for a long holiday soon after.
11–13 May 1929: Congress Assembly, Youth Assembly and Student Women's Assembly are held. The Chattogram Volunteer Vahini puts up a show. Subhas Chandra Bose meets Ananta Lal Singh, Ganesh Ghosh and Tripura Sen secretly. On the last day there is a fight and a police complaint is filed against Ananta Lal Singh, Lokenath Bal, Naresh Ray and Tripura Sen under Section 147 of the IPC. It is scheduled to be heard on 23 October 1929.
12 June 1929: Bhagat Singh and Batukeshwar Dutt are sentenced to transportation for life for throwing bombs in the Central Legislative Assembly. The breaking news is that Bhagat Singh is

being implicated in the murder of Superintendent of Police J.P. Saunders and a new trial is about to begin. Jatin Das is arrested in the next couple of days.

13 September 1929: Jatin Das dies.

21 September 1929: Elections are held in Chittagong. Sukhendu is stabbed by goons on the day the results are declared. Surjya Sen and his boys leave for Kolkata to prepare for the BPCC elections.

23 October 1929: Ananta Lal Singh returns from Kolkata to attend the hearing in Chittagong. He is sentenced to four months in jail and has six months time to present himself at the jail. He returns to Kolkata and appeals to the Calcutta High Court.

November: BPCC elections are held in Kolkata. Subhas Bose wins by a narrow margin defeating J.M. Sengupta as Congress chief. Motilal Nehru orders a detailed inquiry. BPCC elections have to be held again and completed before the AICC meeting on 21 March 1930.

15 October 1929: Pledge taken – DO AND DIE.

December 1929: Tegarts are back in India.

22 February 1930: A fight with Karunamoy Dutt of Municipal School takes place. The police name Tegra, Tripura and Bidhu Bhattacharya as conspirators. Ananta Lal Singh and Ganesh Ghosh force the boys to turn themselves in.

7 March 1930: Ananta Lal Singh reports to jail. His appeal to the Calcutta High Court comes through and he is released on 14 March 1930.

12 March 1930: Gandhi begins his Satyagraha Movement.

14 March 1930: Ram Krishna Biswas suffers extensive burns and goes into hiding. On 25 March 1930 he is sent off to a hideout in the interiors. On 26 March a case is registered on his name under the Explosive Substances Act but he is not to be found.

24–26 March 1930: Colson spends this time in Chittagong reorganizing the Detective Branch schedule. From 2 April 1930, Johnson is scheduled to institute the revised system.

8 April 1930: A police patrol appears to be hunting for Tarakeshwar Dastidar (Phutu) and Ardhendu Dastidar who have suffered burn injuries one or two days before.

11 April 1930: The date of action, i.e., 18 April 1930 is finalized.

18 April 1930: The Younies embark for Chittagong.
18 April 1930: The Chittagong Armoury Raid takes place.
19 April 1930: Alexander Burnett arrives in Chittagong as a member of the SVLH.
22 April 1930: John Younie arrives at Chittagong Circuit House having left the family at Barisal.
22 April 1930: The Battle of Jalalabad takes place.
22 April 1930: The Feni incident takes place.
24 April 1930: Amarendra Nandi is shot dead at Chittagong.

ACKNOWLEDGEMENTS

Chittagong: Summer of 1930 owes a great debt to Ananta Lal Singh, Ananda Prasad Gupta, Suresh De, Pritilata Waddadar, Kalpana Dutt and Charu Bikash Dutt who left behind graphic first-hand impressions of the times; to Ananda Prasad Gupta's niece Manju Mohanty who first told me the story the day Ananda Prasad Gupta passed away in London and then very promptly arranged for the family copy of *Chattogram Bidroher Kahini* to be sent to me; to Sunanda Gupta, wife of Ananda Prasad Gupta, and Sunanda's sister Krishna Dutt who enthusiastically filled me in on the details of young Ananda's life, the stories of the family and his Thakur-Ma and Gobindo-da; to Sanhita Nag, librarian at New Delhi Kali Bari, who helped search for relevant material and kept the books of Ananta Lal Singh ready for me to borrow; to Arati Sarker, Geeta Sinha and Ajit Sinha, the children of Nand Lal Singh (Sinha) and Sucharita Sarker, the granddaughter of Nand Lal Singh, for their inputs on the family; to Surajit Ghatak for the many introductions he was responsible for, especially the one with Himadri Bal, son of Lokenath Bal, which resulted in the collection of several details about Lokenath and Tegra; to Suvagatha for his encouragement and help with locating police documents; to Chandreyee Bhattacharya and Swapna Mitra who helped with locating several important documents from the archives at Shaheed Surjya Sen Bhavan, Kolkata, run by the Biplab Tirtha Chattagram Smriti Sangstha; to Dr Dorothy Younie who carefully preserved the correspondence between John Younie and herself and to Elspet Norton for permission to rummage through and use the collection of letters preserved at the archives in the British Library, London; to Lady Kathleen Tegart who wrote an account of Sir Charles Tegart's life and deposited his papers to the care of the University of Cambridge; to

Kevin Greenbank, curator at the University of Cambridge; to James Tegart and Robert Tegart who, by way of sharing the name, have been interested in Sir Charles Tegart and sent me their collection of newspaper clippings and photographs; to Malcolm Kennedy for his *The Diaries of Captain Malcolm Duncan Kennedy, 1917–1946*, which I found on the Internet; to Subrata Bose, the son of Sarat Chandra Bose, for the details on his father; to the National Library of Australia that has made its newspaper archives available on the Internet.

I owe a great debt to the following institutions: Biplab Tirtha Chattagram Smriti Sangstha; British Library, London; and the University of Cambridge.

Photo credits: revolutionaries – Biplab Tirtha Chattagram Smriti Sangstha; John Younie – British Library, London; Tegart Collection of crime scene photographs – Centre of South Asian Studies, University of Cambridge; Sarat Bose – Sarat Bose Academy Calcutta.

For their support and assistance I owe many thanks to Nirmal Bernadette Kumar, Pramada Menon, Brinda Bose, Sujata Raghubir, Kaushik Chatterjee, Ranabir and Medhavi Majumdar; to Dr Chittaranjan Sengupta and Dr Santana Sengupta for their painstaking editing; to Shantanu Ray Chaudhuri, Labanya Unni, Antony Thomas, Shuka Jain and Amrita Chakravorty of HarperCollins India and last but not least to my mother, Jayashri Bhattacharya, who read the rather difficult Bengali texts out to me, laughed and wept as she shared with me the dreams and experiences of the young people that set out to free India.